Naked Greed
A Novel

by
Gerald Seaman

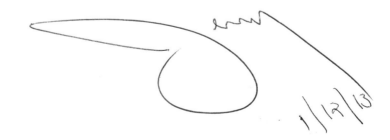

To my daughters Sara and Jennifer
and my bride Carol of 30 years.
They have put up with the foibles of a
would-be novelist for far too long.

Thanks to my good friend and fellow writer
Roger Hale
for combing through this manuscript and
offering invaluable suggestions.

"Our modern, technological society is fair-weather oriented. Agriculture, transportation, the economy, even our homes are no guarantee against the cold."

*

"Twenty-first Century man treads on a tenuous thread. The slightest natural aberration upsets his progress – threatening disaster and even death."

*

"Man lives in blind faith that modern technology will provide him with an uninterrupted life-support system. Nature can raise havoc with this."

*

"How vain of man to even consider the possibility of controlling the weather. As it is now, he cannot even predict it."

CONTENTS

"It is quite possible a storm center could stall and the interaction of very frigid arctic air on a massive influx of moist, tropical air, could condense into enough snow to totally immobilize a large geographic area."

from a national weather broadcast

WEDNESDAY, DECEMBER 19

Deep in the womb of the underground nerve center at Scan-Man headquarters, the activation of Scanner XII was one minute away. The morning launch had been accomplished with precision. Now a new challenge was being faced.

"Sixty seconds and counting, fifty-nine, fifty-eight ... "

The frantic activity of the day had now settled down to the numbing tension of the final moments of countdown. Nat Webster, the Control Room chief, felt his head about to split with anticipation. It had been building throughout the day. It was a pain that was quite familiar that began at his lower neck, worked up into the base of his skull and then spread into his cranium. It had now reached his eyes. He felt like puking. A churning stomach always accompanied these headaches.

The entire project now raced through his mind -- the months of total dedication he and his team had devoted to bringing the Energizer and its Searoc Beam to these final seconds. The project had cost him his marriage.

"Fifty-three, fifty-two, fifty-one ... "

Webster's faded red shirt was wet. Perspiration stains spread under his arms and along his spine. Tie loosened, sleeves rolled, he stood with arms spread-eagle on his desk, eyes following the motions of each technician at the terminals. Five years of his life were wrapped up in this project. It had started when he discovered it was mathematically possible to reflect the sun's energy into a beam of light onto the earth that in turn could act on the atmosphere and modify global weather patterns.

As with some ideas, the concept was easy enough once he believed it could be done. He envisioned endless beneficial uses of weather modification. Never more would there be droughts with the resultant damaging of crops and shortages of food. Precipitation and fair weather could be controlled around the world. Hurricanes could be diverted or dissipated. Floods and other natural disasters resulting from normal atmospheric movement could be eliminated.

But, there also was the down side, Webster felt. The Searoc Beam could be focused to a pinpoint, much like a laser. As such, it could drill a pinhole through three inches of armor and, when slightly expanding the focus, the concentrated rays of the sun could reduce a military tank to a flow of liquid steel. Relative to this, he had heard talk among the directors that the Searoc Beam had great military potential.

Not if I have anything to do with it, Webster thought.

Webster's concept of the Searoc Beam was significant enough to alter the course of history, literally. The Scan-Man board of directors jumped at the idea of producing the Energizer and offered Webster anything he needed to accomplish his plan. But the project must be kept top secret, the board warned him. That was his only restriction.

He became consumed with the project, resisting the temptation to assume the role of God Himself. All he could think of was how beneficial this project could be -- how many lives could be saved -- how food would never more be a problem.

"Damn I stink," Webster thought, raising his armpit toward his nose.

"Forty-nine, forty-eight, forty-seven ... "

All had gone well for the first four years and Nat Webster presented the Scan-Man directors with the plans and a working model of a Solar Energizer that produced what he called a Searoc Beam. The go-ahead was given to manufacture the Energizer and a date was set for the first trial. There were a couple of minor setbacks, but finally the day had arrived -- today.

"Those guys don't make life any easier down here."

Fifteen feet above the Control Room in the observation deck behind soundproof glass stood several well-dressed executives wordlessly peering down on Nat Webster's territory. Webster hated having an audience watch him work. Maybe he should do a jig to give them some real entertainment.

One of the observers was Chandler Harrington, Chairman of the Scan-Man board. Earlier today he had spoken with Webster.

"Nat. This is the big moment for all of us. It has been you, however, who has carried the ball the whole length of the field. We're now within inches of a touchdown and your fans in the board room are on their feet howling triumphantly. You. Yes, you, Nat Webster, have been our hero. There's not a shadow of a doubt that the $1.3 billion has been well invested. You're our offense. Get that TD now."

The praise was great, Webster thought, but he had to keep from laughing out loud at the man's metaphors.

"Forty-five, forty-four ... "

"The longest sixty seconds of my life -- the birth of my baby." Webster was happy, but his sick headache of anticipation was threatening to squelch it.

The Scan-Man Control Room was buried 82 feet beneath the surface of Peters Airfield and the Scan-Man building itself. From this room a network of a dozen "weather" satellites were controlled, nourished and milked for information. In this one large room were housed the millions of circuits that connected Scan-Man to its celestial robots perpetually circling the earth. On command from this room to any one or all of the satellites, weather patterns, temperatures, humidity, air currents, pollution, atmospheric pressures and even surface temperatures of specific points on Earth could be read and transmitted back. Seventy-four percent of the Earth's atmosphere could be monitored at any given moment.

Huge flat wall screens carried the pictures returned from the monitor cameras in outer space. At this countdown, however, only one screen was the focus of those in the room. To the untrained eye, this screen looked like TV picture pixels gone bad. The image was predominately black, but with gradual lighting to the left.

To Webster and his technicians this picture was quite familiar. It was the North Atlantic Ocean, showing also portions of eastern Canada and all of Greenland. It was a nocturnal view -- but this was soon to change.

"Thirty-nine, thirty-eight, thirty-seven ... "

Webster had confirmed the mission was going as he had planned – contrary to Harrington's plan -- harmlessly out into the North Atlantic. This was certain to foil Harrington's Phase I operation to inundate Europe with snow. We will catch them in their own net, he assured himself. The Icelandic Low was working in his favor. It had changed its position slightly during the previous evening.

He was no meteorologist, but Scan-Man's Ellen Bloodworth was. He knew he could count on her expertise to help him plan this operation and teach him the fine points of the upper atmospheric conditions which would make his plans work. During their professional interaction, their relationship developed into friendship and then into something deeper.

"Thirty-six, thirty-five ... "

Two hundred feet above Webster were Scan-Man's two well-known antennas, landmarks in the area for miles around. Via these, all information was sent and received. Dish-shaped, each rotated 360 degrees and inclined to 179 degrees, enabling them to focus precisely on the satellite from which information was relayed.

There was so much to this project, Webster thought. The millions of details that, with his team of experts, brought them to this highly satisfying point.

"Thirty-four, thirty-three, thirty-two ... "

Feeling a little better, he chuckled to himself as the countdown progressed and turned his head briefly to glance at the men who stood above. One of them actually waved. Little did they know.

"Fifteen, fourteen, thirteen ... "

OK, my friends, Webster said to himself. We are ready to announce Scan-Man's presence to the world.

Then. "All is go," he spoke calmly to his technicians.

"Three, two, one ... "

Lever down.

The screen on the wall suddenly came to life. All eyes turned to it.

"Ah, you beautiful baby. How you work!" Webster shouted. "Just look at that!"

Several hundred square miles of the darkened surface of Greenland had become bright as day. A large area in the middle of the screen was now lighted, similar to the light from a theater spotlight shining on the floor of a darkened stage.

"Mark thirty seconds into activation," a technician said without a trace of emotion.

Webster turned to his distinguished audience above and gestured toward the picture. He could see them talking and that their conversation was animated, obviously pleased.

Harrington's voice then came over the intercom.

"Good work, Nat. Like clockwork. Will you join us in the board room for a celebration drink?"

"No thanks Chandler. We've just begun down here. It'll be a few hours before we can trace its effects. I'll be in touch."

Nat Webster turned his back. His head throbbed. He needed a bowl of chicken noodle soup.

*

The sun has ceased to rise for more than three weeks. Even the moon has dropped below the huge peaks along the horizon, faintly silhouetting the icy ridges. It is December 19 and soon there will be only darkness and an intense cold known to native Greenlanders as *kausuitsug unua*, or the polar night.

In northern Greenland a tiny village 500 miles above the Arctic Circle is startled into activity by a light from the sky nearly as bright as the sun in mid-summer. And at Thule Air Base an alarm sounds that scampers all personnel to alert status. The crew aboard the International Space Station also witnesses the event. They send an alarm to Houston headquarters.

The light is steady and it sends a warmth that would be welcomed were it not for the fear and confusion generated by the mystery of its source. The unnatural sun illuminates an area of several hundred square miles. It burns for precisely one hour, heating the air above the surface of the snow and ice to 72 degrees Fahrenheit. The light then disappears and the polar night returns.

14

The warm air rises rapidly, with increasing volume like a monstrous underwater bubble. As it rises it creates turbulence in the previously stable, frigid air mass. The warm air pushes upward through the cold like an invisible blanket covering the upper half of Greenland. It forms a giant, swelling cumulus. This sudden and unnatural warming phenomenon over so large an area creates a spectacular low-pressure system. The expanding warm air violently displaces the cold air and pushes it southeast.

High over the North Atlantic, south of Iceland and east of the southern end of Greenland, is a natural global weather condition known to meteorologists as a Weather Control Area. This particular one is named the Icelandic Low and, in its normal position, acts as a magnet, attracting weather disturbances moving off the North American continent.

On December 19 a massive cold front that has just left the coast of Greenland nudges the Icelandic Low. The Low begins its journey southwest.

Some five days earlier, a storm had formed in Northwest Texas, a low. It traveled southeast to the Gulf of Mexico, picking up warm, tropical air. It then swept northeast through Louisiana, Mississippi and Tennessee on a direct path toward New England.

As it progresses, it meets cooler air, and the storm intensifies, producing precipitation that changes from rain to snow as it reaches Connecticut.

The front moving up the coast from the Gulf is an ugly surprise to Webster. He wonders if he had been too hasty in his decision. He is now greatly concerned he may have set loose a meteorological tiger.

*

The reaction was immediate. The startling light, reflecting off the Greenland's snow cover, slashing into the

15

total darkness, was not lost on meteorologists, astronomers, astronauts and the personnel at Thule. Frantic messages quickly spread world wide questioning the source and purpose of the event.

The Associated Press picked up the story. It was immediately relayed to media worldwide. The news will reach the public on December 20.

*

Thirty minutes later, Nat Webster's antiquated, rattling VW bus was traveling east on Great Road in Hollandson, Massachusetts. Winter dusk had turned to darkness. The street was coated with a thin layer of snow. Traffic was light on the westbound lane and the view was clear. A slight depression on the accelerator and the VW accelerated suddenly, black smoke issuing from its twin tail pipes. The vehicle moved faster and faster. The accelerator would not release. The brakes didn't seem to respond either. The VW weaved from side to side, losing traction and then total control. It crossed the double center line and collided with the under section of a gasoline transport truck. Sparks flew. The tanker was pierced and the highly flammable liquid flooded over the VW and burst into flames. The driver was immediately unconscious.

A sedan that had been following the VW from a distance witnesses the violent scene. It slows but the shocked driver doesn't dare go near the conflagration. He drives on with a mild sense of guilt for not attempting to help..

The truck driver escaped, called 911, and stood by helplessly. The victim under the truck has already become immolated.

*

The dispatcher's voice was monotone. Without a trace of emotion she announced the accident and the need for emergency equipment on Great Road.

16

Maggie Billings heard the call on the police scanner in the news office and yelled to her husband. "Get your act together, Phil. It's out on Great Road, east. Probably a fatal. Don't forget your big flash."

Phil Billings emerged from an adjacent office, cigarette dangling from his lips, and pulled a coat over his shoulders. "For God's sake, Maggie! I know what to bring." He was hungry, and irritable as a result.

"Bring back a good shot." She ignored Phil's temper.

"Ya. Ya." He slammed the door behind him.

Maggie turned back to her laptop, but then paused when the scanner announced the need for extrication equipment at the scene. She wondered if she should have gone also. Phil was not one for blood and violence. She dismissed the thought and returned to the story at hand. She'll call the police chief later and get the details.

THURSDAY, DECEMBER 20

The newspapers and television news have their lead story. Speculation runs wild. "Have we been attacked by aliens?" "Is God communicating with us?" "Is a superpower flexing its muscle?" "Have we been hit by an asteroid?" Some people are frightened. Others pass it off as a blip in their daily life. Everyone wants a definitive answer.

The chief suspect is the United States. The State Department denies it. NASA and the CIA are also suspect. They also deny involvement.

No one has an answer. Scan-Man is mum.

*

The stars have just melted into the bleaching sky as two figures in sweat suits run in unison past mile five of their six-mile course. They are obviously experienced runners for their pace is controlled and their breathing regular. The cool morning air condenses their breath into mini steam-train bursts. The country road is hushed except for the bark of a lonely dog and the drumming of their feet on the snow-dusted pavement. Not a word has been spoken for the last forty minutes, nor will one be exchanged until they reach Thompson's Truck Stop.

The older woman had accepted the other's challenge more than two years ago. At 32, Maggie Billings had begun to fear the deterioration she saw in other women her age. Although she had always been slim and in good health, the exertion of a short sprint, or the simple bending to retrieve an object from the floor, produced an unpleasant dizziness. She stopped smoking. Regular running had now brought back at least part of her youthful vigor. She felt good.

Ellen Bloodworth, eight years Maggie's junior, had been an athlete in high school and college. Basketball and track made fast foot movement a way of life. She was a tall woman, close-cropped curly black hair, African-American, chocolate smooth skin.

After six miles, thirty-eight minutes from the start, they pushed through the doors of Thompson's. The corner booth was empty but already set with their breakfast -- orange juice and unbuttered toast. Everything was on schedule.

Petty conversation was not essential. They intuitively knew each other's thoughts after the habitual morning run. The first few minutes were spent regaining normal breathing and inventorying the other Thompson regulars.

Thompson himself came over to their booth and broke the silence. "Mornin' black an' white," Jack's long-time pet name for the duo. "You heard the news."

"What news is that, Jack?" Ellen asked.

"About the, what is it? – the 'Hole in the Night' they call it."

"No. What about it?" Maggie asked.

"Last night – in the middle of the night – this bright light came down from the sky. Nobody knows what it was. It's all over the news."

"I wouldn't worry about it, Jack," Ellen said. "It's probably nothing."

"I don't know. I worry about space aliens."

"Humbug, Jack," Ellen continued. "I know Scan-Man launched another satellite the other day."

"I dunno," Jack continued. "I also hear them convention people are comin' in today. There's a awful lot of deliveries goin' up there these last few days."

Jack was a thin, boney man, balding. He wore his usual smile through his white Hemmingway beard. Shirtsleeves were rolled, revealing wrinkled tattoos, and burn scars from years of attending the short order grill. His apron was a stained record of the morning's business, served to the truckers and laborers who were already on the job well before much of white-collar Hollandson was awake.

"It's a big thing, Jack," Maggie said. "The management's been looking for this day ever since they opened."

"You goin' up there?"

"Yes. Later in the day to check it out."

"I hear the Pulitzer winner scientist is comin'. What's his name?"

"Chabus. Fred Chabus. He's quite a guy they say."

"Ya. I been readin' about him. There was a story about him in *Readers' Digest*."

"He's done wonders for space technology, that's for sure, Jack."

"And what's happenin' with you, Ellen? You goin' to give these space guys some good weather?"

"I wish I could," Ellen smiled. "But I only track the weather. I don't make it."

"Well, glad you can't. It scares the hell out of me if somebody could play God."

"I wouldn't worry about it, Jack. Mother Nature wouldn't allow it if I tried."

"I don't know." Jack was skeptical and shook his head. The *Readers' Digest* story made it sound real -- all that, what is it? Cloud seedin' stuff, and the floods and the drought -- I don't know."

"You're serious. Jack?" Maggie said with surprise looking briefly toward Ellen. "Are you really worried about that?"

"You bet your booties I am. I don't put nothin' past them scientists. They always got to fool around with God's work."

"That's progress, they say."

"Hah!" was Jack's response. "Progress!" He reached for Maggie's glass. "More orange juice?"

"Please." She touched Jack's arm. "Hey friend. Don't look so serious. You worry me."

"I'll do my best." Jack returned to his post behind the counter.

Ellen turned to Maggie. "Your story on this convention has the town all shook up. I can't believe all the preparation the hotel went to in getting ready for this."

"The first convention is always hardest, I guess," Maggie sighed. "They want to make an impression. This means hundreds of thousands of dollars to them. They hope this will bring them back next year and that other conventions will follow. Without conventions, I'm told, a hotel's profits can be marginal."

Jack returned with the juice. Ellen raised her glass.

"Here's to the continued success of the Hollandson Motor Hotel." And with a nod to Jack, "And may those scientists keep their hands off Mother Nature."

They each laughed and Jack disappeared.

Maggie Billings and her husband Phil were owners of the Hollandson Weekly *Bulletin*. They purchased and brought it from irrelevance nearly five years ago. Today it flourished and was considered mandatory reading for everyone interested in the local scene.

Phil was the financial guy responsible for the advertising. He also had a hand in the photography. Phil was often envious of the attention Maggie received generally. At parties, he thought, who wants to talk with the sales manager and moneyman. It's the editor who had the exciting information. This had been a continual rub that irked Phil. It was just that Phil was not as outgoing as his wife..

Maggie was the editor. She was generally considered a remarkable woman who had overcome most of the obstacles, real and imagined, that interfere with the success of many women. Tough-minded, intelligent and aggressive, she also possessed a femininity that could be disarming to her male counterparts. Long working hours and an active social life had not diminished her attractiveness. She was a stunning woman.

Maggie was the optimist, a believer in the ultimate goodness of mankind. She was confident in herself and her capabilities. She didn't acknowledge her possible limitations or potential barriers. In short, Maggie had proven herself to herself as well as to Hollandson.

Although her position on the *Bulletin* prevented her from seeking public office, she was very much a political person. She was never hesitant to express her opinion, or support the candidate whom she felt could best serve the town. Her and Phil's newspaper was a respected voice in the community.

Ellen Bloodworth rented one half of Maggie's large, antique colonial on Great Road in downtown Hollandson. During her two and a half years there, she become close to Maggie, sharing many professional and personal confidences. She was one of Scan-Man's meteorologists and worked at their headquarters on Peters Airfield in Hollandson.

Ellen's function was to analyze meteorological data collected from Scan-Man satellites and observatories scattered around the globe. She had a wide range of sophisticated equipment at her disposal, the company being one of the largest weather interpreters in the world. Scan-Man's size and importance had not been diminished by its intimate association with the federal government. The company generated many devices used by the Apollo and other space programs.

Ellen's professional specialty was winter precipitation, and snow was, not coincidently, her favorite playground. She spent much of her vacation time mountain climbing, and did it with distinction. Next year she was scheduled to tackle Mount Everest as part of an all-woman team, provided of course, the political situation in Tibet remained stable.

They ordered another glass of juice.

"What were all the sirens last night, Maggie? The racket woke me from my before-work beauty nap."

"A fatal on Great Road. A car smashed headlong into a gasoline truck at high speed. I thought it might have been a bad house fire. I was tempted to go. Phil said it wasn't very pretty. The body was pretty much consumed. It was someone who worked at the Airfield, according to the chief."

"From the Airfield?" Ellen was buttering her toast. "Who was it? Maybe I've heard of him, assuming it was a him."

"Let's see." Maggie pondered. "Webster, I think it was. Nat Webster."

Ellen's jaw dropped. She leaned toward Maggie. Her toast fell out of her hand. "Are you sure that's the name?" her voice rising to panic.

"What's the matter?" Maggie asked, startled by Ellen's sudden reaction. "You know this man!"

"Well tell me!" Ellen wailed. Every head in the diner turned in startled response. "What happened?" The wail was louder. Tears burst from the corners of her eyes and ran down her cheeks.

Maggie was totally taken off guard by her friend's emotional response. She had never seen Ellen react this way.

Ellen leaped to her feet, bumping into the table. "Where'd they take him?" she asked, her voice shaking. "Where can I find him?"

Maggie stammered. "He's, he's at the hospital morgue, I guess," she tried to explain. They ... "

"Oh, shit, shit, shit," Ellen cried. "I gotta go."

"Well, look. Let me go with you. I ... " Maggie stood, reaching out to Ellen.

"No. Thanks. I'll go alone." She pushed Maggie aside. "I can't believe it. It's not true."

Ellen ran from the restaurant, oblivious to the universal attention given to her.

Maggie sighed and collapsed back into the booth, head in her hands.

Jack stumbled out from behind the counter and over to her. He self-consciously put his arm over her shoulder. "What's goin' on, Maggie?" he asked gently.

*

Maggie was puzzled about her friend. Back at the house she went directly to the shower. The hot water felt especially good this morning and relieved some of the tension of the last half hour. It was a gentle massage that awakened every pore. She soaped herself thoroughly, inhaled the steam and felt very much alive.

Ellen's shocked expression repeatedly appeared before her. Obviously Webster must have been very close, Maggie thought. She had seen Ellen with a man on a couple of occasions but had never been introduced and Ellen never spoke of him. She wondered if Webster had been Ellen's boyfriend. Could he have been her lover? She felt a twinge of loneliness deep inside. What was it between the two of them? Why had she never mentioned him?

Maggie had often wondered why an African American woman as attractive as Ellen didn't have a male companion or even spoke of men. As she remembered Webster, or whomever she was with, he seemed ruggedly handsome and maybe 10 years older than Ellen. Strange, she thought.

Under the influence of the shower, Maggie's mind drifted to men in general. She had tried to avoid the thoughts of love and lovers. She and Phil had a tiff recently over something stupid and he was now sleeping in the guest room. They were trying to work things out, but it was very difficult. Why were marital spats so often about stupid little things? Why were couples so critical of each other to the extent that they hurt the one they loved?

At the newspaper they were mutually dependent. He, as Business Manager, was responsible for bringing in money that kept the paper afloat so the Editor could write and edit. But dependency does not a good marriage make. Somehow, it seemed, something was missing from her life. Ellen's apparent secret brought this point home hard.

Could she ever really love Phil again with her original passion? Could she love anyone again? She had good old dependable Phil. She hadn't had the opportunity to have a one-night stand with anyone else. Phil was her first love – and her only love. Now they are sleeping apart for some stupid reason, or unreason!

She had her newspaper and her many friends and that had pretty much kept her mind occupied. She didn't have time for the effort love demanded. Hmmm, she thought. Maybe that was the problem. She could be too involved with others. Perhaps she and Phil didn't do enough of anything -- together.

Thinking now about Ellen and Webster sparked her romanticism. Was there someone out there whom she could love, who could satisfy her desires -- if indeed her desires could be reawakened?

As she soaked her hair and let the shower beat against her neck, she examined her breasts. This had become a regular part of her fitness program. She noted they were firm, small, yes, but firm. Her hand dropped to her stomach that she now tightened and pressed. Sit-ups had helped here. There was very little flab, just enough, she thought, to avoid boyishness.

The buttocks was the problem. Just a little too much droop. She didn't like the effect her posterior presented when she wore jeans. But then, she had less rear end than she had a year ago.

Vain, Maggie. You're very vain, she repeated to herself. But, if I don't care about my body, certainly no one else will. Go ahead Maggie. Be vain. But keep it to yourself.

"Damn it," she said, stepping out onto the bathmat. The loneliness was a little stronger now.

She looked at her face closely in the mirror. She saw high cheekbones and the easy tan she carried year round -- that outdoors look which became more pronounced each morning after her run. Her hair was short, reddish brown and curly, a new cut recently acquired, easy to manage and drew many compliments. So far there were no gray hairs. She had no facial blemishes either, except for a few minor indentations on her forehead, a result of childhood chickenpox. Her teeth were a part of her joy also. They were white, even, and all hers.

Ah, yes. She was developing a few wrinkles, but they were smile wrinkles -- always excusable. It was the frown or scowl wrinkles that were unacceptable, or frowned upon. She smiled to herself.

Suddenly Ellen's image appeared again. Maggie wondered how she could comfort her. Did Ellen want comfort? Would Maggie be interfering in a realm Ellen preferred to keep private?

She decided to let Ellen make the next move.

26

*

Three men sat shoulder to shoulder in the rear of a large limousine. Two were dressed in business suits, the third in an Army uniform liberally decorated with ribbons, insignias and a pair of stars on each epaulet. On the brim of his hat were the 'scrambled eggs' of his rank. The car was traveling at moderate speed on the 128 beltway that arcs west of Boston, Massachusetts. There had been very little conversation except for casual references to everyday concerns. Soft background music and the sizzle of tires on the wet pavement were the only other sounds.

One of the men in a business suit spoke, lowering his voice to indicate a change in topic to more serious matters.

"We've known each other for a long time, John. I think we trust each other in a way few men can in our business." He was aware that he sounded awkwardly formal.

John Ruben, the Army General, acknowledged with a nod, fighting an uncomfortable sensation of self-consciousness.

"The reason I say this with such gravity is that I have something of the utmost importance to tell you. What I have to say is, by necessity, top secret for the next few days. I am telling you now because I want you to be the first in your command to know. You'll find this will be to your advantage later, should General Stringer choose not to tell you anything."

The speaker cleared his throat, shifted slightly in the seat and continued.

"Yesterday, as you are well aware, we sent up Scanner XII, the most sophisticated satellite we, or anyone else, have produced for scientific purposes. In addition to the meteorological technology it carries, however, is a device that, militarily speaking, is more potent than any military weapon ever devised. This device is uniquely subtle, yet no more

27

harmful than a drought, a flood or a snowstorm. In short," and the man cleared his throat, "this device is the first viable weather modification instrument ever created."

The man sat back with a satisfied smile, realizing he had finally exposed his cards but was not yet assured of the reaction he expected. He waited.

"What do you want me to say, Chandler? Tell me more."

Chandler Harrington leaned forward again. "Hank and I have been working together for some months now. Only he, as our Agency contact, myself, and a handful of technicians at Scan-Man are cognizant of this instrument. A still smaller group is aware that it was installed in Scanner XII. The reason for this secrecy is obvious.

"The device, or instrument, I refer to is called a Solar Energizer. Officially its use is for refueling or recharging satellites as well as a quick burn destruction on the obsolete models. But, it has one additional purpose, and that is to modify the weather at any spot on earth at our command!"

"Jesus, Jesus," the General murmured.

"At this very moment Scanner XII has set into motion a weather disturbance that will rock central Europe. Snowfall, to an extraordinary depth, will begin to fall on Berlin, Paris, Rome and other large cities within the next couple of days. After this has occurred we plan to ask for a private meeting with the President, the chiefs of staff, and perhaps a few trusted members of Congress. By this time they will have read about the storm. They will have shaken their heads and expressed sympathy for the poor Europeans. But they will also realize that Mother Nature is Mother Nature and that there are mild winters and there are harsh winters and there is nothing anyone can do about it. What they will not know is this was planned and that it happened according to plan."

The General's eyes were glassy, fixed on only a blur of the speaker. His ears heard things he did not want to hear.

"Frankly, Europe was not our first choice for this demonstration, but we needed a technologically sophisticated area, an area that was most capable of coping with a natural disaster. And again, Europe's latitude was more practical at this point in our development than the lower latitudes."

Harrington paused. His talk now took on a sense of urgency. He felt his audience was fully captured.

"The President has to be impressed with the military advantages this will give the United States. Nuclear proliferation has voided any possibility of reasonable control by our government.

"The beauty of the whole idea of our device is its subtlety. Weather is a wholly natural phenomenon. Other than the primitive act of cloud seeding, no other weather controls exist -- until now. It's imperative that the idea be kept secret for many reasons I can't go into now.

"As I said, I wanted you to know in advance. You can watch the foreign press with a different perspective than that of your peers."

The General did not respond immediately.

Finally. "So this is why you've been preoccupied lately," he said. "You finally came through with it. It's really a viable concept." He paused thoughtfully. "But why do you have to be so damned secretive? Why can't this be an up front operation?"

Hank, the man from the Intelligence Agency spoke for the first time. "We have our reasons, John. Those reasons need not concern you. Your position in the overall picture should be your concern. It'll be another star on your shoulder if you play it right."

"Just what do you want me to do?" the General asked with the slightest trace of a grimace.

"I believe," the Agency man continued, "that with your position in the Pentagon and mine at the IA, coupled with Chandler's reputation at Scan-Man, we can present the President with some goddamned convincing arguments for investing in the technology."

The General turned his head and looked out the window. It was a dreary scene, bleak and depressing. Huge, wet snowflakes spattered against the window, fell to the road and were crushed into oblivion. He tried to think of where he went wrong in his career. He had compromised himself too often with these civilians.

"But you already have the technology!" the General said.

"We want the government to pay in full for this technology. To you, it doesn't exist. We want them to pay us to create it – as if we never had it."

"And you want me to say we need it," the General said with disgust. "You have to give me time to think about it," he said sadly.

Harrington's response was dry and harsh. "You have ten minutes. The code name is 'Hot Spot.' We'll fill you in later on the details." He rapped on the window to the driver who acknowledged the signal and speeded up.

General John Ruben developed an instant headache. Why me? he thought. How many times can my arm be twisted before it breaks off? God, I hate myself. I am a fucking, yellow-bellied shithead!

*

"Then who was it?"

"I have no idea. But I thank God it wasn't Nat!" Ellen had recovered.

"How can you be sure it wasn't?"

"That's a long story, Maggie. I feel very guilty for not having told you of my friendship with Nat."

30

The two women were sitting in Maggie's office at the *Bulletin*. Ellen was still dressed in her running suit and now had her hands wrapped around a mug of hot coffee.

"The problem is, I don't know where Nat is," Ellen mused. "After I left the morgue, oh what a horrid place, I called his apartment and then his office. The office had just gotten the word that he died. I didn't argue with them. They thought I was nuts asking for him after that bit of news -- if anyone should have known, it was I. He just seems to have disappeared."

Maggie leaned across her desk and looked compassionately at her friend. "Ellen. Let's back up a bit. Do you want to tell me about you and Nat?"

"I don't know why I didn't before this."

"First of all, how did you know this man wasn't your friend? It's my understanding he was mutilated beyond recognition."

"Nat and I are very close. I've known him this way for two years. We met at Scan-Man. Since he was divorced from his wife we've spent a lot of time together. We live separately because he has been very busy with getting Scanner XII assembled, launched and operational.

"You're right about this body being mutilated. But I knew it wasn't him. It's somebody else. But since I'm not next of kin, nobody believes my identification. I think they thought it was humorous. But they can believe what they want! At least I know."

"But wasn't it Nat's VW that crashed? How do you explain that?"

"That's what they say. That's why they think its Nat. They also said the VW was speeding, and that settled it for me. Nat never drives fast. He drives like a little old man. In fact there was a joke around the office that the reason he never went home was because by the time he got there it

31

would be time to turn around and come back." Ellen smiled at the anecdote.

"Did Nat act strange the last time you saw him? Did he act upset or was he depressed about anything?"

"You don't believe me either!" Her tears flowed again. She reached for a tissue from the box on Ellen's desk and dabbed at her eyes.

"Come on, Ellen! I do believe you, but if we're going to find Nat and find out who this mysterious dead man is, we've got to know who to look for."

Ellen regained her composure. "Yes, I admit he has been very depressed and despondent -- for the past couple of months. It's his job. It's really getting to him. I've tried to get him to move in with me. But he's stubborn. I think I could really give the support he needs. Sometimes I think he would be embarrassed living with a Black woman. But then I've never noticed a problem when we're out in public together.

"Nat is a very affectionate man. We make great love together. We fit like Yin and Yang, although I'm a couple inches taller than him. He insists we'll get married when things calm down."

"What about the job? What's depressing him?"

"This he won't tell me. As close as we are, he never discusses any details about what he's doing. He said it's classified. He says he doesn't want to burden me with his problems.

"He's a brilliant man," Ellen continued. "Beyond ourselves, his obsession in life is his job. He's been at Scan-Man practically since it was founded. He's been the brain behind some of the company's most advanced technology. He's a shirtsleeve guy. He turned down several chances to take a desk job. He fulfills his dreams in the lab and at the drafting table. He's a creative genius who's rotten at delegating responsibility.

32

"Nat and I see each other two or three nights a week and sometimes on weekends. His favorite game is to make me feel important by prying information about my end of the business. It's ridiculous! He probably knows more about meteorology than I do! His end of the business at Scan-Man is inventing and perfecting gadgetry for his satellites. Although he'll never admit it, I know that most of the hardware floating around upstairs comes from his drawing board.

"I wouldn't call it depression. He has been very quiet these last few days. I often wonder if our relationship is falling apart, even though he assures me it isn't and that he needs me all the more. Now that I think about it, he did mention a few days ago he felt he was heading for a crackup -- a 'mental breakdown,' he said. I tried to get him to forget his job, to quit if it was going to wreck his life -- our lives.

"But he said it wouldn't last much longer. He'd soon be free. I don't know what he means by that. I assume it means he's finishing up this project and he'll soon be free from it."

"Was there anything else?"

"I'm afraid there is, and it hurts me to tell you this. I never take him seriously about it, but it's a subject that apparently fascinates him. He spoke of suicide."

"He finds suicide 'fascinating?'" Maggie asked incredulously.

"Maybe not 'fascinating,' but interesting. Now look! Don't jump to conclusions!" Ellen was becoming agitated again.

"I'm not," Maggie said soothingly. "Please don't think I'm prying. I just want to help you find Nat. There's obviously something strange going on here. I'm also very curious about who the dead man is."

*

Press time was noon, less than two hours from now. Maggie had one more story to write and several to edit. Meanwhile the phone continued to ring and last minute news items from local clubs were littering the In Box. There were final decisions to make on national and international stories that stuttered uninterruptedly on Doris' keyboard. There was a persistent someone in the waiting room with a "hot" story about the renovation of an historic home in Lexington.

She buzzed her secretary. "Look, Doris. This has to stop. Reschedule some of these people. Either that, or let's forget about going to press today."

Doris smiled knowingly, closed the door and spoke to the woman in the waiting room. Maggie was a great boss. It was just that every Thursday morning at 10 she panicked. Doris was accustomed to it.

The phone rang. It was Police Chief Paul Wilson.

"How many times have I told you not to call me in the morning unless you have news," Maggie chided Wilson.

"I wouldn't call you unless I did. Why else would I call you? I'm a married man."

"Seriously, Paul. I'm out straight. What's happening?"

"I thought this might relate to your story on the accident. Your friend Ellen was in a little while ago and she says the victim is not Nat Webster."

"That's right. I just found that out an hour ago."

"But I'll bet you didn't know this," the chief said teasingly.

"What!"

"We finally located Webster's ex-wife early this morning. She came in and positively identified the body as her husband."

"Wow!" was Maggie's reaction. "That is interesting, Paul. Who are you going to believe?"

"I have no choice. Although your friend appeared absolutely certain after close examination, and Mrs. Webster, with one quick, squeamish look, made her positive ID, we have no choice. She was his wife."

"Did you ask Mrs. Webster why she was so sure?"

"I asked both of them that. They're both just 'sure.'"

"OK, Paul. Thanks for the tip."

"Sorry to bother you, Mag."

"And don't call me Mag!" She shouted into the phone.

The chief snickered and hung up. He enjoyed needling the editor about her name. "Maggie" was bad enough. "Mag," he knew, was unbearable.

*

The noon whistle blew. Maggie closed her laptop. Ready or not, the Weekly *Bulletin* was going to press.

*

The Hollandson Motor Hotel is approached from the intersection of Route 128 and Great Road by a half mile curving drive, lighted on each side by white globes atop tall posts. The drive winds gracefully up to a fieldstone entrance that is covered and able to accommodate several vehicles at a time. Guests are greeted by doormen who escort them through electric glass doors to a spacious lobby embellished with a huge Oriental rug beneath a chandelier of mammoth proportions. Brick and fieldstone interior walls and floor complete the impression of splendor and solidity.

To the left of the entrance is the Cloven Hoof Tavern, open to both guests and locals who stop in for an evening of entertainment and relaxation. To the right are gift shops featuring Fifth Avenue stores displaying furs, fashion clothing and jewelry.

Directly ahead is the Garden Room, the central gathering place. This is a tropical outdoor environment,

35

covered by a massive dome of glass and metal girders one hundred feet above. Two acres in area, the Garden Room contains dining and drinking locations at ground level and on elevated South Pacific-style grass-roofed platforms. Buffet meals are served from stainless steel counters along part of one wall. Scattered through the Garden Room are several fountains, mini waterfalls, a brook, swimming pool and a dance floor. Connecting each of these are meandering, crushed rock paths, lined with shrubbery, exotic trees, gas lamps and park benches. It is a manicured dream island within the protective womb of a heated structure.

Along the other walls of this "room" are the guests' suites that overlook the scene from a tier of five balconied floors. A fourth wall provides entrance to the convention hall capable of seating more than a thousand for dining, dancing or lectures.

Taxis and limousines from Boston's Logan International Airport had been arriving all morning and many distinguished guests were now lined up at the front desk performing the dreaded but necessary ritual of checking in.

Dashing among them, carrying out token bits of courtesy, was Vito Pazzita, manager of the Hollandson Motor Hotel. He was a nervous little man -- short, but rotund. Yet he was very fast on his feet. Vito's mind was always two steps ahead of the project at hand. Thus, a meaningful conversation with Vito was impossible, for his train of thought was already on what was to come next and next and next. Some would describe him as obsequious, but the truth was he was more eager to serve than to flatter. He wanted each of his guests to have the very best service.

This was a significant week for Vito. This was the most important event of his career in hotel management. The arrival of the guests this day marked the beginning of the hotel's first national convention. The success with which Vito handled it would determine if it returned next year. And, if this convention was memorable, more national conventions were sure to follow. Success also meant a promising future for the manager.

During the afternoon he had greeted Dr. and Mrs. Fred Chabus, current President of the National Scientific Association, the organization sponsoring this convention. Vito personally handled the couple's check-in details, bypassed the bellhop and attempted to escort the couple to their suite. Chabus modestly objected to the personal attention, saying he preferred to go about the procedure at his own speed, speaking with his associates along the way.

Vito wouldn't hear of it and bulldozed them through.

Puff, the doctor's wife, smiled at the way her celebrated husband was overruled, and waved goodbye to him as she turned away to speak with a friend across the hall.

Later, President-elect Dr. Robert Krentzler, arriving alone, was also met by Vito. Although Krentzler acknowledged his presence, his six-foot-eight frame passed Vito over with disdain. By sheer height alone, Krentzler was able to do his own bulldozing. His abrupt and commanding voice and gestures accomplished what was left. Krentzler enjoyed intimidating people, including his own colleagues.

*

Maggie Billings and Puff Chabus were chatting over drinks in the Garden Room on the Tahitian Atoll when Dr. Chabus found them.

"Doggone it, Puff," he said in exasperation and in deference to his wife's companion. "I've just spent the last half hour traipsing through every mile of this hot-house trying to find you." He collapsed on a stool at the bar with exaggerated exhaustion.

"If you'd refrain from letting hotel managers run your life ... " Puff began.

"Vito's a nice guy. He's just a little, ah, eager."

Puff turned to Maggie. "Freddie, I want you to meet my friend Maggie. Maggie Billings. We just met in the lobby while you were being carted away by your manager. She's editor of the local paper, but she says she works off the record also."

Maggie extended her hand to Chabus who took it warmly. "Did my wife pick you up, or did you her?" He laughed. "Puff picks up people like lint."

"Fred Chabus!" Puff scolded. "Maggie's not lint!"

"Excuse my dangling simile. What do you do on the paper, Maggie?" he asked with a relaxed charm.

"Oh, about everything," she responded with as much modesty as she could dredge up. "I'm covering the NSA meeting this week. It's a big deal for our small town and our first real convention. And, of course, it's newsworthy."

"Oh, they're newsworthy all right. Hang around," Puff warned as if the distinguished group would conduct a panty raid later in the evening.

"Count on it. I'm just here for an overview today. I'll be back tomorrow to attend some of the seminars." Leaning toward Chabus, Maggie said, "You have some fascinating topics lined up."

"I'm glad you think so."

"You've recently won the Pulitzer Prize for your research on Dish Antennas, isn't that right?"

"Yes. It was really an honor."

"Oh, Freddie. You're so darned modest," Puff cut in. "I'm Freddie's PR person. He never takes credit for anything. Yes, he spent five years, five long years on the project. At times I felt like an antenna."

Now that Chabus had arrived, Maggie wished his wife would evaporate.

"In all seriousness, it was a difficult time," Puff said. "The prize money made up for a lot of it though." She obtrusively toyed with a large diamond, a gesture Maggie chose to ignore.

A pause followed as Chabus lighted his pipe. "Maggie," he began thoughtfully through the gray smoke. "You didn't happen to know a man from this area by the name of Nat Webster, did you?"

The mention of the name struck her with a thud in the chest. Her heart pounded noticeably. "Then you've heard."

"Yes. It appears to be the talk of the convention."

"Frankly I hadn't heard of him until last night after his accident." Thoughts rushed through Maggie's head. What did this man know about Webster?

"Who's this you're talking about, Freddie?"

"A colleague of mine. I don't think you met him. He was in San Francisco last year at NSA. He died last night in a car accident."

"Good grief!" Puff gasped. "Did you know him well?"

"Quite well. We collaborated on the Scan-Man reorganization here in town many years ago."

"Scan-Man reorganization?" Maggie asked.

"Yes. Nat and I were part of a group that geared the company up for Kennedy's space ambitions."

Maggie's interest intensified. "I have a good friend who was close to Webster. She's just been through hell over his death. In fact she refuses to believe he's dead."

"A natural reaction for someone close to a victim," Chabus reflected.

"My friend said he was a brilliant man. It seems he was totally involved in his work."

Chabus nodded. "That's Nat."

Maggie paused, phrasing and rephrasing her next sentence. "There's some speculation his death was related to his latest project."

Chabus sat erect and looked squarely at Maggie. "Whose speculation?" he asked sarcastically, "Yours?"

Maggie was embarrassed. She'd screwed up. "I'm sorry. I'm told that Webster had not been himself for the past several months. According to his friend he spoke of suicide."

"Who the hell is this 'friend?'" Chabus' temperament had changed dramatically.

"His girlfriend. She said she watched him deteriorate over the last few months." Maggie felt herself being backed into a corner of her own making.

"So you're suggesting Nat killed himself?"

"Possibly. Possibly because of his latest project."

"I don't believe it. I think that's a lot of bullshit." Chabus sat back on his stool as if to reinforce his statement.

Puff interrupted. "You two chat for a bit. I see a dear friend across the way I haven't seen in an age." She looked at her husband. "Don't be too long, dear. You have to circulate. You know what I mean?"

"OK, OK, You run along. I'll catch up."

The women nodded to each other and Puff went on her way, waving and beckoning to her friend.

"You know something about Webster's latest project?" Maggie pressed.

"I know quite a bit about it." Chabus' answer was short.

"Look, Dr. Chabus. I'm sorry if I jumped to conclusions. I take it back. But for my satisfaction can you tell me something about Nat Webster?"

40

Chabus slowly regained his composure and returned to sucking contentedly on his meerschaum. He gazed at Maggie thoughtfully then took another sip of his martini. "The details of Webster's project are classified. Why do you want this information?"

"Purely personal. If you're worried about my being an editor you can forget it. I won't rest until I can tell my friend why Webster died."

Chabus continued to eye Maggie as he struck another match and relit his pipe. "I trust you. I think I can read your sincerity."

"Thank you," Maggie said, refraining from releasing the sigh built up within her.

"Webster was a funny guy -- a brilliant mind. Even when he was in high school he was experimenting with rocketry and aerodynamics. He also played with optics. He had a wide range of interests and he excelled in all of them."

"He worked for Scan-Man for a long time?"

"Oh, yes. He brought the company to its feet. He's been ... He was a director at one time and has been with the company since its infancy."

Chabus appeared to Maggie to be in deep thought. She listened for several minutes, hesitating to interrupt to ask the question that most deeply interested her. What about his most recent project?

"Yes, yes. He has spent the last two or three years, I understand, developing what are called solar energizers. This is essentially a method of permanently fueling satellites while in orbit. Theoretically this method makes the life of a satellite, a space station, or even a rocket, infinite. Imagine not needing conventional fuel in space. Imagine charging space vehicles with solar energy. Imagine, once free of gravity, to have an infinite supply of energy to power your space ship to any destination.

"This was Webster's project. This is what we talked about last year at NSA. The way he described it, it seemed to be a realistic scheme. He even showed simulated models of his energizer last year. Unfortunately I haven't kept up with this in the last few months."

"Do you know of any reason why Webster might have been severely depressed lately?"

"Nat always took things very seriously, Maggie. He was also under a great deal of pressure. Scan-Man is notorious for the demands it makes on people."

"I wasn't aware of that. My friend, who also works at Scan-Man, never mentioned that."

"Ah, Maggie. But is your friend entrusted with billions of dollars of space gear? Is your friend responsible for returning men from space missions? Does your friend have the burden of knowing, because of the flick of a switch, as simple a thing as that, four Americans in the Triade Project missed their mark and their bodies are now rocketing into infinity? Webster carries that burden."

The *Bulletin* editor gulped and looked at Chabus genuinely shocked. "I ... I had no idea. You mean Webster ...?"

"Few people do," Chabus said gravely. "I trust you will keep that bit of information to yourself."

"How could such a blatant error have been kept from the public?" Maggie asked, ignoring Chabus' last comment.

"You imply that all blatant errors are revealed to the public. They aren't. There are ways, Maggie Billings. There are ways. Believe me."

Maggie's brain tumbled in a confusion of unanswered questions. The Nat Webster story was a bombshell. Why did Chabus reveal Webster's error? Was it true, or was it to test her? Just who was Chabus?

"Why wasn't that disaster made public?"

"I can tell you no more, Maggie. At least not now."

Chabus smiled and stood. "I would like to see you later after things here quiet down."

Maggie stood. Chabus' voice was strangely husky. He was standing awkwardly close and she could feel his body heat.

She had to learn more from this man. "I'd love to," she answered, easing away from him. "And we haven't begun to discuss your accomplishments -- which I assume are public information."

"Yes, my dear, they are." Chabus took her hand with a warm smile. "I look forward to your company later."

Maggie shook her head as if to clear it of the jumble of information she had just absorbed. She watched Chabus wind his way across the Garden Room waving and nodding to one person and another. "Incredible," she said as she regained her presence of mind and turned in the opposite direction.

Passing the convention registration tables, she picked up a program and flipped through it. She noted that one of the featured speakers was from Scan-Man -- an Edward Randolph, listed as President of the company. The name was vaguely familiar. Was he a Hollandson resident?

She suddenly became acutely aware of how little she knew about that giant company located in her own back yard. She felt a twinge of guilt. She, the editor of the local newspaper, the person who is looked up to as the bureau of information in the community, knew nothing about a hierarchy that appeared to help shape world events. It was damned embarrassing.

She resolved at that moment to place Scan-Man near the top of her investigation list. There was a story here. The convention was an obvious place to begin. Chabus was the obvious man to help her.

*

Normally Marsha Randolph telephoned her liquor order, but since she was in the vicinity she decided to do it in person.

"Ah, Mrs. Randolph. So good to see you. What can I help you with today?" The storeowner flourished.

"Hello Walter." She handed him her list and briskly turned to scan the shelves. "Give me a case of each of these," she said, referring to the list. "I want them delivered tomorrow."

Walter quickly looked over the list and smiled. "No problem, Mrs. Randolph. We ... "

"And I'll take the Tangurey with me now. Put it in the car."

"Certainly. Certainly. Anything else Mrs. Randolph?"

"Don't be such an obsequious ass, Walter," she flashed at him then turned toward the door. "Put the gin in the car. I'm in a hurry."

"Yes, Mrs. Randolph."

*

The Randolph home was set well away from the Road, in a pine grove on a rise overlooking the Winniposkeg River, a dairy farm in the valley and the hills beyond. The driveway was long, unpaved, steep and winding. It discouraged strangers from passing the "No Trespassing" sign at the entrance.

The house itself was a copy of a Frank Lloyd Wright design the Randolphs had seen during one of their visits to the Southwest. It was a single story, except for the second floor bedrooms at one end. It was constructed to fit into the contour of the hillside. Its length was enormous, yet because of the harmony of the architecture with the landscaping, there was little awareness of size. Brown, weathered exterior blended with the natural surroundings, with large picture windows looking out upon the pleasant scene below. Beyond

44

the hilltops to the east were the upper stories of the taller buildings of Boston.

The Randolph house was acknowledged to be one of a kind in New England. Soon after it was built, a cover story in Boston Globe Magazine unveiled its charms to a million readers.

The garage doors opened as Marsha's sleek Maserati approached. There was an empty bay next to where she parked and in a third bay was a Lincoln SUV. At the rear was yet another car, perhaps an antique, protected with a drop cloth.

Marsha breezed into the house by way of the kitchen. "Alberta. There's a case of liquor in the car. Have Francisco put it away."

"Yes, Mrs. Randolph," was the monotone response.

Alberta was the elderly black cook who had been part of the elder Randolph household. She was reassigned to the young couple following their marriage ten years earlier.

In the master bedroom Marsha tossed her coat across the bed and turned into the bathroom. She removed three capsules from a container and swallowed them, one at a time, with a glass of water.

She returned to the kitchen. "Have you seen Robert?"

"He don't get home from school for another hour, Mrs. Randolph." Alberta continued her work without looking up.

"Oh, that's right." Marsha spun on her heels and went into the living room where she poured herself a gin on the rocks. She sat, kicked off her shoes and, with a private sigh, studied the growth of moisture on the side of the glass.

*

A crowd had gathered at the Cloven Hoof Tavern. It was dark, lighted only by the glow of red shaded recessed ceiling lamps and the dim white lights from the bar.

Cushiony vinyl chairs circling tiny tables filled the room. Along the oval bar a stutter of stools supported top-heavy burdens. The decor, and the intensity of the many muffled conversations, gave the room an air of escapism which patrons found exciting. Two waitresses kept busy shuttling drinks through the nearly impossible obstacle course of both sexes determined to enjoy themselves.

Irene Stitch was earning $100 an hour in tips this evening. They had told her the convention was a moneymaker. That kind of money more than paid for the bruises she suffered bumping between the chairs. Somehow it compensated as well for the occasional pinches she endured.

She began her work just prior to Thanksgiving. She had seen an ad in the *Bulletin* soliciting extra help for Thanksgiving Day. She and a few of her friends signed up. Although some of them had since quit, she stayed on. It was a job, and she was saving to buy a car. Her parents had promised her a car if she graduated from high school. That was last June. She did graduate, but the promise never came through. She should have known.

One nice thing about the job was the other kids who worked at the hotel. Although Vito was a pain most of the time, he was easily ignored. She and the others frequently had their own parties in one of the empty rooms. Nobody ever knew the difference as long as they didn't make too much noise.

If these tips kept coming all week, Irene figured she'd be able to buy her car after first of the year. Then she'd quit the job.

*

Frank McCullough turned his old Chevy into the dirt drive of the barnyard and eased into the shed. It had been windy and cold at the landfill -- four hours of monotony -- not like Saturday mornings when the children arrived, accompanied by their parents on trash day. That was the day he handed out penny candy to a hundred or more shy, giggling faces. He loved Saturdays.

Today, however, he had finished carving another link in his famous wooden chain, hand hewn from the slim trunk of a young oak. This was his conversation piece -- nearly everyone, week after week, asked Frank how he was progressing on his chain. On Saturdays he rarely had time to work at it and that was just as well. That was the day he displayed it to all who cared to ask.

He emerged from the shed, an ancient, tanned, weather-beaten hulk of a man. His face was deeply creased, but the lines were those of a man who had had a happy life, the lines of a well-used smile or laugh. He was dressed in never-polished work boots, faded green trousers, a checkered wool shirt over which he wore a sleeveless down-filled windbreaker. Frank wore his character on the outside.

High thin clouds stretched between the horizons. There would be no snow tonight, he thought, just another stove-hugger. He had been worried about the tulip bulbs he planted a few months ago along the edge of the house. Without snow the frost would penetrate deeply, possibly in spite of the mulch he had spread over them.

Mabel, his marriage partner of sixty-one years, waved to him from the kitchen window as he headed toward the barn to perform his daily ritual of chores. Rolf, the golden retriever, nearly thirteen years old now, wiggled and wagged his way out to meet Frank who patted him on the head and thumped him affectionately on the ribs. Oh, how Rolf hated to leave his bed in the hay next to Buttercup's stall.

Buttercup was the heifer. Raised lovingly, she was nevertheless doomed to occupy the freezer shortly. Two years was her lifetime, and then another calf would replace her in the spring. Then there was Henrietta, the inexhaustible milk supplier -- the single cow in the barn that once housed forty. And finally there were the 140 or so hens, all egg layers, and a dozen assorted cats that kept the ravenous mouse population out of the expensive grain.

Frank's last task was to collect the eggs in two large wire baskets. Eight dozen was a reasonable production to expect in this weather.

On the porch at the back of the house Frank set down the baskets and surveyed the landscape. How proud he had once been of this farm. Fifteen or twenty years ago it had been a thriving dairy with eighty acres of well tended pasture, a freshly painted house and out buildings. He was reluctant to admit it, but for the last few years he had been unable to keep up with all the repairs. Somehow things had slipped past him. It now took all his energy to tend the garden, care for the animals, cut wood and work fifteen hours a week at the landfill.

He leaned into the door. Mabel was waiting for him with a come-see-what-I've-done grin. He followed her into the kitchen and placed the egg baskets on the counter. There on the table was a six-tiered wedding cake, two feet tall. The base frosting was white, dotted with yellow, pink and blue decorations. Garlands circled the upper edge of each layer and at the top was the traditional wedding couple with two of Frank's hand-carved sugar wedding bells. He turned to Mabel and winked. Those wedding bells were the most delicate project Frank had ever attempted. He had carved, oh, so very gently, each bell down to paper thickness, so that each was translucent. And this was done with those big, ugly, earth-oriented hands.

"Do you think they'll like it?" Mabel asked with a coy timidity that carried the message that this was her masterpiece.

"Mabel," he said, tucking her tiny frame under his arm, "they'll go -- how do they say it now? They'll go bonkers." They laughed, turned and placed their arms around each other.

Mabel lived in and for her kitchen. She scorned modern aids and still carried on with her mother's tried-and-proven utensils. No gadgetry for her! Her joy, over and above the canning and preserving of Frank's garden vegetables, was creating cakes of every description. Initially as a hobby, it had developed into a business. Advertising solely by word of mouth, over the fence and across the clothesline, people came from forty miles to purchase her creations.

"Well, you got done in plenty of time," Frank said. "They ain't comin' for it till the day after tomorrow."

"No problem," Mabel said. "Into the cooler it goes so the frosting don't get soaked in."

*

The Randolph family was unusually buoyant at dinner this evening. Each had pleasant expectations for the next few days. The dining table was exquisitely set for the evening meal. It was the one time during the day when they were all together. A linen tablecloth was the order of the day along with a second-best set of china and silverware. The centerpiece tonight was a bouquet of six yellow roses set in a nest of babies' breath. Two red candles were placed at either end. The room lights had been turned down to a mellow glow. It was romantic, a relaxing scene that Marsha knew Randolph preferred.

Ed and Marsha sat at either end of the table and Robert, their nine -year-old, at one side. Alberta served from opposite Robert, standing. She and Francisco would eat by themselves in the kitchen after the family had finished.

Randolph, as Marsha called him, was smiling to himself. His wife had noted the smile for the past five minutes and had expected him to say something about it during one of the pauses in her monologue. She finally asked.

"Months of headaches have finally left my desk and are now 220 miles above us," he began.

"Oh?"

"Scanner XII has been launched and it's working to perfection."

"That's the new satellite with all the fancy whatchamacallits built into it that you've been stewing about for weeks?"

"That's the one. The directors are pleased and Harrington is beside himself. Everything has worked out just perfectly."

"I read in the *Bulletin* that your man Webster committed suicide. That was horrid! Why do you suppose he did it?"

"What's suicide, mother?" Robert asked.

"It's something you're too young to know about," Marsha said. "Please eat your peas before they get cold."

"Did the article say 'suicide'?" Randolph asked with surprise.

"No. But anyone who drives that recklessly has to be committing suicide."

"Well, I don't know. Probably never will. I really hated to lose the guy. I've known him for quite a few years. A strange guy and he could really be a pain sometimes."

"What do you mean?"

"He never wanted to go along with company policy. You might say he was an independent cuss."

"Why'd the company hang onto him?"

"Because he was smart. He had some good ideas."

"He wasn't very good at parties. He was a bore," Marsha added, recalling the only Randolph party Webster had been invited to -- seven years ago.

"I didn't think you'd remember him."

"I always remember party bores."

Randolph chuckled. "And how are things coming for Saturday night? I noticed you have the pool decorated."

"Yes. I've been working overtime with Alberta. We have all the food, and I ordered the liquor today."

"How many guests this time?"

"Twenty-five couples, I hope. I expect we'll get the rest of the answers tomorrow."

"Good. I want to make this very special. We have a lot to celebrate. You have acceptances from everyone at Scan-Man?"

"They're always the first to answer. I hope we get all the fun ones too."

"You don't like my associates from the office?"

"Of course I do," Marsha answered quickly. "It's just that I like to have some of my friends too -- people who can talk about something other than whatchamacallits and space stuff."

"Well, you'd better like them. That's our bread-and-butter. We have to always show our best side."

"Count on it Randolph dear. I'll be my regular, charming, adorable self."

Thanks to Robert, the conversation changed course.

"Tomorrow, after school, Francisco is going to help me cut a Christmas tree. We're going to get a real big one."

"Don't get it too big, Robert, or we'll have to cut a hole in the ceiling." Randolph chuckled again.

"Oh, father!" Robert said, looking down at his plate. "I don't mean that big."

"Will it be bigger than last year's tree?" Randolph was having fun.

"Oh, much bigger," Robert said with a huge smile. "This high." Robert stretched his arm over his head, rising from his chair simultaneously. When he returned to his chair his elbow hit his plate, knocking it to the floor. It broke.

"Robert!" Marsha shouted. "You go to your room this instant!" She immediately regretted her flash of temper, but it was too late.

The boy burst into tears and ran from the table. The spell was shattered. Alberta, silently standing at the side of the room, returned to the kitchen for the dustpan and brush.

"Sometimes I think you are too harsh on that boy," Randolph commented.

"Sometimes I think you don't discipline him enough!" Marsha shot back. "You just play with him. I'm the one who has to be the bitch!"

"Well you certainly are!" Randolph jabbed.

Marsha jumped up and left the room. It was that time again. She couldn't afford to lose that edge. Her nerves just let go every time. She swallowed three more pills, washing them down with water.

*

"OK. The selectmen's meeting is called to order," Bob Sivolesky announced with characteristic drama. "The first order of business is to announce that we won't meet next week because of the holidays. And, Roy here is heading for the sunny South and has said we can freeze our butts off." He ended with a laugh.

"Where are you going Roy?" Maggie asked. Roy Langer was junior member on the Hollandson board.

"This isn't for publication, but the lady and me are visiting the daughter in Alabama. Actually it could be quite cold down there. I understand the South had a bad fall."

"It can't be any colder than here," Warren Coulter added. "But I'll be right behind you. I'm going to Orlando."

"My God," Maggie exclaimed. "The selectmen's job must pay pretty well!"

"Sure. A dollar a day and all the headaches you can take," said Sivolesky.

The selectmen were forever using the standard joke of how little they were paid for the problems they faced. And it was true that they were each paid an annual salary of $365 for the elected position.

The board met every Thursday evening. Maggie relished the meetings for this was where she acquired the political meat each week for her paper. For five years she had sat in the selectmen's office one night a week as a reporter, and she was as much a fixture as the chair she sat on.

The regular business of bill paying and permit signing having been accomplished, Sivolesky, the chairman, acknowledged the Army captain who had been sitting stone-faced through the previous five minutes of less-than-dignified governmental management by the trio behind the desk.

"Can we help you captain?" Sivolesky asked.

Coming to attention, the Captain stood. "Yes. Thank you, sir."

"Pull up a chair and be comfortable. Loosen your tie of you want, captain." Sivolesky smiled.

"No. Thank you. I'll just be a minute."

Maggie couldn't help but smile also. The board always had to have its fun.

The captain stood tall, slim and straight. Dressed fastidiously in uniform and highly polished shoes he was a dramatic contrast to the selectmen who rarely took any pains to impress the public with their wardrobe.

The captain explained that for the first two weeks in January the Army would be experimenting with aircraft guidance systems and the town could expect the activity of a large number of low-flying aircraft.

The noise of the coming and going of airplanes had always been a sore point with Hollandson residents.

Although Peters Airfield had preceded ninety percent of the current population, the traffic of helicopters and large transports could be noisy and irritating on an otherwise peaceful afternoon in July.

"I suppose it's useless to object," Sivolesky said.

"I'm here tonight, sir, to inform you of our activities, sir. The commander knows the town's feelings and he says he will make every effort to keep the noise to a minimum."

"What exactly is this guidance system?"

"I'm not at liberty to give details, sir, but it is a new technique of guiding aircraft through zero visibility conditions to PGTD, sir."

"What is PGDT, captain?"

"It's PGTD, sir. Pinpoint Ground Touchdown."

"Is it better than what commercial airlines now use?"

"Oh, it's much better," the captain said, forgetting himself momentarily. "It's an entirely different principle based on sound rather than radio waves. But I've said too much already."

"Probably similar to the principal of sonar?" Sivolesky went on, ignoring the captain's discomfort.

"I'm not at liberty to say."

"Ah, ha!" Sivolesky exploded, hitting his fist on the table. "I'll bet it is! What do you think, Roy?"

"I think we'd better thank the captain and let him go." Langer was less vocal than Sivolesky.

The captain turned for the door.

"Oh, captain," Sivolesky said.

The captain turned. "Yes, sir?"

"Was that one of your men who had the accident last night?"

"What accident, sir?"

"Oh, never mind. There was a fatal accident on Great Road. I heard it was somebody from the base."

54

"I don't know. Sorry, sir."

"Well, thanks anyway, captain."

"Maggie cut in. "I heard he was from Scan-Man, Bob."

"Scan-Man, eh? Too bad." Sivolesky returned to his papers muttering. "Why the hell he was driving a heap like that so fast beats me."

Maggie followed the captain out the door and into the hallway, squeezing past Molly Battinni who was just entering.

"Captain. My name's Maggie Billings. I'm with the *Bulletin*."

She handed him her business card.

"I'm sorry, ma'am, but I can't comment any further."

"I'm not after a comment, just to introduce myself. I'm a friend of Commander Heathside. I'd appreciate it if when you see him you give him my card and say I said hello."

"Certainly will, ma'am." The captain smiled.

The Army base at Peters Airfield was public relations conscious. At least once a year, usually Armed Forces Day, the local press was invited to dinner with the commander where they were given the opportunity to learn more about what the Army was up to and, conversely, the Army learned from the press if they were making headway with the public. At one rare occasion Maggie played golf with Heathside and since then they had become casual friends.

"I'd appreciate it. And, by the way. Don't pay any attention to the selectmen's comments tonight. They're in a jolly mood, with the holiday and all."

"Thank you, ma'am."

Maggie returned to the room where the board was coping with Molly, the perennial director of the Annual Winter Carnival. How she originally became interested in this winter activity Maggie never found out. Certainly she couldn't participate! She was only four-foot-six and appeared to be as wide as she was tall. But Maggie knew her to be a superb worker, vigorously and noisily in the background, pushing, cajoling, urging and swearing at various individuals, eventually pulling the whole complex event together.

"Yes, I'm back here again," her voice boomed. "I come in this office only once a year and it's always for the same reason."

"Let me guess," Sivolesky said.

"You undernourished potato peel! You know damn well why I'm here."

"Wait. Yes. I've got it!" Sivolesky teased. "I'll bet you want a parade permit."

"I don't know why I bother," Molly sighed. Turning to Maggie, "This bunch of jokers -- I don't know how this town survives."

"We survive on momentum, Molly," Sivolesky continued.

"Our forefathers did such a good job in Lexington and Concord and here in Hollandson, we're still riding the wave."

"Personally, I think you're under the wave," Molly smiled.

Maggie laughed out loud, unable to hold it back.

"I heard there won't be any snow this year," selectman Coulter said, joining in on the fun.

"I've done my snow dance, boys. It wouldn't dare not snow."

Everyone laughed, including Molly, as each envisioned her performing a snow dance.

"But anyway, the news tonight said it was going to snow although not very much. But, then, who can believe the weatherman?"

"It'll snow, Molly. It'll snow for you," Maggie said with as much confidence as she could carry in her voice.

"We've decided to hold the parade regardless this year, whether it snows or not. Last year, you remember, it was a bust. All the floats were wasted because nobody wanted to get them wet. But this year we'll parade rain, snow or whatever."

"Good for you," Sivolesky said. "And you've got your permit."

"Thanks. Now then, will all three of you ride on the Float of Honor?"

"I guess I'm the only one, Molly," Sivolesky said. "These two characters are leaving us behind. You know. Southern vacations."

Molly feigned a glare at Langer and Coulter. "OK then. We'll begin to assemble in the municipal lot at one-thirty. I'll look for you there, Bob -- promptly! Good night, gentlemen."

"Night, Molly," they sang in unison.

"And Bob. Don't forget the tree lighting ceremony. Sunday at six. Say a little something, OK?"

"I'll be there," Sivolesky assured her.

The final appointment of the evening was with the road superintendent, Bud Kelly. The board knew what he wanted. For two years they had listened to what he wanted.

"I should probably not bother you fellas with this until after Christmas, but something's got to be done. Right now I got two plow trucks down -- one with a blown cylinder wall and the other with broken steering linkage. And then there's the front-end loader. It ... "

"Hold it. Hold it!" Sivolesky interrupted. "We've been over all this before. You've got a budget. Get them fixed."

"Bob," Kelly began patiently. "These are our two oldest trucks. We've spent a fortune on them already. How much more can I spend on these old hulks? It's cheaper at this point to buy a couple new ones. But you've put me off for two years."

"I'm sorry, Bud," Sivolesky said. "I really am. Expenses are up all over, in every department. We have to cut somewhere. We can't cut education. We can't cut salaries, although that might be a good idea. We can't cut fuel oil and a million other things. Cost of living's shot up twenty-three percent. Sure I know it's throwing good money after bad, but we just can't do nothing about new equipment until the May town meeting."

"I just wanted to remind you that winter is here," Bud said with a touch of sarcasm. "I need all six trucks in working order. The loader too. The clutch is going."

"Do what you can, Bud. We've got no choice but to make repairs. I'm sure we can squeak by this winter."

"Ya. Just like we squeaked by last winter!" Bud added.

"How's everything else?" Sivolesky asked, changing the subject.

"All's great, I guess. I've just had all my thoughts on this equipment. I tell you, I lose sleep over it."

"Well don't, Bud," Sivolesky said with sympathy. "You can only do the best you can. That's what I was taught when I was a kid."

The selectmen turned to other business.

FRIDAY, DECEMBER 21

"I sure didn't expect to see the black an' white here this mornin'."

"Jack. I thought you knew us better than that," Maggie said, removing her mittens and rubbing her hands." A little below-freezing air and a smattering of snow never hurt anyone."

Jack shook his head and muttered something about crazy people who run. "I'll get your orders."

"That was invigorating," Ellen sighed. "My lungs are frosted, but it was worth it. It gets my mind off Nat. I tried to reach him again last night, but no luck." Her exuberance of a minute earlier faded. "He didn't show up at work yesterday, either. He's never missed a day, until now."

Thompson's Truck Stop was steamy. Maggie watched the drops of condensation roll down the huge windowpane next to the table.

"But I did some checking around last night," Ellen continued, perking up a little. "It seems I'm alone in believing Nat was depressed. I spoke with a couple of guys in the Control Room and they said just the opposite, that he was at peak excitement, just nervous about the project he's been on. This was his 'baby,' as they put it."

"Did they say what the project was?" Maggie asked, hoping to confirm what Chabus had told her.

"They were very open about it. The satellite was Scanner XII and it contained a number of classified instruments he had developed. They were new and exciting to

Nat, and quite naturally he was nervous and concerned that they function perfectly. No details, of course."

"And then Nat left his job, speeded his VW to 70 mph and hit a truck?" Maggie said skeptically.

"I admit it does sound strange -- uncharacteristic."

"Ellen," Maggie said in a sudden outpouring. "I want you to know that I believe you when you say it was not Nat who was killed in the crash. Please understand. But, we have to look at the accumulated evidence, as circumstantial as it may be. First of all, we know it was Nat's car. Secondly, you told me that he was depressed, that he was separated from his wife. Normally that leads to depression. You also said he mentioned he would soon be free, that he was heading for a mental breakdown, and he had spoken, not of suicide, but that he couldn't live with something that happened at Scan-Man. And, I almost forgot. I learned yesterday from the chief that Nat's wife, although estranged from him for several years, identified him as her husband -- shortly after you'd been there.

"All of that, to me, is pretty strong evidence that it could, and I say 'could,' have been Nat who died."

Tears appeared and rolled down Ellen's cheeks. She continued to look at Maggie, but said nothing.

"I also had an interesting conversation yesterday with a former colleague of Nat's at the hotel," Maggie continued as gently as she could. Chabus was his name. He told me a little about Nat. He worked with Nat at Scan-Man for a period of time and has seen him off and on at of the National Scientific Association. He told me something about Nat's project, or at least the last project he knew Nat to be working on. It was a 'solar energizer', he said, something they use to refuel rockets and space vehicles. I really didn't understand much about it and he said couldn't go into details because of its classified nature. But, more importantly, he told me, as I think you

60

have also, Nat took his work very seriously and that Scan-Man could be very demanding on its people."

"What's so unusual about that," Ellen cut in. "Don't you and I take our work seriously and find it demanding?"

"It's the way he said it. I got the impression Nat was under a very heavy burden -- a burden, perhaps that might drive him to do something uncharacteristic."

Maggie knew she was hurting Ellen, but she just couldn't allow her to continue to believe in the hopeless. She wanted to believe Ellen desperately, but evidence was stacking up against it. Ellen's only grounds for believing Nat was still alive was her examination of a body that was badly burned. That examination, Maggie felt, must have been a very emotional experience for her, perhaps emotional enough to cloud reality.

She wished she could tell Ellen the story about the astronauts that Chabus had told her -- that Nat carried the burden of knowing he was responsible for their deaths. But, for the time being anyway, she couldn't. Besides, it would serve no useful purpose. It would only hurt Ellen more.

Ellen was sobbing now, her face in her hands. Maggie reached across the table and tried to comfort her. "I'm sorry I said those things, Ellen. I really am. I certainly don't want to hurt you."

Ellen looked up, pulled a handkerchief from her pocket and blew her nose. She then wiped her eyes on her napkin.

"OK, black an' white, here it is." came the booming voice of Thompson. Then, noticing Ellen, and Maggie's look of concern, "What the hell's the matter here?" he added in a softer tone.

"It's OK, Jack," Ellen said. "I'm just having my regular morning cry." She attempted to smile.

"Christ," Jack answered with lumbering sympathy, "this is the first mornin' I noticed."

"Thanks, Jack. Your food will fix me up."

Thompson decided he'd better go away. He didn't understand crying women. "OK," he said skeptically. "If you need anythin' else, just hollah."

Thompson left.

"You're probably right," Ellen conceded.

"I hope I'm wrong!" Maggie said with a smile.

An extended silence reigned as the women nibbled at their toast. Each was deep in thought. It was Ellen who spoke first.

"I agree that what you say certainly indicates Nat took his own life, but there's another way of looking at it." Ellen's face reflected the seesaw of emotions she was experiencing. "Granted. It was Nat's car: but someone else could have been driving it for some reason. It does seem strange, especially since the accident coincides with the time Nat left the Control Room. And, Nat never drove recklessly. So, someone else must have been driving, because that was the body I saw at the hospital. "That's my logic, anyhow.

"And there's another conflict," Ellen continued. "I know Nat was depressed, yet the Control Room boys say he wasn't. He was just excited. I know he was excited also, so obviously Nat never brought his depression into the office.

"Yes, Nat is separated from his wife, for several years, but since I've known him, this never bothered him. His depression has only shown up within the past few weeks so I don't think it's related to his wife.

"He did say he felt he was headed for a mental breakdown, and he did mention suicide, but I think I know him well enough to believe these were only expressions of his unhappiness with what was going on at work. He never expressed these thoughts in a context that I took seriously.

"And," Ellen smiled broadly. "I find it very interesting what you say about Nat's wife. I'm not a bit surprised that she identified the body as Nat's. What does she have to lose? If Nat has disappeared, yet it looks as if he has died, she is in line to collect his interest in Scan-Man. It's my understanding that his piece of the company could easily be several million dollars!"

Maggie looked at Ellen with renewed interest. She was surprised at Nat's financial worth, although she was not convinced Ellen was right in her reasoning. Much of what she said made as much sense as Maggie's arguments.

Ellen was now smiling. At least she was completely convinced.

"I'll go along with much of what you say," Maggie began. "But we have a few problems, no matter which way we argue. Nat is missing and, there is the problem of an unidentified body."

"On that we can agree," Ellen said.

"I also have a strong feeling that something very strange is going on." Maggie thought back to Chabus and his astronaut story. "It is quite possible that Nat's disappearance could be related to the project he was working on."

"I'll go along with that, too."

"So the project is our only hope. Otherwise we're at a dead end," Maggie concluded.

"If the authorities believe Nat is dead," Ellen reasoned, "they certainly won't send out a missing persons *Bulletin.*"

Maggie again dropped back into thought. "Hmm ... Do you have access to the Scan-Man files, or at least some of them? Do you think you can check out the files to find out exactly what Nat was up to?"

Ellen was hesitant. "I can sure try, but I don't have access to the classified stuff. If Nat's project was classified, that's probably where the information would be."

"Are there any people at Scan-Man who could help you?"

"No." Ellen was emphatic. "The Control Room guys were the only ones who might have had any contact with Nat's work at my level, and I think I have exhausted that resource."

"It looks like the files are our only alternative then."

"I'm worried about him," Ellen said. "I just can't believe this is happening. Where could he possibly have gone, and why? Why didn't he let me know? I thought we were very close."

Maggie smiled. "It's funny. Those were my very thoughts about you when I learned Nat was a good friend of yours and you had never told me about him. Now that I understand your relationship, it all makes sense."

"So you're saying that once I find Nat, everything will fall into place once he explains it."

"Let's hope so." Maggie leaned back in her seat.

"Me too. I'm going to wash up and return to the office. There has to be an answer."

*

Frank McCullough, paused on his back steps and looked up at the clouds. Sure enough, he thought, we're in for some snow. "Come on Rolf. We've got some work to do."

Rolf hobbled lamely down the steps and lazily followed his master, tail swinging from side to side.

In a shed at the side of the barn were several cords of stove-size wood, split and neatly stacked. Outside the shed, in a jumble resembling a river log jam, were several more cords cut to four-foot lengths. Since early fall, just when it began to turn cool, Frank, accompanied by Rolf, had taken his tractor and wagon and began the annual cutting and hauling of hardwood from his woodlot. This was at the far end of the field and near the edge of his property along the Winniposkeg River. The woodlot had increased in size substantially since he had given up farming, now taking over a good portion of the land that had once been maintained as pasture. But this new growth would take several more years to mature enough to be of practical value. His original five-acre lot would continue to serve his needs for years and there was no reason to believe Frank would ever exhaust the supply.

Near the shed, under a heap of canvas, linoleum and discarded burlap feed bags, was Frank's homemade sawmill. A 30-inch circular saw was at one end of a long table. At the other end was an ancient "one-lunger," a single cylinder gasoline engine, sparked by the coil from a Ford Model-T. Most of the fundamental parts had been collected from the landfill over the years and Frank's genius had been assembling the parts into a workable whole.

He now tinkered with the engine and soon, awaking with pops and bangs, it started and gained momentum. The saw was soon in operation, connected to the engine with a patched leather endless belt. Work went fast. The four-foot lengths were fed against the saw blade and a sizeable pile of stove lengths was built up within a half hour.

He then shut down the saw and turned to his wood splitter. This consisted of a modern gasoline engine taken from a retired go-cart and this operated a hydraulic cylinder. With the forward motion of a lever, a wedge was effortlessly driven into and through the length of stove-size wood. The lever was then reversed and back came the wedge ready for the next piece.

Frank had the system down to a science. He created tools that worked for him, yet he was not dependent upon them. They helped make difficult work easy. And because he built them, he could repair them as well.

He devoted a half hour per day to his woodcutting and splitting operation. He believed a half hour of work every day is better than four hours once a week. "It takes the curse off ugly jobs," he was fond of saying. Wood was the McCullough's prime heating fuel, reinforced by several tons of coal in the basement, "just in case."

*

Ellen Bloodworth worked at Scan-Man's Interpretation Room, located forty feet below the surface of Peter's Airfield and two floors above the Control Room. It was here telecommunications technicians and engineers received and digested data from meteorological satellites, ocean buoys, reconnaissance flights and ground stations around the world.

Ellen was one of twenty-three specialists who controlled the heart of this information center that felt the weather pulse of more than three-quarters of the earth.

She liked the variety and sophistication of her vocation. She enjoyed the feeling that she was part of a spearhead for all space technology. She continued to be awed by the intricate functions she was able to perform at the touch of her fingertips.

Minute by minute, twenty-four hours a day, every day of the year, a shift of Scan-Man personnel monitored the world's weather variations. Minute changes in cloud movement, sea temperature, wind direction, barometric drops and rises were recorded automatically by a bank of computers. When significant changes began to occur, a technician was alerted and the human eye and ear would take over to interpret what that change might mean. Rarely did a combination of events ever repeat. The challenge for Ellen was to piece together the complicated puzzle and arrive at a satisfactory answer.

Despite the vast complexity of Scan-Man's meteorological programs, Ellen was aware that it represented only a fraction of the company's interests. Many of these other interests, she understood, were in cooperation with the federal government, and her access to them was severely limited. Yet she was not discouraged. She knew that in time, having proven her value to the company, she would be promoted to a more responsible position.

During the Christmas holidays, Ellen was scheduled to work the nine p.m. to five a.m. shift. She was lucky; she'd have her days free.

Following breakfast and a shower, Ellen returned to Scan-Man. She went directly to her workstation, nodding to surprised fellow employees to whom she had turned over her shift only four hours earlier.

Since talking with Maggie, Nat's project had grown in importance to Ellen, and now dominated her thoughts.

In retrospect, Nat had not simply avoided discussions with her about his most recent activity at work; he was positively secretive about it. There was a distinct, yet subtle, difference between the two. She was certain of it. Nat was secretive!

She had known all along that he was very much involved with Scanner XII. That was no secret. It was to be a bold new venture into weather technology, the details of which she had been briefed on several times. She too was excited about Scanner XII. It promised to broaden her technical capabilities. It was a weather satellite, and the Interpretation Room personnel would therefore be closely associated with it.

Maggie had learned from Dr. Chabus, however, that Nat had also been developing something called an Energizer.

It would be used for re-fueling rockets in space. This was the project Nat had been involved in as of a year ago.

The question foremost in Ellen's mind had become, was the Energizer part of Scanner XII's inventory? If it was, what did it have to do with weather and the other functions XII served? Certainly re-fueling space vehicles had nothing to do with meteorology!

From her desk, Ellen retrieved the Scanner XII technical manual and flipped through its pages to the inventory listing. In alphabetical order, the word "Energizer" jumped out at her. There was no explanation of its purpose, nor did she expect one. She knew, and the Control Room boys confirmed, there were other classified instruments on board XII and it was quite likely the Energizer was one of them. It had been her assumption previously that the classified instruments were weather-oriented as well.

"Now at least I have a good idea of what I'm looking for." Ellen said to herself with some satisfaction.

She returned the manual to her desk and took the elevator up to ground level where the company library and file rooms were located. Her friend Jim Naugler was on duty.

"I'm not sure what I want, Jim. I'm just going to browse around." She was cautious, wanting to avoid the possibility of revealing her mission.

"You're not supposed to do that, Ellen. Maybe I can ..."

"For God's sake, Jim!" Ellen lashed out. "I'm researching a project. I'm here on my own time. I'm not taking anything out of here." She then caught herself as she saw Naugler step back in surprise. "I'm sorry. I guess I'm just tired."

"Why, sure, Ellen. Of course. I was just trying to help."

"I know. Thanks. But I'll be sure to call you if I have any questions."

Naugler kept very good records. Everything was cross-referenced. She found Webster's name immediately, but that was the easy part. Under his name were dozens of file cards with the hundreds of projects he had worked on. One of the hazards of working here for so long, she thought.

She turned over card after card until she came across "Scanner XII." Listed under that were several sub-headings, and "Energizer" was one of them. Again there was no description, but to the right of the Energizer heading was the file reference number. Unfortunately it was preceded by the "S" prefix that denoted classified information. She had not yet earned her clearance for sensitive material.

"Damn, damn, damn," Ellen mumbled.

Naugler looked up from his desk. "What's that Ellen?"

"Huh? Oh. Nothing, Jim."

This had to be Nat's project, she guessed. She took note of the reference number, replaced the card file and left the library, barely acknowledging Naugler's farewell. Ellen felt stymied. She was dead-ended, it seemed. Unless ...

The trace of a smile crossed her face and her pace picked up. She returned to her workstation and withdrew a requisition form. It was a long shot, but it might just work.

Supervisor signatures were required to remove any file information from Scan-Man headquarters for examination at home or elsewhere. Classified documents, with supervisor approval, could be examined, but only in specific reading rooms.

Ellen filled out the form and requested the reference number listed in Webster's project file. She intentionally omitted adding the prefix 'S', however. She carried it to her daytime supervisor.

"Ellen. What brings you in today?" Steve Whebley asked.

"I'm up to my neck, Steve. I came back to retrieve a file to look over at home. I thought I had taken everything I needed this morning, but, you know how it is."

"What are you up to?"

Ellen's brain worked quickly. "Oh. It's just a recap of the Azores Observatory. We're still running into inconsistencies."

Ellen placed her requisition sheet in front of Whebley and handed him her pen.

"This isn't the Azores reference number," he puzzled.

"You're sharp today, Steve," Ellen smiled, perspiration beginning to break loose under her arms. "You're right. But it is my own input to Scanner XII."

"As long as Margo agrees, it's fine with me." Whebley signed the release and handed it back.

"Thanks, Steve. You saved my day."

Margo Chin was Ellen's nighttime supervisor. Whebley had assumed Ellen had her permission to remove this document.

She returned to her workstation, sat down and carefully inscribed the letter "S" in front of the reference number.

She returned to the library again and handed the requisition to Naugler. He scrutinized it, looked at Ellen, shrugged his shoulders and led her to the document room. Designed as a fail-safe system, Ellen recognized the potential hazards she was creating for herself by crossing the wires. She felt somewhat secure in the fact that Margo Chin had completed her shift with Ellen. It was unlikely she would return this morning and be questioned by Whebley.

Naugler retrieved several thick manila file folders. Ellen felt her wet blouse cling to her spine. She wondered

70

how much time she had before someone would become suspicious. Was there any chance Whebley would check with Naugler to see if she received the information she requested? Competition between work shifts was often furiously aggressive. Would Whebley want to know what Margo was asking Ellen to research?

No chance, Ellen thought. I'm just nervous and feel guilty for being so devious.

"Thanks, Jim."

He led her out of the document room, closed the door, and ushered her to the classified reading room. She would now be alone.

"Call me when you're through." Naugler left.

She opened the first folder and flipped through its contents. Memos, letters, diagrams and hand-written notes appeared to concern the design of the Energizer.

The second folder contained memos to the Scan-Man directors about solar energy itself. The Energizer would be used to convert solar energy into a concentrated beam, multiplying the sun's energy value.

Fascinating, Ellen thought. But how does this explain Nat's secrecy?

A third folder described potential uses of the beam. Included were many more memos from Webster urging the company to pursue production of the Energizer. The name coined for Energizer's beam was "Searoc Beam," although no explanation was included in the file explaining the derivation of the name,

Page after page reflected Webster's enthusiasm for the project. The rocket refueling was finally described. More pages detailed its value as a component to fuel automobiles, heat homes and offices -- in short, to obviate reliance on petroleum products for energy.

She became immersed in a description of Searoc's use on homes whereby an antenna would be used to collect the sun's energy, thereby making expensive solar panels and disks archaic.

Another block of papers described how the concentrated energy beam could be used for weather modification, thereby revolutionizing farming and providing moderate weather to most of the U.S., eliminating most of the weather extremes now experienced.

Mind boggling, Ellen thought.

Yet another folder. It contained a memorandum, signed by the Scan-Man board of directors, agreeing to fund Webster's project. The Army was mentioned. Pentagon officials' names were listed. The Searoc's importance to "national security" caught Ellen's eye.

Conscious of the time, Ellen felt rushed. She flipped rapidly through page after page, stopping momentarily as specific words caught her attention. The words "Hot Spot" particularly stood out.

Oh, if she only had time to read this material, she thought. She had been at it for more than an hour already and to digest all this material would take an entire weekend.

A final folder was thin. It appeared to wrap up the project. The Energizer would be installed in Scanner XII.

"That confirms it!" Ellen said out loud, startling herself by the echo in the small, boxy room. The Energizer and Searoc Beam must be part of Nat's most recent project, she concluded, to herself.

She had to leave. She was tired, not having slept for almost twenty hours. The vast amount of technical information, most of it well beyond her understanding, filled her head in a jumble.

One question still bothered her. How did this relate to Nat's disappearance? There was no question now that this had been the project Webster was working on. What had she gained this morning? Was she better off now than she had been last night? What does this project mean?

It was 10 a.m.. She went to the door and called Naugler. She had to speak with Maggie. Maybe she had some ideas.

*

Maggie arrived at the hotel during mid-morning. She felt a twinge of guilt for taking time away from the office. There were more important stories she should be following.

The frantic and light-hearted atmosphere of yesterday had vanished and a business clime had taken its place. Men and women with somber faces crisscrossed the lobby at a brisk pace carrying folders of papers and attaché cases.

She stood with several NSA people in front of the schedule of events posted in the lobby. Some hurriedly took notes and then rushed off. Others arrived and took their places. Maggie sighed. None of the topics captured her imagination.

Strictly scientific, she thought. Ellen should be here, not me. But then a name caught her eye and her interest sparked. Fred Chabus was speaking. She checked her watch. Yes. She was just in time for at least part of his lecture. Why not?

The large hall was packed. Maggie considered herself lucky to find a seat even though it was near the rear of the hall. She promised herself she'd stay only a few minutes -- just to hear how the man sounded professionally.

" ... And I do hope you all get a chance to visit the site before the proceedings are over," Chabus was saying.

"Although the Scan-Man complex preceded the Andover, Maine station by several years, it was not until 1991 that we began to plan Scan-Man itself. Andover in 1961 was a

73

pioneer in remote ground stations -- the world's first commercial earth station to serve as an international satellite control center. Andover was the foundation of an idea we carried much further. And, whereas their operation is commercial, Scan-Man's is linked closely to the federal government -- and many of its projects are therefore highly classified.

"The first part of our-design was to shield our antennas from the electronic interference Andover achieved geographically. This was accomplished through a maze of circumferential grids that filter the locality. This, of course, gave us the advantage of locating in a populous area.

"Secondly, and Peters Airfield had plenty of open area, we installed our uniquely designed dish antennas -- one 200- and the other 249-feet in diameter. These extraordinarily large antennas give Scan-Man an unbreakable hold through loud signals. The resulting potential will allow us to track a space vehicle, and send and receive signals, beyond our solar system!

"Trunk lines have been cumbersome and impractical. Therefore all transmissions to and from Scan-Man are via satellite, whether it be to or from the next town or on the opposite side of the globe. It has been considerably less expensive to install mini-antennas atop buildings than to install trunk lines.

"Under the old system, NASA executed its own liftoffs from Cape Canaveral and control was not picked up by Andover until the final rocket firing. But during the last year, Scan-Man has been able to command the entire rocket package from here in Hollandson without the necessity of changeover. Scanner XII's firing was executed from here just last Wednesday.

"Geosynchronization has been thought to be highly accurate when measured in thousandths of a degree. Our technology has narrowed that to near perfection.

"This brings me to my favorite topic: the popularly known dish antenna. For the past five years ... "

Three quarters of an hour later, Maggie was still listening. Chabus was exciting. She noted the audience was absorbed in his talk as well -- that they appeared to hang on his every word. He spoke with authority, but with added humanitarian warmth. His smile was captivating and, although the talk was technical and meant little to her, Maggie could not draw herself away.

She felt something uniquely attractive about this 40-something-year-old, something worldly, sophisticated, genteel that drew her toward him. This bothered her.

Maggie always prided herself on her self-control. She had nurtured and perfected a manner that gave her the upper psychological hand in person-to-person relationships -- except for those times with Ellen and other close friends when she could relax and be her real self. But what was her real self? This often troubled her.

Did she too often try to dominate? Phil had once accused her of attempting to castrate him. Ellen had once mentioned Maggie's superwoman tendencies threatened their friendship. Ellen would not be dominated. She'd accept competition gladly but warned Maggie of her tendency to push others to their limits. Ellen let Maggie know she was her own woman. Period.

The lecture ended while Maggie continued to sit, deep in thought. She was startled out of her introspection by a tap on the shoulder. She turned. It was Chabus. He was smiling.

"You were at my lecture?"

"Yes. And I didn't understand a word."

"Why'd you come?"

"Should I be honest?"

"Why not?"

"You fascinate me," Maggie said, slightly embarrassed. "My curiosity was stirred after our talk yesterday. I wanted to see you in action."

"Well, you saw me in action."

"And I was fascinated. I just regret you had to inform me about an industry right in my own back yard."

Chabus shuffled his papers and looked around. "I'd like to continue this conversation this evening. Are you free? I'm sorry but I have to run now. Another one of these blasted lectures."

Maggie was surprised Chabus allowed himself to be tied to such a tight schedule. "Sure. Yes. Fine."

"Good. I'll meet you here in the lobby at eight."

Maggie nodded.

"Oh. By the way," Chabus added. "One of your local people is speaking in a few minutes. Randolph. Ed's with Scan-Man. You might be interested."

"Thanks. I am interested. I'll follow up on it."

"Very good. Until tonight." Chabus walked rapidly down the hall, nodding and speaking to people without letting up his pace.

Ed Randolph was already at the lectern when Maggie entered the hall. She was startled by his youth. He looked her age or younger. She had expected an older man to be President of a giant, international company.

During the first few minutes of his talk, Maggie labeled Randolph to be diametrically opposite Chabus. She began to understand how he had taken command of Scan-Man. He came across as a tough-minded, hard-driving man. He spoke with an authority that would not allow questioning. She automatically disliked him, yet was perturbed at herself for making a judgment on so little evidence.

"... Just think of us as your monitor of all activity on this planet, and above the planet, for that matter. Scan-Man is the giant in international electronic monitoring. We are capable of literally counting the automobiles on the freeways and can identify their makes and models. Militarily speaking, it goes without saying this is an invaluable asset to our nation. Our eyes in the skies have limitless potential.

"How do we do this? We have a worldwide network of eighty-four satellites performing a variety of functions. We, of course, carry the normal telephone, television, tracking, telemetry and data transmission, but we also can monitor the weather locally over seventy-eight percent of the world. Now, when I say this, I mean we can accurately measure weather conditions in, let's say, Massachusetts, from the ground surface temperature, water temperature, radiation hot spots, etc. We can read the surface barometric pressures and wind speeds -- all of which was formerly a landlocked function. Although this has not yet been commercialized, we expect it will be available to the public within two years.

"Weather prediction and modification has always been a primitive craft. Scan-Man has now provided the technology to elevate it to a science.

"The temptation is gnawing at me to tell you of our most recent achievements, for which I am very proud, but the government would not approve. For the time being, the most exciting part of Scan-Man's program is classified. You, who have the clearances, are always welcome to review our activities.

"Two days ago, Scan-Man launched the world's most sophisticated satellite. This eye in the sky measures sixty-eight feet in height and has wing-like extensions or more than 229 feet. Its weight is less than 500 pounds, which is an important factor in space transportation. Its capability is immense. It can handle 50 billion separate transmissions an hour -- a far cry from the so-called sophisticated models launched in 1980.

"How do we digest all the information we are capable of retrieving? We have an acre of computers, located eighty feet underground in solid ledge. The computers separate the wheat from the chaff. Naturally we are not interested in anything but a fraction of the data we receive second by second. The computers are programmed to intercept and interpret significant changes from the norm. If there is a buildup of automobiles where there shouldn't be a buildup, we hear about it. If the weather changes for the better or for the worse, we learn about it. If we are interested in a particular geographic location, we follow every change, regardless of its apparent insignificance.

"What about the clutter of 'dead stars' and orbital trash above us? For several years there has been concern that this garbage will come down on our heads -- very much like Sky Lab did in '79. We've taken care of that problem by reducing all trash to dust. The capability of Scanner XII, which carries a unique optics system, transforms energy from the sun into concentrated heat -- heat hot enough to incinerate all manner of elements. Similar to a laser you say? Yes it is similar, but our system has a much more concentrated beam. Originating in the ..."

Randolph had statistics at his mental fingertips. His company employed fifty-six thousand scientists worldwide. He praised NSA for its dedication to science, but then let it be known as well that, thanks to Scan-Man, it was the company's laboratories and bankroll that provided the opportunity for science to create and develop exciting technologies.

Maggie was honestly stunned at Scan-Man's boasted accomplishments. She was again reminded that such an influential company was located in her town and she had never acknowledged it in the *Bulletin*. She recognized there was meat here for an incredibly exciting story.

My God, she thought. The world is being controlled by someone in my own back yard. How little we know about the internal workings of these influential companies.

*

Phil Billings arrived at the hotel separately from Maggie. His mission was to capture the convention in photographs while Maggie concentrated on the story. He and Maggie usually worked independently, yet somehow the efforts of the two meshed every week at press time. Photography was the enjoyable part of the paper to him. Managing the business end was the bread and butter -- a tedious necessity.

Billings was not a happy man. He frequently blamed Maggie for this, claiming she dominated him and forced him to be number two at the *Bulletin*. He claimed she was always in the spotlight. She received the attentive glory of the public. Who wants to talk advertising at a party? They all flocked around Maggie for the latest news and gossip.

He had become a negative man, and he realized that. Their relationship nagged at him. Whereas Maggie tended to seek the bright side of events and situations, Billings took the opposite view – probably just to needle her. When Maggie pointed out that he was his own best enemy, he retorted that it was necessary -- the newspaper business could not survive on wishful thinking and an everything-will-be-lovely philosophy.

When it came down to facts, he knew he was essential to the *Bulletin* whether anyone else realized it or not. His camera and his ability to make money were the things that gave him his identity. Even Maggie admitted he was a good at what he did.

Their marriage had settled down to an arrangement of convenience in recent years. He and Maggie now slept in separate rooms and had not been sexually active for months. Although it was never a subject open to discussion, each knew they would stay together longer if they continued to go their separate ways. Ten years of marriage had made their life together a habit. Each knew his responsibilities to the family and the business. For the most part their co-operation was mechanical, from cooking meals to office work. It was all habit. Billings had learned to prefer it this way. To break up the habit of either their marriage or their business would be disastrous for both of them.

Yet he was unhappy. Mechanical living had little excitement. On the other hand, to seek out excitement meant altering his habits. So, he just let events happen -- passively. He lit a cigarette.

"Phil? Phil Billings?" He heard a female voice.

He turned and saw a woman he didn't recognize. She hesitated and then waved to him. He shuffled through his inventory of faces but could not attach a name to the face.

The woman came toward him. She was short, perhaps up to his shoulder, and attractive. She was dressed in a knee-length cocktail dress with a low neckline. Strange, he thought, so early in the day. She was slim, had generous breasts beneath a low neckline. Billings couldn't help dropping his eyes to them. Her hair was cut pixie-short and her lips were painted bright red. She was well tanned.

Gradually she began to appear somewhat familiar.

She laughed. "You should be ashamed for not recognizing me. I'd know you anywhere. It's been a long time, Phil. You remember Puff Kingsley?"

Billings slapped himself on the forehead in an exaggerated gesture of recognition. His pulse quickened as old memories returned and his inventory fell open in place. "Puff!

You son-of-a-gun! What are you doing here?" he said enthusiastically, dropping his cigarette and stepping on it.

She reached up and put her arms around his neck, her breasts pressing against him. Billings was mortified and felt clumsy as she hung on him, his camera dangling in his hand.

She pulled away, having enjoyed his embarrassment. "I'm here with my husband for the convention. I'm Puff Chabus. Freddie is President of this lavish affair. You know what I mean?"

"I just can't believe it," Billings said. "How many years has it been?"

"More than I care to remember. You know what I mean? How've you been?"

As they talked, standing awkwardly in the hallway, Billings' mind backtracked to his college days in Boston. Puff and he had dated for two years and had shared his one-room lodging for six months. They had very seriously considered marriage after graduation, but then something came between them. He had accused her of being too ambitious after she had told him she was leaving him for a medical school student. It was a bitter separation for Billings. It had destroyed his morale for many months. He had genuinely loved Puff, but in the end he realized she had used him to meet his friends. Eventually, he simply shrugged his shoulders and chalked the relationship up to a worthwhile experience.

At least that was his superficial reaction. Billings was unsure of himself. Should he ignore Puff now that he remembered the disappointing past she represented, or should he play it by ear and see what comes of the chance meeting?

"Everything's just great, Puff. My wife and I run the local newspaper here and ... "

"I can't believe it," Puff interrupted in a high-pitched voice. "Of course. Your wife's name is Maggie. I met her just yesterday. She's quite a woman. You know what I mean?"

He'd forgotten how chatty Puff was, how flattering she could be. "Yes," Billings agreed with an undercurrent of sarcasm that was not lost on Puff. "She's quite a woman." He lit another cigarette and offered one to Puff.

"No thanks. Are you free for drinks later on? I'd just love to talk over old times. Freddie's tied up with all these dumb meetings and I just can't bear another session with the girls. You know what I mean?" The words gushed out, packaged in her melodious voice.

"Well, I ... "

"Oh come on. Don't give me that bashful stuff any more."

Billings weakened and agreed to meet her. At least he told himself he weakened. He was not quite ready to admit he still found Puff very attractive and sexy. The old memories brought new life to him. He felt a new excitement stir in him that he thought had long been dead.

"I have to run now Phil," she sang. "Don't you dare stand me up." Again she laughed gently in a way that he still found captivating. She turned and seemed to skip away, the hem of her dress dancing up and down.

*

Ellen and Maggie arrived at the *Bulletin* office simultaneously. Each was excited about their respective discoveries.

"I've got a good hold on Nat's project," Ellen said, "but I'm afraid I'm no closer to discovering where he disappeared."

"Let's compare notes."

"The Energizer is Nat's project and there seems to be no question that it's being carried on Scanner XII. I checked the inventory sheet and it's listed."

"That's progress," Maggie said. "What's its function?"

"Essentially it converts rays of energy from the sun into a beam of energy called a Searoc Beam. I don't have any idea what 'Searoc' means, but that's what it's called.

"This beam is apparently very powerful and is a substitute or alternative for petroleum fuels. It's an advancement over the solar cell collection of energy. Nat's plan uses only an antenna which energy passes through."

"That really sounds far-fetched," Maggie commented.

"Far-fetched or not, that's what I read," Ellen said. "And that's not all. Another use for the energizer is weather modification. According to what I read, the Energizer can moderate the seasons by eliminating extremes in weather."

"Then weather modification is another function of Scanner XII."

"So it appears." Ellen said with a nod. "It also appears this is a military project. There were memos which concerned the Pentagon, and the Army was mentioned." Ellen paused. "Oh, Yes. 'National Security' was also used along with something called operation 'Hot Spot.' I can't imagine what that means, but those were specific words that caught my eye. It all sounds extremely important."

Maggie was thoughtful. She doodled in the margin of the sheet of paper on which she was taking notes. "I heard two very interesting lectures this morning. One was given by Dr. Fred Chabus whom I told you about. The other was by Ed Randolph. Between the two of them, and from what you've just told me, I think we can conclude Nat was working on a very important secret project, the impact of which is just sinking in on me.

"Randolph mentioned an optics system that transforms the sun's energy into concentrated heat, a heat powerful enough to burn metal to dust. Your mention of 'Hot Spot' seems to confirm this. 'Hot Spot' sounds like a code name of some sort. The component, I guess we can call it, that performs this function sounds as though it might be the Energizer. You called it a 'Searoc Beam?'"

"Right," Ellen answered. "But it's called an Energizer on the inventory sheet."

"I suppose that doesn't make much difference," Maggie pondered. "What else did you learn?"

"I went through the material very rapidly," Ellen admitted. "I could have spent hours on it, but I was afraid of being caught. It was a pretty risky thing I did. I short-circuited the classified file system. If had been caught, I'd certainly be fired."

Maggie thought some more. "I don't want to blow this whole thing out of proportion, but one man has been killed and another has disappeared over something that is going on at Scan-Man. Although 'national security' is an over-used term, especially in government circles, it sounds very important when attached to the type of project you describe.

"This sounds to me to be something far superior to common solar energy as we know it. Although Chabus and Randolph only hinted at what this Energizer is, they were emphatic about its great importance. Although I can't guess at how this Energizer works. When you mentioned weather modification, it struck me. Weather modification is an extremely sensitive issue."

"I know," Ellen said. "You start fooling around with Mother Nature and she bites back."

"Still, we're guessing," Maggie said. "Think back, now that you've read the files. Does anything Nat said to you ring a bell?"

84

"I've been trying to recall. I was thinking this morning as I read the files that Nat was secretive about his project -- secretive in a sense that was different, rather than how one might act about regular classified materials."

"What do you mean?"

"He asked me many questions about meteorology over the months, as if he was interested in what I was doing at work. These were technical questions of an inquiring mind. Since none of my work is classified, and since I was eager to show him how much I knew about my specialty, we talked a great deal about it. Now that I think about it, however, it was almost as if he was taking notes. Basically it concerned how weather is generated, how it develops, where it goes and what influences it."

"To me," Maggie said, "it looks like the Energizer may indeed be weather oriented. Do you think so?"

"That's coming through now, loud and clear," Ellen agreed.

"And if it has to do with weather modification, it seems to me that it would be classified information, of interest to the Pentagon, and would certainly be related to national security."

"I can see your point."

"It's a pretty powerful machine that can turn metal into dust. But I can't see how a beam of energy capable of doing that is related to weather modification."

"My imagination is going wild too," Ellen said, a bit discouraged. "I don't think we know enough to come to any conclusions."

"I agree. So I guess we should dig a little deeper."

"I don't see how any of this relates to Nat's disappearance, either."

"Neither do I," Maggie said. "This project sounds so exciting I can't imagine Nat being depressed. Why is anyone ever depressed, unless he's doing something he doesn't like, or is placed in a position of compromise? This project was Nat's 'baby,' they said. Why would he be depressed about it?"

"I have no idea, Maggie."

A long silence followed. Ellen sipped her coffee and Maggie doodled with her pencil some more.

"I guess it's back to the files again," Maggie finally said. "Do you think you can find out some more details?"

"I doubt it. I don't think I could get away with it again. I'm still nervous about this morning."

"Maybe I can find out something," Maggie said. "I'm meeting with Dr. Chabus again. Maybe I can also arrange an interview with Mr. Randolph. Since talking with Chabus yesterday, I've had this powerful urge to find out something, anything, about Hollandson's largest industry."

"Lots of luck!" Ellen said. "How do you expect them to tell you things that are classified?"

"Not everything is classified," Maggie reasoned. "There's the Scanner XII program. I can ask innocent questions about that."

"I can tell you a lot about that."

"You're right," Maggie said. "Start with this. You said you've been tracking XII. I assume you track it eight hours a day."

"Yes. That and other hardware. The other sixteen hours are recorded."

"Has anything peculiar been happening?"

"I haven't paid much attention since I haven't known what I now know." Ellen said.

"Do you have any way of going back over your records?"

"Sure. In fact I can easily check the records of the other shifts also. But what's that going to tell us?"

"I'd study the records closely. Look to see how the satellite is being used. It may be too early, since it went up, when?"

"The first part of the week," Ellen said. "All the tapes of Scanner XII are stored in the library. It will be easy to review them." Ellen's eyes widened with excitement. "Why didn't I think of that?"

"Probably because you're tired. When did you last sleep? A little rest might give you some inspiration."

"By God," Ellen said, not listening to Maggie.

"Calm down," Maggie cautioned. "Don't get excited yet."

*

Nat Webster's funeral was simple and took place at the Woodside Cemetery in Hollandson. The obituary notice had appeared in the previous day's *Bulletin*. It too was simple; the way Webster would have preferred it. A light snow covered the ground and the twenty or so people who gathered, pressed in around the grave under the small canopy.

Maggie and Ellen took note of the people present. Several Scan-Man employees, including Ed Randolph. Also present were Webster's ex-wife and two children, now adults, as well as a number of people from town and from Lexington and Concord whom Ellen said Webster had known from his infrequent local activities.

The service was said by a young Unitarian minister, a friend of Ellen. He was a personable, intellectual type who said he wished he had known Nat from the background Ellen had supplied him. Mrs. Webster had not wanted a minister or a ceremony, but Ellen said she would pay all costs for the entire funeral if his ex would arrange it. Mrs. Webster readily agreed.

Heads bowed, the minister read the eulogy.

"Nathaniel Webster leaves us this afternoon in body but not in spirit. A man dedicated to science, he achieved far more toward the betterment of humanity in his lifetime than most earthlings imagine achieving.

"Nathaniel was an innovator, a leader in the development of communications which now tie the nations of the world together in a network that may someday lead to mutual understanding. His inventiveness ... "

Maggie noticed Randolph winced at the reading of Webster's achievements. She thought she also detected a wink between him and one of his companions. Were they mocking the ceremony? Had they known Webster better than Maggie and Ellen were aware?

And Mrs. Webster seemed to be taking the occasion lightly. Of course. She had walked out on Webster. She had refused to see Webster during the three years they had been divorced. The Webster children, although now young adults, stuck by their mother. It would have signaled treason to visit their father, according to Ellen.

Webster left no known will.

"... But Nathaniel, despite his achievements, was a simple man. He was not a glory-seeker. He was content to work his wonders in the background ... "

The Scan-Man group had become restless. A bored look had taken over Randolph's face. Maggie wondered about the true relationship between him and Webster. She wondered about Fred Chabus' comment concerning Webster and his accidental sending of the astronauts into oblivion. How had this catastrophe affected Webster's relationship with his family and with Randolph?

Ellen appeared to be the only genuine mourner. She stood beside the minister staring grimly at the unadorned coffin. Tears appeared on her cheeks.

Maggie was not even clear about Ellen's relationship with Webster. Until yesterday, for more than two years, Ellen had kept that segment of her life secret from her close friend. She loved him, Ellen said, and had been his close companion. Yet it was totally separated from Maggie's friendship with Ellen.

The ceremony finally came to a close and the coffin was lowered. Maggie had an overwhelming desire to interview Randolph and Mrs. Webster, but she could see Ellen needed her more at the moment.

They remained at the site until the others had left. Only the work crew stood by, in the background, smoking, talking quietly, patiently, waiting for the last of the mourners to leave.

A breeze picked up and snowflakes were blowing under the canopy and onto the top of the casket. There they melted into bubbles of moisture. Maggie pulled Ellen away.

"That was a beautiful service, Ellen."

"If it was Nat, he deserved it. Someday I hope I can tell you what that man means to me." Ellen placed her arm around her friend's waist. "I will not believe Nat is dead. It is only because I can't prove otherwise that I went ahead with this service."

*

The schoolyard was a din of confusion and excitement as the children burst through the doors of Hollandson Elementary School. It was Friday. It was the first day of Christmas vacation. And, most important of all, it was snowing.

As the school buses left the yard, they were pelted with snowballs thrown by the walk-home students. There were no repercussions. It was all in fun. No one was hurt.

Snow. It was late this year. Normally it fell before Thanksgiving. It was a month late. But now the prediction was for six to twelve inches -- that would be enough for Winter Carnival on Sunday -- the big Hollandson winter event. The children always looked forward to it.

*

The two Hollandson service stations rolled out racks of snow tires and taped snow tire posters to their windows. But the only reactions they received to the snow so far were requests for free windshield scrapers. One attendant scratched his head in amazement as he recalled how year after year car owners wait until heavy snow before they mounted their winter tires. Every January it was the same thing -- a last minute rush. For some strange reason, he thought, drivers believed this is the year it won't snow. They acted surprised and indignant each year when it finally did snow.

*

At the firehouse, the crew installed chains on the emergency vehicles. This was standard procedure whenever three inches or more snow was anticipated.

*

Bud Kelly's sand trucks were loaded and ready to roll. One of his spreader engines was giving him problems. It was old and should have been replaced years ago. The other engines started well, but it was not without a prayer that they would continue to run.

Kelly was also trying to decide if he should attach his plows. His weather eye could not yet determine if it would be a six-inch or a twelve-inch storm. It would soon be dark. The commuters would be driving home. It was important that the roads be clear. In the back of his mind was the selectmen's warning that snowstorms cost money. They didn't want Kelly wasting money on overtime pay if the snow was going to melt the next day. If only a few inches were expected, salt mixed with sand would save plowing and wages.

Kelly decided to wait a little longer.

Molly Battini hung up the phone. She had called her Winter Carnival directors and told them the snow looked good and to spread the word that work could begin tomorrow morning on the parade floats. Snow sculptures would start in earnest at the field about 9 a.m..

*

Ed Randolph was deeply troubled. During the late afternoon he had been informed that an unusual weather pattern had developed over the North Atlantic and was moving southwesterly toward the North American continent. Normally Randolph would not have been specifically notified of such a weather condition. This time, however, he had personally requested his meteorologists track all disturbances that developed in the North Atlantic and to keep him informed of their progress in detail.

He could not believe the report when he first heard it. He sent Margo Chin scurrying back for additional details. When the storm direction was confirmed, Randolph slammed his fist on his desk and told his secretary to call an immediate meeting of the directors.

"I'm sorry, Mr. Randolph, but do you realize what time it is?" his secretary asked." It's after 5:30 and it's storming badly."

"Are you telling me no one is here?"

"Yes, sir. They all left a little early on account of the storm."

Randolph was famous for his temper. He bristled at inefficiency. He fired any employee who gave less than total devotion to the job. A job to Randolph was not one that followed the clock. A job began when there was a task to be done and ended when that task was completed.

For him, the job was never-ending. As a result he surrounded himself with efficient machines and electronic gadgetry. His office was a communications center. It extended to his limousine and into his home. He could conduct business anywhere in the world either through conventional ground lines, or via his company's satellites. The directors of Scan-Man were tied into Randolph's lines also and could be connected for conference calls. This was only appropriate and reasonable for the managers of the world's largest and most sophisticated communications corporation.

Randolph's desire for a face-to-face meeting was now frustrated. He excused his secretary and pressed the "general alert" button. This activated the call buzzers for each of his directors in the office, at home or on their mobile units. Conversations were automatically scrambled and unscrambled at each end of the line.

Randolph now waited for the acknowledgement lights to blink on. Within thirty seconds, all but one was glowing.

"Where's Chandler?" Randolph asked.

"We've had difficulty getting through to Washington today, Ed," a voice said. "They've had a front pushing up through there."

"We've hit a snag on an Hot Spot," Randolph began. "I don't know the details yet but it sounds serious. I'm calling a meeting for ten tomorrow. I want everyone involved in the project at that meeting."

"Can you brief us?"

"It has rebounded. It may mean a switch to Phase II."

There were gasps of surprise from the other ends of the line. "Are you telling us Hot Spot has backfired?"

"It looks very bad. The storm appears to be moving in this direction."

"What the hell happened?"

"This is what I'm going to find out," Randolph said. "I want each of you to have some answers. I also want you to give detailed thought to the consequences of Phase II. Be ready with some explanations of why Phase I backfired and what we're going to do about it. Ten in the morning in the Board Room."

Randolph's face was gray. The Health-Club tan had disappeared. The muscles of his jawbone rippled as he clenched his teeth. He wondered about Nat Webster. Could it be? Could it be possible that Webster had something to do with the rebound?

It was 6 p.m.. There was little else he could accomplish at the office without the others present. It was also Friday night, Randolph remembered, and his wife wanted to talk with him about the details of the weekend party.

That annoyed him. Why couldn't Marsha take care of the party herself? He had enough problems of his own. Now, with the nightmare of the Scanner XII rebound to cope with ... How the hell could it have happened? It was so thoroughly planned out!

*

Turk, Randolph's driver, stopped the car and rapped on the window behind the front seat. Randolph pressed the intercom button.

"I'm afraid the drive is not plowed, sir."

It was dark. The snow was thick and damp. Randolph was determined he would not walk up the long drive to the house. Where was Francisco? He called Marsha from the car.

"Francisco has chores to do for me. The drive is Turk's"

"Goddamn it ... " But it was fruitless. She had hung up.

Randolph was snow-soaked and very angry when he entered the house fifteen minutes later. He flew into a rage at Marsha's independence and total lack of consideration.

"Yes, yes, yes," she said, acknowledging his complaints. "You're a very busy and important man. You're involved in worldly events, etc., etc., bullshit!" She followed him into the next room. "It just so happens that I have things that must be done as well. We agreed long ago on division of labor. The drive is your problem. The guests -- most of them your friends -- are my problem, and they'll be here tomorrow."

Randolph marched into the den. He knew it was useless to continue the argument for it would only degenerate into a bloody battle. Still, it raised his blood pressure well beyond the effect this afternoon's event had on him. God! He thought. She's impossible. Probably been at the pills again.

He poured himself a bourbon.

Dinner was served in silence. Robert talked about what he wanted Santa Claus to bring -- but neither Randolph nor Marsha paid much attention. Robert was accustomed to this. Ever since he could remember, his parents sat through silent meals. He had learned to content himself by simply talking, and hoping that one of the other would acknowledge him occasionally with a nod or a grunt. He understood the problem. His parents were very, very busy people. They did important things.

But, he knew he could always talk with Alberta.

*

Maggie was a half hour late for her appointment with Chabus. This didn't bother her because she disliked standing in lobbies waiting. Besides, she suspected he would be late also. She smiled to herself as she entered the hotel lobby, brushing the snow from her coat. Chabus was seated on a couch talking with someone. She walked directly to him. He stood when he noticed her, and after an introduction and a brief chat, the third party excused himself.

"How about a drink. Maggie? You look as if you could use one."

"Thanks for the compliment. I'm glad I spent three hours at my dressing table preparing for this occasion." She laughed in her infectious way. Thirty minutes earlier she had been at the office. She had rushed home, freshened up, stepped into a bright red jumpsuit and full-length rabbit fur coat and traversed the slippery roads in her 4-wheel-drive. "It's been one heck of a long day, Dr. Chabus. Although I'm in training, I'll take you up on that drink. But only one."

"In training?" Chabus asked as they walked toward the tavern.

"I run every morning, or at least I did. With the snow prediction, I suspect that will be curtailed." She unbuttoned her coat. Her suit accentuated her stature and slim figure. She was again very conscious of her height next to Chabus.

"You look very athletic and fit. I ought to begin running."

They entered the Cloven Hoof Tavern and chose a table in a corner. Chabus helped her drape her coat over the back of the chair, noting with pleasure Maggie's soft auburn hair and delicate skin. A very beautiful woman, he thought.

"I'm afraid ninety percent of your lecture this morning was lost on me. My ignorance of matters celestial is astounding. Anything beyond the treetops is outside my experience."

"You're very modest. I like modest people." Chabus said in his deep, sonorous voice that Maggie liked. "Tell me about yourself. What are your interests?"

"Oh come now! Let's not dwell on me. You're the one we should talk about. You're the one with the Pulitzer Prize and the international reputation."

"Let's compromise and forget our professional capacities."

The waitress arrived, took their orders and left.

"Before we do that," Maggie suggested, "let's pick up where we left off yesterday. I want to hear more about Nat Webster."

Chabus shuffled in his chair. "What more is there to tell?"

"For one, you dropped a bombshell on me yesterday -- about the cover-up of Webster sending the astronauts off into space. Now Webster is dead. You could give me some insight into Webster."

"I suspect nothing would be gained by it."

"I'd like to determine that. I have reason to believe he may have committed suicide. If this is the case, he has at least one close friend who would like to know the reason. Your story might help set her mind at ease." Maggie felt a recurrence of the discussion of the same tension she felt yesterday during a same topic.

"Who is your friend?"

"Her name is Ellen Bloodworth. She's a close friend, girlfriend, of Webster's. They've spent a good deal of time together since he was separated from his family."

Chabus pulled his meerschaum from his suit coat pocket thoughtfully, packed it, lighted it, and looked directly at Maggie for several moments. She felt he was reading her mind, feeling for her motives, testing her sincerity.

"OK," Chabus relented. "But make me a promise not to print any of this in the paper. This is for your benefit and your friend's alone. I'm telling you this against my better judgment and experience in a world that frequently can't be trusted. But I can read your sincerity. This is not flattery. You are a remarkable woman. However you use this information eventually, please protect your source." He looked her directly in the eyes once again, reached across the table and gently touched her arm.

96

"I'll agree to that," Maggie said without avoiding eye contact. She was pleased with herself at having Chabus open up.

The waitress returned with the drinks and Chabus ordered a second round. Maggie declined.

"To Nat Webster," Chabus said, lifting his glass. "May he find peace wherever he is."

Maggie played the game.

"You must understand the politics of a corporation the size of Scan-Man. It is international in scope. The directors of a company this size, particularly a company that produces military weaponry and space gadgets, wield tremendous international influence. The structure is so complex, and interwoven with a multitude of smaller companies, they are nearly a government in their own right. In fact, their power may exceed that of the President or even Congress, each of which has the disadvantage of public scrutiny. Scan-Man is a closely held corporation and can operate silently and secretly. It is so complex -- and I can't stress this enough -- that no federal bureaucracy could begin to understand it."

Maggie was transfixed by Chabus' words. Once more it struck her, and Chabus confirmed it, that she knew nothing and never heard anything from this giant that was located right in her own small town. Sure, she was aware of the many hundreds of people who worked in the complex. She was aware of the layoffs and the hiring, depending on the ebb and flow of government contracts. But that was all superficial. And, why should she know anything about this company? No interesting news ever escaped it. The company appeared no more interesting than any of the hundreds of other companies that lined Route 128.

Maggie sipped her drink. Her tension had subsided as Chabus' words poured out. She noted his use of the words "silently and secretly." She wondered if he might go as far as saying "clandestinely."

"Scan-Man operates, in a way, very similarly to the CIA. It is very necessary for them to have a spy network. Clandestine work is necessary for survival sometimes. Ideas are created and developed and wrapped in a cloak of secrecy. Ideas are stolen. Spies infiltrate competing companies. Spies attempt to in infiltrate Scan-Man offices. Billions and billions of dollars are at stake. It's a real world of espionage and counter-espionage on the corporate level."

"Are you still affiliated in any way with the company?" Maggie asked.

Chabus leaned back in his chair and smiled. "No. No. I haven't been for years. But in my line of work, I'm in touch with the 'advance guard,' you might say, of a dozen different companies. Scan-Man happens to be one of the more interesting because of its leadership in technology, and because I was affiliated with it and continue to know people there with whom I have worked."

"How well do you know Mr. Randolph?"

"Not well at all." Chabus cleared his throat and relit his pipe. "He's a relative newcomer who climbed up through the management ranks very rapidly. He's a tough man -- a real hard driver."

"Ambitious?" Maggie asked, probing.

"No question."

"Unscrupulous?" Probing further.

"What are you after?" Chabus leaned forward again. "It would be a serious charge to attach that label to a man."

"I know," Maggie said with an even voice. "That's why I asked you."

Chabus smiled. "Well, I wouldn't go so far as to say he was unscrupulous. Let's limit it to ambitious."

"I apologize for sidetracking you. You were going to tell me more about Webster. How long has he been with Scan-Man?"

"Webster joined Scan-Man shortly after it was formed. He was an important force in developing the company. I'd go so far as to say he was a major influence. You recall my talk this morning. Webster worked directly with me in developing the Scan-Man remote ground station. It was a coordinated effort. I worked on the ground control while he developed the satellite technology. Webster has devoted twenty years to Scan-Man. He was a director for much of that time.

"Then came the accident. He really screwed up. In layman's terms, he pushed the zig button when he should have pushed the zag. It was an important mission. Sending four Americans aloft is never taken lightly. Fortunately the incident received little or no press. The public had become jaded by that time. You watch men shot into space three or four times and you've seen it all. The press was therefore less than interested.

"As a result, the incident could easily be covered up. The astronaut families were given a plausible story and a handsome income for the rest of their lives, and they kept quiet. They were aware of the risks beforehand, anyway. It was simply an unfortunate incident, a patriotic sacrifice for God and country. They didn't hold anyone responsible.

"There was also an implied threat involved. Remember, these are military families that have been conditioned to discipline. It was the old, familiar national security line. Any breach of secrecy on their part and they would endanger their country. It was effective."

"Was Webster involved in this threat?"

"Indeed he was," Chabus said with a knowing smile.

"That changes my opinion of him if he was part of the cover-up." Maggie was suddenly angry for having felt sympathy for Webster up until this point. She realized now that her feelings had been with Ellen, and by extension Webster.

"I'm afraid you misunderstand," Chabus hurried to add. "Webster was one of the victims. The company used Webster's mistake against him."

"Scan-Man threatened Webster?" Maggie couldn't believe it.

"Yes."

"Why did he allow it? What was the threat?"

"I don't know the specific threat. All I know is the company subjected him to a great deal of pressure. Why he allowed it, I don't know. Our minds work in strange ways. The company, or I should say Webster's work, was everything to him. The fear of losing that can become greatly exaggerated in the mind. But I'm just guessing at this. All I know is Webster felt, and showed, the pressure."

"How did you learn about all of this?"

"Webster and I, as I said, were colleagues at one time. We exchanged ideas long after the ground station was completed and I went on to other things. We explored the unknown together at NSA meetings and elsewhere. We questioned the impossible together and made it possible. The official split came between us after this incident. We ... "

The waitress brought a second drink for Chabus. He ordered a third. Maggie declined. She was still working on her first.

"After undergoing the trauma of this, Webster underwent a psychological change. As a perfectionist, as a scientist, he hated himself for his stupidity, his carelessness. He withdrew and we each went our separate ways, except for the annual NSA conventions.

"He resigned from the Scan-Man board of directors and submerged himself in his laboratory where he was working on the development of practical solar energy, as we discussed. His marriage failed, bitterly, and his children deserted him. It was tragic."

"What's happened since then?"

"I don't really know. As I said, the last time I spoke with Webster was a year ago at NSA. We talked about his Energizer and he seemed pretty enthusiastic about it. It seemed like a good project that had a lot of promise. And that's the last I heard of him -- until arriving here."

There was a pause in the dialogue. Maggie's head was bursting with the excitement of all Chabus had told her. How much more would Chabus tell her? How far could she go?

"What do you know about Scanner XII?"

"What do you want me to know about it?" Chabus countered.

"The news reports said it was a weather satellite. Do you think there might be a connection between it and Webster's Energizer -- the Searoc Beam?"

"I thought you didn't know anything about this stuff," Chabus chuckled, crinkling his tanned face.

"I don't. I just hear stories," Maggie returned, smiling.

"Who knows?" Chabus threw up his hands dramatically. "There may have been a relationship. I know Webster did plan to send the Energizer aloft within the year. But as to whether it was on board or not, I'm out of touch with that."

"Can you tell me something about the Searoc Beam itself? Just what is 'Searoc'?"

"My you are quizzical. No, my dear. Not any details. It was just that Webster had marvelous plans for heaven on earth. He envisioned controlling the weather to meet every one's satisfaction. Frankly, although it's all possible, I have always felt it's rather a utopian scheme." Chabus paused. "Searoc is an acronym for 'Solar Energy Amplification by means of Radiant Optical Conversion,' if I remember correctly."

"That's a mouthful," Maggie said. "His ideas then were plausible? The Searoc Beam was something that could alter weather patterns?"

"Oh. By all means. But the idea of making everyone happy with the weather is like expecting everyone to get along with each other."

"From what you've told me," Maggie reasoned, "I see nothing to drive a man to suicide, unless he was unable to cope with company pressures."

"I don't think that could have influenced it. That was his inspiration. But if he were to be fired from his job, that might have influenced him."

"It's not likely he'd be fired," Maggie said. She began to sense Chabus' restlessness. He had now finished his third drink and appeared to be holding his alcohol well. She decided to continue a little further. This opportunity might not arise again.

"Does 'Hot Spot' mean anything to you?"

Chabus shuffled in his seat again. He seemed uncomfortable. "Your questions are very probing. I'm amazed at your source. I had the impression this was classified information."

"It seems as though I only know the questions," Maggie said. "Questions, I don't believe, are classified."

"Good point."

"I'll lay it right on the line, Dr. Chabus," Maggie finally said. "I do not believe Nat Webster killed himself. Although this belief is tenuous, the more I learn about Webster and his company, the more I suspect foul play."

Chabus laid his pipe down and leaned forward with renewed interest.

"Since speaking with you about the company and about Webster the man, I believe he did something that displeased the company. Scan-Man, in its clandestine way, might have felt it would be best if Webster was no longer around."

"Do you know what you're saying?" Chabus gasped.

"I know very well what I'm saying," Maggie said firmly "We are speaking here about a major project -- possibly one involving weather modification. That's not kid's stuff! What if Webster had disagreed with company policy for one reason or another? What if he threatened to leave Scan-Man to take his ideas elsewhere? If, as you say, his Energizer was plausible, and the company wanted to keep the project a secret, and Webster disagreed, to what lengths would Randolph react?"

Chabus studied the woman across from him. "I want to invite you up to my room. We can continue our delightful conversation up there. You intrigue me. You excite me."

"Thank you. You're very flattering," Dr. Chabus. "I am charmed by you as well. But that is not my style on a first date. Besides, I don't think Puff would approve."

Chabus laughed. "That's a shame. I wanted to probe your mind."

"Pardon me if I have misunderstood," Maggie said toyingly. "My mind is not what I think you'd probe in your room."

"Oh, Maggie. You are a prize."

Maggie laughed out loud, leaned forward to meet his face eyeball to eyeball. She whispered. "Say what you will about Randolph. You know the answer as well as I. A Scan-Man operative might kill Webster!"

*

"It's so exciting to run into you, Phil, and then find you're in the newspaper business with Maggie. I think it's so lovely that you two work together on a life career. I know of so many couples that never see each other. And then there are other marriages that are so humdrum, nine-to-five, home at six, watch TV and go to bed. You know what I mean? It must be super to be doing your own thing together."

Billings nodded and lighted a cigarette.

"How nice," Puff commented. "Whew! Can you please put that stinky thing out?"

Surprised, he crushed the cigarette in the ashtray.

Puff and Billings met this evening at the Tahitian Atoll. Since their arrival, Puff had talked without respite. Billings had listened, nodded, shook his head and occasionally laughed or responded with a yes or no.

He simply enjoyed watching her, not really listening. Puff rarely said anything worth listening to. She was expert at gesturing. Her monologues were fired with enthusiasm and spirit.

Tonight she wore another short cocktail dress, again slung low at the neckline. Her petite body fit into it like a little girl's. She wore stockings and spike heels. Bracelets completed the picture of the delicate, sexy little lady Billings had always remembered.

This was the girl he had always wanted – the helpless type. Someone he could pick up in his arms and swing around in a moment of joy, someone he could cuddle like a doll on the dance floor -- and in bed.

But she had left him for a stranger. That was sixteen or seventeen years ago when he was twenty-four or five. She must have been nineteen or eighteen, somewhere in there.

Puff had now swung back into those early years.

"Remember the times we had on the Charles River, and the concerts at the Hatch Shell in July? You know what I mean? Those are some of my best memories she crooned. And dancing. We danced everywhere from the Hill Billy Ranch to the Parker House. Those were the good years, Phil, and you taught me a lot."

She paused, looking up at him with dewy eyes. "Do you realize I was a virgin when I met you? Well I was. I admired you. You know what I mean? You were the older man in my life. I looked up to you."

Billings cut in. "Older man! Hell, there's only five or six years difference!"

"True, but at my age, a young innocent of nineteen, you were the man of experience. You had been around the world. You were an Army man and we were a world apart in experience. You know what I mean? I must admit you were a very good teacher. From you I learned values. I learned to appreciate the beauty of a moonlit night, the excitement of Tchaikovsky concerts at Symphony and the pure pleasure of an afternoon in the Museum of Fine Arts.

"From you I learned who Nietzsche was and how I feared his Superman philosophy. From you I learned the plots of Dostoevsky novels. You taught me to see beyond the obvious."

"You flatter me, Puff. I had no idea I had made such an impression."

"I know you didn't. You were too modest. In fact you were downright self-defacing. You know what I mean?"

"That was me. Old self-defacing Phil," he mimicked. He reached for a cigarette, but then changed his mind.

There was another pause and another drink was ordered.

"Tell me what happened after I left, Phil. What did you-do? What've you accomplished?"

"I'll be honest, Puff. I've been going downhill since you left. When you left, the bottom dropped out."

"You're serious," Puff said, puzzled. "I had that effect on you?"

"Yes. We had a beautiful student/teacher relationship, if you want put it that way. I suppose I was subconsciously trying to bring you up to my experience level."

"I understand. I enjoyed every minute of it, if you know what I mean. You were so creative, so intelligent, so ... imaginative."

Billings looked her dreamily. "Why did you leave?"

"Because you weren't Jewish."

Billing's jaw dropped in astonishment. "That is what came between us?"

"That and other things."

"Like what?"

"As a provider, you showed no promise."

"Provider?"

"Yes. You know. Money. I didn't believe you could ever provide me with the material things I craved. You know what I mean?"

"You never mentioned this then. You never mentioned material possessions."

"Of course not. I wanted you for something else. And when you're young you don't need material things."

"You used me then."

Puff tossed down her drink and signaled the bartender for another.

"Phil. You could never understand the necessity of money. I love money and all the things it stands for. I love the security, the prestige, the house, the clothes, the cars, the country clubs, the people, the parties, the life, love and fun it brings."

"Yes. I understand."

"I don't think you do. I don't think you give a damn about those things. But a woman has to have them. Without

106

them she grows old fast. Wrinkles appear before she's thirty. Money helps me keep young, feel young and swing with the young."

"Then why did you find me attractive?"

"I told you. You launched me with a basic foundation."

She giggled and smiled at Phil. "Do you realize how often I've used Nietzsche, Dostoevsky and Tchaikovsky among my friends? I can't tell you how impressed they've been."

"That's horrid!"

"Of course it is, but it works. And let me tell you another secret." She leaned toward Phil confidentially. "You remember your New York Times *Book Review*? I never have to waste my time wading through all those books. I simply read the reviews and I'm in. And I get a jump on my friends."

"Shit, Puff. You've twisted and corrupted everything we did together."

"You're still very idealistic. You know what I mean? I'd say that I could now be the teacher. Our roles have reversed."

"You could be right."

"You have to be practical, Phil. You have to know where it's at. Your wife. I think she really knows where it's at."

"We can leave her out of it."

"I'll bet Maggie just leaves you in the dust," Puff giggled again. "I'll bet you love being a little puppy dog following Maggie around."

"Puff!"

"Mark my words, Phil Billings. She's going to walk out on you also if you don't come back to reality."

Billings was confused. He reached for his cigarettes, and then changed his mind. What the hell was Puff doing?

She was mixing truths and untruths and coming out with all truth. It hurt. He was a puppy.

"Does your husband give you everything you want?"

"Pretty much."

"Do you love him?"

"Love doesn't enter into it. Ours is a marriage of mutual need. I provide for his social needs and he provides money and prestige that satisfies those needs. Sure he's twice my age and a clumsy lover. So what!"

"What about love?"

"What about it? Love is a figment of man's imagination. Two people find each other attractive, for whatever reason. They like being with each other. They may or may not make a commitment to marriage. Being together becomes habit. A habit can be tough to break."

"Yes. You learned to philosophize, but your pessimism is astounding."

"I'm not a Romantic," Puff insisted.

"You were once. You just said so. Remember the moon, the music and the concerts?"

"Romanticism is drug. Fortunately I was able to kick it."

Where was the little girl I knew? Billings pondered. What has she grown into, sitting across from me in her little girl dress? How could I have misjudged her so completely? Perhaps Puff was right. Perhaps I am an impractical romantic who has never been a provider. What happened to me over the years? Where have my values gone? Where is the man Puff reminded me I used to be?

Puff was watching Billings look at her. "Do you still feel anything for me now?"

"Certainly, but it's not like it used to be."

"Explain."

"You are a very attractive woman, physically. Intellectually, you're a cripple."

"You never said that before."

"I guess there's a lot we never said to each her. I think I was in love with your body rather than anything else you had to offer. You were my Lolita."

"Who's that?"

"Google it."

"I like to have men stare at me. They're not going to stare at my brain!"

"I can understand that, and it's good for you. I'm glad you ran off, but I wish we'd had this conversation sixteen years ago."

"We couldn't have." Puff said. "We didn't have the experience. You now have Maggie. I have Freddie. We're both very lucky."

"You've made me finally realize that."

"Do you want to go to bed with me now, just for old time's sake? I'd really like it, Phil." She watched his eyes as she shifted in her chair and raised her short dress up her thigh.

Phil looked away. "I had that in mind an hour ago, but I don't think I want to now."

"You're being bashful again," she teased, leaning forward and placing her hand on his thigh.

He looked her in the eye now. "No, Puff. It's not bashfulness. I think I'm beginning to see things differently." He stepped down from his stool, leaned toward Puff and kissed her on the cheek. Her face was cold and he felt her makeup powder come away on his damp lips.

"Goodbye, Puff." He left her seated at the bar.

Billings felt good. He was smiling. He pulled out his handkerchief and wiped the powder from his mouth. Back to reality, he thought.

*

The jet stream has formed a deep trough. It extends south from the frozen tundra of northern Canada to southern Connecticut. Here it turns out to sea before swinging north again. It carries a frigid, dry air mass. Meanwhile, a stream of moist, tropical air from the Gulf of Mexico has moved rapidly north along the Atlantic seaboard.

The two contrasting air masses meet and converge into a giant low, and form a counterclockwise disturbance that grows to several hundred miles in diameter as it continues north and intensifies.

The cold, polar air concentrates and sinks. It forces the tropical air, which is much lighter, to be displaced, rise and disperse. The higher the warm air now rises, the colder the air it meets in the upper elevations. Here it condenses and forms cumulus clouds that in turn produce precipitation.

The precipitation falls, crystallizing into snow when it reaches the colder, polar air near the earth's surface.

*

The Icelandic Low, stirred into motion by an unnatural disturbance in Greenland, approaches the New England coast from the northeast. It has become a violent storm in itself -- best known as a Nor'easter. Its air mass is moist, a characteristic picked up from the North Atlantic Ocean. This storm forms a blockade to the opposing storm attempting to force its way up through New England.

Both storms halt their progress, like two heavyweight Sumo wrestlers in center ring, grappling to see who will dominate the other. It is a battle that will be a fight to the death, and it will be of several days duration.

*

"Maggie arrived home before Phil and was surprised at his absence. After showering, washing and drying her hair, she went downstairs to sit beside the woodstove to continue reading the novel she had neglected for the last few days. But

110

she couldn't concentrate. Chabus, Webster and Scan-Man wandered between the printed lines of her mystery book. Truth once again proved to be more fascinating than fiction.

Phil then walked into the room and interrupted her train of thought. He walked directly to her chair and kissed her on the cheek.

"My, you smell clean and fresh," he remarked.

"And you look lovely."

"Thank you. I wish I could say the same for you."

Phil smiled. "Maggie," he announced. "You see before you a changed man."

"Oh?" She looked at him with suspiciously.

"Something happened to me tonight that has changed my life."

"Let me guess," Maggie mocked. "You fell into a snowdrift tonight and froze your dingus."

"Be serious, Maggie."

"I've tried to be serious for the last several years," she retorted. "You're always making these promises. You're always reforming. You're always going to change your life. Let's forget the words and see the action."

"You're right on all charges. I accept them."

"Then you're not going to tell me what happened?" Maggie said, a little bit disappointed.

"Not necessary. But I can assure you I am now a changed husband."

"Including smoking?"

"Including smoking."

"Showering?"

"Every day."

"I hope I can believe you this time."

"Count on it," Phil said confidently. "Now tell me about your day."

Maggie was astonished. "You have never asked me that, ever! Do you really want to know what I did?"

Taking advantage of the opportunity for whatever it was worth, Maggie related what she had learned from Ellen and Chabus. Phil listened intently, concentrating on her every word and phrase. Maggie was encouraged and told her story in detail.

"How do you get yourself involved in these things?" was Phil's first question. That's incredible." He then reached for his cigarettes, as Maggie waited for a response. He walked over to the woodstove, opened the door and tossed the pack into the fire. "Do you think you can trust Chabus?"

"I asked myself that question on both occasions," Maggie said, her attention now divided between Phil's behavior and her story. "I have no reason not to believe him."

"Do you think Webster is alive or dead?"

"I don't know. But if I were to guess, I'd say he was alive. I have no grounds for that, except Ellen's identification."

"The weather modification business scares me," Phil said thoughtfully, "especially on nights like tonight when the wind is whistling, blowing the trees around, shaking the walls, beating against the windows, piling the snow high against the house, making travel difficult or impossible. It can be scary as hell. What would it be like if crazy men and their computers begin to tamper with it?"

Phil stared silently at the stove. Maggie watched his face. "I'd rather be subjected to a nuclear blast than take the chance of fooling around with the atmosphere."

"It is a frightening subject," Maggie agreed, "although I can't say I'd prefer a nuclear confrontation."

Phil continued. "I just imagine the most frightening storms I've seen or read about, right here in New England – the snowstorm of '78, the tornadoes, floods, ice storms. The list is endless. But they were natural disasters. Think how many fold worse these could be if somebody screwed up the weather cycle. Imagine the Arctic ice cap shifting to New England, or the other way around, the ice caps melting and the oceans rising!"

"I know." Maggie said, impressed by the first decent conversation she had had with her husband in years. "It's all possible. Climates could shift ninety degrees in any direction."

Phil brought the subject back on course. "So Ellen's going to check some more at Scan-Man?"

"She's going to try. But she feels kind of edgy about it."

"I don't blame her, after what you've told me."

Conversation dropped, as both reviewed their thoughts.

"I guess I'll be off to bed now." Maggie stood and stretched. "Are you coming up soon?"

"Phil smiled "I'll be up. But I want to take a long hot shower and wash this grubby hair."

"Boy, I am more curious about what happened to you today."

"Better left unsaid. I'll see you shortly."

SATURDAY, DECEMBER 22

It was not until shortly after one, Saturday morning, that Ellen was able to take a break from her terminal and go to the file rooms. Recordings by Scan-Man weather satellites were maintained as permanent visual records of atmospheric activity around the world. Fortunately for Ellen, these records were readily accessible. Each record contained one day's readings from each satellite, stored on data banks. Logically, she decided to begin her review the day of the launch.

Scanner XII moved into orbit Wednesday morning, December 19. It was not operational, presumably, until that afternoon when geosynchronization had been achieved. Wednesday night Ellen had been on duty monitoring XII, but she recalled nothing extraordinary. But what happened between geosynchronization and the beginning of her shift -- the same time period when Nat disappeared?

Thursday's records were already filed. An hour ago she had turned in her segment of Friday's records to be merged with the other Friday segments. But, there was no Tuesday, of course, since Scanner XII had not been launched. But Wednesday's record was missing! There should have been a segment of the day XII was first operational.

Ellen's first thought was someone was studying it. But there were only two work stations other than her own which were operational tonight, and they were monitoring live. They could not have been taken from the Interpretation Room because that was against procedure.

Maggie had warned her of frustration. Could the missing record have some significance? Was she jumping to conclusions?

"They picked that one up yesterday afternoon," Paul Kreig, the night librarian, told her a few minutes later.

"But they're not supposed to be taken out," Ellen protested. "Couldn't you have made a copy?" Ellen was visibly shaken.

"Hey. Calm down," Kreig said. "I get my orders. The big boys wanted it, so the big boys get it. I don't argue."

"The 'big boys'? Who the devil are the 'big boys?'"

"Mr. Randolph sent his executive assistant down after it. It was very unusual, I must say. I don't ever recall anyone requisitioning those records except you people. It was such an unusual request, Jim Naugler pointed it out to me when I came on tonight."

"When are they going to return it?"

"Hell! I don't know." He turned to the file of requisition forms and slowly flipped through them. "Ah. Here it is. Damn! He didn't fill in that blank!" Kreig was puzzled and an annoyed. Someone had violated his procedure.

"Well," Ellen remarked. "I guess you can't fool with the 'big boys.'" She laughed. "Can I see the requisition?" She examined it. "They asked for something else also -- something with an 'S' prefix." Her heart thumped. It was Nat's file that she had requisitioned and looked through yesterday morning!

"So?" the librarian asked. "Why are you so interested in this particular record?"

"Why shouldn't I? They've taken away the tools of my trade. How can I function properly when my records disappear?" She handed the requisition form back to Kreig.

"Oh. Wait! Let me see that again for a minute." Ellen remembered something. She pushed her way in front of Kreig and flipped through Friday's requisitions. "Are all of yesterday's slips here?"

"Yep. For the past two days. They're not filed until Monday."

Ellen re-examined the small pile thoroughly. The requisition she had filled out and faked in order to see Nat's file was gone!

As she returned to her terminal, she saw Margo Chin approaching and motioning to her. Oh, God! She thought. They're after me already about the requisition.

"Where the hell have you been?" Margo asked, not in anger, but as if she was under a great deal of strain.

"Sorry, Margo. I had terrible stomach cramps and ... "

"Never mind that now." Margo spoke rapidly. It was very unusual for her to be perturbed. "We've got problems. Go to Recap right away and then come back and monitor 5Z4.2. Let me know how things progress." She then dashed off.

The Recap meeting was in progress. Stills were being shown on the projection screen featuring the East Coast of the U.S. and Canada. Four other telecommunication specialists were present watching quietly.

" ... And so we come up with a very erratic and unusual phenomenon. What happens when the two fronts meet we can only surmise. One thing is certain," the speaker said. "We can expect an abundance of precipitation."

Ellen's trained eye read the situation with a bit more pessimism. In her opinion there would be a hell of a lot of snow falling over the New England states.

"Any questions?"

Ellen spoke up. "What's the origin, Wally?"

"The North Atlantic."

"This development seems a bit sudden for the usual nor'easter."

"That's what I mean by an 'unusual phenomenon.' This is a freak storm."

116

"Any clues as to why it sprung up so fast?"

"That's the mystery. We haven't been able to determine that so far."

"Can't we follow it back on the records?" Ellen continued. "That's Scanner XII surveillance, isn't it?"

"We did. It seems that the germination of the storm and the geosynchronization of XII coincided. In other words, we weren't operational in time to record the event."

There were too many mysterious circumstances surrounding XII and the weather, Nat's disappearance, the body in Nat's car, the information gleaned from Nat's classified file. All of these seemed to be related and fell into the time period of Wednesday afternoon/evening. Ellen now strongly suspected XII was responsible for germinating this nor'easter.

"Wally. Did you review Wednesday's records?"

"Sure did. It was negative. This is a freak. No two ways about it."

So that's where the record is, Ellen mused. But where's Nat's file?

The briefing continued, but Ellen's thoughts wandered. When it was over, she spoke to Wally privately. "Did you review Wednesday's records personally?"

"Not the whole thing, I have to admit. For some reason they gave me a copy. The word is, the directors reviewed all the records when they heard of this storm. For some reason, I think they edited Wednesday's stuff." Wally then looked around as if he had said something shameful. "Look, Ellen. I didn't say that, OK?"

Ellen returned to her terminal to track the storm with her fellow employees. Isn't it interesting how the directors have suddenly taken a personal interest in a nor'easter? Ellen thought. It's as if they had some kind of vested interest in it.

She smiled widely and foolishly to herself. It all began to make sense.

Her train of thought changed. Her smile disappeared. She had dozens of questions, two of them overrode the others. Where was Nat? Why was this storm created?

*

December 22, the first day of winter; the northern hemisphere is experiencing its winter solstice; the time of year when the least amount of sun is received -- the shortest day of the year.

The word solstice means "sun stands still," because the sun stops its apparent northward or southward motion and momentarily stands still before it begins to move in the opposite direction.

The sun is nearest the earth during the northern hemisphere winter, therefore it is not distance that is responsible for the difference in temperature during the various seasons.

The difference is to be found in the angle of the sun in relation to the Earth and the length of time it remains above the horizon.

During the summer the rays are more nearly vertical, and therefore more concentrated, whereas in the winter, because of the sun's low angle, the rays are spread out over a larger area – similar to a flashlight beam shining across the top of a large beach ball.

*

Maggie and Ellen did not run this morning. The snow had accumulated to twelve inches and was still falling heavily at 6 a.m. They met instead in Maggie's kitchen at the table next to the picture window. To Maggie's surprise, and initial annoyance, Phil joined them.

"I'm disappointed," Phil said with dubious sadness. "I wanted to run with you all."

Maggie looked at him closely. "You're serious!"

"Of course I am. I did my stretching exercises before I came down."

Maggie turned to Ellen and winked, but Ellen's thoughts appeared to be far from the kitchen table. "Let me get the Java."

Maggie poured the coffee and then sat opposite her friend, next to Phil. "Tell us about it, Ellen. Last night I brought Phil up to date on what's happened so far."

"The whole thing is weird," Ellen said in a trance-like voice, staring into her coffee. "It's like a surrealistic painting, and all of a sudden I seem to be in the middle of it."

"You learned something new last night," Phil concluded.

"Did I ever!" she answered, shaking off the trance and looking at Phil. "I don't know where to start. First of all, we're in the midst of a 'freak' storm that's going to dump at least three feet on us."

"Three feet! That's a big storm, but why is it a 'freak?'"

"It's a storm that has no explanation, according to Scan-Man. But I think differently. I think Scanner XII generated this storm by means of the Searoc Beam we were talking about yesterday."

"You're saying we're into weather modification? The storm is manufactured? You think the Searoc Beam is operational and this storm is the result of it?" Maggie's face was an expression of disbelief, yet one that also held a hope that what Ellen was saying was not true.

"That's what I'm saying. It hit me last night." Ellen took a quick sip of her coffee, apparently relieved to have spoken the most pressing thoughts on her mind.

"Something very strange is going on at the company," Ellen continued. "Randolph confiscated the records which probably contained data of the storm germination. They've taken Nat's file, too, the very file I looked at yesterday. They also took my requisition slip, the one I faked in order to see that file -- so they now know I saw that file.

"For some reason the company directors have a personal interest in this storm. Based on everything I've seen and read to date, it all points to Scanner XII and Nat's classified project. Why else would they be interested in this particular storm?"

Phil whistled. The thought was incredible.

"I'll have one of your cigarettes," Maggie said to him.

Phil laughed. "I guess we're both out of luck. Or maybe we're lucky. I'd be smoking two at a time if I hadn't thrown them out."

After a pause, Maggie spoke. "I had a long conversation last night with Dr. Chabus. You and he seem to think along some of the same lines. Scan-Man may indeed be up to no good. Apparently they are capable of dirty tricks. I'm not surprised you believe this is a manufactured storm. The Searoc Beam was designed to do just that, according to Chabus."

Tension was high at the table. Each wanted to speak at the same time. Minds were racing. Imaginations were flying.

"I kept asking myself all last night," Ellen said, 'Where is Nat?' and 'Why would the company want to create this storm in their own backyard?' It just doesn't make sense."

"I don't want to discourage you, Ellen, but after my talk last night, I'm convinced Scan-Man wouldn't hesitate to put someone out of the way if he interfered with company policy some way."

"You've said it very discreetly," Ellen nodded. "You mean they might kill Nat if he got in the way."

"Bluntly. Yes."

"I have the feeling we're going off in different directions here. Can we pull it all together? I don't fully understand." Phil poured himself a coffee and asked with a circular motion of the pot if the others wanted more.

"From what I understand you two have said," Phil continued, "you think Scan-Man is up to no good, that they've created a storm through the use of Nat's invention. It's quite possible that Nat got in the way of their plans and, if so, they might have killed him.

"And Ellen said something earlier we didn't pick up. She said the company knows she saw Nat's file, the classified file."

Phil looked closely at Ellen. "Are you worried about them doing something to you?"

"No. Of course not." She shrugged, her eyes avoiding Phil's.

"You're not worried?" Phil said. "From what Maggie tells me, you've seen Nat's plans for his weather modification gimmick. I have the impression the company would frown on that."

"They'd frown alright!" Ellen admitted.

"Then you *are* worried about some kind of retribution."

"Not necessarily," Ellen said.

"What do you mean 'not necessarily'? That doesn't mean anything. Everything is 'not necessarily'." Phil was irritated. "People usually use that phrase when they don't want to admit they're wrong."

"OK. So I'm worried, although I find it very hard to believe they'd try something," Ellen said. "This whole thing sounds like some kind of mystery novel. I've read part of it but I'm too spooked to continue on to the end."

"I understand precisely," Maggie said. "When real experience begins to compare to fictional experience, we often

121

find it difficult to believe the real. I think we have something very serious here, and we'd better move very carefully -- especially you, Ellen"

"I think we're making too much of this." Ellen's voice indicated little conviction.

"That's not what you really believe," Phil said. "I think you're afraid to believe what's actually happening."

"You're right, Phil. I am afraid. I don't want to believe the evidence."

"Just what evidence is that?" Phil asked.

Ellen looked at him in surprise. She then looked at Maggie. "There is no evidence. There's not a damn bit of evidence! Phil's right. All we have are bits and pieces here and there. There's nothing concrete. We're basing our beliefs on what Maggie's heard and what I've seen and heard. But the files are gone. The record is gone. Nat's gone and we have nothing."

"Couldn't that be exactly what they want?" Phil asked. "With no concrete evidence we can't do anything. We can't prove anything."

"Tell me some more about the storm, Ellen," Maggie said. "If what you say is true, we'd better get things into gear here."

"Margo Chin, my supervisor, was all shook up about something last night. After I returned from the library, she had me go to the Recap Room where I learned about the nor'easter we're expecting. There is a 'freak' storm, as they explained it, coming towards us from the North Atlantic. They were not able to explain its origin. It seems that the Wednesday record, the one that Randolph took, was edited. In other words, it looks as if the origin of the storm may have been edited out. This tells me they are trying to hide something. I was told that satellite coverage over the area, where the storm was germinated, was not recorded that day.

Geosynchronization was not achieved until after the storm was formed. I believe the storm was recorded, taped before geosynchronization, and that Nat's Energizer did its weather modification act before Scanner XII geosynced.

"So, this snow that you see before you," and Ellen gestured dramatically toward the window, "is generated from a storm that has moved up the East Coast from the Gulf of Mexico. Very shortly it will meet with our North Atlantic nor'easter, right over our heads, and it will be a battle royal. Although the meeting of two storms is not unusual, the lack of explanation of the Atlantic storm, and the timing of the collision between the storms, will make this a beauty, or a 'freak', as they say."

Maggie gazed out the window. "You say that Margo Chin was all shook up about something?"

"Yes. Something isn't going right. They seem to be very concerned about this storm, from the directors on down."

"Why do you suppose they'd be upset about it," Phil asked, "if it was something they planned?"

"Unless it was something they *hadn't* planned!" Maggie said with emphasis. "Isn't that one of the great fears about Man's fooling with the weather – that we can't be assured it will perform as we wish it to?"

"It does seem strange they'd direct a huge storm at their corporate headquarters," Ellen said.

"Did you say three feet are predicted?" Phil asked.

"I think I said 'at least three feet'," Ellen clarified. "We spent most of the morning alerting emergency centers, and sending warnings over the web."

Phil chuckled. The women looked quizzically toward him. "I know this isn't funny, but I just have to agree with Ellen about her surrealistic painting metaphor. Here we're saying that Scan-Man has gone to great lengths to create this storm, and then they seem to be greatly concerned about it. Now they're alerting everyone to it. Does that make sense?"

"Have we forgotten about Nat?" Maggie asked. "We've wondered where he disappeared, but have we asked ourselves how he might be related to this?"

"Good point," Ellen said. "Another thought I had last night was how everything, it seems, happened last Wednesday. The satellite was launched; Nat disappeared; a storm was generated in the North Atlantic; a mystery person was killed. Wednesday's records were taken and edited. Nat's files about his Energizer were taken ... "

Maggie had her own ideas, but she was not yet ready to voice them to Ellen. It looked to her as if Nat Webster had generated the North Atlantic storm, saw that it wasn't going to work according to the way he planned it and then committed suicide because his 'baby' had failed. It was more than he could bear after so much dedication over so many years.

"But we still have no evidence," Maggie said in answer to Ellen. "If we want to pursue this, and I think we should, we have to be aware of the dangers. Sooner or later everything has to fall into place, evidence and all. Just be careful, Ellen."

Maggie thought back to Chabus' statements about Nat's experience with the astronauts and the resulting threats Scan-Man made to their families and to Webster. She wondered if her friend really was in danger.

"I hate to end this discussion, but you need your sleep Ellen. I must notify the town about this nor'easter." Maggie shook her head. "Bud Kelly might go into shock and something similar might shake up Bob Sivolesky."

"All I can say is 'Groan'," Phil said. "Three feet of snow! I just think of the disaster we had in '78. I hope we learned something from that and don't have a repeat."

*

The Town Common was alive with the activity of both children and adults. Amid the heavily falling snowflakes and gusty winds, the sculptures were already taking shape.

Molly Battinni, a giant sculpture herself, accentuated by her heavy, snow-covered wool coat, shuffled among the competitors offering words of encouragement and praise. Her enthusiasm was contagious and it sparked renewed activity and increased cheering and jeering between groups.

She was affectionate with each of the younger children, placing her arm around one and then another whenever convenient. She wiped running noses, tightened the laces of loose snowsuit hoods, and admonished the teenagers for leaving their jackets unzipped.

"You'll catch your death! Tommy put you hat on! You don't even have a sweater on!"

"It's hot, Mrs. Battinni. I'm working up a sweat!"

"All the more reason to zip up. This wind will blow right through you."

A fifteen-foot-long dragon had taken shape. Not far from a ten-foot-high snowman. Some other piles left identification to the imagination at this early stage.

"I have food coloring in the car when you're ready for it," Molly said.

"Think the dragon should be red or green?"

"Try red. It'll look real mean," she laughed.

She left the common and walked toward the town garage where some of the parade floats were nearing completion.

*

Ed Randolph's face rippled with rage as he stood and addressed the two young men sitting across the table from him and the other directors.

"I want to know what the hell happened in that Control Room last Wednesday! I want to know in precise detail what happened. What did that idiot Webster do to the mission of Scanner XII?"

The young, but experienced, technicians had worked with Nat Webster in programming the Scanner XII mission, yet now they were speechless, entirely taken aback by the august presence of the board of directors and their President who was incredibly disturbed about something.

One of the young men spoke. "Well, sir, we have the print-out here which should pretty much explain the computer functions. We ... "

"I don't give a shit about the print-out! I want to know from you what Webster did down there!" Randolph slammed his fist on the gleaming mahogany table.

A director sitting next to Randolph placed his hand on Randolph's sleeve and said softly, "Easy, Ed. We won't get anywhere this way."

Randolph sat, attempting to regain control. Meanwhile the other director spoke.

"We've had a backfire, a rebound in the mission Mr. Randolph is speaking about. We're trying to find out why it backfired. We thought, since you worked closely with Webster, you could help explain what happened."

"Well, sir," the young man began again. "At this point in time we find we were told very little about the mission. We only did what Nat directed us to do, sir."

"Webster himself," the director interrupted. "Did you notice anything at all unusual about his behavior?"

"On the day of the shot?"

"Yes."

"He didn't appear weak at all. He seemed unusually nervous. He even looked sick ... We were pretty busy at the controls ... "

"Yes. Yes. What else did you notice?"

"He was sweating, and ... talking to himself, I think."

126

The men around the table looked at each other.

"Then would you say Webster was, er, not in control of himself?"

"No. I'd say," and he turned to his companion for confirmation, "I'd say he was in perfect control. All of his commands were rational. Right, Jim?"

Jim nodded.

"I think he was just very nervous over the mission, and perhaps he wasn't feeling too good. He's complained a lot about stomach trouble and chronic headaches."

Randolph cut in. "I'm told that one of our meteorologists, Bloodworth, Ellen Bloodworth, was asking questions about Webster after he smashed himself up."

"Yes."

"What did you tell her?"

"Gosh. Nothing, really."

"What in hell do you mean by 'nothing really?'"

"She asked me if I thought Nat had been depressed lately, and I said no. I said I thought he was excited about the mission -- nervous."

"Anything else?"

"I told her we'd launched Scanner XII and that it contained some instruments Nat had developed. But that's all."

"Are you sure?"

"Sure. Hey look ... "

"Don't 'Hey look' me!" Randolph exploded. The consequences of the rebound were wearing heavily on him. It was his company. He felt personally responsible for those under him.

"Sorry, sir."

"Are you certain you told her nothing more?"

"Yes, sir. I mean no sir. That was it."

"You realize, of course, that you have no business giving out any information to anyone."

"Yes, sir. But ... "

"Your work here is highly confidential. You keep everything to yourself."

"But Ellen's one of our own. She's our meteorologist. We work for the same company."

"She was prying into your business. She would have been briefed on the project at the proper time. In fact she had an interim briefing a month ago."

"Yes, sir."

Randolph turned to the rest of his board, "Any questions? If none," and he turned to the young men again. "You can return to your stations."

The technicians rose hesitantly and left the room.

*

The directors redistributed themselves around the table and waited patiently, talking softly among themselves. Ed Randolph, the President of Scan-Man, still frustrated by the previous meeting with the technicians, waited as well. Ten minutes passed before Chandler Harrington, chairman of the board, entered the room, walked around the table greeting everyone and took his place, standing, at the head of the table.

He fit the stereotypical board chairman image found in Fortune magazine -- tall, white-haired, tanned, dark, pinstriped, three-piece suit, white shirt and regimental tie. His heavy black eyebrows turned up like horns.

"Gentlemen," he began. "We have pretty much exhausted speculation over last Wednesday's tragedy. It is quite evident now, painfully evident, that the ball was dropped when Nathaniel Webster balked at our plan -- right under our eyes."

There was a murmur of agreement.

"We are forced now to pass the ball over to Phase II which I will cover briefly in order to refresh your memories. Alternative plans are not ever to our liking. They could destroy this company's image and credibility if practiced too frequently. We can take comfort in the fact that our mission remains safely under wraps. This reminds me of the great FDR's words, "The only fear we have to think is fear itself," or some such. So let's keep that in mind and proceed.

"Following this meeting, I will call Washington and arrange a team meeting with the President and his top military, foreign and domestic advisors. This meeting should take place at the earliest moment. I will fly to Washington, soon after I place this call, to set this play in motion.

"While I am doing this you will return to your respective offices and destroy all material relevant to Phase I. Phase I never existed!" Harrington emphasized his last statement.

"I am taking with me the video records of the Greenland activity that were logged on Wednesday by Scanner XII. This is our proof, our concrete evidence of foul play by an unknown foreign power. It is convincing evidence that is certain to impress the President. I fully expect to return from the Capitol with the full cooperation of the Executive and Congressional branches of our great government and a multi-billion dollar contract in hand."

Smiles and nods around the table.

"I thank you all for your cooperation," Harrington concluded. "May God be with each of us."

Harrington beckoned to Randolph, picked up his attaché case from beside his chair and, as the other directors rose from their chairs and stood silent, he and Randolph walked to the door.

"Do, you know this Bloodworth female?" Harrington asked, confidentially. "I've never met her. We've got to do something about her. I don't like the way she's been nosing around. We can't take chances."

"I'll take care of it, Chandler," Randolph nodded.

*

Bud Kelly was a worried man. The prediction of two feet of heavy snow was going to be a problem. Already one of his good trucks had broken down and he needed all of them to keep the roads clear.

He paced the chilly, wet garage, occasionally checking on how the crew was progressing on the broken drive shaft. He cussed. The crew cussed. And the phone rang for the fifteenth time this morning. He stalked back to the office hoping it would stop ringing by the time he reached it.

"Kelly here. Yes, Mrs. Randolph. We're working on it. We'll get there as soon as we can. OK. So long."

Some of the back roads had not been plowed at all today. Mrs. Randolph, down on River Road, was complaining as had some others. But what could he do? No use staying here, Kelly thought. He had patched together two other trucks -- the ones with the blown cylinder wall and the defective steering linkage. He hoped they were still at work. The front-end loader was in use at intersections around town.

Christ! This stuff is piling up fast! he thought.

*

Phil picked up two egg salad sandwiches at Thompson's and brought them to the office. He announced his arrival and joined Maggie in her office. His thoughtfulness surprised Maggie -- another courtesy he hadn't performed for quite a while.

They sat together and chatted shoptalk. Phil said he couldn't believe how fast the snow was piling up. They talked of their plans for the balance of the day. It was developing into a very busy Saturday.

Maggie's editorial yesterday, criticizing the selectmen for their inaction on the highway department equipment, had inspired a number of phone calls and emails. Selectman Sivolesky had been irate and had asked what the devil she was trying to prove. She simply acknowledged Sivolesky's call and said her viewpoint would stand as printed.

Phil laughed and said he had enjoyed Maggie's editorial stance.

Other e-mails Maggie received were from citizens who asked what could be done. She referred them to the selectmen who were the only ones who had the power to release the needed money. Bud Kelly's problems today and the poor condition of the roads proved Maggie's point.

Phil spoke of his observations around town taking pictures of the Winter Carnival preparations and how the Carnival may in fact become buried in the white stuff.

Maggie spent a few minutes viewing Phil's photos through the rear of his camera. "There's an awful lot of white in these," she chuckled.

For one of the first times in many months the two enjoyed each other's company in the office. This enjoyment was not vocalized. Just below the surface was the fear that the harmony would not last, but that it was nice to have it while it lasted.

*

The supermarket at Crosby's Shopping Center was first to notice the crush of panicky customers. It came imperceptibly at first, shortly after the late morning news. It intensified after the 1 p.m. report.

George DeMoss, the manager went to the phone when he saw the situation becoming rough. Most of his cashiers and packers had gone home and he was down to only three open registers. DeMoss should have anticipated the crowd and had all eight open.

"I need an officer down here, Sergeant. Right away. Everyone's panicking at the crush of people."

"I'll do what I can, sir, but most of our men are on traffic control. We're tied up with some bad problems out here."

"I need someone down here before they tear this place apart!" DeMoss' voice was urgent.

"I'll do what I can."

DeMoss hung up and continued to survey the scene from his raised office overlooking the store. Tempers were flaring as customers jockeyed for positions in the three register lines. As the lines lengthened and became tangled, customer's tempers flared. Seeing no logic to the cash register lines, some abandoned the wagons in place and went home. Those with carts already in line told others the end of the line was behind them. Those cutting in shouted and returned the gestures.

It had become everyone-for-himself and DeMoss could see that his standard system just wasn't working. He descended from his observation nest determined to create some order. A single line feeding into the registers should be the answer.

"Everyone will be served," he shouted to the noisy group, ignoring their individual complaints. "Unless we have some order none of you will be served."

He walked over to where the lines had backed up into a single tail. He patiently blocked off further progress of carts and told the shoppers how the lines would form. Where brief arguments broke out, he attempted to settle the dispute.

"The line will form in this direction," he pointed. "Now, please. Let's be patient and you'll all get what you want. I apologize for the delay, but we could not anticipate this rush."

He signaled to his assistant manager and told him to bar the entrance doors until the present problem was cleared.

DeMoss was sweating. He disliked conflict. He was a peace-loving man. Squabbling customers made him very nervous. He just didn't know how to handle them.

The police never arrived.

*

Smitty's gas station was another scene of confusion. Cars waiting for fill-ups extended 100 yards in two directions along Great Road. Smitty recognized the danger of idling cars along the main road under these conditions, but what could he do?

As if in answer to Smitty's thoughts, a sand truck, unable to maneuver when it came up behind the stopped car at the end of the gas line, slid into it at twenty miles an hour. This produced a domino effect on the icy road. Six vehicles, one after another in the line, crashed into the vehicle in front of it. Two of the vehicles in the middle, rammed both front and rear, buckled the line out into the center of the road, blocking all traffic.

Smitty winced, shook his head, and called the police.

The cruiser and the ambulance were already at the intersection of Great Road and Pine Street. A car, attempting to beat a red light, slammed into another that had proceeded innocently on his green signal. The latter had been hit directly in the door of the driver's side and the victim complained of severe back pain. The ambulance crew spent more than twenty minutes removing the driver for transportation to the hospital. Meanwhile traffic was backed up in four directions.

*

Maggie and Phil, alarmed by the increased activity on the police scanner, decided a tour of the town was necessary.

"It's times like these that I feel like a leech," Maggie said, wiping the condensation from the windshield with the back of her hand. "I feel so useless. This is an emergency situation and all we've doing is feeding off it."

"It's our job," Phil reasoned. "We're recording it all for posterity. We're fulfilling a need."

"So do whores and bookies," she retorted.

"My, my you're cynical today. Why the change?"

"People are panicking. People are hurt. The police, ambulance and highway crews are breaking their butts trying to help, but the storm's getting ahead of them."

"What do you propose?"

"That's it. I just don't know," Maggie sighed.

*

Vito Pazzita posted the notice on all exit doors and in conspicuous places in the lobby.

"All air and pubic carriers are cancelled. Police ask all guests to remain in hotel until roads cleared." Haste had made waste in his typing of "public."

As he returned to his desk from this mission, the first outraged guest was waiting for him. "I need a cab now. I must return to New York tonight. This is an emergency!"

Vito shrugged his shoulders. "Sorry. Even if there were cabs it wouldn't do you any good ... No planes."

"Look," the man said. "There's got to be a way." He then leaned toward Vito and lowered his voice. "I'll make it worth your while."

"You don't listen to the news. Everything's shut down, Mr.? ... "

"Hopkins. Look. I can see cars moving down there. What is this? Some kind of prison?"

"I'd like to help you, Mr. Hopkins, but my hands are tied. You can leave the hotel anytime you want, but I can't help you. Now please excuse me." Vito hustled off into the hallway.

*

Traffic along both north and south lanes of Route 128 had slowed to a crawl. Plowing by the State had been adequate but the road surface was slick and additional snow was accumulating fast. This was the first snow of the season and most drivers were showing caution by driving slowly.

It was also the first day of the Christmas holiday traffic rush. Plans had been made for travel to relatives and friends over the long, four-day weekend and families were anxious to get a head start on the storm despite the warnings being broadcast.

Bumper to bumper, the traffic extended for miles along the notorious highway. Headlights tried to pierce the approaching late afternoon December darkness. Thousands of windshield wipers attempted to sweep the freezing water from the defroster-blown windows. Visibility was very poor and worsening.

By 5 p.m. the traffic had come to a halt in the southbound lanes. Vehicles fortunate enough to be in the position to do so, exited, with the hope of bypassing the obstruction by using side roads. Dozens took the Hollandson exit, contributing to the already congested conditions. By far, the greater number of drivers either waited patiently for the obstruction ahead to clear, or waited impatiently because they had no choice.

One problem was a jackknifed trailer truck near the Massachusetts Turnpike exit ramp. It had overturned and scattered its load of steel I-beams across the highway.

Cars and trucks all along Rt. 128 attempted to jockey for apparent better positions, changing lanes where possible, and pulling up close behind the vehicle in front. Finally, movement ceased altogether. The snow fell steadily. No plows could get through. Windshield wipers swung back and forth in apprehensive monotony.

*

Chief Wilson's blood pressure had climbed forty points during the last three hours. He couldn't feel the difference, but he knew it was building.

Officer Commerwitz had radioed in the Rt. 128 traffic interruption. The chief said he didn't want to hear it. It was the state's problem. But he finally relented and threaded his way out to the Great Road overpass.

He parked on the bridge, stepped out of the cruiser wearily, and walked over to the rail. "We've got a problem" he said to Commerwitz with understatement as he faced a gust of biting snow chips. Shaking his head, remembering nightmares of not too long ago, he added, "This is goddamned jolly. Remember '69 and '78?"

"Nope. I'm a lot younger than you. But that's why I called you, chief. I thought you might want to get ready for it -- just in case."

At a standstill for more than a half hour, and unable to determine the cause of the problem, some drivers deserted their vehicles to walk in the direction of the jam-up. They spoke to each other, sympathizing with mutual frustrations.

Hoping their cars were temporarily safe, other drivers, stalled in the breakdown lane, carefully locked and abandoned their vehicles. Near an exit, they planned to walk to the warm haven of a restaurant, motel or garage where they could wait in comfort until the problem went away.

Those in the travel lanes dared not leave their cars, fearful of being towed during their absence when the traffic started moving again.

Activity near the exits increased as time passed. Vehicles above the exits jockeyed to leave the highway. Those immediately below the exit attempted to back up or make a u-turn so they too could escape from 128.

Frozen, snow-covered windows provided little or no visibility. This, along with impatience, resulted in fender bending and another blocked lane. Many cars were without snow tires.

Now an eighteen-wheeler blocked the exit ramp to Hollandson. Its tires spun in place against the slight upgrade.

*

The telephone rang. Frank McCullough answered it.

"I'm sorry to tell you this so late, Mr. McCullough, but our big wedding plans have been changed because of the storm. I hope you haven't gotten the cake ready yet because we won't be needing it. We're going to have a simple wedding tomorrow, since nobody can make it in this weather. I hope you don't mind."

"I understand, young lady. Don't you worry none. You give our happiness for the weddin' to the groom. I bet you'll look real pretty comin' down the aisle."

McCullough replaced the receiver and looked solemnly at Mabel. She was placing the supper dishes on the kitchen table.

"Who was that, Frank?"

"Bad news. They ain't comin' for the cake." He walked over to his wife and put his arms around her. "They changed the plans. I guess they ain't got no one to eat your cake."

Mabel pushed him away. "Don't be so mush-mouthed about it. My heart ain't broke. You just got yourself a Christmas present," she chuckled.

"Well, if you ain't somethin! Maybe we can have the kids in to share it."

"Or divide it up for the neighbors," Mabel added. "Shame to let it go to waste."

137

"All that work."

"Oh hush yourself! There's worse things in this world. It's only a cake. Pour the coffee and set yourself down."

*

"No! We have no more rooms," Vito was saying to a group of ten people who had just walked through the hotel doors. "We're full up."

"We'll share the same room. All we need is one for the night. We had to leave our cars back on the highway." It was a plea. The group was wet and exhausted.

"I'm sorry. We're full up with a convention." Vito tried to sympathize. "You can patronize the bar and the restaurant, we just don't have any rooms. Period!"

The group stepped away from the registration desk to confer among themselves. They decided to go to the Garden Room for a hot meal and further discussion.

*

The Mitchells were greeted with the warmth they expected. For Marsha Randolph it was a well-rehearsed welcome.

"Frankly, Ed, I didn't think we'd get through," Ralph Mitchell explained as Randolph helped him remove his coat. "Have you been out in the streets? I've seen better roads in the Yukon with ten times the snow!"

"I've called the road crew three times already today," Marsha answered. "All they have is excuses and 'We'll be by as soon as we can.' Sometimes I wish we lived closer to the city."

"You can't mean that," Elaine Mitchell said. "You have such a charming home."

"It's charming once you get here," Randolph said, "but sometimes that can be a problem."

The two couples walked into the living room. A large Christmas tree now stood in the corner where Turk and Robert placed it that afternoon. The Randolphs liked

138

decorations. The tree shimmered and blinked and a music box at the top of the tree played *Silent Night* while a rotating star cast its beacon around the circumference of the room. Glitter and artificial snow hid nearly all the green.

"My, what a lovely tree," Elaine exclaimed. "Where'd you get it?"

"From our back yard, of course," Marsha explained. "It's one of the advantages of living in the woods."

Randolph ushered Mitchell to the bar. He wished he could be relieved of having to listen to the man.

"By jingos, I need a drink or two," Mitchell said. "It'll relax my heart condition. You know, I consider myself real lucky to get off at that exit just north of here. As it was, I spent an hour sitting, and then jockeying for position, sitting, and finally pulling off. I then took the back roads to Hollandson, got lost and ... oh well. We're here. I don't know how ... "

"How many guests do you expect, Marsha?" Elaine asked.

"That's what I don't know. We invited twelve couples. Six have called to say they just couldn't make it. Conditions apparently are worse closer to Boston."

"The way it's mounting up, the others had better get here soon, or ... oh well."

"I'm concerned too. I'd hate to think I knew anyone marooned on 128 right now."

"OK, everybody! Here's a toast," Randolph interrupted. "May technology triumph over the evils of nature and deliver us from this pestilence."

"You're so damned romantic," Marsha quipped.

"There are romantics and realists," Randolph said, defending himself from his wife's sarcasm. "The romantics dream dreams. The realists live them."

"Very well put. Ed," Mitchell said. "That reminds me of a story about a guy I knew in business school ... "

Marsha saw her chance for a temporary escape. She went to the kitchen. "We're going to hold up on dinner till nine, Alberta. We should know by then how many guests we'll have."

"Yes, Ma'am."

"And check on Robert. I don't want him out in the mix tonight. Keep an eye on him and get him to bed on time.

"Oh. And what the devil is that! How many times have I told you not to paprika the eggs? I hate paprika. Let them add their own if they want it."

"Yes, Ma'am."

The Randolph home seemed particularly comfortable tonight. The floodlit scene through the windows was picturesque, if not poetic. Elaine had turned her chair towards the snow falling among the evergreens. It was as if she was watching a wide-screen TV.

Marsha nervously looked at her watch. If more guests didn't arrive shortly her dinner party would be a disaster. Why was it the bores always arrived first? She went to the bathroom. It was pill time again. She returned. Elaine continued to express her admiration of Marsha's home -- a sure sign of boredom and, undoubtedly, condescension.

Marsha prayed the Stevensons would arrive soon. Now there was an exciting couple! Young and absolutely crazy. She invited the Stevensons to all her parties. They were the one constant she could depend on. They had become a crutch. If they let her down tonight, she'd never forgive them.

Randolph remained cornered by Mitchell. He was the old man on the Scan-Man board directors, extremely conservative, reluctant to try new ideas, but he had an abundance of influential friends, men in government who

140

controlled lobbies that could swing money votes in Scan-Man's direction.

"Quite a show you put on this morning," Mitchell said, his jowls tightening into smile. "Have you heard from Harrington yet?"

"Not yet. Quite possibly we'll hear something tonight."

"Tell me honestly, Ed. Do you think Harrington has a chance?"

Randolph looked at Mitchell with puzzlement. "I'm surprised at you. You know Chandler much better than I and I'm certain he can handle it."

"He's got a heavy assignment."

"Have you ever known him to bother with a light assignment?"

"We've never played for such big stakes."

"I don't know about that. I'd call our Apollo contract a nice nest egg. Get yourself another drink Ralph."

Randolph walked toward the window to view the storm, glad to have escaped Mitchell temporarily.

The phone rang. Marsha answered it. "Alice. Where are you? You're not finking out?"

"We're at the Hollandson hotel, with a million others. We had to ditch the car. You wouldn't believe this mess."

"Oh my God. Are you alright?"

"Just wet, tired and dirty. You ever walked a mile through a snowstorm in two inch heels?"

"I'll be right over to get you."

"Are you sure you can make it?"

"I can sure as hell try. I need you here desperately. I'll be right over."

Marsha turned to make the announcement. "Hey everybody! Another country heard from. That was Alice.

They had to abandon their car and I'm going to go over and get them."

"No way, Marsha," Randolph cut in. "We'll send Turk in the 4-wheel drive."

"But Ed."

Randolph lowered his voice. "You're not going to stick me here. Turk will go. I'll speak to him."

*

Steve Kramer sat ramrod straight in the cab-over-engine seat. He couldn't relax for a moment. He looked down on the plow and tried to see ahead, beyond the area where his headlights pierced the blowing snow. The defroster wasn't working correctly and he had to keep wiping the windshield with his handkerchief. The plow was inefficient at low speeds, but there was no way he dared shift out of first gear. His path had become a zigzag around the obstructions of deserted vehicles.

He was tired. He'd been working steadily since five this morning. He thought of the overtime money he was earning, but now, spent from hours of concentration, a bed meant more to him than money. Two plows, he thought. Two damned plows for the whole town. There was no way they could keep up with this stuff. He was really doing this for the super. Superintendent Bud Kelly had told him about his problems with money and the selectmen. He had told the super he ought to quit. He'd quit with him. The whole crew would walk off the job!

Kelly wouldn't hear of it. "Think of the people. The townspeople depend on us. We have a responsibility."

Kramer laughed. "As if they gave a shit. They ought to get us some goddamned new equipment!"

Bud Kelly was too good a guy, Kramer thought. He was only working these extra hours because of him. He wiped the windshield again and pulled into the highway barn for a break.

*

The waiting room outside the President's office at 1600 Pennsylvania Avenue was hushed. Fifteen men and one woman awaited the arrival of the chief executive. Only two of those waiting were aware of the reason for this hastily called, top-secret meeting.

Chandler Harrington sat in icy silence, his attaché case flat in his lap, his hands folded on top of it. He was smugly pleased with himself for having arranged this meeting so quickly. He was satisfied with the reflex the name Scan-Man commanded. Yet he had never quite become accustomed to the respect he received as chairman. Inside, he was still slightly self-conscious and therefore somewhat uncomfortable. He smiled to himself as he thought how it was that no one ever really becomes an adult -- just an older child.

Next to Harrington was General Armand Stringer, Chairman of the Joint Chiefs of Staff. Beribboned and polished, he too sat erect and silent, staring straight ahead. Stringer had a reputation for independent thinking. During the height of the Iran Conflict, he was the first field grade commander to recommend getting out as gracefully and quickly as possible.

Secretary of State Philmore Buttrix was leaning toward Defense Secretary Hatfield Coge, speaking discretely and earnestly. Cote was shaking his head slightly as if disagreeing with Buttrix. The U.S. was currently mediating between two South American countries, one of which claimed to have perfected its own atomic bomb and said it wouldn't hesitate to use it on its neighbor if the latter didn't listen to the reasonable claims of the former. Buttrix and

Coge were the negotiators. They suspected this meeting concerned that issue.

General John Ruben appeared very uncomfortable. He talked to no one. He kept crossing one leg over the other and then vice versa. The look on his face was pained. It may have looked to others that he needed a bathroom visit.

Others in the room included congressional leaders, Sen. Harry Woark, Chairman of Ways and Means, Sen. Evelyn Robinson, Majority Leader, Rep. Bob Herman, Democratic Leader, Teddy Rosenfelt, Majority Whip, and several presidential advisors. It was the cream of the nation's decision-makers, asked personally by the President to attend an "urgent matter of national security."

The door opened and the group jumped to its collective feet. A staff member motioned them into the Oval Office where they were seated in a semicircle. A moment later, the President entered and the group stood once again. He motioned to take their seats. The President alone remained standing -- in front of his desk.

His face was lined, almost pasty and tired. His hair before the election three years ago had been black. Today it was sprinkled with gray. The attempt at a smile failed as he looked around his office. He felt tired, and indicated this by sitting on the edge of the desk and allowing himself to relax into a slump. There was no public pretense in this private meeting except, perhaps, for Harrington who noticed the President's personal photographer in the shadows.

"Thank you all for interrupting your busy schedules and holidays and coming here this evening on such short notice. I'll not waste your time.

"It appears that we are faced with a grave matter involving the security of this country, indeed, the security of the free world. This morning I received a call from Mr. Chandler Harrington, chairman of Scan-Man, the company

144

we all know that revolutionized surveillance satellites. You are all familiar with the Scanner Program. Mr. Harrington briefly outlined to me a recent event that changes the perspective of our entire way of life. But I shall let Mr. Harrington amplify briefly."

The President and Harrington exchanged places. Harrington placed his attaché case on the desk, close at hand.

"Thank you, Mr. President.

"It's not my place at the moment to anticipate the consequences of our discovery, although it was this anticipation that brought me here. I will only present the evidence as I interpret it. I'll be blunt.

"Last Wednesday our company launched Scanner XII, the most sophisticated satellite to date in our series. During the day the optics of XII picked up the activity of what appears to be an act of weather modification. I have with me a DVD of what we now call a 'Hole in the Night', whereby some ultra-sophisticated mechanism, from we don't know where, initiated a weather transformation, action and reaction, on the surface of Greenland. The results of this action began what appears to be an immense storm that at this moment is contributing a giant snow dump on the New England states, including our very own facility in Hollandson, Massachusetts.

"In short, it looks like New England is being inundated by a giant storm that was artificially created. We do not know the source of the power that initiated the storm. Our scientists can only conjecture that some foreign power has the means to do this. Some foreign power has technology advanced enough to modify world weather patterns which are capable of phenomenal destruction."

Secretary Buttrix interrupted. "We have all heard of this event. We have all listened to and read all the conjecture about this event. How can you be certain this is the work of a 'foreign power?'"

"I did not say I was 'certain.' We don't know who or what created it. No natural phenomenon that we know of is capable of creating this effect."

Harrington looked across the group with a small smile on his lips, "I assume the United States has not clandestinely undertaken weather experiments of this magnitude."

The listeners looked questioningly at each other. The President spoke. "I think we can all be assured that the United States is not. Please show us your evidence, Mr. Harrington."

An aide went to the projector that had been set up in anticipation of the showing. Harrington unlocked his attaché case, removed a DVD and handed it to the aide. A murmur of apprehension ran around the room as the screening was readied.

The first few seconds of the video were black, but with a gradual lighting to the left. Suddenly the center of the screen brightened and landscape could be seen reflecting a light from something as bright as the sun. The group watched in silence for several minutes, seeing quite clearly the topography of a section of Greenland.

Harrington spoke as the video continued. "Cameras from one of our satellites that monitors earth captured this scene that continued for a full hour. This was not a flash in the pan, if you'll excuse the metaphor. Then the light went out as suddenly as it appeared."

The observers were confused. Mumbles were heard that they didn't understand what it was all about.

"Mr. Harrington," the President said. "I am as confused as the others. Please explain."

146

"Much of Greenland has been in total darkness, twenty-four seven for the last few weeks," Harrington began. "Darkness, and an intense cold known to the natives as *Kausuitgup gna*, or polar night, has fallen. Nearby is Thule Air Base. They witnessed and were the first to sound the alarm about this 'Hole in the Night'. It appears that astronomers and scientists worldwide who have heard these reports find the effect baffling.

"At precisely eleven in the morning, Eastern Standard Time last Wednesday, this area was illuminated by a light that was reported to be as bright as the sun and many times warmer than that climate usually experiences. The light burned for exactly one hour. One whole hour! You have just seen an abbreviated version of that light on the surface of Greenland.

"Needless to say, it was startling for everyone in the vicinity, including those at Thule. The natives in the village panicked and thought the world was ending. Our own people lived one nightmarish hour of disbelief themselves.

"The light covered an area of several hundred square miles. This we could measure from what you have seen on the DVD. Surface temperatures were recorded in the high nineties. The barometer fell significantly, indicating the formation of an extreme low as warm air pushed aside the below zero air and rose, creating an immense atmospheric turbulence.

"The ice cap began to melt, and clouds developed with incredible speed. In short, the weather process was speeded up as if it had shifted into high gear. Then, an hour later, the light went out and the cold polar night returned to normal.

"Our satellites are unable to determine the light's source. They described the weather as balmy and strangely misplaced.

"Now, it is only because of Scanner XII that we were able to confirm this event. We had launched XII and were still positioning it in proper orbit when this tape was taken. It was only by chance that we have it. Normally there is no reason to conduct surveillance over the northern latitudes.

"So there you have it," Harrington concluded.

The room burst into vocal activity. Everyone had questions. Harrington sat and the President returned to his desk.

"Mr. President!" Senator Woark stood. "This is the most incredible story I have ever heard. It is right out of the pages of a science fiction novel. I remember reading ... "

"Senator," the President interrupted. "You doubt the story?"

"It, well, it sounds too fantastic to be true."

"Mr. President." Defense Secretary Coge spoke. "I have no doubt that it happened and it frightens the hell out of me. It does appear that someone has a technology, as Mr. Harrington says, that far exceeds ours."

"I've had a little more time to reflect on this than the rest of you," the President began, "and I think it is imperative that we each think long and hard on what this may mean. Let me briefly give you my thoughts.

"This seems to me to be a deliberate tampering with the weather system. The very act violates informal international agreements against such tampering except for local cloud seeding and the like. A large scale attempt, such as this appears to be, has the potential of completely destroying the delicate balance of the atmospheric system. It doesn't take much imagination to visualize what that can mean.

"I firmly believe that a government has plunged ahead with this technology clandestinely and contrary to all codes of human ethics. They are testing their technology in a sparsely populated region of the globe. They are aware that our
148

satellites do not conduct surveillance in that area. Obviously they were unaware that Scanner XII would wander over Greenland at that time.

"New England is now being affected by this phenomenon with the most devastating consequences. If it had not been for Scanner XII's chance encounter, the storm would have been shrugged off as another of Mother Nature's wicked deeds.

"Most of all, I believe we are now at the mercy of a foreign power that has the potential, it seems, to alter our weather pattern. This could have a detrimental and withering effect on our people and our food crops.

"We have just witnessed an event as startling, and perhaps with greater long range consequences, as Sputnik!"

Pandemonium broke loose.

"Gentlemen, please!" The President was firm. "It's 4 p.m. now. I'm going to ask you all to leave. Collect your thoughts, and return at nine this evening. Reflect on this. Take notes and return. We will discuss this in full at that time. I need not remind you of the necessity of absolute secrecy. No leaks! There is enough panicking out there as a result of the publicity it has already received."

"Mr. President." It was Sen. Woark again. "I see no need to delay discussing this. I can see right now the evidence is inconclusive. I ... "

"Sen. Woark," the President said. "Please bear with the rest of us then. Thank you."

*

Ellen Bloodworth had difficulty sleeping during the day. Nat, the storm, the ethics of Scan-Man, Scanner XII, the publicity of the Greenland event and her own future at the company flashed through her head in an endless film strip. She dozed, awoke, tossed and turned and dozed again. She wondered just how much of this nightmare she was imagining.

What should she do now? What were her obligations, her responsibilities? Should she continue to look for Nat? Was Nat lost? Was he in trouble? Did Nat want to be found? Why didn't he contact her? If he loved her he would. If he didn't he wouldn't. He hadn't. The whole business was driving her insane. She felt like screaming.

She got up, took another shower, drank a glass of milk, returned to bed, directed her thoughts to her upcoming Tibetan adventure and peacefully dropped into a sound sleep.

*

Now rested, Ellen decided to walk to work. Her little car would never negotiate the route to Peters Airfield. The snow was now more than two feet deep, and the roads were in horrid condition.

As expected, the walk was stimulating. There was no traffic. It also gave her time to think, to dream, and to look forward to her expedition.

Being properly dressed made all the difference. She imagined herself to be on the side of Mt. Everest. The wind, the driving snow, the below freezing temperatures and the resultant wind chill factor enhanced her fantasy. The storm was an excellent pseudo-Himalayan environment.

Ellen was expecting correspondence from her climbing colleagues any day now. It would include the travel timetable and the plan of coordination that would pull the whole operation together. It was a monumental task, but the women had learned from the experiences of previous expeditions.

The age-old problem of money had been the initial hurdle. The estimated cost was several hundred thousand dollars for the complete package. But an all-woman team had captured the hearts and pocketbooks of the publicity-hungry sponsors. They could expect heavy press coverage of the climb. By the same token, Ellen was aware of the pressure that would be placed on the women to complete the Everest climb. They were representing more than themselves and their sponsors -- women in general were watching from all parts of the world to see them win in a sport formerly reserved for men only. The anticipation of the event exhilarated her more than any previous experience.

She was ready for it. She was in excellent physical condition. She could not afford to allow the situation at Scan-Man depress her. The guard at the door was taken aback by Ellen's arrival. He greeted her heartily and commented that she had more energy and enthusiasm than he ever had. If he had it to do over ...

Ellen hung her snow clothes to dry and went to the washroom to make herself presentable. She showered and changed into the clean skirt and blouse she had brought in her knapsack. Now, hair combed, face freshened and sporting just a touch of Chanel No. 9, she walked briskly to her workstation.

A note on the console outlined her instructions for the night. She sat down, ready to tune in to the pulse of the world. She reached for the "on" switch and a stabbing pain shot up through her right arm. That was the last she remembered.

She fell to the floor.

*

"I have been asked to be spokesman for this group, Mr. President," Secretary of State Buttrix began. "We have drawn some conclusions."

It was a very different climate from that of five hours ago. Even Sen. Woark nodded his head in agreement.

"There is no need for drama here tonight, Mr. President, although it does sound like the unfolding of a frightening play. In speaking further with Mr. Harrington and learning more about the intricacies of weather, there can be no doubt that we are up against a formidable enemy.

"Several things bother us. The most troublesome is this -- we don't know who it is. We suggest an immediate confrontation on the floor of the United Nations. We must find out who we are up against.

"Secondly, we must consider ways to counteract the use of what we can only consider a weapon of mass destruction. Sophisticated weather modification technology can purposely alter the climate of the northern hemisphere. For example, by warming the arctic by only a few degrees, the general circulation of weather will be changed dramatically. The temperate zone can be changed to arctic conditions in a matter of days. The most frightening part about this is -- it could be done unwittingly! The paths of hurricanes can be altered; the amount of precipitation could be altered -- rainfall distribution could be thrown all out of whack.

"Until now, in any case, no one has been able to confidently predict the specific consequences of a large scale tampering with the atmosphere. No one can predict the dire ecological changes, the inevitable ecological modifications. We can right now see what is happening in New England. It appears that they are in the midst of an unseasonably heavy snowfall that is raising havoc with the region.

"Mr. President. The most impressive part of what we see here tonight is the subtlety of the technology. Whatever it is that is causing the present disturbance is hidden. It can manipulate our weather and create artificial effects without ever ... "

"Mr. Buttrix," the President interrupted. "Thank you. We all know how mismanagement of the atmosphere can disrupt everything. What I may not have made clear before is what are we going to do to stop or counteract this? Have you considered this?"

"Yes, Mr. President. Two things. One, we must address the United Nations and appeal to the country which is doing this. Two, we must take immediate steps to devise our own system that is able to compete with this unknown. We suggest a plan on the magnitude of the Apollo Program, or the Atomic Energy Program of the 1940s. Time is of the essence. Indeed, we may have no time!"

Buttrix finished. The room was heavily silent for what seemed like several minutes.

"I certainly agree with much of what you have said," the President began, "but you haven't told us how you plan to do it.

"I seriously question the wisdom of acknowledging we are aware of this device. I wonder about the effect it would have on this unknown government to have them know we don't know who they are and that we feel helpless. Would they retaliate or retreat? We don't know. I question taking the chance. By keeping what we think we know under cover, and by disbursing our intelligence and by pursuing counter technology, we may stand to gain much more.

"I certainly agree we should plunge ahead immediately with counter technology. No expense should be spared. Time is critical.

"Mr. Harrington. Can you give us your thoughts on this?"

All heads turned to Harrington who until this moment had remained silent.

"Very frankly, Mr. President, I certainly think we have the resources to move in that direction. I see no reason to believe anything is impossible."

"Do you think we have the technology to compete?"

"We have seen tonight that it can be done, by someone quite likely less technologically advanced than us. Yes. Certainly we can compete. It means adjusting our focus and thinking in ways that have been unthinkable until now."

"What do you mean?"

"The way I see it, warfare has suddenly moved into the space age. We have seen the use of a super powerful beam generated from what we have to assume is a man-made satellite. Our evidence shows a sun-like beam of light illuminating and heating a large geographical area. This in itself is mind stretching. But further, does this device have other capabilities? Are these other potentials more deadly?

"This we don't know. This is where we have to think the unthinkable in order to meet the challenge that is facing us."

"Now, Mr. Harrington," the President said. "Can this be accomplished without showing our cards?"

"I believe we can proceed along the same lines as we have in the past with other military hardware. There are ways of doing this."

"How do the rest of you feel?"

There was general agreement.

"OK then. Since this is a matter of the utmost national security, I must demand there be no leaks." The President eyed each person in the room. "We all understand the potential consequences of a leak. I need not say more on that score. We will meet again tomorrow at 2 p.m. to firm up plans. I realize the time is short and the holidays are upon us. I do think the gravity of this threat must supersede everything else.

"Thank you for coming."

*

Maggie received the call about 9:30 PM and immediately set off for the hospital. There had been no

154

explanation over the phone, just that Ellen had asked her for a ride home and, "I'm OK. Don't rush."

She was impatient nevertheless. What had happened? Why was Ellen in the hospital? She gunned the Chevy Blazer along the snow-rutted road, giving an extra burst of acceleration to explode through a three-foot drift. Abandoned vehicles made it an obstacle course -- a hazard. She imagined the dispair Bud Kelly must be experiencing at this point. None of his plows could ever navigate this road. It took Maggie a half hour to cover the two miles.

Ellen was in the waiting room. She looked pale and weak. Heavy wrinkles cradled her eyes.

"You look terrible. What happened?"

"I was zapped by my console -- an electrical shock. All I remember is reaching out for the 'on' switch. I woke up in the hospital. "

"Are you OK?"

"I'm fine. Just a little burn on my hand." Ellen showed Maggie the bandage. "It burned the end of my thumb, nothing important."

A nurse crossed the room and came up beside Ellen. "She's very lucky." She looked at Maggie. "She could have been killed. That was a very powerful jolt she received. If it hadn't been for her excellent health, she might have had cardiac arrest."

"Have you any idea how it happened?" Maggie asked.

"Nope. Margo found me lying on the floor. She called an Army ambulance and they brought me here. Margo said they couldn't find anything wrong with the computer."

"She really should spend the night," the nurse added. "The damage could very well be more extensive than we've been able to observe so far."

"Thanks anyway," Ellen apologized. "I have to get back to work. They're short-handed -- no pun intended."

"No way," Maggie said. "You look as though you need a long rest."

"Truthfully, I do feel rotten. My head is splitting. I guess I do look forward to a few hours of sack time."

During the ride back to the house, Ellen expressed her perplexity over what had happened. "It just doesn't make any sense. Those are fail-safe machines. Sure they carry a lot of current, but why should something go wrong? For a while I thought it had something to do with the shower I took just before sitting down at the machine. But then, I've never had any repercussions before."

The trusty Blazer bounced along, its engine muffled by the deep snow. Maggie's eyes never left the tunnel her headlights cut through the night and the slanting snowfall.

Maggie had her suspicions about the cause of the accident, but they were too far out to mention to Ellen. It was just possible this was an attempt to get rid of Ellen. It looked as if the job was neat and clean. The machine could have been shorted out before Ellen used it and then repaired or replaced immediately afterward. She wondered if Ellen was thinking the same thing but was also afraid to voice it.

Ellen's thoughts were on Margo Chin. She was still puzzled at Margo's response when she regained consciousness in the hospital. Very subtly, Ellen received the impression that Margo was disappointed when Ellen awoke. Margo appeared irritated. Instead of showing relief, her reaction seemed the opposite. But Ellen couldn't be sure. The feeling was illusive, shadowy, faint. It was just enough to warn Ellen to be cautious of Margo.

*

"What I want to achieve here is unanimity," Defense Secretary Cohen was saying. "You've just heard Mr. Harrington give us his proposed 'Energizer' package. Yet I still hear grumblings among you."

156

The meeting was in a mini-amphitheater just off the War Room, deep within the Pentagon. Cohen was disturbed by the dissatisfaction he heard among the service branches about trading their favorite futuristic projects for another fuzzy idea called the Scan-Man "Energizer."

"Looking objectively at the New England debacle," Cohen continued, "I'm surprised you can't see the totally effective submission this enemy, yes *enemy*, has done to this region. How can you doubt the effectiveness of Harrington's package for our inventory simply amazes me."

"We don't doubt its effectiveness, Mr. Secretary," General Stringer said. "We question Scan-Man's ability to duplicate, or improve upon it. We hesitate to scrap some really top-notch projects which are already in the blueprint stage for Mr. Harrington's, if you'll excuse me, pie-in-the-sky."

Harrington stood. He was angry. May I answer that, Mr. Secretary?"

Cohen nodded.

"General. Why do you choose now to doubt us? You are well aware of project after project we have completed for you. Why now? I'll come through on this one also because my name is Chandler Harrington; because I have personally assured the President we'll put together a competitive package; because my company has never failed any of the branches of the armed forces."

A Navy Commander stood. "I don't for one minute see how your so-called Energizer can compete with the Trident, the MX or any one of the nuclear packages. The Energizer is ... is ... so soft."

Harrington smiled. "Thank you. You said it. I think the word you were struggling for was 'subtle'. The hardware you speak of is conventional barroom brawl stuff. It carries with it the dangers of retaliation, of atmospheric pollution, of destroying the entire world. Warfare, gentlemen, has now

157

moved into the space age. The future belongs to space. The longer you resist it the further behind the United States falls. Our enemy, whoever he is, has given us a subtle warning that I think we'd better heed. We too have to move our thoughts into space -- into the space age.

"Scan-Man is already well into that space age. Remember, without my company's satellite, we would not have suspected the New England atrocity. With this technology that Scan-Man will have for you within the year, we will be able to subdue entire countries without losing a single man, without firing a single shot, without despoiling the rest of the world! That's important, dammit!

"And consider this. We'll do it, and the enemy will never suspect its source. He'll have no reason to suspect it's anything but a natural disaster.

"Gentlemen. You have just witnessed the destruction. Now just imagine what is going on among our people in New England. Without much imaginative effort you can see the tragic physical and emotional damage taking place. To our own embarrassment, New England has been subdued. A proof of our enemy's success is that we can do nothing to counteract that snowfall! We can do nothing to prevent the thousands of deaths that are inevitable during the next several weeks.

"Do you see what I mean? You can't knock that effectiveness!"

Harrington poured a glass of water but set it down without drinking from it. In a more even tone, he continued.

"I have been in touch with Scan-Man scientists in Hollandson today, via Scan-Man satellite I might add, since conventional lines are not operational. In just the last twenty-four hours my men have learned much about the effects of the disaster taking place right at the goal line. They are already at work on technology for our new Energizer. In a matter of months, we will be able to duplicate that New England storm

158

– anywhere on earth. We too will be in command of the weather, able to modify it to suit our needs."

Harrington's voice now rose to a crescendo. "And don't tell me this isn't the most effective, subtle, devastating and truly magnificent instrument devised by man!

"Are there any doubters in this room?"

*

The Stevensons were exhausted but tremendously relieved to have finally reached the security and warmth of the Randolph's home. The whole day had been an ordeal, including the ride with Turk in the Jeep from the hotel. Marsha rushed up to Alice and Peter and hugged them both in the doorway.

"Thank God you're safe," she said. "And look at you!" Marsha continued, stepping back. "What happened?"

"It's a long story." Peter said. "We'll tell you later."

Alice Stephenson stepped into the room and displayed in mock fashion-model gestures her torn gown and hose and battered high heels.

"Fortunately I had my fur. Without that I would have perished. Peter and I and a whole bunch from the highway had to hike at least a mile. And, when we got to the hotel they didn't want to let us in! The place is jammed with people of every description. I don't know how Turk found us."

"She's right," Peter added. "We couldn't get into the bar or the restaurant. Both were full they said. So we had to mill around in the lobby with hundreds of exhausted, irritated, frustrated and smelly travelers. Where they're going to eat and sleep, I have no idea. Having Turk show up was like escaping a bad dream."

"Both of you follow me," Marsha said. She led the Stevensons down the hallway to the bedroom. "You can change into our clothes. There's no need for formality

159

tonight. It looks like we're the party -- just the six of us. Most of the others have called in saying they couldn't make it, for obvious reasons, but I'm worried about the others who haven't called. I hope they're not stuck somewhere along the way."

The Mitchells, being out of hearing distance, Marsha said, "Thank God you're here. I know I would have died a slow death with the Mitchells. Perhaps we can liven up this place." Marsha took out some fresh clothing for each of them.

"Ed's on the phone with Washington. I don't think he'll be too long. Dinner's ready when you are. Believe me, there's plenty to eat."

*

The general circulation of air is the cause of the Earth's climate. The sun, the frozen arctic, the steaming tropics, the oceans, all contribute to immense masses of air moving hundreds, or thousands of miles, rising, sinking, whirling, battling ferociously where cold meets warm air masses, forming huge horizontal waves, that develop into gentle breezes in some areas and hurricanes elsewhere. Condensation is formed and falls as rain, snow, hail, fog and other forms.

There is a mystery about it that continues to challenge scientists. No precise long-range weather forecasts are yet possible, for the weather is an entity unto itself and it governs our everyday life.

*

Randolph's Washington call was from Chandler Harrington. Harrington was ecstatic over the results of his presentation to the President and members of Congress.

"Things look very good from this end, Ed, but you know how I feel about the proverbial counting of chickens. When the government gives a quarterback pass to that check, we can count ourselves successful."

160

"I've got to hand it to you, Chandler. Deep down I never thought you could carry off Phase II."

"As I say, we've still got a long way to go. Another huddle is scheduled for noon on the 24th. In the meantime all the others are head-to-head in conferences working up plans. They have me moving from group to group lending my expertise. If this wasn't so damned serious, I'd laugh. I'll give you another call tomorrow night about this time. I may need some file information."

"I'll be here. You can count on that. You wouldn't believe the snow. It scares the hell out of me. How much longer do you think this'll keep up?"

You're asking me? You're supposed to be the expert on Webster's files. You're the one in charge of XII now. You'd better damn well learn how to operate that Energizer."

"OK, OK. So far it's been my worst enemy. I'm trapped here at home. My only contact with the office is by phone. The files are at the office. We've got XII geosynched until we need her again, at which time we'll know her operation inside out. I've got Margo in charge of it."

"That reminds me," Harrington said. "Have you moved yet on that Bloodworth female?"

"Yes. Tonight was the night. I'll hear from Margo later on."

"It's important, Ed. She knows too much."

*

With Ellen delivered to her apartment, Maggie returned to her side of the house. She was concerned about Phil. It was uncharacteristic of him to stay out this late. It was unusual for her to be home and him out. Generally it was the other way around. The house felt empty.

She stood in the unlighted parlor in her robe and watched the snowfall in a diagonal blur across the beam of the floodlight illuminating the yard and driveway. Her arms were

161

crossed, holding tightly to the warmth of her robe. The wind turned briefly and kicked up a flurry of flakes against the window. The sound was nearly imperceptible, like the whipping of feathers against each other.

She tried to estimate the height of the drift against the side of the garage. It looked about six feet. Yet other parts of the drive were bare where the wind blew consistently up the path where Phil had shoveled earlier in the day.

Many thoughts crossed her mind. Perhaps Phil was stuck somewhere. He was on the snowmobile. Perhaps he hurt himself. She returned to the kitchen and reheated the coffee pot, just in case he returned momentarily.

Over another coffee she thought about Ellen and the strange events taking place at Scan-Man. Why was it that after all her years in Hollandson, Scan-Man was becoming so visible? Why all of a sudden? Why did these things happen at inconvenient times? She would thoroughly enjoy an interview with some Scan-Man people, but after the holidays would be soon enough.

Still no Phil. Maggie picked up the phone again and dialed the police station. The dispatcher answered.

"He went out on a call with officer Commerwitz. There are a lot of problems at the 128 intersection."

"Have him give me a call when he gets back, will you please?"

Maggie went to the window again. Without four-wheel drive, motorists were certain to have problems. She saw a lone pair of headlights moving slowly along Great Road. She could not tell what type of vehicle it was.

Reluctantly, she went to bed.

*

Vito was losing control. Forces more powerful than him were dictating conditions he found unsavory. Dozens and dozens of uninvited guests were camped out in his lobby,

162

sprawled on his delicately upholstered couches and chairs. Others were stretched out on the floor, wrapped in blankets, defiling his half million dollar Oriental carpet.

True, the tavern was producing unprecedented receipts, and the Garden Room was turning a handsome profit as well. But this was the only advantage to a captive population. It was all so disorganized and untidy.

Many of the transients carried little or no money. These were the problem people. Earlier in the day he had tried to lock his doors against further invasion, but that attempt was only momentary. The old, the miserable and the sick had turned into an ugly mob threatening to break through his picture window.

Vito felt he was a victim of circumstances. He was unabashedly sorry for himself. Why did this have to happen to him -- especially during his first convention -- a time when everything seemed to be going so well?

Then came the children crying. Vito crumbled inside whenever he heard a child cry. It was the crying that eventually urged him to serve hot broth to anyone who wished it. Bread and a variety of restaurant leftovers were also made available to those who could afford nothing better.

Now, as he sat at his desk, he prayed the town would come up with an adequate shelter by morning. He could not continue to function amid this chaos.

SUNDAY, DECEMBER 23

Consider how totally intermeshed are the earth, the sea and the sky. The combined effects of the three dictate a cyclical behavior in every living thing. When this cycle is broken or interrupted, living things experience hardship. Death is inevitable for those not fit to survive.

*

The Randolph party, just after midnight, had already become a drag. Marsha felt it in the pit of her stomach. Six people do not make a party that was planned for fifty.

Ed and Ralph, Marsha noted, were head to head, deep into some irrelevant topic that had nothing to do with partying.

Elaine's head was nodding. Her eyelids were heavy and she was about to give in to their weight. Peter had been slowly circling the room, studying each and every object d'art in the Randolph collection. He was now staring, blank-faced, at the Christmas tree.

Marsha and Alice were sharing a joint of marijuana. They were the only users of the contents from the little yellow box that now sat on the fireplace mantle. Marsha was working overtime to achieve a high. She wanted to keep away from the pills tonight for they usually didn't mix well with alcohol. She wanted to enjoy the entire night.

Abruptly, she jumped from the couch and went over to Peter. He had dropped an Electric Light Orchestra album into place on the turntable. The music began. Peter turned to Marsha and they began a slow dance.

*

The room felt cold when Maggie awoke. It was still dark, but she could see the snow falling beneath the light of the street lamp. Her first thought was Phil. She pulled on her robe, slid into her slippers and went across the hall. He had not come home last night.

Not to worry, she thought, and went downstairs to build a small wood fire to take the chill off the house. He's all right, she said to herself. I won't fuss about him. And I haven't heard from the chief. I'll wait a while before I call the station.

But fuss she did, until Ellen knocked on the door between their living quarters and joined her for breakfast.

"You look tired this morning," Maggie said. "You didn't sleep well last night?"

"I slept fine," Ellen answered, good-humouredly. "It's just that I went to work for a couple of hours this morning."

Maggie was astounded. "You nut! I suppose you walked both ways."

"How else? I have to keep in shape since we're not running any more."

"I guess your shock therapy didn't adversely affect you."

"That didn't," Ellen said, becoming serious, "but I got more of a shock this morning."

Maggie looked at her friend inquisitively.

"That shock was intentional. It was meant to put me away."

"Ellen! How'd you learn that?"

"A friend told me he saw Margo, my supervisor, working with the maintenance man on my machine. The coincidence between that and my accident made him suspicious."

"Why do you suppose she did it?"

"I think it relates to my requisition of Nat's confidential files. I think Randolph, or one of the big boys, put her up to it. She's pretty thick with them. They must think I know something they don't want me to know."

"Well? You do, don't you?"

"Perhaps. But this whole thing scares me more than ever. Think I ought to go to the police?"

"Wow! That's a problem. I don't know what they could do. This whole scheme is a hell of a lot bigger than our Hollandson Police Department. This sounds like federal problem to me, with international consequences. I've got to think about this one. But I sure wouldn't go back to work until you find out what's going on."

"I was afraid you'd say that. I love my work. Now it's gone up in smoke, or should I say snow."

"At least you haven't lost your good humor."

"No. I have to return to work -- at least once more."

"Why?"

"If I leave," Ellen said with determination, "I'm leaving with Nat's files. I'm not going down without a battle. I'm sure there's something more important in those files -- something I missed. They took Nat from me. If I go, I'm taking Nat's files."

"But you said they were gone. You said Randolph had requisitioned them."

"Right. And I think they might still be in his office."

It was a somber breakfast. Although Maggie didn't encourage Ellen to return to Scan-Man, she didn't discourage her either. She could easily understand her feelings. If their roles were reversed, she'd do the same for Phil.

Ellen updated Maggie on the weather. An unbelievable five feet of snow could now be expected.

"I hope you're wrong," Maggie said.

"So do I. But I wouldn't have said it if I hadn't believed it."

Ellen decided she'd make another attempt at sleep.

It didn't seem like Sunday morning. To Maggie, events were crowding in and making each successive day seem like an eighth or ninth day of the week -- similar to a fourth dimension. Although the life of a newspaper editor had always been exciting, this past week, Maggie knew, would stand alone. She wanted to keep herself busy, and her mind off Phil. She'd return to the office. The *Bulletin* publication schedule no longer existed, but there would be an abundance of solid news once the weather returned to normal. In the meantime, the news had to be written.

*

An elderly couple had been marooned in their car on an isolated section of 128. Traffic had long since stopped flowing. When they were first mired, the man exited the car, surveyed the area and decided there was no sign of life within sight. It would kill them both if they attempted to walk in snow this deep.

They had now been stranded for more than 24 hours. No help had come along. Their car had run out of gas several hours ago – no more heat. As the couple hugged each other to keep warm, the snow swirled around their vehicle nearly covering it. The windows were frosted on the inside from their breaths. Thinking ahead, they had kept an open space outside the door by periodically opening and shutting it so they would be able to escape when help came -- if help came.

The man kept poking his wife to keep her awake. "Don't go to sleep, Sweetie. We have to stay awake no matter what." She objected whenever he shook her and curled into a tighter knot.

A faint sound found its way into the car. The man cocked his head. Was he hearing things? He thought he heard a sound of something other than the wind. It sounded like an engine. Yes! The faint sound was an engine.

He pulled on his wife's arm, "Hear that? Do you hear that?" but his wife didn't respond.

The sound was getting louder. It was heading toward them. "Wake up Julie. They're coming after us. Wake up." And he shook her again, but she just groaned.

The sound of the machine was quite distinct now.

"I'd better get out and flag it down," the man said. "They'll never see us in here."

He pushed on the door. It only opened a few inches. He pushed harder and it opened a few more inches. The sound was loud now – definitely an engine. He was elated. One more time he pushed and this gave him just enough room to squeeze out the door opening. Oh, how stiff he was. He felt half frozen. His limbs could barely move from being immobile for so long.

Outside, he found the snow a lot deeper than he thought. When he stood up straight it was up to his chest. He wanted to climb up above the snow, but his efforts were futile. He just kept sinking in. It was too soft. He then tried packing it under his feet, stomping on it. His breath was short. It was an effort to breathe. He couldn't do it.

Now the man tried crawling. He had to find the engine. He was not dressed for this weather. Hatless, gloveless, and wearing only a light jacket, the wind penetrated and drifting snow hit every pore of his exposed skin. His shirt was pulled out exposing his belly. Again he tried to raise himself above the snow level to signal for help. His form was absorbed into the whiteness.

As he looked around he saw nothing but white. The car was out of sight. He could see no trace of it. The wind rapidly filled in his snake-like track. He had lost his bearings. He adjusted his course to meet the machine that grew ever louder.

He was soaked. His belly stung. His hands and feet were numb. "Oh, God, help me," he moaned into the wind.

The engine noise grew still louder and the man's anticipation of meeting with it tensed him. He bristled with concentration, fighting against the involuntary and violent chattering of his teeth and the vibrating of his arms and thigh muscles.

The roar was a huge piece of mechanical equipment. He felt he should be able to see it very soon. It should be coming straight for him.

He was puzzled as to just what kind of machine could make this sound. It certainly wasn't a plow. Apparently it was moving very slowly. No plow could get through this mess, even though its route seemed to be the median strip where it could avoid the abandoned vehicles.

The man tensed still more. The sound of the storm was now drowned out by that of the engine, grinding and hissing -- most definitely a hissing -- steady and even. What kind of a monster was this?

Fear took the place of curiosity now, and multiplied the shivering spasms. Fear of the unknown. Just feet in front of him, yet he couldn't see it because of the whiteout. The man's mouth twisted in a conscious effort to hold it closed, to keep it from jackhammering his teeth together. He gripped his arms around him, attempting to hold himself together, to keep his body from falling apart from excessive vibration.

Suddenly! There! There it was! It towered above him, no more than twenty feet away. His eyes opened wide in disbelief at what was bearing down on him. He had to move. He had to get out of its way. Stopping the machine was no longer his concern.

He swung to his right and tried to churn through the snow. But progress was ever so slow for an old man -- infinitesimal compared to that of the aggressor bearing down on him. His breathing was heavy, his heart pounding. He fell once, got up, fell again.

He looked back over his shoulder. It had whirling fan blades that chopped into the snow and hurled it out the chute at the top, forming a gigantic arc. The wind, blowing against this arc sent a fine shower.

The whirling blades were nearly on top of him. The sound was deafening. The man was exhausted. He had no strength to move another inch. He slumped into the snow. His shirt was pulled up. His stomach bloodied from scratching over the snow. His hands red and raw. His hair frozen and crusted.

The man was now quiet -- unmoving -- bent in earnest prayer.

There was no pause in the drone of the engine, no quiver in the hissing, spinning blades as they bit into soft flesh and bone and spat it out the chute over the cab. Hardly a stain was left in the expelled snow when it came to rest along the median strip.

The driver, exhausted from the constant strain of peering through icy windows at a featureless landscape, had stretched his limbs, just for an instant, without leaving his seat. Unnoticed to him, a single spot of red touched the windshield, just for an instant, before the wiper blades did their job.

"Jesus," the driver said. "This is a nightmare."

After an hour of producing nothing but false starts on her typewriter, Maggie locked the office and walked the two snow-covered blocks to the police station. Maybe Phil had checked in by now.

Great Road was well plowed. A front-end loader was widening it still further by pushing the snow banks onto the sidewalks. The wind blew relentlessly, causing great swirls of snow to dash up and down the length of the nearly abandoned road. Maggie pulled her scarf tighter around her nose and cheeks. It was doubtful if the Sunday papers would come through from Boston this morning, she thought.

At the intersection by the stoplights, Maggie noticed Bud Kelly's pickup. He was poking at a storm drain with his shovel.

"You going to be able to keep ahead of it?" she asked.

Kelly laughed, pausing in his efforts. "If it stopped right this instant, we'd catch up in another day or so. If it keeps up, we're in deep sh-, ah, deep trouble. We've got to spend all our time on the main roads. You know the rest of the story."

Maggie did. As Kelly had predicted, his trucks broke down. With an allotment of five, the highway department had only two trucks in operation.

"You seen Sivolesky today?" Maggie shouted into the wind.

Kelly paused again and turned to Maggie. "Hah! He won't show his face around here. He'll be lucky to get out of his driveway!"

She couldn't help but smile as she pictured Sivolesky's home on the unplowed outskirts of town. "You mean ... "

"What's a guy supposed to do?" Kelly said with a grin. "We can't show favoritism."

Kelly returned to his task and Maggie continued on, around the corner, to the police station. The path to the door was unshoveled, yet well packed from the passing of many feet.

Chief Wilson looked exhausted, Maggie noted. "You look like you haven't slept in two or more days."

"Yes, yes. I know, Mag. That's because I haven't slept in two or more days. How in hell can I when everyone's crawling up my back?" He swung his feet down from the top of his desk.

"Unless you get some sleep you won't live to see the end of this storm. And don't call me Mag!"

"You want to take my place?"

Maggie smiled. It was another of the games between them. "I always give you a 'yes' to that question but you never take me up on it. I'd love to be queen for a day."

"Ah you newspaper people are all the same," Wilson continued, playfully. "You always think you can do everyone's job better than they can. What do you know about police work?"

"I know how to pour a coffee. That's all I ever see you doing." Maggie walked over to the coffee maker and poured herself a cup. "God, this stuff smells strong!"

"Go ahead. Drink it. It'll put hair on your chest -- that's the first requirement for the chief's job," Wilson chuckled.

"You haven't seen Phil, have you?" Maggie asked, becoming serious.

"Sure. He's been in and out of here all night. He's working with the rescue crews on 128. They've come across a number of CO_2 and hypothermia cases, even some frostbite. You haven't seen the mess out there? What kind of a newsperson are you, Mag?"

"I'm afraid I haven't. Tell me about it."

"I can't. You have to see it for yourself. It's a nightmare. Frostbite, exhaustion, exposure and shock. It's been a steady stream of people, totally unprepared for this weather, walking the mile or more from the highway."

"You're sending them on to the school?"

"Can't keep 'em here."

"Looks to me like we're in deep trouble." Maggie sat on the edge of the chief's desk, wincing at every sip of her coffee. "Have you heard the weather lately?"

"That's all I've been hearing. We're going to get three feet or so."

"If that's all we get we'll be lucky. I have it on good authority we can expect five feet or more."

"I don't like your authority."

"Would you believe Ellen Bloodworth?"

Wilson looked up attentively. "Really? That's a Scan-Man prediction? Jesus!"

Maggie was interested that Wilson appeared to take the word from Scan-Man so seriously. He obviously knew more about the company reputation than she did. "Why are you so impressed with their prediction?"

"I'm more troubled than impressed. Scan-Man usually updates us on unusual weather conditions. If what you say is true, it bothers me that I haven't heard about it. Usually it comes in as text message."

Maggie looked in the direction the chief gestured and saw the message across his computer screen. "When did you last read that info?"

Wilson smiled wearily. "You're right. It's probably there."

"The point is, the storm is blocked and we're in for a serious accumulation." Maggie said. "I know the road department is already in trouble. I know you're in trouble.

The school's in trouble. We need to call a general meeting and pull ourselves together."

Wilson twisted in his chair. "Well, look. I don't think we have to get too excited too soon. We've only got a couple feet of it out there. Weather forecasts have been known to be wrong. I sure can't believe we're going to get anywhere near five feet. Who ever heard of a five-foot snowfall in a single storm? Besides, if there was an emergency, the Governor would call it."

"You're incredible," Maggie said, looking down on him from her perch. "It wasn't two minutes ago you were complaining how bad things were, that you hadn't any sleep, that the school was a mess, etc. Why are you now backing off?"

"Why? Because I don't hear any of the other towns complaining. Sure we've got a pileup on 128. But we've had that before and we've survived. Let's just not get too panicky yet."

"Well I'm going to take a look around on my own." She swung down from the desk and returned her coffee cup to the counter. "In the meantime, you might dig out your emergency plans for coping with a crisis like this."

"Are you speaking as a reporter or a citizen?"

"Don't get uppity. I'm simply a concerned human being who smells a disaster slowly descending. It's going to cramp our style, Paul, unless we figure out how to cope with it. I hate to admit it, but the Emergency Preparedness Committee has never come up with any plans for coping with deep snow. We're on our own."

"OK, Mag. I'll come up with something."

"And don't call me Mag!" Maggie hovered over the chief's desk with a threatening gesture. Wilson feigned a cringe. "Get out and get some fresh air," she said. "It'll do you some good."

*

The town garage was a colorful spectacle. Seven floats were in the final stages of completion. A flurry of eager youngsters crawled over them, shouting and laughing, chiding each other over whose float was the best, the biggest, the prettiest. The excitement echoed and brought life and warmth to the damp, poorly heated building.

Several adults, not nearly as warm or jovial, stood behind the moisture-covered garage door windows and peered without enthusiasm at the whirling flakes and rapidly mounting ground cover. A large figure suddenly appeared through the maelstrom, heading for the door.

Molly Battinni burst through the metal door with a crash and strode to the center of the floor where she could be seen. Expectant silence replaced the joviality.

"I'm sorry to tell you this, kids. I know how hard you've worked. The Carnival has to be cancelled, or at least postponed. The storm is simply too intense. I've just talked with our selectman, Mr. Sivolesky, and he agrees. As a matter of fact, he can't even get out of his driveway this morning!"

Sighs and exaggerated groans of disapproval followed her announcement. "After all this work?" "A winter carnival is supposed to be in the snow." "How long will it be postponed?" "We cancelled it last year too -- because of rain!"

"I know all the work you kids have done," Molly continued. "But there is no way we can carry this off. One look outside should convince you. The floats would be wrecked in minutes by the wind. It seems strange, but we have too much snow. The back roads are blocked. Many of your friends are not here this morning because of this. I've just been to the Common and the snow has covered all the detail of the sculptures."

The adults reinforced Molly. "She's right, kids. Maybe if we postpone it till next Sunday ... "

175

"But we can't. My dad needs his truck this week. I'll have to take all this apart and begin all over!" Tears came to the boy's eyes.

"We'll work something out, Michael," Molly assured him. "But the Carnival is just not possible today. There are troubles all over town."

The youngsters' expressions fell to uncomprehending disappointment.

"And I'm afraid I have some more bad news," Molly continued. "The tree lighting ceremony this evening has also been cancelled. The snow has damaged the lights and the wiring."

"You're full of good news." someone quipped.

Molly's expression turned grave. "I have to tell all of you that this storm looks real bad. I've just talked with the police chief and he says the trouble is widespread. He asked me to tell you all to go home and prepare for the worst. chief Wilson said he has heard this is a freak storm and it may last for days."

The mood of those in the room also turned serious.

"Go home. Shovel yourselves out. I promise we'll have the Carnival as soon as we can. We won't cancel it this year. It's just that now is not the time for it."

The group filed toward the door. A thunderous gust snatched the door from a boy's hand, slammed against the wall and sent the boy to the floor screaming with pain.

A broken arm.

Oh, God, thought Molly. She had not intended to have her speech punctuated like this.

*

The first signs of activity for the new day were just taking place at noon at the Randolph house. Of the three women, Marsha was the only one up. She staggered into the kitchen holding her hand to her forehead.

176

"'Jesus, Alberta," she said to the cook. "Fix me a double seltzer."

Alberta was grumpy. "You people sure left this place a mess last night. It took Francisco and I all mornin' to..."

"Oh stop the complaining." Marsha shot back. "What do you get paid for? You want me to clean up first so your job will be easier?"

"It just seems to me that ... "

"I don't want to hear it!" Marsha shouted, wincing at the renewed pain in her head.

Alberta was silent. She slid the seltzer contemptuously across the counter top and returned to her dishes. She avoided looking at Marsha's glare.

As Marsha drained the last of her drink, Turk came through the door from the garage. He was wet and looked very tired.

"Ah. You're up, Mrs. Randolph. Don't look like your guests are goin' home today. There's no way they can get out."

"What do you mean?"

"You looked outside?"

"No I haven't." she snapped, irritated by the feeling she was being corrected by her house help.

"The radio says most of the traffic is stopped. Only a few of the main roads are plowed."

"Oh, goddamn!" Marsha went to the window. Snow had drifted against the side of the house. The birches were bent low. The wind was gusty. Visibility was only a few feet. She turned to Alberta. "Got enough food for another night?"

"Yes, ma'am. We got a freezer full. Alberta makes sure of plenty of food always. Never can tell ... "

"OK, OK! Put a menu together and we'll go over it."

"I called the police station," Turk said, "and they said the radio was right. Nothin's movin'."

"Where's Robert?"

"Outside," Turk answered.

"'Outside?' Get him in here! He'll catch his death."

"He's OK, Mrs. Randolph. I bundled him up. He's with Francisco," Alberta added.

"I don't care!" Marsha stamped her foot like a spoiled child, and then raised her hand to her forehead again.

Turk left the room to retrieve Robert.

"And have him clean his room. I expect it's a mess."

"But," Alberta began.

"Don't start lecturing me on how to raise my son!"

"Yes, ma'am."

Marsha Randolph returned to her room where she lay on the bed, her arm over her eyes. It would be a couple hours longer before she could face a new day. Last night had been such a disappointment.

*

Ed Randolph was irritated and becoming increasingly restless. An hour ago he had called Margo Chin for a progress report on events at Scan-Man. She had nothing favorable to report. Margo had said the attempt on Bloodworth's life had failed. In fact, Bloodworth had recovered to such an extent that she had returned to work for a couple of hours early this morning."

What ddid he want her to do now? Margo asked.

Randolph didn't know. He needed time. He would get back to her. Something had to be done before Harrington called tonight -- before Bloodworth relayed classified information along to others -- if she hadn't already.

What was the status of the storm? Randolph had asked. Margo said it continued to be stalled. There was no indication of when this condition would break. Couldn't Scanner XII be activated to break up the pattern? Margo didn't know. She would have to check with the Control Room and get back to him.

178

Randolph called Mitchell and Stevenson to the den where they now sat. Regarding the activation of Scanner XII, Randolph suspected he might be in an embarrassing position. Who among them was familiar with the operation of the Searoc Beam?

The three exchanged blank looks. No one of them could immediately recall anyone on the board who was familiar with this phase of operations. Unless one of the Control Room technicians was familiar with it, there was only one individual they knew who could operate it – Nat Webster.

"So that leaves us up the goddamned creek," Randolph said. "So much for Scan-Man back-up knowledge. How did we ever let Webster carry the only basket of eggs?"

"I'll tell you how," Mitchell said. "The project was so big, so intricate, so unique, we forgot. All we saw was the big bucks."

"You're not giving us very much credit, Ralph," Stevenson said. "You make it sound as though the project is washed up.

"OK, you two," Randolph cut in. "You're both right. First of all, the weather pattern can't hang over us forever. It was simply my hope to break it up sooner than if we waited for natural forces. Regardless, it doesn't affect the project. We still have Webster's plans and his outline of operations. Assuming the CR technicians don't know any more than we do, we'll just have to go back to the classroom. At least that's better than starting from scratch."

A fruitless discussion followed and Randolph's mind wandered. He had to have a concrete answer for Harrington.

What if Bloodworth showed up for work again tonight? How is she able to get to work and he can't? He realized he should have remained at headquarters until he had answers for Harrington. He had thought Chin could handle the situation alone.

Finally, he asked the others to go get something to eat. He needed to be alone for a while. He had to decide on his next move.

*

Their strength and alertness had been fading after working nearly twenty-four continuous hours. The giant snow thrower had revealed another car on Rte. 128. Inside was an elderly woman curled up in the passenger seat. She was alive, but just barely. Their responses were suddenly electrified. Phil and the others in the crew once again worked quickly and efficiently.

She was suffering from a typical case of hypothermia. Her exposure to cold because of inadequate dress had slowed her metabolic processes. Her body temperature was reduced and she was in great danger of frostbite and losing her fingers, toes or even limbs. If not treated quickly and gently, the woman was in danger of losing her life.

A blanket was handed through the door and Phil spread it out between him and the victim. Conditions were cramped as he kneeled on the floor. He carefully picked her up. She was lightweight and bony. He laid her on the blanket and slowly extended her legs that moved with difficulty because of the stiff knee joints. The waiting crew eased the blanketed woman out the door, onto a toboggan and strapped her down. A snowmobile then towed it off the highway, up to the top of the bluff and to the hotel.

The crew shuffled on to the next car, the next truck and next car. They were becoming chilled themselves. Hopefully a replacement crew would soon be along.

*

The woman carried no identification. She was taken into the hotel lobby and placed alongside a couple dozen other victims of exposure, exhaustion and carbon monoxide poisoning. They were tended by EMTs, volunteer doctors, nurses and others who were willing to donate their skills to help others during what had become a crisis in the last few hours. Blankets were retrieved from the rooms, hot soup was served, but the lack of proper medical facilities and medicine became increasingly evident as the makeshift hospital grew.

Vito Pazzita was angry. The relief he had expected this morning had not materialized. The chaos he visualized was coming to a boil, and his carefully orchestrated hotel mechanism was running down. Disorganization and unplanned occurrences devastated Vito's sense of security. Everything had to be in its place, for in Vito's world, there was a precise place for everything. There was no place for these patients in his hotel.

He liked to think he could accept pressure, but today Vito could not. The Governor was expected by mid-afternoon. The press would be accompanying him. TV cameras would be scattered throughout the hotel capturing the minutest detail. There was no way he could allow the very gateway to his prominent hotel to be cluttered with dirty, sick, non-paying humanity. Should this disharmony be broadcast nationally, he was certain to lose his job and end up as a common bellhop once again.

Vito called the police station. The chief answered.

"I want these people removed from my premises. They are all trespassers and are here against my will. They should be taken to where they can receive proper care."

"At the moment, Mr. Pazzita, your hotel is the best place for them. We have no other facilities. Believe me, the town is grateful for your help in this emergency."

"I can't have it. The Governor and the press are due here at any moment. This is a big event. I have a big convention. I have hundreds of guests who have paid a lot of money for the best accommodations."

"I'm sorry for the inconvenience these helpless people are causing you," Wilson continued, becoming impatient and feeling the warmth of anger rise. He also knew Vito somewhat and decided to take a different approach.

"I'm surprised at your lack of compassion. You say the press is coming? I'm amazed you can't see how you can take advantage of this. Frankly, I see this as a chance for real glory. This, to me, illustrates your great compassion for suffering humanity. When the press sees what you have done for these helpless victims of circumstances, they will rush to your side. This is a great human-interest story, Vito. You'll be the hero of this storm."

Vito suspected the chief might be putting him on, but the voice was low, sincere and authoritative. Wilson had some good points. Maybe he could turn this to his advantage. What if the press found out that he had kicked these people out? That too would be a disaster.

"Think about it, Vito. In the meantime I'll see what I can do to find other accommodations."

"OK," Vito responded as if his mind was elsewhere. "I think I can handle the situation through the rest of the day." Then, changing to his comically gruff tone again, "But I want them out of here tomorrow morning."

"We'll do our best. You are a compassionate man. No doubt about it!" Wilson hung up.

*

Maggie drove the snowmobile at full throttle. Conditions along Great Road were nearly perfect for speed -- a two-inch accumulation on a packed surface. Pedestrian traffic was very heavy as the adventuresome took to foot and skis to sightsee and exercise. To the left and right were six- and seven-foot snow banks. Businesses were plowed in. Gas

182

stations were closed. Crosby's Shopping Center was an arctic island. Thompson's Truck Stop, the diner, seemed to be the lone oasis between town and the famous industrial route. She was tempted to stop for a coffee, but she was on a mission.

The falling snow appeared now to be icy particles. They bombarded Maggie's cheeks like tiny needles. They tick-tick-ticked off her goggles and she squinted, attempting to see further ahead.

Route 128 appeared quickly. Several vehicles were parked on the bridge and spectators leaned over each of the railings observing the scene below. Maggie could see the wide path where the giant snow thrower had passed, but that was already filling in with drifts.

Visibility continued to be poor as the snow fell and whipped through the air in billows. The few cars and trucks that could be seen below were nearly covered with blown snow. Each was a frozen corpse, immobile in its own isolation. Beyond this was nothing but a wall of billions of flakes, hastily descending and delivering a cold, gray dampness.

She swung the snow machine around and steered down the embankment onto the highway. Closer now, it reminded her of a typical auto junkyard in winter. Some vehicles, with doors still open, were collecting the drifting snow.

She slowly zigzagged between the silent vehicles until, by chance, she came across a rescue party. They had just discovered a victim and did not notice her arrival. Attention was directed to the inside of the car. The back door had been pulled open and two of the workers were inside performing CPR.

Looking closer, she was startled to recognize her husband. He was breathing for the victim while the other man rhythmically compressed the victim's chest. Maggie had to look away.

The victim's face was cherry-red, the signal flag of carbon monoxide poisoning. The lifesaving attempt was finally abandoned. The cold of the extremities, the paper feeling of the skin, were indications the victim had been dead for a short while. The attempt at CPR failed to stimulate the heart and the resultant pulse. Artificial breathing produced no promise of recovery.

"No use. No vitals. So young, too." They eased the body from the car and placed it on the toboggan.

"I really wonder if we should bother with him now," one man suggested. "There might be some others just up the way. We should be saving the live ones. Know what I mean?"

"Goddammit!" said another in frustration. "What a hell of a job! I don't know. I hate to just leave him here."

"Calm down, Bill," another said, placing an arm on his shoulder. "He'll be OK. Let's put a handkerchief on the antenna and we can pick him up later."

To this there was general agreement. The boy's body was gently returned to the car. A groan of escaping air passed through the victim's vocal chords. The door was closed, and the party headed on to the next vehicle.

Phil looked up, recognized Maggie, and gave a tired smile.

"Are you OK, Phil?" Maggie asked. He looked horrid. His eyes were bloodshot, his face lined and dark.

"Maggie." He put his arms around her and rested his head on her shoulder briefly. "I'm ready to sleep for a year."

"Let's go home."

"Not yet. We're just finishing up here. A relief crew is on the way."

"Come on home soon," she pleaded. "I don't want you to be a victim."

184

"In a little while." He kissed her then shuffled off to catch up with the others.

Maggie revved up the machine and turned back toward town. She was of no use here. If she had used her head, she thought, she would have brought hot coffee and doughnuts to the men. Then, shaking her head, oh, dumb me! I knew I should have stopped for donuts at the diner.

*

"It's much worse than I imagined," Maggie told Chief Wilson. "I see no choice but to call a general meeting and get ourselves organized. It seems now we're going in different directions. Heard from our selectman today?"

"Yep. He was in a little while ago. He's running around on a confiscated snow machine. He's furious about being snowed in! Afraid I don't have much sympathy for him, and I think he now knows he was wrong. Knowing him, though, he won't admit it. He'll blame it on the other two."

"What's he up to?"

"Checking around."

"What do you think about a meeting?"

"Fine with me," Wilson nodded. "I did some checking after you left. I'll finally admit you're right. Now if we can pull all of us together ... "

"Have any plans?"

"Nope."

"Then we start from scratch. I'll find Sivolesky and see if we can put the meeting together."

"Watch it!" Wilson warned. "Your editorial is still fresh in his mind."

"Good," Maggie said, and returned to the street, pausing over which direction to travel. She decided to go home and telephone rather than face the elements all afternoon. Besides, Phil might return and he'd be very hungry.

185

"Well, Rolf. Looks like we got another good ol' New England blizzard. Not bad shovelin' though as long as we keep ahead of it."

Frank McCullough leaned on his ancient wooden shovel and spoke into the wind to his dog. The path was clear half way to the barn. Each shovelful was thrown to the lee side, allowing it to blow away. Slowly, methodically, he inched his way to the barn. Rolf was well protected from the wind by the walls of snow his master had dug through.

McCullough paused again, his back to the wind, collar turned up, earmuffs down. "It's peaceful, Rolf. I always like a good storm. Makes a nice blanket against the house. It keeps the drafts from blowing in under the sills."

He cut the snow away from the barn door. It rolled open on well-oiled wheels. Rolf ran past him and once inside shook himself lustily. McCullough followed, stamped the snow off his boots and closed the big door.

"Remember when this old barn was full of cattle, Rolf? Remember how warm it was from the heat the herd gave off? Now all we have is Buttercup and Henrietta and they can't begin to do the trick."

McCullough reached for the pitchfork and speared a bundle of hay into Buttercup's manger. He then scooped a wooden quart measure of oats from a barrel and emptied the container into the heifer's feeder.

"Well, old girl. Hang in there. You'll stay inside today." He massaged behind the animal's ears and then scratched her head where her horns had once been.

The chickens were at the other end of the barn. McCullough picked up a wire basket and walked from nest to nest reaching, one by one, for the eggs.

"A-ha! This weather agrees with you girls. Looks like we got about nine dozen today."

A smile on his face, the old man filled the feeders with grain. He then scattered oyster shells over the grain to insure hard eggshells. Egg basket in hand again, he and his old retriever returned to the house. The kitchen was hot and dry and smells of something good escaped from Mabel's oven.

"Think I'll just let the Chevy sit at the end of the drive till tomorrow. No point in shoveling it out the way she's driftin'."

Mable nodded and continued her work at the kitchen counter.

Frank took a couple lengths of wood from the wood box and placed them in the stove. He then rubbed his gnarled hands together over the heat. Turning to the eggs, he washed and weighed them and finally packed them in boxes according to size.

"Egg business is goin' to pot. Not many customers in this weather."

*

Early Sunday afternoon each of the New England governors received a secure message from The White House.

National Weather Bureau forecasts extreme snowfall for Northeast. Weather advisory of urgent nature. Suggest declaration of immediate emergency procedures.

Alert and mobilize all available personnel and equipment. National Civil Defense already on alert. Federal Government ready to aid in every way possible. Disaster Assistance Administration ready to move in with Army personnel to aid in rescue and relief efforts and equipment to assist in clearing streets and highways.

Direct line open to White House. Request you keep this office advised of changes in conditions.

Reaction to this communication was mixed. Maine and Vermont governors were incensed by it. To them it was direct interference with state sovereignty.

"So it's a bad storm," was the reaction. "Every three or four years we have unusually heavy snow."

They shrugged it off.

New Hampshire, Connecticut and Rhode Island were eager, on the other hand, to accept any free handout the Feds had to offer. It was expensive coping with winter's heavy snows, they said, very draining on the budgets that were already lean. Declaring an emergency was certainly the practical way to go. The National Guard should be called out simultaneously. Overtime expenses for state and local personnel could then be kept to a minimum.

This particular Sunday was not the most convenient to reach Massachusetts Governor Kelly Fitzwilliam. He was, at the time the message was received, on route to Hollandson to speak before a distinguished gathering of scientists. He had been preparing for this public appearance for several days. It was his chance to be in the national spotlight.

During the day his aides had asked him when he was going to call an emergency -- just as was done way back during the Blizzard of '78. Fitzwilliam ignored the inquiries. Each town, he said, was declaring its own emergencies, including Boston. Everything seemed to be well in hand, he continued. He would wait until he returned from his speech tonight to make the declaration.

It would look bad, he thought, for him to declare it now and then travel to Hollandson and back for this appearance. He would be accused of dastardly conduct by the press.

In his absence, another aide received the Presidential communication at the State House. Admittedly lacking in experience, and shaken at having received a message from the number one office in the country, the aide called the Governor's cell phone but there was no response. He next telephoned the Hollandson Motor Hotel.

No, the Governor had not yet arrived. The aide, wanting to insure personal credit for reporting the event to the Governor, gave the hotel operator his name and asked that the Governor call him as soon as possible.

The operator misspelled the aide's name and placed the message on her side table for the clerk to pick up. An hour later, a harassed clerk picked up the message and stuffed it in the key box for one of the Governor's staff.

*

Phil Billings gunned the throttle of the snowmobile and pushed through, rather than over, the snow bank into his driveway. The machine immediately sank into two feet of fresh snow. He twisted the throttle again and the powerful machine churned up a white cloud all the way to the garage door.

Maggie heard the noise. She ran through the ell to the garage where she raised the door from the inside, surprising Phil at the welcome. He drove the vehicle over the snow drift in front of the door and into the shelter. Maggie pulled down the door, shutting out the violence of the wind.

She helped him remove his helmet and wet, snow-caked jumpsuit.

"God I've missed you, she said with a worried laugh, throwing her arms around him.

Pleased and embarrassed by the unaccustomed attention, he said, "Let's go inside. I'll tell you about it over a cup of hot soup."

*

"You wouldn't believe some of those jokers." Phil was saying. "During the afternoon and evening yesterday, we spent most of our time attempting to convince people to abandon their vehicles. They just wouldn't believe the seriousness of the situation. They clung to the hope that the snowplow would soon be along."

189

"I expect many of them were in shock," Maggie offered.

"That came later. For those who refused to leave, we told them we were going to tie a red ribbon to their mirrors -- so we could find them in the morning when they were unconscious."

"That's terrible!"

"Why? In most cases that little action was enough to get them to leave. For those who didn't, sure enough, they were the ones who were in trouble last night and today."

"I couldn't believe the things you were doing at the scene, Phil. You were great. I never saw you act with such decisiveness as with that CO_2 victim. Frankly, I don't know how you did it. He looked so horrid!"

Phil chuckled. "I don't know how I did it either. I suppose there's something to be said for numbers. Since yesterday I saw victim after victim and I guess I became used to it. And then, it's the urgency of possibly saving a life that starts the adrenalin pumping. You don't stop to think about what he looks like. What I couldn't get used to were the kids. I just can't bear the anguish of a suffering child. It sends me up a wall."

"Any idea how many cars you searched?"

"No idea. There are hundreds and hundreds of vehicles out there. It reminds me of the February '99 storm, except I think they only received about twenty inches." Phil paused. "What's the latest word on this storm?"

"No change. As far as I know it's just going to keep coming." Exhaustion overtook Phil as Maggie brought him up to date on events since they last spoke. His lids drooped with increasing frequency and his head nodded.

"Hey, partner," Maggie said. "You'd better sack out."

"Wake me when it's over. At this point I don't care about anything but sleep."

190

*

A meeting of Hollandson officials took place in the Town Hall at two-thirty. It was not without difficulty that most of them came to the meeting as a result of Maggie's phone calls. Traveling was daunting without the right equipment.

Selectman Sivolesky opened the meeting and it was immediately apparent his good humor of last Thursday was now absent. There was also an undercurrent of hostility in the room between departments. Each was aware of the sad condition of the roads. The blame rested squarely on the selectmen's shoulders and Bud Kelly wasted no time in reminding Sivolesky of his short-sighted policy of allowing snow removal equipment to deteriorate. Fire Chief Bradford joined Kelly and told Sivolesky he'd better hope there were no house fires or ambulance calls within the next few days. They wouldn't be answered.

"OK, OK," Sivolesky finally said. "I hear you all. We're all tired. But we aren't gonna get anywhere at all if we don't work out some solutions. I don't want to hear any more complaints. I've got enough of my own. I wish to hell I'd gone to Florida this week, or better yet, South America.

"But I'm stuck right here in Hollandson. We gotta live with each other. With a bit of cooperation we can. Now let's forget past mistakes and pull together. Any suggestions?"

"Yes. The roads, "Chief Bradford said. "How are we going to clear them?"

"Well, I suggest we mount plows on the fire engines. I seem to recall this has been done in the past."

"No way," Bradford said, loudly. "Your thinking is forty years out of date."

"'No way, bullshit!" Sivolesky shot back suddenly, jumping to his feet.

191

The fire chief leaped up from his chair also and pointed his finger at Sivolesky.

"I said 'no way.' You're not going to destroy this town's expensive fire apparatus because you don't have the foresight to fund the highway department. Fire equipment is for fires. Period!"

"Well. So much for cooperation," Sivolesky sighed. "Anyone have some constructive suggestions?"

"I hear they've got some big equipment comin' in from Buffalo," Kelly said. Someone laughed. "Ya. That'll be here by Easter."

"How about the Peters Airfield?" Sivolesky continued. "They must have some heavy equipment. You know anyone over there any more?"

"Ya," Kelly said. "I know the gate Sentry."

The school committee representative was also angry. "I don't see how you people can joke when people's lives are at stake. We need immediate relief. We've got some mighty sick people over at the school. I hear the hotel has a lot of people too. They all need food and medicine."

"There are many things we need, John," Sivolesky said. "I don't want to hear needs. I want to hear solutions."

The room fell silent. Finally it was Maggie who spoke.

"Let's get one thing straight right off the bat," she began forcefully, anticipating criticism. "I do not represent the press tonight. I am a concerned citizen of this town and, by the way, the officially appointed Civil Defense Director. I would like to suggest some solutions.

"I made a few phone calls this afternoon and I'm pleased to say we have a distinguished guest among us. He's Buzz Cavioli, owner of Cavioli Trucking. He owns a fleet of heavy trucks and plows. He normally plows for the state. Since the state has not yet called him because he is at the end of their call list, his men and equipment are available to us at

192

modest cost. I'd like to suggest we ask Bud Kelly to coordinate the plowing with Mr. Cavioli and begin work immediately.

"Roads are our number one priority, for without them no other plans are possible. With us also is Ronnie Smith who owns a couple of wreckers. From my observations, abandoned cars will have to be towed before the plows can even get to many of the back roads.

"Number two problem is the school. As soon as the driveway to the hotel is cleared and the CD folding cots from the fire station are set up at the school, I suggest the ambulance begin a shuttle from the hotel to the school."

"Why can't we take them to the hospital?" someone asked.

"I've called Memorial Hospital. They're short on staff and every bed is already filled. They also won't release any of their medical supplies because they don't anticipate new supplies in the near future.

"Finally, I'd like to see a committee of five among us work together on acquiring food and medicine. We're going to need a lot of it at the school."

"And just where do you think we're going to get that!" Sivolesky asked sarcastically.

"You got up on the wrong side of the bed today," Maggie smiled, looking at the selectman. Everyone in the room laughed. "There are several sources of food. One, and the most immediate, is from the homes of the people here in town that are willing to donate staples. The ultimate source, if this storm worsens, will be the shopping center."

There were several audible surprises in the room.

"So, as you can see, there are food sources when the situation becomes extremely critical. Cooperation with the local pharmacy may also be possible if the need arises."

The meeting ended shortly after Maggie's talk. Nearly everyone wore a smile as they returned to their respective chores.

"I owe you an apology, Maggie," Sivolesky said, as he caught up to her at the door. I've been pig-headed and stupid. I just never anticipated a storm like this."

"We all have our days, Bob, and I doubt if anyone anticipated this storm. But it is true we do have an obligation to keep the town's equipment up to snuff. Let's just hope tonight's plans work out."

*

The President met once again with his advisors, Scan-Man's Harrington and others. It was a very grim gathering that sat once again in a semi-circle in front of the President's desk. There was no indication it was only two days before Christmas.

The tragic news from New England was that all records for snowfall had long since been broken. Five to six feet of precipitation had laid the states to waste. There was no machinery available that could keep up with the downfall in such a populous region. Man's own technology, the car, truck and bus now effectively blocked all further attempts at efficient road clearing. Roofs were collapsing, power was out, people were dying by the hundreds from exposure in their unheated homes. Humanity in general was simply not able to cope with the weather.

"We have been in direct contact with five of the six New England governors," the President said. "Only Massachusetts' Kelly Fitzwilliam seems to be unavailable, but we are working through the Lieutenant Governor O'Brien. We are sending in men and machinery from neighboring states and from the west. Unfortunately it's a slow process. Air transport is out, at least until the snow stops."

194

"Mr. President." It was Secretary of State Buttrix. "Anyone with a smattering of history can see the potential enemy we face. A monstrous future has been hatched and the U.S. is no longer in the position of divine favor. In a spirit of international trust and SALT treaties, we have allowed our nation to become susceptible once again. The New England experience today is just a hint of warning -- very much like Truman's atomic bomb to Hiroshima! Our question now is, when will the Nagasaki bomb fall?

"During the 1940's, we had time to create the bomb. During the 1960's we had time to create satellites. We are now facing a weapon far more sophisticated, subtle and devastating than anything yet imagined. Last week we considered ourselves masters of our fate. This week we are the humble servants of an unknown master."

"Very dramatic, Senator Buttrix," the President said, "but also very true. Let's now get down to the task at hand. What is out next step?"

Defense Secretary Hatfield Cohen stood. "I suggest we have Mr. Harrington proceed with all possible speed. I think General Stringer will agree with me that, of all potential contractors available, Scan-Man has the most experience and satisfactory results over the years. Certainly we can't throw this project open to other companies -- at least not if we're to maintain some degree of secrecy.'"

"How long do you envision this project taking?" asked Representative Evelyn Robinson. "A year? Five years? Ten?"

"Naturally that's a difficult question to answer, Evelyn," Harrington replied, "because it depends on so much. I think it might be better, under the extreme circumstances, for you to tell me when you want a working prototype."

"Can you work that way?" Robinson asked.

"Ask our friends in Defense. Given ample funds, working room and federal cooperation, I blush to say that we have performed miracles."

General Stringer confirmed this. "Army was stuck with a program developed by a competing company that only lived up to half of our expectations. That was two years ago. We pulled the project away from them and gave it to Scan-Man, telling Scan-Man they'd have to maintain the same schedule the other company had, but which was already one year behind. Three months and two hundred million dollars later, Scan-Man completed the project, on schedule, and saved the taxpayers a billion dollars." The general lifted his chin with a jerk, as if to say, "I told you so."

"How much time do you think we have?" the President asked.

"This we don't know either," Buttrix said. "What is the motivation of the enemy? Was this his first move, or one of a series? Was it even an error on his part? Or, my friends, is this just an giant blip in the weather cycle?" He paused.

"We have to examine this from every angle," he continued. "Maybe we shouldn't try to compete with this unknown ... "

Chandler Harrington stiffened in his chair.

" ... If we can assume the source of the power is from a satellite," Buttrix said, "is there a possibility we can attempt to destroy it Mr. Harrington? With all your eyes in the sky, isn't it possible to track down our, excuse my metaphor, heavenly enemy in space?"

"I'm afraid not, Mr. Secretary," Harrington said with a condescending chuckle. "It's a mighty big area out there. There are hundreds of satellites and thousands of pieces of space trash circling our earth, new, used and abandoned. We're not quite into the Buck Rogers, or should I say, Star Wars era. Chasing down enemy satellites, at least today, falls into that

196

category. Even if we could, we don't know what we're looking for."

Buttrix pursued the matter, irritated by Harrington's poorly concealed superior attitude. "Scanner XII appeared to be in the same general neighborhood when it recorded the so-called Hole in the Night. If you knew it was still in that area, could you adjust Scanner XII to take an inventory of the space hardware around it?"

"No," Harrington answered. "XII isn't built for that. The information you saw the other day was part of its normal function. To rebuild XII to scan the upper stratosphere or beyond is a very different project. And also, the results would be dubious at best, unless, of course, we caught the enemy in mid-performance."

As Harrington spoke, General John Ruben was filled with disgust. The whole deceitful plot Harrington so skillfully wove filled Ruben with remorse. Why had he agreed to go along with it? he asked himself. Because of the photos? Hell, the photos didn't amount to a damn next to this plot. How could he have allowed the threat of his embarrassment to undermine his ethics? He looked around the room. Who else knew the truth? Was he the only one? Could it be that Harrington was now counting on him to reinforce these ideas? Well, Harrington could handle it himself. He wasn't saying anything.

On the other hand, Ruben couldn't believe that he was the only one in on the plot. Why him? He heard his colleague, Stringer, speak up. Could he be in on it?

"With the growing importance of satellites," Stringer was saying, "for early warning, communications, navigation, reconnaissance and meteorology, the United States will have to develop some type of extensive satellite defense."

Harrington simply looked at Stringer and nodded. The General was known for daydreaming into side issues. Ruben looked at Stringer. No. He wasn't part of it.

"Why would altering a satellite to scan the atmosphere and beyond be any more of a difficult task than creating a weather modification function to compete with that of our enemy?" Robinson asked.

Harrington shifted in his chair. "Hypothetical questions are never easy to answer. I suppose I should retract my earlier statement of saying it would be difficult to build a space scanner, and say that we certainly could. Space, optics and weather are our forte. Weather modification equipment is a specific goal I am certain we can tackle, perfect and put into use. A space scanner, although I'm certain it will have its uses in the not-too-distant future, promises no hope of solving our present dilemma. Our goal is to tackle the enemy on his own ballfield. We're going after a touchdown. I believe we ought to proceed along lines that offer the most practical solution."

Cohen and Stringer nodded their heads in agreement.

"I've given this matter a great deal of thought," Senator Woark said. These were the Ways and Means chairman's first words of the meeting. There followed general mumbles indicating Woark was not the only one who did the thinking.

"I've given this matter a lot of thought," Woark began again. "Just what makes any of you think this powerful light is from a man-made satellite? I'm inclined to believe the source might be from a UFO of sorts."

A groan reverberated around the room.

"Now just hold on a minute here!" Woark continued, angered at the challenge to his credibility. "We're here to consider every angle of this thing. Don't go knocking this theory down until you've at least considered it." He glared at his peers with a turn of the head.

"You will all have to admit what you saw on Mr. Harrington's tape was unworldly, strange. The effects it had on the earth have been highly powerful, like nothing we have developed with our own advanced technology. I maintain that that light and heat source could have come from a space ship of interplanetary origin." Woark paused. "I challenge anyone of you to prove me wrong."

All faces in the room were smiling, except the President's.

"All new technologies are unworldly," Senator Robinson said. "Think how startled we were when we learned of the Sputnik."

"Its source was known," Woark snapped back.

"OK then," Robinson continued. "Think what the Japanese thought when the atomic bomb was dropped. Certainly that produced an effect that was unworldly and as much of a terror as the present situation."

"Its source was known," Woark again said with emphasis. "I repeat. We know nothing about the source of this Hole in the Night."

"The Senator has a good point," the President cut in. "Although I'm not ready to subscribe to his theory of extra-terrestrial space ships initiating this phenomenon, I don't think we can simply cast it aside as impossible."

"Thank you, Mr. President." Woark smiled self-contentedly and leaned back in his chair.

"I think we've tossed this around long enough and we must now come down to basics," the President continued. "I think we agree on several points. Number one. We do not want it known that we are aware it exists, at least not at this time. Number two. We want to develop our own technology that can compete with whatever this is. Number three. Time is at a premium, it seems.

"Mr. Harrington says he wants us to give him a time limit. I'd suggest one year. During that time he should come up with a practical working model. Does that seem reasonable, Mr. Harrington?'

"It's a good start, Mr. President."

"That's not what I asked. Can you produce a working model within a year?"

"This is the time frame I have been tossing around," Harrington said. "To work within that frame we'll need up front money of $41 billion."

Harrington's statement elicited several gasps.

"But we can do that in four installments," Harrington quickly added. "I have a proposal with me already prepared." He handed a copy to the President. "I can easily make installments changes."

More disgruntlement.

"Gentlemen," Harrington continued quickly, hoping to delay or prevent any budget discussions. "Do you have an idea of the immensity of this project and the speed and manpower required to do it? It could very well cost you twice that much or more. But let me hastily remind you of the cost of Apollo, the C5A, and hundreds of others. Why is this project any different?"

"He's right," Buttrix said. "A lot lesser projects have cost our citizens many times more."

"Members of Congress," the President said. "Can you come up with the money?"

Senator Woark spoke. "The money is no problem. It's the secrecy, combined with the justification of the money before Congress and the public, that will be difficult. What will we tell everyone?"

"Gentlemen, the answer is simple." It was Senator Robinson "I suggest we take the money from Defense, since this is indeed defense. We'll simply have to suspend some of the current projects which, of course, are now obsolete."

"Mrs. Robinson!" Stringer exclaimed indignantly. "We have to continue to spend more for defense. You can't just scrap everything for a single project."

"It's not how much you spend that concerns me, General," the lady Senator said, smiling beneficently, repeating the principle she had preached for years. "It's what you are spending it *for* that concerns me, General. What good are your missiles, your tanks, your ships, your airplanes, or for that matter, what good is any of your hardware in the face of our present enemy? I'll answer you. None. I suggest to this room that all Defense spending for development be suspended and earmarked for the Scan-Man project. Without it, gentlemen, we are a nation without a defense."

Applause and smiles now filled the room, except for those representing military factions.

The President interrupted. "I do believe we have gone as far as we can go today. There seems to be unanimity. I suggest we let the money issue rest until after the holidays. Let's plan to meet once again just after the New Year. In the meantime I want to wish all of you a pleasant holiday.

*

Vito Pazzita's jaw dropped thirty degrees off the horizontal when he was told the governor and his retinue had arrived. He stood immobile, paralyzed, not believing his big moment had arrived.

Recovering, he dashed to the lobby where he saw only what looked like a group of newly arrived refugees. He glanced at his tall, gangling clerk. "What are you talking about!" he spat out in disdain. "Where is the governor?"

The clerk poked Vito in the ribs and motioned to the newly arrived group. Vito swallowed hard. He now recognized the governor beneath his snow-covered coat and fur hat.

"Oh, your excellency," he said, arms outstretched as he approached Kelly Fitzwilliam. "Welcome to the Hollandson Motor Hotel." Then he mechanically added, "I hope your trip was pleasant."

Governor Fitzwilliam and all other heads turned to see the source of this ridiculous greeting. Could this little man be making fun of the governor?

Aware of his sudden center-stage position, Vito now felt self-conscious and embarrassed by his remark. Before his question was answered, he stepped up to the group and apologized for the crowded condition of the lobby and the totally disheveled appearance of the hotel.

"I hope you'll forgive me, but we've had problems with ... " and Vito waved his arms around indicating his uninvited guests in the lobby. "We've had problems and I'm trying to get the police to handle it. Let's take care of your bags. He snapped his fingers for a bellboy, but none appeared. "Well, let me show you to the ballroom. Leave your bags here. Oh! You have no bags ... "

The snow blown group remained in place. Fitzwilliam then told one of his aides to deal with Vito while he, the aides close behind, stopped to talk with several of the medical volunteers as well as some of their victims.

The "lobby people," as the regular guests had come to know them, told the governor of their individual tragedies on route for the Christmas holidays. They complained about inadequate snowplowing, spoke vehemently against the poor medical care they were receiving here and the absence of emergency facilities. The press took notes and snapped pictures as Fitzwilliam listened sympathetically and spoke of how fortunate he was to be here to "personally witness the problems first hand." He said he could readily sympathize

202

with them, for his own journey west from Boston this afternoon had been an immense ordeal -- an act for which he would undoubted be criticized. But, he said, duty came first.

Fitzwilliam promised the lobby people that all state snow removal crews would soon be working overtime to keep ahead of the storm. He assured the people, with appropriate facial adjustments, that "conditions will improve just as fast as possible." Many gave a serious nod of approval and gratefulness was returned to the governor for this comforting assurance.

By now Vito had returned with the aide in tow. He stood next to Fitzwilliam, attempting to draw his attention away from the lobby people, the riffraff, and on to more important matters. But, it was not until the press lost interest that Fitzwilliam straightened and turned to the hotel manager. "Where have the TV crews set up?"

"They, ah, I don't know ... " Vito stumbled.

Fitzwilliam's aide cut in. "They aren't here yet sir. It looks like the weather frightened them off."

Superficially, the governor carried his disappointment well. But then, he had little choice under public scrutiny. Fifteen minutes later, in the privacy of his suite with his aides, his Excellency, Massachusetts Governor Kelly Fitzwilliam said, "Goddamn the bastards! Didn't you tell me they'd be all set up for my arrival?"

*

Maggie was glad to be home once again. The meeting with the town officials had drained her, yet she was pleased she had maintained her sang-froid -- a quality that had not come easily over the years.

Not surprisingly, Phil was still asleep. She went to her own room, kicked off her shoes, and sprawled on the bed. Pleasant thoughts were beginning to march behind her eyes when the phone rang. "He's here," said a voice at the other end.

"Is that you Al?" It was her freelance reporter who covered weekend events for the *Bulletin*. "Who's where?"

"The governor! You know. The guy elected to run our state. He's here at the hotel. You wanted me to call." Maggie was incredulous. "How'd he get here, by dogsled?"

"Would you believe it? No. He got here a few minutes ago and is positively ripping that the TV crews never showed."

Maggie laughed. "Fitzy is often blind to the simple frailties of others. Well, look. You've just ruined my potentially peaceful evening. Keep on the governor's tail. I'll be over in a little while."

*

It was four thirty and dark before Maggie arrived at the hotel. She hid the snowmobile in the woods, well away from the temptation of would-be thieves. Chief Wilson had warned her that snow vehicles had suddenly become extremely valuable assets, the only practical means of transportation. Reports of stolen vehicles had become common during the past twenty-four hours.

Maggie's first sensory perception on entering the hotel was the strong smell of body odor. The lobby was crowded -- reminding her of a bus terminal prior to a major holiday. Crying babies, running children, yelling mothers, impatient fathers -- people waiting, hours on end, for the storm to terminate and the holiday season to resume.

The governor was not difficult to locate. His stage voice rang loud and clear in response to questions asked of him in regard to the storm. His promises astounded Maggie, as they always had.

Maggie was tall in relation to the crowd, and she stood conspicuously dressed in her rabbit fur coat open at the front revealing a daffodil yellow jumpsuit. Fitzwilliam recognized her almost immediately and came toward her, leaving a wake of admirers behind. He greeted her warmly, with an enthusiasm and a kiss that was not justified, Maggie thought, by the two or three times they had met.

"I appreciate your enthusiasm, Fitzy," she responded, sarcastically, "but keep in mind the *Bulletin* has only fifteen thousand circulation."

"As usual, Maggie, I'm warmed by your candor. You're so damned refreshing. I wish all the press were like you. I'd know exactly where I stood with them."

Maggie's acquaintance with Fitzwilliam began nearly five years ago when he ran for re-election against a popular liberal. Fitzwilliam had stopped in Hollandson and Maggie had interviewed him. She had disliked the governor at first sight and, despite her principles of reportorial objectivity, set them aside on this occasion and produced a caustic story. This was her first and last experience of being captured and controlled by political emotionalism. She had since regretted the story.

Fitzwilliam and his followers were able to use the criticism to their favor. By turning the other cheek with a smile, the re-elected governor now invited Maggie to state functions, some of which she surprised herself by attending. But it was Fitzwilliam's genuine insincerity and hollow warmth that Maggie could never warm to. He was a blowhard in Maggie's estimation. He'd do anything for publicity, including today's example of driving through the century's worst blizzard to speak before the National Scientific Association, an engagement that had promised to give him some national press.

Maggie could never bring herself to be sincere with the governor. Her conversations with him, and thoughts about him, were laced with a sarcasm over which she allowed little control.

Fred and Puff Chabus soon joined them and Maggie made the introductions. Maggie participated in the exchange of a few sentences, but soon decided to forego the competition with Puff. She stepped aside and turned her attention to the lobby people whom she was encountering for the first time.

*

It was 5 p.m. before Ed Randolph psychologically forced himself to call Margo. He had never felt so shaken in these abilities. Since noon he had been attempting to invent a way to dispose of Ellen Bloodworth. He felt like a mystery writer plotting a foolproof scheme. If it hadn't been for the pressure he felt exerted on him by Harrington, this might have been an interesting cat-and-mouse game. As it was however, Harrington was going to call at 10 p.m. and would want to know if Bloodworth had been "taken care of." Randolph had let him down once already, and it was not going to happen again.

Yet he was operating by what could only be considered remote control. He was not at the scene. He had to work through Margo. She was his puppet, yet he could not control her actions.

Margo was tough. She was tenaciously loyal to the company, and she could be totally unscrupulous. But, was she capable of murder? Randolph recoiled at the word he had avoided using until now. But murder it was. Murder it had to be.

Randolph's indecision had wasted five hours. Everything he imagined turned out nasty in the end. It was essential that Scan-Man come out clean. Harrington would revolt at anything less. Yet time was running out. Each minute he wasted, was a minute taken from Margo on the other end.

Murder was not the only crushing pressure Randolph was experiencing. The storm had isolated him from direct control at Scan-Man. The storm could now be considered out of hand, with no one at the helm of Scanner XII directing the Searoc Beam. The eventuality of the storm could not be known. It promised only to be devastating. Something had to be done to bring it under control. But was it possible?

Corporate pressure was an accepted fact, and Randolph usually thrived on it. The pressures that had come about as a result of Scan-Man's venture into weather manipulation were another matter. But it had taken every ounce of self-control to hold himself together this afternoon.

"Regarding Bloodworth, Margo," Randolph told her now, "I'm placing the responsibility for her on your shoulders. I cannot plot such a scheme from this distance. I have every faith in you, Margo. You will be amply rewarded for your loyalty to the company. Carry it out and get back to me before ten tonight. Be careful."

Chin's response to Randolph was a firm "Yes Sir."

Thus Randolph passed the proverbial buck and temporarily eased his own burden. Margo's response surprised Randolph. As if she already had a plan in mind, she accepted the burden with no further comment on that issue.

Margo then reported to Randolph she could find no one with the knowledge to activate and operate the Searoc Beam. But then, there was only a skeleton crew in the office. It appeared to Margo that Nat Webster had been the prime mover and operator. Everyone reported to him. He held the ultimate key.

"That key," Randolph said, "is in the classified files now locked in my desk. I know you have a lot on your mind, but I want you to begin studying those files. Get familiar with them. I need you to guide Webster's technicians through this operation."

Randolph's voice was low and self-assured. It oozed the confidence he wished to pass along to Margo. Inside, Randolph was the young, ambitious, nervous executive, ready to scream out his frustrations. His world had never felt so delicately balanced, so precarious.

But he was the President of Scan-Man. He knew what was expected of him as chief executive officer of a global company. He would see that he achieved the goals that Harrington expected of him.

"Call me before ten."

*

The ballroom rang with the chatter of conventioneers, each attempting to be heard over the other. The cash bar was dispensing drinks at a rapid rate, lubricating and intoxicating.

The planned formal dinner was not going well. Much of the hotel food supplies had been given to the lobby people. As a result, food was limited to snacks and sandwiches. The chaos was rapidly building. Liberal quantities of alcohol served without food promised to be explosive.

Fred and Puff Chabus sat at the head table with the Governor, an aide and two other speakers. Chabus was slowly tearing apart his napkin as Fitzwilliam and Puff, leaning forward on either side of him, conversed animatedly. He nodded at Maggie as she energetically waved to him from across the room.

Then, about 7 p.m., the ballroom lights flickered, went out, came on again, and then went out once more. A woman screamed. Several men guffawed. Chatter turned to uneasy speculation as the problem continued. Optimistic conclusions ranged from a blown fuse, to a knocked down wire.

The candles at each table, in their various colored containers, lent an eerie luminescence to the room.

Vito immediately stumbled from the room, and in the dim glow of the emergency lamps went to the front desk. He called maintenance for an explanation, but no one answered.

Maggie saw Vito leave and hurried after him. Her rapid departure caused others to look up and wonder if they too should leave.

Chabus stood. "Ladies and gentlemen," he began, speaking at first into the dead microphone. Then, pushing it aside, "Please keep your seats."

He spoke louder, yet still a few of his colleagues ignored him! "Please keep your seats. Relax. Have another drink. We'll find out the problem in a few minutes."

The kitchen crew emerged and stood along the wall in the ballroom waiting for something to happen. There were no candles in the kitchen.

"Thank God for the candles," Maggie said as she caught up to Vito at the main desk.

"Goddarn him!" Vito said emphatically. "He's never here when I need him." Maggie looked at her cell phone battery. It was at half charge. She called the police station. The dispatcher answered. "No. The chief's not here. Yes. We're on emergency power. Looks like the whole town is out. Calls from everywhere."

She next called the electric company. A weary voice on the other end said, before the question was asked, "Yes. We're aware of it. We're doing everything we can."

"Is it a general blackout?" Maggie asked.

"I'm not allowed to say."

"What? You ... " and the phone disconnected. Sure as can be, she thought. It's a general blackout.

Vito was shouting into the front desk phone. "What do you mean you don't know what's the matter? You're on a payroll to know these things. You ... "

Maggie placed her hand on Vito's shoulder and whispered to him. He hung up the phone. He looked at her and his face sagged.

"We don't know how long this is going to last," Maggie said confidentially to Vito. "We have to assume it will last a few hours. I'd suggest getting everyone back to their rooms before the emergency lighting batteries run out."

Vito turned and dashed off.

"Wait, Vito! What are you doing?"

The lobby people were milling around, apprehensive, restless, worn and hungry. One shouted out to Maggie, asking what was happening.

"Quite obviously we've lost our electricity," Maggie said impatiently, not intending to sound sarcastic. "Other parts of Hollandson are dark also. It may be a while before they're repaired."

"Ya. I guess so," one of them remarked and then added, loud enough so all the other could hear. "No repair crew is gonna fix anything in this storm."

"Please, everyone. Just be patient. The electric company says they are working on it." Maggie then hurried after Vito. The ballroom was in an uproar. Chabus was still attempting to calm the din. He had not been very successful. Larger groups had now made up their minds to leave. They pushed past Maggie and Vito, deaf to all suggestions. Maggie was against the wall, and watched in disbelief as these highly educated scientists panicked! It was not literal, blind panic, but a refusal to be organized, coupled with a determination to leave the room. Vito was at the opposite wall, now a bit panicky himself.

When the initial wave passed, Maggie crossed over. "What did you do?"

"I just told them to hurry back to their rooms before the emergency lights went out." He shrugged his shoulders, freeing himself from guilt of the alarm he caused.

In the lobby, people patiently waited for elevators that would not appear. Others crossed the lobby and climbed the stairs to the mezzanine, cautiously watching their footing in the dim light. Others moved on to the Cloven Hoof Tavern and the Garden Room.

Maggie crossed the ballroom to speak with those still at the head table.

"That idiot!" Puff was saying. "He must have had training in mob dispersal." She then noticed Maggie, who told the others the little information she knew.

"Well. I guess we just wait it out," Puff said with a shrug. "Join us upstairs?"

"Thanks. No," Maggie answered quickly. "I want to keep tabs on what's happening down here."

*

The phone in the Chabus suite gave a weak, hesitant ring. Lack of electrical current placed the phone system on emergency power.

"Is the governor with you Dr. Chabus?"

Fitzwilliam took the phone and listened, responding with blunt, guttural punctuations. The conversation ended with, "I'll be back as soon as I can arrange it."

He looked at the others. They in turn watched him in the flickering candlelight, waiting for an explanation.

"I'm needed in Boston. This storm -- this blackout -- is a lot more serious than my advisors realized. Something got screwed up. I missed an earlier message."

"What's the situation, Kelley?" Chabus asked.

"My Lieutenant has declared a State of Emergency and has called out the National Guard. Boston and all along the New England coast is at a virtual standstill. No emergency vehicles can move. Boston, the coastal cities and towns have never had this much snow. There's nearly three feet of it along Beacon Street!" He paused and shook his head.

"I must return. I must return to my duties now." The governor had a flair for the dramatic, even when justified.

*

The singing from the candle-lit Cloven Hoof Tavern was just loud enough to reach the lobby. A drift of bored people began to flow in the direction of the merrymakers.

*

The governor's aide met Fitzwilliam in the lobby. "There's no way we're going to drive, sir. I've just been outdoors. The car is buried and the road isn't plowed."

The governor stamped his foot and mumbled something about imbeciles between gritted teeth.

*

Maggie decided to spend the night at the hotel. Nothing would be gained by fighting her way home through the drifts in the darkness. It was already 8:30 p.m.. Whatever had to be done could wait until morning.

She called Phil, wishing now that she had charged her cell phone before the electricity was lost.

"I know you're exhausted, but I have foumd this beautiful room on the fifth floor overlooking the Garden Room. True, it has no electricity, and it's a five-storey walk-up, but the candlelight is romantic and well worth your time and effort. I'd love to have your company."

"Sweetheart, I'd love to join you, but I also want to keep an eye on things in town. If this blackout persists, our troubles will have severely multiplied. Most people will have

212

lost their heat. Many will have lost their cooking capability. TV communication is gone. Water and sanitary facilities will be curtailed. The potential problems are incredible. I should get over to the school now that I've had my beauty sleep. I'm taking your Blazer out since you have out snowmobile.

"OK, OK. You've convinced me. I'll sleep alone tonight,"

Phil was right, Maggie thought. A chill passed through her as she realized the temperatures in her room and the hotel lobby were dropping.

"Is everything OK at the house?"

"No problem. I just stoked the coal fire and she'll go another twenty-four hours. Between you and me, we'll be the warmest place in town."

"Yes. And we're not taking advantage of it," Maggie said sadly. "Well, take care of yourself. I'll be home in the morning. I have a feeling I'll need that warmth."

As she returned off the phone and checked her battery power, her mind wandered. What problems would the loss of electricity cause at the hotel? She looked out her window. Without the floodlights, she couldn't see the storm. Another shiver ran up her spine.

*

The singing in the tavern increased in volume as more and more of the curious arrived. A smile crossed Maggie's face as she listened to the fun and jocularity drifting up from below. Perhaps a quick nightcap wouldn't do any harm, she thought. It might even help her to get to sleep.

She paused at the tavern door, looking over the shoulders of others waiting to enter. It was a mob scene. She was reconsidering that nightcap when someone tapped her on the arm. It was a short, young man, on the chubby side, but well dressed in a neatly pressed suit and tie. Maggie looked down at him.

"Sorry to bother you, ma'am, but the Governor says he must see you. It's urgent."

"Urgent?" Maggie asked, puzzled. "What's the problem?"

"That's all he said, Ms. Billings. Can you meet him in his suite?"

"I suppose." She followed the little man down the hall.

*

The Governor greeted her with a broad smile and a handclasp. "Thank you so much for coming. You don't know how I appreciate this."

"To tell you the truth," Maggie said. "I came reluctantly. I was just about to have a nightcap and retire early."

Fitzwilliam literally jumped and turned to his sideboard. "Well I guess I can fix that very easily."

"Just a small glass of dry wine."

The room was dimly lighted with a couple of candles and a portable gasoline lantern. It was a spooky light that cast long, black shadows. A group she could only assume to be aides were seated around a table in an adjoining room playing cards. The little man who brought her was standing over the others, watching.

"Perhaps you're wondering why I've asked you here," the Governor began in his typical, well-worn stage lines.

"Yes," Maggie responded tersely, with a nod of her head and an upraised wine glass.

"Bluntly, I must get back to Boston as soon as possible," he said, watching closely for her reaction.

Maggie smiled. "That I can assure you will happen."

"Oh?" Fitzwilliam was surprised and pleased.

"It may not be until next week, but I assure you it will be as soon as possible."

Fitzwilliam showed a slight trace of irritation. "Please don't play with me. I must get back to Boston so as to lead the Commonwealth out of this tragedy. You are the only one I know who has contacts here and might arrange transportation."

Maggie sighed. "You dragged me all the way up here to ask me that question, Fitzy." she said, teacher to child. "There's a raging blizzard out there! The snowfall has now surpassed record depths. It's a disaster. It's ... "

"You need not dwell on the obvious," Fitzwilliam cut in. "Perhaps it would help if I told you I have a communication from The White House instructing me to contact the President's office regarding this emergency." He handed her the note he had transcribed from his phone conversation with Boston.

"Why can't you respond from here?" Maggie asked.

Fitzwilliam's head dropped and he looked at the floor. "The message is six hours old. I'm not sure it's accurate. All my paperwork is in the office." He was pleading.

Maggie could read the frustration in the Governor's eyes -- the idea that he was missing his big chance to confer directly with The White House. Knowing the man, Maggie understood his drive to step into the flickering national limelight – the big time.

"There's something you're not telling me."

"Damn it, woman! Why is it you see me so clearly?" He appeared angry. "OK. So O'Brien has already declared an emergency for the state." He leaned forward and looked earnestly at Maggie. "I can't let that sonofabitch run the show!"

Maggie would not allow herself to laugh his face. He had spilled his deepest feelings to her. He had come clean. She had to respect him for that.

"You ask the impossible but I will check around. I certainly can't promise anything."

"How soon will you know?" he asked eagerly.

"Fitzy!" she said in exasperation. "I haven't even put my thoughts together. Give me another wine and I'll retire to my boudoir and get to work." Another wine, Maggie thought, would comfortably put her to sleep for the night.

*

The view from Maggie's fifth floor balcony, overlooking the Garden Room atrium, was even more pleasant than she had imagined. Vito's description was modest. She looked down from the top story of rooms, directly beneath the atrium's huge dome of glass. The scene was a very spacious artificial outdoor environment. It was an enjoyable perspective -- an aerial view -- of a tropical island with dozens of flickering candles and flashlights wandering its winding paths. Most of the tables were occupied and the waiters and bartenders appeared to be busy. Someone carried a portable radio and it broadcast gentle music, quite fitting for this island of safety.

Maggie looked up at the atrium dome, with its giant, supporting girders. All was quiet. She tried to imagine how much snow that structure was now supporting.

Wine glass still in hand, Maggie left the balcony and went into her room where she imagined she could think more clearly without the distraction of the balcony scene.

How was she to arrange to return the Governor to Boston? Why did she even allow herself to let him think there was a possibility it could be done? The answer to the last question was much easier to answer than the first. Maggie never admitted defeat. She would return the Governor to Boston if she had to spread her arms and fly!

Fly, Maggie thought. The only thing that could fly in this weather might be a helicopter. They are frequently used in rescue operations at sea in high winds. Why not here?

Commander Heathside, her old golf buddy! The man who was always anxious to maintain good relations with the press! He had helicopters at Peters Airfield. She hastily set down her wine glass and reached for her cell phone. She had his personal number. Heathside answered as if he expected bad news.

"Roger. This is Maggie Billings. Sorry to call you so late. How are you guys doing over there?"

"Maggie old girl. Good to hear from you. We're fully occupied with this white crap."

"Funny. We've got the same white crap over here too."

"We've got to keep Scan-Man cleared as well. Apparently they're having their own problems. But they still have their lights on. Looks like their latest rocket got off OK."

"We've got an emergency situation over here."

"Of course you do. Everyone has a goddamned emergency situation."

"Mine involves the Governor."

"Oh. Him."

"Well, it involves the White House too."

"Uh Huh. Tell me about it."

Maggie told him about the Governor and the call from The White House and how there was no alternate way to transport. Would a flight by helicopter be possible?

"It would be suicide, Maggie. The winds are too strong. There's an icing problem. Visibility is near zero. Navigation is impossible."

Maggie smiled. "It sounds as though you're trying to discourage me. I thought helicopters were used all the time for rescue operations under adverse conditions."

"It's my opinion that this blizzard can be categorized as something well beyond typical, adverse conditions." The static on the phone increased, emphasizing the commander's point.

"Would it be possible? I realize it would be rough. But would it be possible?"

"Anything is possible."

"I'm glad we agree on that point." She searched her mind for arguments to present. Finally, "I understand your people are testing a PGDT guidance system." She waited for the commander's response.

After a pause Heathside said, "So?"

"Wouldn't this be the ideal conditions to check it out? Isn't this weather fitting with its design?"

"Not exactly." The commander laughed. "Heavy fog is what that was designed for."

Maggie was really pushing now. "Can't you call together some gung-ho volunteers and really put this system to its test? After all, it can be justified since the mission is indirectly related to a call from your commander-in-chief in the White House? Actually, I can't believe that you're not taking advantage of this record-breaking weather to test your equipment."

"Maggie! Our equipment is being tested to the utmost as we speak. We're clearing the base and we're doing our best to help the National Guard. We're not sitting on our asses here!

"You don't give up. But you've got a point. I might have some jackasses here who want to prove their manhood as well and our equipment. I'll tell you what. I'll speak to some of my men and see what they say. But, that's all I can promise. It may indeed be possible. Call me first thing in the morning."

"Thank you, Roger. First thing." The phone snapped and crackled. The battery was lower still.

*

Only a skeleton crew was on duty at Scan-Man. Because of this lack of personnel and the switch to an internal power supply, most satellite functions were temporarily suspended and efforts were now concentrated on the storm eighty feet above.

Satellite input showed the northeastern U.S. and eastern Canada enveloped in solid cloud cover from Manhattan north and the Berkshires east. Two large lows had converged over eastern Massachusetts and were stalled. It appeared they would remain stalled, for there was no other weather movement within 1500 miles. There was no evidence indicating when the weather pattern would break. Ellen Bloodworth didn't even want to consider the potential snow depth.

Ellen was restless. Her job tonight was a drag. All day the thought had gnawed at her that Nat Webster's files might be in Randolph's office upstairs. To her, Nat's files were Nat. They represented all he stood for and worked toward. The files might also provide a clue as to where Nat had gone or where he might be hiding.

She could postpone the decision no longer. There would never be fewer people around. She left her machine and rode the elevator up to the ground floor. She then switched to another that carried her to the fifth floor of the Scan-man tower.

It was here the normal office functions were conducted and where the corporate offices were located. Ellen had visited the above ground facilities only three times since she joined Scan-Man, and Randolph's office only once.

The hallway was darkened, except for the exit and the elevator buttons. Ahead, dim lights shined through office doorways. All sounds were muffled by the carpeting.

Randolph's office was large, sumptuously furnished and ghostly vacant. Papers and file folders were stacked on a very low shelf that ran the length of the brown-tinted wall window. Ellen felt that, since the material she was looking for was current, it had to be either on or near Randolph's desk or, she feared, he may have taken it home to study. Her hunch was Randolph was already familiar with the material and therefore had not taken it home. But it was also possible he had given it to someone else.

There was nothing familiar to Ellen on his desk or near it. She tried his top drawer but it was locked. A heavy screwdriver, conveniently forgotten on a table at one end of the room, solved that problem. There was nothing in the top drawer. The folders wouldn't have fit, anyway. Nothing in the top left drawer. In the middle drawer, however, she recognized the material immediately. Her heart thumped. That idiot! She thought of Randolph, not believing her luck.

She gathered the folders lovingly and sat to briefly skim through them and make sure everything was there. Seconds had turned into minutes, however, when she was startled by the click of the elevator doors down the hall.

Quickly, she grabbed the folders and ducked under the kneehole of Randolph's desk. She listened for footsteps but could hear nothing.

The wait seemed endless. She was not even sure anyone had exited the elevator. She felt foolish hiding, and was about to move when the toes of two shoes abruptly extended under the front of the desk, just nudging her leg. They were women's shoes and they were large.

Ellen held her breath as she stared at those shoes that kept moving as the woman apparently examined the top of Randolph's desk. Ellen tried to remember how she had left the top of the desk. Neat? A mess? Did she shut the drawers?

The shoes then disappeared and Ellen was unable to tell which direction they went. She listened, hearing her own heart beat, but there was no clue, no sound.

"OK, Ellen. You can come out now." It was Margo Chin's voice. Sweat broke out across Ellen's forehead and the palms of her hands. What the hell am I going to do now? she thought. Does she know where I'm hiding? Is she just guessing I'm in the room?

She continued to wait, silently. Her heart seemed to skip every other beat. If discovered, how would she handle Margo? Would they fight? Could she take on Margo? How agile was she? Although Margo was a big woman, one could never tell her capabilities.

"I said, come out from under that desk," Margo said. Her voice was different, Ellen thought. It sounded strangely repugnant. It was not the voice she knew.

Ellen took a deep breath. She crawled, leaving the folders behind. Cautiously, she peered around the side of the desk and came face to face with the screwdriver she had used a few minutes earlier.

"Get up!"

As Ellen prepared to rise, she saw Margo's feet and legs move into an offensive position. Ellen rolled away and bounced to her feet. The screwdriver dug into the carpeting where she had just been kneeling. Margo was still gripping the handle. Ellen was unbelieving. What the hell was going on?

She looked at Margo and her face was contorted, as if she was psyched up or was trying to smile following several Novocain shots in the jaw.

Before Ellen could move, Margo was again pointing the weapon at her, holding it tightly at waist level.

"Hey! Hold on, Margo! What's with this?" Ellen stepped behind Randolph's swivel chair, put her foot on the back of it and thrust it full force along the carpeting toward Margo. It hit her sharply on the calves. Margo grunted, but it didn't stop her.

Ellen was now against the window. The desk was between her and the door. A file cabinet was on the other side. She reached for a heavy book lying on the low window ledge and threw it. Margo ducked. Ellen looked for another object, turning her head. Then Margo, screaming an inhuman guttural noise, dashed toward her, screwdriver raised high. Ellen crouched at the last second and caught Margo at knee level. She tumbled over Ellen and her head crashed against the window. Margo dropped, landing on a small steel sculpture of a lightning bolt that was set on the low window ledge.

Ellen leaped out of the way as Margo fell and saw her torso land atop the sculpture and then roll to the floor. She now lay on her back with the inverted piece of art erect, penetrating her chest.

Stunned, Ellen rushed to Margo's side in horror. There was nothing she could do. Margo was already lifeless. The screwdriver was still in her hand.

Ellen was shaking violently. What to do now? She thought. She looked around expecting to see someone else checking out the commotion. All was silent.

Ellen moved for the door, stopped, and returned for the folders. She had gone through too much to leave those behind. She decided she would not call for help – yet.

*

Time was running out. It was 9:15 p.m. and Margo had not yet reported in.

Pressures on Randolph continued to mount. The blackout had been unnerving. His home communications system was now useless so he had to switch to the mobile unit that had limited distance capability. Turk was now monitoring it.

Shortly after the power failure, he had called Scan-Man and was relieved to learn that the transition to emergency power had been satisfactory. He knew, however, that their own power generation was not sufficient to maintain all systems. With operations therefore greatly reduced, the data files were losing information that would be needed for studies and comparisons later on. The Earth continued to rotate inexorably and spew forth data second by second. Since data was not being captured and recorded, it was lost forever.

Against his better judgment, Randolph had mixed a third martini. His nerve ends were jangling, yet he somehow maintained a cool exterior. The party, the people, the restricted atmosphere battered him on one side. Scan-Man attacked him on the other. He was now uncommunicative.

"Why is it, in this modern, technological age, Marsha, you just happen to stock a thousand candles in your closet?" Peter Stevenson asked.

"That's easy," she laughed. "Primitive instincts, I guess. Perhaps somehow I know deep down, that with all this technology in the world, the whole bubble will eventually burst and we'll all be sent back to basics."

All of them laughed, except for Randolph whose thoughts were elsewhere. "That's good, Marsha," Stephenson said, smiling. Then, turning to Randolph, he added, "Do you agree with that, Ed?"

Randolph looked up, hearing his name. "What's that? I'm sorry. I'm thinking about Harrington's phone call."

"Come on, Ed, you old party pooper," Marsha said. "Can't you ever leave that job alone. Let's forget all the problems of the world and live it up tonight!"

*

It was 9:55 p.m. Randolph radioed Scan-Man from his mobile unit. There was no response after repeated tries.

"Damn her!" he said to himself. "What's going on over there?"

He couldn't imagine why Margo hadn't called him back earlier. She had nearly five hours to carry out her missions. He should have had at least some word that something was happening. Harrington would be calling momentarily. He needed answers.

In a virtual panic now, he ran through the house to the phone in his office, continuing to leave Turk stationed at the radio. He dialed the direct line to the Interpretation Room.

After several rings, someone answered.

"Let me speak with Margo Chin," he said abruptly.

"She's not here. I haven't seen her for an hour or so," the voice said, matter-of-factly.

"Well find her!" Randolph shouted.

There was a long pause at the other end. Cautiously and inquisitively, the voice asked, "Who's calling?"

Regaining control, Randolph apologized. "I'm sorry, but this is very important. This is Mr. Randolph."

The voice suddenly became all business. "Certainly, sir. You want me to find Margo. This might take some time. Do you want to hold?"

"No. Have her call me immediately."

"Yes sir."

*

At 10:05 p.m. Harrington's call came through at Turk's station. The phone crackled and for a moment and Harrington's voice was indistinct.

"Repeat," Randolph said.

"Did you know Bloodworth was a good friend of his?" The voice now came in strongly.

"Friend of whose?"

"Webster's, damn it!"

"No. But she was at the funeral and shed more tears than his wife."

Then came the inevitable question. "What's the story on Bloodworth?"

He stammered. "I ... I really don't know. I can't reach Margo. Something strange is going on. With this storm ... "

Harrington interrupted. "Don't let anything happen to her. She's very valuable to us now. She was a close teammate of Webster's. She may be able to manage the Energizer."

"Don't let anything happen to who?"

"To Bloodworth, Damn it!" Harrington barked.

"But you told me ... "

"I don't care what I told you. She's very important to us now that Webster's gone."

Randolph was thrown-off his equilibrium. "I really need some help up here. The storm is real bad. How are we going to shut it off? The power is cut back and we're on internal ... "

"We each have our little problems, Ed," Harrington said forcefully. "I'm working my butt off down here. This is going to be very, very important to you and me and the company. I expect the same of you. As I said before, I don't care how you do it. I'm not interested in your problems. I want results, not excuses."

The phone hummed and buzzed and Randolph could no longer hear his Washington caller. He swallowed hard. A flash of pain ran up a nerve and into his head.

"Hello. Hello." It was Harrington again.

"Yes, Chandler. I'm here. I got most of what you said. Things are going real well up here -- a bit of snow flurry activity, but nothing to get upset about -- nothing we can't completely control."

"I'm glad to hear that, Ed. You had me worried for a minute. I'm all the way down here and sometimes I get nervous when I hear doubt in my people's voices. No one ever said either of our jobs would be easy."

"I understand."

"We're meeting with the President again at noon tomorrow. I expect something concrete will materialize. I wish you were here for the excitement. Being stuck at home must really be a drag. The storm up there has really thrown these people into a shock. It's the best thing that could have happened to sell this project. The proof is in the pudding, they say." Harrington laughed heartily.

*

Shortly before midnight, following a gradual increase in temperature, the snow ended and a light rain began to fall into the four-foot accumulation that now lay on the ground and rooftops. Word spread quickly of the change in precipitation and hopes were raised that this might finally be the end of the storm and that the treacherous white blanket might soon be beaten down and washed away.

The rain fell with increasing volume, silently, into the soft snow. As the water was absorbed, the snow depth was reduced, making it more concentrated, heavier, lethal.

Imperceptibly, the effect of the greatly increased weight was felt on the sleeping town. Flat-roofed wooden buildings were the first to feel the effects.

226

MONDAY, DECEMBER 24

The hike back to the apartment from Peters Airfield took more than three hours. For Ellen, this was the truest test of her physical readiness for the Tibetan climb. Each foot of the way she fought the fierce winds and deep snow. She relied heavily on her outdoor instincts to carry her through the darkness.

Snowshoes made the otherwise impossible journey practical, although near the end, when the rain began, the webbed feet took on altogether different characteristics. For the last half mile, the combination of melting and wet snow stuck to the webbing and accumulated, making them cumbersome and unwieldy. Yet without them, she would have submerged helplessly.

Although the exercise stimulated her physically, she felt psychologically drained. The grotesque but brief scuffle with Margo had unnerved her. The horror of blind attack and bloody demise had not been dulled by the storm. Yet the satisfaction of having escaped alive and, with Nat's files, helped ease the incomprehensibility of it all.

The knowledge that her job at Scan-Man was unofficially ended contributed to her enervation. She had loved her work, but for the time being at least, it didn't appear she was welcome.

For three hours the potential problems arising from her confrontation with Margo occupied her mind. The storm seemed to take on secondary importance. Her mind became a swirling eddy of potential problems. She wanted desperately to talk with someone about them.

She didn't know what to do about it. Yesterday, Maggie had advised not going to the police. But now the situation was infinitely more complicated. Had she envisioned this happening, might that have changed things? Who should she report it to? If she did report it, how would she explain her presence in Randolph's office?

Ellen was quite sure no one had seen her leave the building tonight. She was reasonably sure no one had seen her arrive at work, also. Even the doorman was absent and the building was open to anyone who wanted to wander in, although in this storm it was unlikely.

Had Margo seen Ellen arrive at work? How did Margo know Ellen was in Randolph's office? She could have followed her, but then the time lag was too great. It could simply have been coincidence, for Margo's office was somewhere in the tower, possibly near Randolph's.

Ellen had cleared herself of all guilt in Margo's death. For this reason she was reluctant to report it. She had been an innocent, or nearly innocent, bystander when Margo had come along. Margo had been the aggressor – on two separate occasions. Ellen could not justify any compassion for Margo under these circumstances.

But was it at Margo's own initiative to kill Ellen? She doubted it. It had be someone higher up -- possibly Randolph himself. If it were him, Ellen still wasn't safe. Someone else might be sent after her.

She wondered who would find Margo. What would be thought about the bizarre situation? What happened to Margo's hand that clutched the screwdriver? Would that be found? Since that screwdriver had been used to break into Randolph's desk, would Margo be blamed for the act?

So many questions. All of them unanswered.

228

It was well after 2 a.m. when Ellen arrived home. She was tempted to awaken Maggie and share her fears and frustrations. Morning would be soon enough.

Her apartment was warm but dark, as if it had been abandoned. She was quickly reminded of the blackout. Phil's coal furnace must be operating, she thought. In the candlelight, however, the thermometer read sixty degrees. But after the last few hours, sixty felt like a heat wave.

It had been her intention to begin reading Nat's files, but she only had time to wash up and sip a cup of hot chocolate before exhaustion overtook her. The distance to the bed seemed endless, and when her head hit the pillow she was asleep.

*

The rain continued throughout the night, sometimes heavily, at other times as a fine mist. The snow layer became a lead-heavy blanket, covering the entire Northeast.

Then, before dawn, the temperature dropped rapidly as the cold and warm fronts altered their positions. The rain changed back to small snow crystals and the sodden snow cover began to freeze into a tough, white armor.

*

It was a little after 6 a.m. when Ellen banged on the door leading to the Billings' section of the house. She had slept soundly for four hours and was now rested, but had awakened out of habit. Maggie should be up by now, she thought.

Groggy, half asleep, Phil opened the door and greeted his surprised tenant. "Sorry," he said with a weak smile, "the custodian is on strike and refuses to stoke the furnace."

"Sorry to wake you, Phil. Where's Maggie?"

"Come on in. I'll put the coffee on." Phil turned and slowly made his way through the dark corridor toward the kitchen. Ellen followed hesitantly. "Maggie's at the hotel. She spent the night there." He yawned. The governor's there and I guess he brought a whole basket of problems with him." He lighted a couple of candles on the kitchen table. Then, looking up at Ellen, he said, "Hey! Did you walk home from work again this morning?"

"I had an incredible night last night, Phil, and I desperately need someone to lay it on."

Waiting for the coffee water to boil, Phil returned to the table and sat opposite Ellen. "I'm not quite awake yet, but I'm ready when you are."

Ellen told her story. Phil became increasingly astounded, reluctant to move despite the screaming kettle. "So, I really don't know how to handle it. I don't know where to turn."

Phil said nothing. He wanted to be sure that when he did it would be the right thing. Instead, he poured the water into the instant coffee, offered Ellen the milk and sugar, and sat again, stirring. He looked at Ellen, and with a smile, slowly shook his head.

"First of all, I think you're blameless," he began. "If you are quite certain you were not seen, I would not report the incident. You can justify this on the many grounds that you have already justified it in your own mind.

"I'll modify that a bit. I would not report it until everything else quiets down. To expect a police investigation when everyone's hands are totally tied up in this storm is ridiculous. The whole story, if we take it from the beginning is so complicated it's mind-boggling. I'd advise you to wait a few days. Certainly don't go back to Scan-Man. The weather is perfect justification for staying away."

"I feel a lot more comfortable after that," Ellen said. "Thanks."

"Why were you in Randolph's office?"

"Oh," Ellen said, surprised for not having told Phil the obvious. "I went after Nat's files. You remember the files I forged the requisition slip for?"

"Sure do. Isn't that the point at which all this trouble started? Didn't you suspect at the time that they might discover you?"

Ellen looked sheepish. "You're right. I did." Then she looked right at him. "I sure didn't know at the time that what I was looking at was important enough for them to want to kill me. I was only looking for clues about Nat. Now I have to study those files. In fact, I should begin right now."

"You have them in your apartment?"

Ellen smiled. "You bet I have them. They're very important to me. I'm going to find out what happened to Nat."

*

The bed bounced violently. It was a tremendous thud -- a single, monumental, dull thump -- much like an underground mine explosion.

Maggie sat erect immediately, puzzled. Her first thought was an earthquake. She prepared herself for a secondary tremor. None came. The room was dark and very little light penetrated the window. She automatically reached for the bedside lamp and turned the switch before realizing the electricity was still out.

There was no heat. The room was icy cold. Something terrible was happening, although she knew not what, and a shiver of the unknown ran her full length.

Seconds later she heard muffled screaming and shouting. She threw back the covers and leaped to the balcony door. Opening it, she was met by a frigid blast of wintry air. Gasping, she stepped back into the room. The atrium roof was gone!

Her heart pounded. Her breath felt squeezed from her chest. Cautiously stepping out toward the balcony again, she looked down. The giant dome, with all its girders, lay in a jumbled heap below, partially covered with mountains of snow.

From her perspective, and through the dim light and falling flakes, she saw a dozen people clustered at the far end of what was, a few minutes ago, the Garden Room. Some were screaming uncontrollably. Others shouted and gesticulated. It was a frozen outdoor scene and the high-pitched voices were muted in its enormity.

She snapped out of it. She was cold, noticing only now that she was dressed scantily in panties and bra. She rushed back into the room and attempted to locate her clothes. Slowly, as she dressed, the realization fully overtook her that a calamity had taken place. Many people may have been hurt as a result.

Fifteen minutes later she was at the entrance to the Garden Room. Looking up, she saw that the entire dome over the area had fallen one hundred feet, burying everything below. The sky was beginning to lighten ever so slightly as the new day's snowflakes, large and soft, fell soundlessly, innocently. At points around the circumference of the room, people with flashlights were already attempting to find crawl spaces under the rubble.

As she stood at the edge of the horror, she saw Puff.

"Terrible! Incredibly terrible! There are dozens of people under there and we can't get at them. I don't know what to do. You know what I mean? I can't find Freddie. Most of them are lobby people, but I know some NSA people are trapped also.

"I don't know what happened," Puff said. "A group of us were having an early breakfast and I had to go to the bathroom, you know what I mean? On my way back I heard the crash. I don't know where Freddie is. Oh, mother of God! Oh, I don't know where to get help," Her eyes eagerly searched the area.

"I've got to find Freddie." She ran off.

Maggie was debating what to do next when she spotted the flagpole figure of Dr. Krentzler. He was walking unsteadily, slowly making his way toward her, climbing over lengths of beam and through piles of snow. Maggie hurried over to him.

"It's nothing," he said in answer to Maggie. "Something hit it." He sat on a beam and Maggie examined his bony shin.

"Were you here when the roof fell?"

"Yes. A bunch of us were about to eat. I'd gone over to the serving counters to help myself, and it happened. There was no warning. It just fell. Poof! I don't see how anyone under there can be alive."

"How many?"

"Oh, God! I'd guess there are fifty of us and I don't know how many lobby people -- maybe fifty more."

"One hundred people!" Maggie gasped. "We'd better see what we can do."

"I think I'll go back to my room to look after this leg."

"The leg's OK, doctor. We could really use you here."

Krentzler swung around and wordlessly hobbled away.

Maggie turned as someone emerged from under the debris. "I've found some of them! This is an entrance!"

Maggie ran over to the spot the man indicated. He had a flashlight. She followed him in. Cautiously they felt their way, on hands and knees in places. Moments later they came across a dozen people lying on the ground, around the base of what Maggie recognized to be the Tahitian Atoll. The raised floor of the atoll had caught one end of a beam that now formed an angle to the floor. Those under this protected area were alive.

Maggie performed a quick triage of the victims and was relieved to learn that only one appeared to be seriously wounded. That was a head injury. The others had multiple cuts and lacerations and possibly broken bones. All were still recovering from intense fright and possible claustrophobia. She helped carry out the woman with the head injury. The others were asked to wait their turn.

Back out from under, she was glad to see some EMTs from the lobby of the hotel. They were attempting to care for some of the victims. They had no medical equipment except drug store-type household kits.

A moment later, pandemonium. Two more caves of victims had been found. Many people were dead, and, according to the reports, others were dying. They needed help. They needed volunteers.

"I'm going for help," Maggie told the EMTs.

"Lotsa luck, lady," was the skeptical response.

*

The lobby was nearly vacant. Those able to do so had wandered to other parts of the hotel. Only those unable to move, and those who were watching over them, remained.

Maggie reached for her cell phone. She was relieved she had some power.

She dialed the police station. The line was busy. She hung up and then dialed again. Busy. A fifth time. Then the battery gave up.

Governor Fitzwilliam's presence at her side startled her as she spun around in frustration.

"Did you come up with anything last night?"

She was shocked. "Are you aware of the catastrophe we have right here in this hotel, governor?"

"I am. But I'm sorry to say it's not unique. I conferred with my office only minutes ago and there are similar catastrophes all over the state -- indeed, throughout New England. Please understand, Maggie. I must return to the office."

Initially, Maggie was aghast at Fitzwilliam's apparent selfishness. Her thoughts were focused on her immediate surroundings. Counting to ten, and reconsidering the broader aspects of the storm, it was narrow-minded of her to discount the governor's plight entirely. The regional scope of the storm was beyond her imagination, beyond her responsibilities, and she was not about to ignore the people of Hollandson for the sake of Fitzwilliam's convenience. Her people needed medication. There was no guessing how many others in Hollandson also needed help.

The thought of a deal crossed her mind. Perhaps she could barter with him. This might be something he could understand.

"I need medical supplies. Can you arrange to provide some for me?"

"What do you mean?"

"I mean I want you to arrange for a quantity of emergency medical supplies. I'll pick them up in Boston with the transportation I arrange for you. My problems are here. Yours are there. Make the trip worth my while and I'll try my damnedest to get you there."

Fitzwilliam only needed a moment to decide. "I think I can arrange it."

The next item, since the first request had gone so smoothly was what she considered a wild idea, but one which could make an infinite difference. "I need a snow cat -- you know -- the kind that is used on the ski slopes."

"For Christ's sake!" Fitzwilliam felt that Maggie was pressing her luck. "Finding an available snow cat in this weather is like ... "

"You're the governor. Can you do it?"

"I'll get to work on it," he said, resigning himself to his fate.

"I need an answer in a half hour. We have to move out quickly."

Heathside! Maggie automatically pulled out her cell phone. Then she remembered.

She called after Fitzwilliam. "Lend me your phone for a few minutes."

She dialed Peters Airfield. "Sorry, ma'am. The commander is not on duty."

"This is a dire emergency. Where can I reach him? This is Maggie Billings."

"Who please?" The phone signal was weak.

"Dammit, officer! Commander Heathside is expecting my call.

Please tell me where I can reach him now." Her voice carried the necessary urgency to stir the duty officer into action.

"Hold on please, ma'am." The wait seemed interminable.

She looked at her watch. Seven. Finally, the Commander answered,

"Roger? Maggie. When can I pick up the helicopter?" She knew this was presumptuous of her, but anything less was sure to get her nowhere. "We've just had a more than a hundred casualties at the hotel. The roof has fallen in, quite literally."

"I'm afraid I haven't acted on your request."

"With all due respect, Roger, I have dozens of people who either need to be evacuated or treated. I can achieve both if I can get to Boston. You gave me some encouragement last night that you would cooperate. If it's any assurance to you, as Civil Defense director in Hollandson, I'll take all responsibility for the consequences. Can you secure a chopper and crew immediately? I have three passengers, including myself and the Governor."

"To Boston? That's a hell of a flight." The phone crackled.

"Can you do it?"

"I can try with volunteers."

"Fantastic! When can you confirm this?"

"Call me at noon."

"How about a half hour?"

The commander chuckled. "You're impossible, but I'll try."

"You'll be remembered, Roger, when we recap this storm in the *Bulletin*. Please do everything you can. Many lives are at stake. Every minute counts."

Maggie's adrenalin was shooting the rapids. She dialed the police station again. Wilson answered with a grunt. She explained the situation at the hotel and asked that more EMTs be sent up.

The chief replied that the hotel was not alone. They were having problems at the school. A gang had volunteered to shovel off the roof, but it was very tough going. The new addition to the school had collapsed, but fortunately it was unoccupied.

"Things are bad all over town. I'll see who I can get for you, but don't count on anyone."

"Well, I'm trying to get emergency medical supplies and transportation. A snow cat would really be an asset. Don't you agree?"

"Yes. So would a sunny day and ninety degrees."

"You can really be nauseating sometimes," Maggie said.

"Hell yes we can use a snow cat," the chief said, dropping his sarcasm. "But where?"

"We'll see," Maggie teased with a chuckle. "This is your friendly CD working."

"Ha! Speak to you later, Mag."

"And don't call me Mag!" Maggie smiled to herself. She needed that light touch every once in a while.

She returned to the Garden Room. The light from a new dawn had just begun to penetrate the snowy skies. To her annoyance, she noticed several of the wounded were stretched out, on the floor. They were uncovered and obviously cold. Snow was accumulating on their clothing.

Muttering to herself, she turned to some bystanders. "Please. Go to the rooms and bring back all the blankets you can find. These people must be covered and moved." Glad to be useful, they rushed off.

Maggie went over to the victims, kneeled, and spoke reassuringly to them. Doing so, she was startled to recognize Vito. He was unconscious and bleeding heavily from an ugly gash on his forehead. She pulled a kerchief from her pocket and tied it over the wound. The bleeding stopped. She checked his pulse and breathing, both of which were rapid. He was cold. She shivered, looked at him again, and shook her head sadly.

Activity at the edge of the room caught her attention. She saw Puff emerge from a cave between the main floor and another level. She was sobbing. Another person had his arm around her.

"Freddy's dead. He was trying to help the lobby people and he died with them." She let her tears flow freely. "This damned snow. Why?"

238

Fred Chabus dead? Maggie thought. The man who had asked her to keep Nat Webster's secret? The man with the brilliant mind? Dead!

More screaming and running. The roof beams had groaned, shifted and settled some more. Volunteers jumped aside. Others rushed out of the caves.

"Let me out of this goddamned place," Puff said loudly, working it into a scream. "Everybody can rot, as far as I'm concerned."

*

The front-end loader groaned under its burden. The driver fought the controls, attempting to take an efficient bite from the icy snowfield that had been a well-traveled road.

It was monotonous work -- very tiring. All day: a hard drive forward with the bucket down, raise the bucket, reverse, turn and drive to the side of the road, dump bucket, reverse, and then drive hard forward again with the bucket down. At this rate he had only cleared three or four miles a day. Meanwhile the snow continued to fall, piling it all up again behind him. He'd give anything for a good look at the warm sun again.

The driver was suddenly jolted out of his daydreaming. A huge red object dropped from his bucket, rolled down the snow bank and hit the front of the loader.

Puzzled, the driver backed up, stopped, and craned his neck out the window. My God! It was a car! He climbed down from his machine to examine the vehicle more closely. It was a sub-compact, bright red and nearly new. Now it was ready for the junk heap. He peered through the broken window and saw nothing unusual.

Scratching his head, he looked again at the little car. Its rooftop was just under snow level. There was no way he could have seen it.

He climbed back up into the cab and maneuvered the bucket so the car was righted and the wrecker could haul it off. He'd have to be more careful, he thought to himself.

*

Ellen now lounged on her couch at home, wrapped in a heavy robe, legs blanket-covered, feet in wool socks. Beside her on the table were a hot chocolate and a stack of Nat Webster's files. She intended to read them thoroughly for she now had plenty of time.

The first folder she opened described the potential uses of the "Energizer" carried by Scanner XII. Its principle was described as "simple," acting as a mini-sun, sending concentrated heat and energy to the earth's surface by means of a "Searoc Beam."

The original concept of the Energizer was its application toward modifying local and regional weather patterns. The beam generated by the Energizer creates heat either at the earth's surface or at any of numerous levels of the atmosphere. The heat generated at the designated elevation alters the physical consistency of the atmosphere, and therefore, the weather. It can drive out a destructive weather pattern or push in beneficial weather.

The potential includes diverting hurricanes and tornados, and softening crop-damaging frosts. Its use can revolutionize agriculture by providing precipitation on an on-call basis. On the grander scale, Webster described "homogenization" of weather -- softening the harsh extremes of drought and torrential rains and providing precipitation and fair weather to areas of respective need.

Depending on the use demanded of the Energizer, weather control could be local, regional or cover several states. The effects on neighboring states or countries not wishing to participate could be minimally affected.

Webster went into great detail describing alterations to the jet stream. The Searoc Beam carried the capability of straightening or deepening the waves of the jet stream. As a result, winters in the northern hemisphere could be moderated by fencing in cold, arctic air, or cooling the summer heat by drawing it south.

A warning, Ellen noticed, accompanied Webster's proposals.

"With restraint, a multitude of beneficial uses could be manifested to ease mankind from the burden of extremes which affect his life, safety and well-being." Used otherwise, Webster wrote, "The probability existed that the entire global weather system could shift out of phase and become an uninhabitable mixing bowl of atmospheric extremes that might continue unchecked for years."

Ellen laid the folder on her lap, tipped her head back, and gazed at the ceiling, contemplating the significance of the material. Could the Energizer now fall into the hands of unscrupulous people? With Nat no longer at the helm of the project, who would now guide it? Was there a danger, not only for her, but also for the world at large? It appeared that if men like Randolph, who seemed to be capable of killing people, commanded the Energizer, Nat's warning might yet materialize.

The whole prospect of weather manipulation in the hands of fanatics, Ellen thought, was a totally frightening concept.

She turned to the next folder.

*

It was 7:30 a.m. when Maggie called Heathside again.

"You're in luck, Maggie. I have a crew of eager hotshots, bored with the storm and being grounded, and eager to demonstrate their manhood. The mission will be entirely in their hands. Frankly, we've been looking for an opportunity to test the new Pinpoint Ground Touchdown equipment. Albeit extremely dangerous, this thick weather is ideal," said the commander, his voice confident. "Under these extraordinary circumstances I can justify the risks. Each of you must, however, sign forms. This is not pleasure cruise.

"It's zero seven forty now. Be at Hanger 12 in two hours. Good luck."

*

Fitzwilliam's chubby aide intercepted Maggie in the corridor. "The governor has good news and wants to see you."

"Good. Tell him we'll meet in the lobby in ten minutes."

*

The Governor was waiting impatiently when Maggie arrived. "It's all set," he said. "Medical supplies will be waiting at Pier One, East Boston."

"And the snow cat?"

"That too. In the terminal building."

Maggie was jubilant. "Good work, Fitzy. And I have a helicopter waiting for us at Peters Airfield. We don't have much time."

"I'll get ready."

"I assume you have a jumpsuit and boots?" Maggie asked with as straight a face as she dared, knowing Fitzwilliam would soon reject her offer.

"What?" he asked, totally uncomprehending.

"I'm just kidding," she said with a smile. "But we will have to jump from the chopper. Probably parachute. The commander says the helicopter can't land in this wind and deep snow."

The governor was beginning to understand.

"Although the visibility will be near zero," Maggie continued, "they have a new piece of equipment that will pinpoint where we hover."

242

Fitzwilliam's countenance progressively faded as Maggie talked. "Have you lost your mind? If you think I'm going to jump out of an airplane, you're on the skids." He tightened his jaw. "Look. You promised me transportation into town. I got you this stuff. Now ... "

"You still have my promise. I propose using the snow cat if you choose not to fly. The cat is more reliable and considerably safer. I should be back from town by late afternoon. If that's convenient for you ... "

"Damn, damn, damn!" He stamped his foot again. "It's nothing but one delay after another. Why can't things be simple?"

"I thought you'd understand," Maggie said, tongue in cheek. "It was you who said the weather was extreme. It was you who took the chance and ventured out here yesterday. I have one alternative. Do you want to borrow my snowmobile?"

The Governor shouted. "No! I don't. I'll see you this afternoon," He turned and stalked away.

Maggie turned on her trusty cell phone. She would call Phil to see if he would accompany her. "Blast! I've got to get this thing charged."

*

Snow is fundamentally related to climate and the coming and going of the glaciers. It is by far our greatest source of fresh water.

*

The snowmobile bucked and leaped through the fresh snow, throwing waves of disturbed flakes up from the runners and over the windshield. Last night's rain had frozen and left an excellent base for the machine. At this rate, Maggie thought, she and Phil were certain to make their appointment at Hanger 12 with ease.

The schedule was tight. When she arrived home a half hour later, she found a note from Phil saying he'd gone for the day. He'd be making house checks with the rescue crews. From the freshness of the tracks leaving the garage, she guessed they had just missed each other.

Checking the apartment, she found Ellen comfortably supine, reading. Reluctant to be interrupted at first, that was quickly changed after the airborne mission was explained.

While Ellen readied herself, Maggie changed into her rugged, wool clothing and windbreaker. She then dashed off a note to Phil explaining what had been happening at the hotel and what her plans were. "Hopefully," her note ended, "we can look forward to a quiet Christmas Eve together."

Now, approaching Peters Airfield, a sense-of excitement and adventure coursed through the women's veins. Ellen saw it as a welcome distraction from the distressing events at Scan-Man. The change would clear her head. Beyond this, it was another adventure in the snow, with a new twist.

From the little Maggie had told her, they were in for a rough-and-tumble copter ride to Boston. It was unlikely they would land because of the high winds and blinding conditions, coupled with blowing snow at surface level. It looked as though a jump would be necessary, either by parachute or with rappel lines. Either way, Ellen looked forward to it.

It was just last fall that Ellen logged her 100th jump at the Sport Parachuting Center in Orange, Massachusetts. Until now, she considered jumping a spring-summer-fall activity. True, she had jumped twice in the winter, on sparkling, crisp days in January when only the whisper of a breeze altered vertical descent to the target. Landing in fresh snow was fun. Shaking it out of the equipment was the unpleasant part.

To Maggie, the upcoming flight and potential jump represented an interesting, even unique, means to a necessary end. If acquiring medicine and a snow cat required a helicopter and a parachute, that's what it would be.

Yes. Of course she was nervous about jumping under unusual conditions. But if Ellen could do it, so could she. She'd follow Ellen's example. Simple – if not totally stupid!

The closest she had come to parachuting in recent years was a hang glider experience in New Hampshire. The *Bulletin* was planning on running a special monthly feature on outdoor leisure activities. The topic of hang gliding took her to New Hampshire, and the desire to shoot some captivating photographs led her to participate by taking flight lessons. She shot her photos on the third flight. Adventure of this magnitude turned her on.

As they approached Peters Airfield, they could see the airport tower between the breaks in the snowy gusts. Beyond that were what looked like the hangers. Off to one side was the Scan-Man complex and the huge antennas. Ellen felt a thud in her chest as she caught a glimpse of the tallest of the Scan-Man buildings that housed Randolph's office. She wondered about Margo, but then abruptly turned her head toward the airfield and sucked in a deep breath of fresh air.

*

The women arrived at Hanger 12 at 9:30 a.m. It was easy to find because it was the only one with activity around it. A large military vehicle with plow was clearing an area in front of the hanger. The wind was blowing wildly across the open field and the truck was jockeying to keep ahead of the snow as it drifted back into the clearing. Horizontal tails blew from the tops of the man-made piles like mini, snow-covered mountain peaks. The wind was cold, penetrating, and

245

individual snowflakes snapped against the women's parkas they ran to the door.

Inside was a cold, metallic world. The hanger was a cavernous echo chamber of mechanical noises. Men's shouting drew the women's attention to a helicopter near the front of the building. Giant stepladders were set up around it and mechanics appeared to be making adjustments. The women walked toward the activity, shaking and brushing snow from their clothing.

Maggie asked for Captain Redford. A hand pointed to a figure studying the tail section of the aircraft.

"Captain Redford?" she asked.

The man turned his attention to the women. Brown, wavy hair swept along the sides of his cap. A short handlebar mustache graced his upper lip. His jaw was muscular. But it was his the eyes that captured Maggie. They were deep-set and commanding. Redford was handsome. Maggie guessed his age somewhat near hers.

"We're ... "

"I can guess," Redford interrupted loudly, a leering smile crossing his face. "You two must be the broads who want the Army to help you commit suicide!"

Maggie immediately bristled defensively. "Don't flatter yourself, flyboy. You stick to your toy. We'll do the rest."

Redford drew back slightly, in surprise. His voice softened. The smile changed to good humor. "Hey, hey! I like you!" he cheered enthusiastically. "We're gonna get along just great!"

"Now that we understand each other, let's start over again. My name's Maggie Billings and this is Ellen Bloodworth. You understand our mission?"

246

"I sure hope so, honey," Redford answered, his face now serious. His accent Ellen tried to place from Virginia or North Carolina. "The commander briefed me."

"Let's check it out." Maggie was all business. She pulled a notebook from her pocket. "This chopper's equipped with the PTLA system?"

"Roger. But as the commander must have told you, it hasn't been commissioned yet."

"What do you mean, captain?" Ellen asked, speaking for the first time.

"Your friend here, if she hasn't told you, is using the Army's experimental navigating system to help us find our way through this white stuff. It's still an unproven system."

"Captain," Maggie interrupted. "We don't have much time." And then to Ellen. "I'll explain later." And back to Redford. "Parachutes for two, and altimeters?"

"All set." Redford said. Then, looking at Ellen with interest. "Ever jump out of an airplane before, honey?"

It was Ellen's turn to bristle. "I get the impression, my dear captain," she said in a controlled voice, "you think we just came out of the kitchen. Do us a favor and knock off the chauvinistic bullshit!"

Ellen was a few inches taller than Redford. She stepped directly up and stared down at him, forcing him to back away. His expression now changed from amusement to anger.

Maggie cut in, reinforcing Ellen. "I thought you got the message a few minutes ago, captain. Let's cut the crap and get on with the mission. This may be a game to you, but it's not for us. Several people have already died this morning and the more we fool around, the more will die. We had hoped with your cooperation we could count on the Army."

Redford was silent. His jaw was clenched, muscles tightening at either side.

"Briefly now," Maggie continued, pretending nothing had happened, while Ellen continued to glare. "We're going to climb above this mess which we estimate to be at 9,000 feet. Is that about it, Ellen? Ellen!"

Ellen turned. "Probably more like 11,000. There are going to be some hummocks to climb over."

"We'll then fly directly east, put the captain's PTLA to work and attempt to land on Pier One, East Boston."

Redford nodded. His expression was boredom.

"But," Maggie continued, "if the system fails, or appears to be inaccurate, it means an alternative. We may have to jump or rappel."

"Well, I look at it this way," Ellen said happily, as much to tease Redford as for any other reason. "This'll be my first jump through snow clouds. It'll be a nice contrast to those boring, sunny, Sunday afternoons in Orange."

Redford cocked his head with interest. "Then you have jumped before?"

"Why? Hasn't everyone?" Ellen said, straight-faced.

"Both of you are jumpers?" He was incredulous.

"Ellen has 300 free falls under her belt and has competed on the U.S. Sport Parachuting Team."

"And just to put your mind at ease," Ellen joined in, "Maggie has several jumps on her record, carries her private pilot's license, and wears a brown belt in Karate."

Redford's jaw softened. "Whew-ee. I'll bet you wear burlap underwear! I like you girls. I'm sorry if I came on strong. But ... "

"We're not the mutual admiration society," Maggie added, "but you gave us the impression you thought we were a couple of lovelies in Maidenforms."

"Let's get ready to move out." Redford looked at his watch. "We'll depart at 1015 hours. Strap yourselves up in ten minutes." He turned and resumed examining the tail section.

Maggie motioned Ellen to step aside. "God! You were great. He's a handsome bugger, but hotshots like that just burn the bedickens out of me."

"I had no idea you'd done any jumping," Ellen said. "I was just laying on the baloney for the Captain's benefit." She giggled. "Burlap underwear... hah!"

"I guess he has every reason to believe it. But no. I've never jumped. If we have to, I'll need some real quick lessons.

"You're a nut!" Ellen laughed. "But seriously. What's this all about?"

"Simple. We're going into Boston to pick up some medical supplies and a snow cat. I called my buddy Commander Heathside earlier this morning and arranged it all."

She then switched to a serious tone. "Ellen. The atrium roof collapsed early this morning. Several people were killed and many badly injured. The place is a madhouse. The governor is still there -- marooned with the rest of them. He's chomping at the bit to get back to Boston and wanted to come on this flight, until I told him he might have to jump. He backed off quickly. He's a pain! The damned fool practically lost his whole caravan in the snow yesterday fighting his way out here. Then he discovered the TV crews didn't show up!" Maggie laughed. "All that effort and no publicity. Serves him right to be stuck out here. The only problem is, he's become everyone else's problem child."

"My night wasn't all that rosy either, Maggie. I think I killed ... "

The helicopter engine started, filling the hanger with deafening reverberations. Maggie looked at Ellen and shouted. "It's like being inside a truck exhaust muffler! Let's go!"

Ellen's last words were lost in the confusion. They ran for the helicopter, shaped like an oval hotdog roll with two rotors atop. They jumped aboard and sat together in webbed seats. Fastening the unfamiliar harnesses took several minutes. Pilot and co-pilot were forward. Behind them was the navigator. Two crewmen sat at the rear of the passenger area. One showed the women how to put on and adjust the headsets and microphone. The first voice they heard was Redford's speaking with a mechanic connected by headset to the exterior of the craft.

Now the hanger doors were opened and the wind and snow gusted in. The side door of the chopper was still open as they skimmed the floor of the hanger to the outside. The downdraft of the rotors stirred up the snow on the runway reducing visibility to zero from where Ellen and Maggie sat. In spite of their heavy clothing, they shivered at the sight of the maelstrom. A winter blast filled the interior until one of the crew rushed forward to slide the door closed.

Redford's voice now spoke to his passengers. "For the ladies' benefit, I'll tell you this is going to be an interesting ride. It won't be your ordinary commute to Boston. We're going to have a few bumps and bruises, but this old baby will take it. She's built to withstand 30-knot gusts, but we'll put her through a lot stronger today. Our real enemy will be ice. Anything could happen. Hang on."

The helicopter was not heated. It was a bare shell, containing only the rudimentary necessities. It was a functional combat machine, designed to deliver troops from one spot to another in the most efficient manner. The troops would be fully laden with combat equipment; each would be filled with fear of the unknown; none of them would have any thoughts of creature comforts. Thoughts would dwell on survival of the next few hours of the mission and what would wait for them on the ground when they hit it after a mass exodus at 2,500 feet.

Maggie herself now felt like a combat soldier on a similar mission. Yes, she was nervous – very nervous. The unknown of what lay ahead was little different from battle. She looked at Ellen and winked. Ellen winked back. Tension eased immediately.

"Functional," Maggie thought. That's all she needed. And Heathside gave it to her. He promised her a capable pilot.

Capable? Hopefully. Obnoxious? Undoubtedly. She could live with the obnoxious.

The rotor speed increased. The shell vibrated. The noise out-screamed the storm. A few words from Redford to the tower. No answer from the tower.

"Seems to be very little air traffic today," the co-pilot joked. "The tower's asleep. All clear, captain."

The rotors spun as if they would pull away from the plane. The wind buffeted the vehicle as its runners pulled free of the ground. Stony, deadpan expressions remained with the crew. It was a sulking look, as if they had come along against their will. Or, maybe they were just bored or, more likely, wanted to appear bored. Redford was all business now. Pilot, co-pilot and navigator exchanged a steady chatter of information. Maggie and Ellen tightened their harnesses and gripped the seat with their gloved hands. Conversation between them was possible via radio, but chitchat was not allowed in flight. Each tried to think of other times in other places.

The chopper began a pendulum rock as it leaned forward into the wind. It bucked and swung. First the tail lifted, and then the nose. Then it seemed to slide to the right and then, with a slam, slide to the left.

"Three thousand," someone said.

The climb was slow, agonizingly. Snow, tiny wisps of it, entered the cabin around the edges of the door. The powdery substance skitted around the floor, and formed crazy patterns. It settled into the handle-holds of the compartment doors on the floor, but then was vibrated out and slithered along to another crevasse.

"Six thousand."

More than half way, Maggie thought, with some relief.

The cabin was dim. The windows were of no use since there was no sun or visibility. A dozen cabin lights glowed along the ceiling, but they were not so much as to give light as to prevent darkness.

Their ears popped again. The plane was not pressurized. A violent motion caused Maggie to hit the back of her head against the wall. Her wool cap helped cushion it. She muttered. Ellen looked at her and winked, as if to say she was enjoying the ride. Maggie forced a smile in return.

"Seven thou ... " and the bottom fell out as if the machine had just plummeted off the edge of a cliff. The chopper turned on its side and blood surged into the passengers' heads. The pilot's voices became a staccato, yet still under control, when a giant hand came up from beneath and caught them. The pressure was eased from the tops of their heads, and dropped heavily into their cheeks, before returning to normal.

Redford's boisterous laugh. "How we doin' back there cowgirls? You asked for it, you got it!"

Maggie pulled her mike down to her mouth. "One more time, cap. This is more fun than a romp between the sheets."

More laughter from the forward cabin. Even the crew in the rear smiled.

"We only lost five hundred feet, girls. Just a little pocket. Nothing serious."

"Thanks for the info, Captain." My breakfast thanks you also."

Laughter was now turning to glee. Everyone felt better.

"Seven thousand." The navigator got it out this time.

The chatter relaxed Maggie. The tightening in her crotch was beginning to loosen. The tension was easing. The chopper seemed to he handling a little better.

"Eight thousand."

"Is the sky lightening up there?" Ellen asked of no one in particular over the radio.

"Won't be long now, sister. We're soon gonna see that sun."

"Nine thousand." The engines were still straining. The snow was no longer beating against the windows. They we now well up into the clouds -- a thick fog.

Definitely lighter above, Maggie thought, peering out and upward. Another drop. Maggie's head snapped back and the pressure returned to the top of her head. Then, just as suddenly, the plane slammed upward and her jaw dropped. She groaned.

"Ten thousand." The navigator sounded either triumphant or he couldn't believe the chopper could gain that altitude.

"We're breaking through," said Redford. Wispy clouds swept by, breaking, filling in, breaking, breaking, filling in.

Then -- it was clear. The clouds, very gradually, were left below. On all sides, however, mountainous thunderheads. It was a relief to everyone to see daylight. The sun's reflection on the crests of the clouds was breathtaking.

The chopper now snaked between the mountains, simultaneously continuing to fight for altitude. Ears popped again.

The engine appeared to be working with less strain. The women turned in their seats as the chopper finally climbed above the last cloud mountain. Their faces met the rising sun. They looked at each other with a sense of great accomplishment.

"Nice going, captain." Maggie said in an attempt to beat the man to his own game. "The commander was right about you. You can fly this bird."

"I'll clue you kids in," came the return. "That was the easy part."

"Have you been in touch with Boston yet?" Maggie asked, not wishing to discuss the difficult part just yet.

"Not yet, princess. Give us a few minutes more."

"Your time is mine."

The big bird flitted rapidly across the top of the roiling cotton fields. Ellen's thoughts turned to her prospective mountain climbing expedition. The top of Everest might offer a similar view of the clouds below. She yearned for the excitement of the climb, the comradeship of the all-female undertaking. She looked back with a sense of accomplishment at her previous expeditions in the Rockies and in Alaska. She had always felt most secure when under her own power, in her own element -- regardless of the conditions. One sure step at a time, one foot in front of the other, she always reached her goal.

Redford was OK. He obviously knew his job. But Ellen felt she was dependent on him and she wasn't comfortable with that. His ego was too large. But then, so was her own. Redford wore his ego on his sleeve. She kept hers inside -- usually.

The radio crackled. They were talking to Boston, a mobile unit at Pier One. Boston seemed excited and Redford had to ask for a repeat transmission more than once. Boston said they had not been able to clear a landing area. The wind was blowing off the water at 40 miles per hour with gusts up to sixty. Drifting, blowing snow had made the unusual situation impossible.

Redford was angry. "Goddamn you turkeys! What the hell do you expect us to do now, pull over to the side of the road and dingle our dongs?"

Boston asked for a repeat.

"Forget it, Boston. Standby ... OK ladies. You heard it. The Boston clearing crews are out Christmas shopping."

Maggie was ready. "OK, captain. Let's see how your new pinpoint landing gizmo works. I want you to take us down as low as you can. We'll take care of the rest."

"So you're gonna do it after all!" Redford said. "I just hate to see something happen to you lovelies."

"Why captain. I'm surprised at you," Ellen chided. "I didn't know you cared."

"Seriously, Redford," Maggie continued. "Have your crew break out the jumping equipment. We want to harness up before you start bouncing this thing all around the sky again."

"Wowee!" Redford shouted through his mike. "You babes are gutsie ... You heard 'em crew. Break 'em out!"

"How far down do you think you can get?" Ellen asked.

"No idea, honey. We can drop until the wind tears this thing to shrapnel."

"I'd like to get down to a couple hundred. Then we could rappel. Looks like you have enough line here."

"Three hundred feet of line," one of the crew said.

"Wowee!" came Redford's voice again. "You girlies turn me on!"

The chutes were brought forward and the women examined them. "What the devil are these?" Ellen asked. "They're those damned combat chutes!"

Redford overheard. "What'd you expect? Jumping is one thing the Army don't do for fun."

Combat parachutes have deep canopies. They don't have the cutouts, or blank gores, that give the sport parachutists forward direction, brakes, steerability and decreased oscillation. They are much larger than sport parachutes, designed to carry a heavy man, with combat gear, at a relatively slow rate of descent. With a wind of any significance, the parachute is at the mercy of the elements, as a leaf is in a breeze.

Ellen was concerned. "I hate to say this, but we'd better either scrap this operation or free-fall. These chutes are just too big. We don't have the weight to guarantee a full canopy opening in this wind. We'll just have no control at all."

"I simply asked for a couple of parachutes. Won't these do at all?"

"Without weight, we're going to either float out into the harbor or just plain miss our target altogether. The jump is going to be difficult enough. A free-fall is fine, but an effective opening, blind, will be ... you guessed it. Hazardous."

Maggie thought for a moment. "This may sound crazy, but what if we both use the same chute? That would certainly give us the added weight.".

Ellen laughed. "You are crazy. You can't do that."

"Why not?"

"Cause you can't."

"That's no answer. If we can get the chopper down to 3,000 or 2,500 feet, we can free-fall to 1,500 or so, open up and count on a soft landing in the snow."

"If we hit the snow and not the ocean!" Ellen added.

"Let's be reasonable."

"Maggie! For chrissakes! You don't know what you're talking about. Let's be serious."

256

"OK. What are you suggesting?"

Ellen was silent. She looked over the chute cases carefully. " At least they have rip cords. I was afraid they might be static line jobs."

"Just think of the experience," Maggie chuckled, trying to make light of a difficult problem.

"What the heck," Ellen finally said. "I'll rig up double harness by clipping on the harness from the other chute. See what you can do about finding an on-shore drop zone. The lower the altitude, the better off we are."

Maggie conferred with the navigator for several minutes. The PGDT was in operation and seemed to be working well. Its readings corresponded with the radio bearings and a positive longitude/latitude could be fixed. The PGDT gave a positive fix of 1/100 of a second, or a three square foot area. The navigator was ecstatic with the results of the new equipment.

She then spoke with the Captain. She told him to proceed as planned, to drop as low as possible. The navigator would request an accurate wind direction and speed from Boston. Knowing altitude, wind direction and speed, Ellen would then be able to calculate the free-fall distance and jump position.

Ellen was rigging the parallel harnesses. "I never thought I'd be involved in stunt jumping. Sport parachuting is one thing. Working with this rig is something else."

The parallel harness under ordinary jumping circumstances would be suicidal. It was inevitable that one of the women would land on top of the other at touchdown. It was therefore critical the landing be soft. The high winds were against them also. A chute may travel a mile and a half from a 1,000-foot drop in a 30- to 40-mile per hour wind. Even when the angle of descent is calculated accurately, the chute, if not collapsed immediately on landing, or released, will drag the person along the ground.

"Boston confirms winds at forty miles per hour, gusting to fifty and sixty. Direction on-shore."

Maggie and the navigator examined the coastal map and the potential approach to the pier. "That parking lot is awfully small for jumping blind," she sighed. "An alternative would be Logan, but we'd never get a pick-up -- it's too far away from the pier." She then beckoned Ellen to the navigator's table and showed her the problem. "We're trying to make a decision without knowing all the facts," she said. "If we have 500 to 1000 foot visibility, this is a piece of cake. What's Boston's visibility?

The navigator called Boston again. "Open and shut. They say it's a quarter mile at times."

"OK," Maggie said. "What's the ceiling?"

"They don't know. Maybe a thousand."

Let's see if we can get below that. We'll decide then."

*

The scream came from the living room. It was Alberta's voice and it rang through the house. No one stirred except for Ed Randolph who smelled smoke as he rolled over.

The scream came again, followed by the words, "Fire! Fire!"

Randolph kicked his wife, but she remained motionless. He grabbed his bathrobe and in the dim morning light. He ran toward the living room.

The smoke became thick as he went down the hall. He shouted for everyone to wake up as he stumbled along.

"The phone. The phone. Call the fire department. Where the hell's the phone? Goddamn it!" Seconds raced by. He found the phone, picked it.

The line was dead.

He was stunned. Smoke was rapidly filling the kitchen. With a violent motion, he picked up the telephone again and threw it at the wall.

He then ran through the house once more, passing Alberta on the way. "Wake everyone up. Quick!" he said.

The fire spread rapidly across the flammable wall-to-wall carpeting and was now going up the front stairway. The smell of burning rug fibers was noxious. Their way was blocked.

"The back stairs!" Randolph preceded Alberta, leaping the stair treads three at a time, stepping on his robe, tripping, falling, up again and nearly falling once more. "Everyone out!" he screamed as he ran. "Quick. Fire!"

The guests were already emerging from their rooms, choking and gasping. Randolph ran to his bedroom. Marsha was still in bed. He threw back the covers and pulled her by the arm to the floor. She cursed and moaned. He tried to pick her up, but she weighed more than he did. He called for help but no one responded. He slapped her across the face several times, wasting precious moments. In desperation, he put her arm around his neck and dragged her to the hall, but it was in flames. He jumped back into the room.

Turning right, then left, thoughts of being trapped racing through his mind, he decided on the window. He raised his foot and kicked. The glass smashed and fell out. He then peered out to see what was below, cutting his hand in the process. He pulled back in and then raised the sash. The snow on the ground was deep. He figured that would cushion the fall. He laid his wife over the windowsill headfirst and then pushed her out. She slid easily, rolled off the porch roof below and landed with a soft thump in six feet of snow.

The fire was in the room now. Foolishly he had left the door open. Flames were dancing across the carpet toward him. A bitter cold wind blew through the window. His choice was either fire or ice. He chose the ice and crawled through the window, fell to the ground, narrowing missing Marsha.

The snow was waist deep, fluffy on top, crusty below that, and the bottom layer was wet. Marsha was now coming around.

She struggled to her feet, not comprehending where she was or why. To her it was a bad dream. It might even be a bad reaction to her pills. Randolph placed her arm around his neck again and they awkwardly lunged and crawled, wincing at the coldness on their bare arms and legs.

Turk was in the garage. He was helping the others into the limousine that was running with the heater turned on full. It would be not be leaving the garage. A wall of snow five feet high blocked the entrance where the door had been raised.

Gasping for breath, Randolph and Marsha slid down the snow wall and into the garage. Breathing deeply, he took stock of who was present. His pulse leaped. "Where's Robert?" Everyone looked around and at each other, but there was no acknowledgement. "Who's got Robert?" he shouted, his face reddening.

Suspecting the worst, Randolph ran across the garage to the house entrance. He grabbed the doorknob, burned his hand and yanked it away. He placed his bathrobe over the metal knob and turned it. A wall of flame burst out, sending Randolph to the floor. Turk rushed over to him. "To hell with me," Randolph shouted. "Shut the goddamned door!"

Frustrated by his first effort, Randolph rushed to the front of the garage, climbed the snow wall and, hindered by the deep snow, pushed and shoved his way through, looking up at the second floor windows as he went. Flames were now breaking through the first story windows and hissing at the snow stacked against them.

At the far corner of the house was Robert's room. Smoke was coming from the open window. He pushed through the snow even faster. There was something hanging out the window. What was it? An arm? A black arm? "Christ!" Randolph gasped. "It's Alberta's."

Moments later, as he continued to stare at it, the first flames leaped through the window and over the arm. Randolph slumped into the snow and cried.

Then, behind him, he heard it. "Father? Father? Why doesn't Alberta come out? I'm very cold."

*

The women unlashed themselves from the cabin and signaled the crew to slide back the cargo door. They pulled on their goggles just as the downdraft from the rotors whipped the snow into the interior. The chopper's descent over Pier One had been smoother than its ascent over Peters Field. The altitude was 1,750 feet and Redford felt he could descend no further. As it was, the chopper was being buffeted to an extreme and the women were expending a great deal of energy simply holding on.

Ellen and Maggie were buckled together. Ellen carried the chute pack on her back and would operate the ripcord and read the altimeter. Maggie would be the passenger, riding below Ellen. Their nerves were tingling, teeth chattering and the wind was snapping at their clothing. Maggie wanted to urinate.

They crawled to the door and held onto the straps at the side and peered down. They were below the clouds. Occasionally the ghost of one of Boston's skyscrapers appeared in the distance. From the charts and from eyeball guessing, the PGDT still seemed accurate. The wind was still onshore.

Redford was to signal when the helicopter was one thousand yards into the harbor. Ellen was quite confident,

261

unless of course the wind dropped or changed direction, that the angle of descent would be accurate to drop them into the huge parking lot or even on the roof of the massive building.

Fortunately the jump was not to be as blind as they had anticipated. As Redford positioned the chopper, the shore became a blurry outline. Just as quickly, a whiteout returned and nothing was visible.

Redford came on the radio again. He had been very quiet.

He was now very serious. The women missed the hot shot Redford. They needed a good fight just about now.

"OK girls. Ten seconds till jump. Good luck."

"Captain? Maggie asked meekly.

"Ya, honey?"

"Is there a lady's room somewhere between here and the ground?"

"Wowee!" Redford shouted. "I love it. Look me up when you get back, sweetheart. I think we can get along good."

"Thanks for the escort, captain," Ellen said.

Down came the navigator's arm. The women pulled off their earphones and jumped, arm in arm.

The tumble through-space was easy. The difficult part was Ellen's. She had to read the moisture-covered altimeter through her equally moisture-covered goggles. It was only a matter of seconds before Ellen nudged Maggie away from her shoulder, positioned the two of them vertically by extending her arms, and then pulled the ripcord. It pulled through easily. There was a rustle, a snap and then a violent shock on the harness.

Ellen looked up automatically to see if the chute was fully opened. She gulped when all she saw were the lines leading up into the whiteness. Beneath her was Maggie, but only whiteness below that.

Vertigo suddenly overtook her. She didn't know whether she was upside down or vice versa. She had never before experienced this discomforting sensation -- the total absence of earthly references.

At 600 feet the weather opened up again and Ellen regained control. The ground was coming up fast. To her right she saw the outline of buildings and they were sweeping directly toward them. She pulled hard on her right lines and the great canopy sluggishly turned to the right. She released them and they were facing the building just as the pair hit the ground. She fought for a foothold, but the still fully inflated canopy pulled them rapidly along the soft snow. They twisted and turned helplessly.

Abruptly and to Ellen's surprise, they stopped. She reached up to her shoulders and, with the harness now slack, released the clips. Maggie was already on her knees, attempting to disengage herself from Ellen. Ellen let out a whoop of joy and relief. She sat up in the deep snow, disconnected Maggie, and threw herself on top of her with a big hug.

"Hey, be careful," Maggie said. "I gotta go pee."

"Still?" Ellen said. "I thought you might have found a lady's room on the way down."

They both laughed and threw snowballs at each other. They only now realized how up tight they had been.

Rolling over, they looked ahead of them. The chute had dragged them up to the wall of a large warehouse. Through one of the windows was a light. Five startled men looked up from their card game as two heavily clothed figures burst noisily into the room.

"Hi there, boys. We're looking for Captain Dietrich," Maggie said as matter of fact. "We could also use a hot cup of coffee."

Thirty minutes later a huge snow machine drove up to the building entrance. Captain Dietrich had accompanied the cat and driver to the building. He gave the women a quick rundown of the medical inventory aboard the machine. It was considerably more than Maggie had dared hope.

The cat was a mammoth machine. The two tracks were each four feet wide, designed, the captain said, for climbing snowy mountainsides, and used commercially for packing ski trails. The wide tracks would support the machine over the fluffiest of snow. Maggie said it was perfect for their needs.

The women's departure for Hollandson was delayed another half hour. Dietrich insisted they retell their jump story for his benefit.

*

A small fire had been started on the fieldstone floor of the hotel lobby. For the first time since the electricity went off, more than twelve hours earlier, real warmth had been created. The sick and the wounded were brought in from the Garden Room to join the lobby people.

The warmth brought hope and some cheer, and the circle increased in size rapidly. The need for a larger fire soon became obvious. The Oriental rug was rolled up and pushed to one side and a big fire was built in the center of the lobby directly beneath the chandelier. A window, five floors up, was opened to allow the smoke to escape, and an order was issued for everyone to gather wooden furniture and other burnables to be stockpiled for fuel.

The wounded, for the most part, were stoics. They rested as best they could in their blankets, with the promise that medicine was on the way. Those whose pain was too great to bear silently were taken to another part of the hotel -- condemned, as it were, to isolation. Although the majority sympathized with them, conditions were bad enough without the added burden of listening to their suffering.

Word had reached the hotel that emergency quarters had also been set up in the Memorial School. The proverbial grass-is-always-greener attitude immediately took hold. Certainly the school had heat, food and better sleeping quarters, the lobby people thought. But transportation was the problem. Snowmobiles were not available and foot travel was impossible. The hotel was isolated. There had been no new arrivals since yesterday afternoon. Didn't anyone give a damn about them?

*

Frank McCullough had just finished clearing the snow away from his car -- just in case the roads are opened up -- when he heard voices in the distance. It was difficult, with his poor hearing, and the vagaries of the wind and snow, to tell from which direction they were coming.

He shrugged, eased himself into the car and started the engine to warm it for the first time in three days. When it had warmed, he shut it off and emerged into the cold. He heard the voices once again. They were closer and he thought he could now detect their direction. The voices were abnormal, as if the people were in distress.

McCullough was hesitant to wade through the deep snow to find them. He just wasn't in condition for that. He decided to wait until they came closer to him. He couldn't guess how far away they might be.

Fifteen minutes passed and he was chilled. Certainly no one would be out on River Road for the fun of it! He shouted.

An answer was returned on the second try. He asked if they needed help. They did. He encouraged them to continue in his direction. Several more minutes passed before two, three, several shadows took shape through the screen of flakes. It was then that he pushed toward them.

He was appalled. It was the Randolph family. They were scantily dressed in nightclothes, except for one big man, their chauffeur, who was clothed well and carried a young boy. The three women wore men's robes and the two other men were dressed in nothing but pajamas. A second boy, called Francisco, who was leading the group, was also fully dressed.

Those poorly dressed were bleeding, and their skin was raw around the ankles and shins where they had broken through the crust with each footstep. Hands and wrists were bleeding from falls as they had lurched along.

McCullough tried to take the boy, called Robert, from Turk but the big man said he was fine and the women should be helped. Slowly, and with great pain, they moved foot by foot, and in a few minutes were in the house.

It was a frightening scene that greeted Mabel. The group was agitated. The pain from their wounds and the stiffness from the cold had chiseled their faces into frozen agony.

McCullough had only seen Ed Randolph once when he had stopped at the house to pick up Robert and castigate his son for not returning directly home from the school bus. It was the same barking voice McCullough heard now -- this time through a nearly immobile jaw.

"Your phone," he said, McCullough had difficulty understanding. "Quick. Man dead. Get help. Use phone."

The words "phone" and "help" McCullough understood. He was not sure he heard the other words correctly. "Sorry, Mr. Randolph. Phones ain't workin'."

Randolph cursed and shook his head. McCullough helped him into a chair. Turk, greatly concerned, stepped quickly over to his boss. "Want me to get help, Mr. Randolph?"

Randolph slowly raised his head and looked at his big chauffeur. "Can you do it Turk?" he rasped. "Do you feel OK?"

"I feel fine, Mr. Randolph. Sure I can leave. Whatever you say."

"Go then. Do whatever you can," Randolph continued, speaking the words hesitatingly. "Get the road plowed. Get a helicopter from the company. Get something, goddamn it! Get me out of here!".

"Sure thing, Mr. Randolph. I'll get back as soon as I can.

Turk pulled on his heavy coat. He borrowed a hat with earmuffs from McCullough and left quickly. "Don't you want something to eat first?" Mabel asked after him.

"I'm OK. Got to get help," were his last words.

During their first few minutes in the house, Mabel had her impromptu guests sit or lie down on various pieces of furniture. They welcomed the wet, warm towels she wrapped around their exposed extremities in an attempt to restore body heat as quickly and gently as possible.

The old couple examined each of their patients and it became evident none of them suffered irreversible physical damage. If there was frostbite, it was minor and would not show up until later. Time and relaxation was what they needed to mend the wounds and the exhausted bodies. The kids, Robert and Francisco, showed no ill effects. They were a great help in maintaining the wet towel brigade. Peter and Alice Stevenson were recovering rapidly. They were simply exhausted. Alice was caught massaging her face and ears as circulation returned with a painful tingle. McCullough warned her to stop or she might damage her skin. "Let the warm towels do the work," he said.

Elaine Mitchell was morose. She had not spoken a word and had kept to herself. She responded to Mabel only with nods or shakes of her head. Mabel could not determine what troubled her.

Marsha was in a daze, not comprehending anything spoken to her. She complained continually until she fell into a deep sleep.

McCullough apologized to the others for the extreme heat. He said he needed the ninety degrees during the day "to soothe these old bones." No one complained.

Randolph was a puzzle. He had been restless since the group first arrived. He still shook violently and no amount of warm towels seemed to send the heat deep enough to calm him. Periodically he placed his head in his hands and moaned. Asked if he was in pain, he answered no, but this was followed by a soft cursing to himself.

In fact, Randolph was very close to a nervous breakdown. Events were stacked so deeply over his head, packed so tightly within his skull, it was threatening his rationality. He felt that if one more thing were to happen, he would go over the edge.

Randolph could only see his problems. His inability to find solutions, because of unforeseen circumstances and events, were beyond his control. The Scanner XII backfire, the snow, Harrington's impossible demands, the house fire, Alberta's death, the bitter walk, Ralph Mitchell's grotesque death in the snow -- each episode flashed before him in an endless slide show.

He felt a scream of frustration developing in his throat. He felt that if he released it in one powerful burst he would be rid of the devil that plagued him. One scream would do it. Up, up, up it came. He inhaled deeply and opened his mouth wide ...

Rationality took over, but not by much. "Damn," Randolph said, loudly, causing host of the heads in the room to turn toward him.

*

Boston was a barren snowfield. Maggie and Ellen avoided the downtown area and headed west. Streets were indistinguishable except for the signs atop shrunken posts. Only the rooftops of some vehicles could be seen, all that was left after the snow had blown in around them. Visibility was less than 500 feet and the women were disappointed by the lack of perspective over the city. Their route took them past North Station, Massachusetts General Hospital and out to the Charles River. They saw no indications of life outdoors. They dared not consider what conditions were like inside the hundreds of unheated apartment buildings and hotels.

Down Storrow Drive, onto Alewife Brook Parkway and finally onto Route 2 west. They were alone in a world that had been inundated by an arctic freeze.

The snow cat, by contrast, was surprisingly comfortable and quiet. It had the luxury of a powerful heater and it cruised at 20 to 30 miles an hour on cushioned springs, snow flying from the treads. Once accustomed to the controls, Maggie welcomed her first respite from the pressures of people -- people with problems. Although not yet noon, they felt the effects of a long and successful morning.

After some miles of meditation, it was Ellen who shattered the spell. She told Maggie of her nightmare conflict with Margo Chin, how she escaped with Webster's classified file and of her talk with Phil about it earlier in the morning.

"What was Phil's reaction?"

"He was pleased that I had come up with the files. He felt ... "

"No, Ellen. I mean about Margo."

"Well, he felt it wasn't my fault," Ellen shrugged, looking away from Maggie. "He thought also I should wait before I report it. The police are kind of busy with other matters right now."

"That's a tough one," Maggie said thoughtfully. "I'd have a hard time recommending one way or another. I'd say it was wrong not to report it, although a delay might be justified. But I'd hate to see you caught without having reported it. Aren't you still jittery about it?"

"It's funny, but I'm not. If you could have seen the animal-look on that woman's face."

"How far did you get into reading the files?"

"Not far at all. Somebody came by and suggested some hair-brained scheme about jumping out of an airplane into a snowstorm."

They both laughed.

Ellen suddenly sat erect in her seat. "Maggie," she said excitedly. "I just remembered. Reading through Nat's files reminded me. Can we stop by his apartment now?"

"Do what?"

"We're going right by it, almost." Ellen said, ignoring Maggie's comment. It's a long shot, but he might have done it. Nat told me a long time ago that if anything should happen to him, I should go to his apartment and look in our secret hiding place. If at all possible, he said, he would leave a note telling me what had happened."

The machine sped smoothly over the snow. For the time being they were making good time and Maggie did not want to stop at the apartment. She envisioned an emotional scene brought on by not finding the note. This would be followed once again by renewed wondering of where Nat Webster could be, if he was anywhere. Maggie was beginning to think of the man as an apparition -- a man who never existed.

270

"Ellen. We're on a mission. Five hours ago I was having my own nightmare. I expect it's not much better now. We'll soon see. Frankly, I dread returning."

"You're right. I guess I've been too self-centered."

Maggie now felt guilty. "Hey, kid. If I were you, I'd be doing the same. Let's get this hotel business over with. We'll go to the apartment later."

*

The party was in Room 413, the Black Room, which by an unlucky fate of numbering was seldom occupied by guests. The word had spread rapidly among the younger hotel staff and each was told to bring plenty of booze, food and blankets. By 1 p.m. eleven kids had arrived, telling no one else of their plan.

It was rebellion. Organization had rapidly fallen apart when they learned that Vito had died as a result of the roof collapse. Basically the young people were tired, fed up with the confusion brought on by the snowstorm, the refugees, the blackout, the roof collapse, the cold, lack of sleep, and the hundreds of unreasonable demands placed on them by frantic adults. The eleven had brought several days' food, thanks to their easy access to storage areas.

The plan was to remain in hiding until the storm was over. "Those suckers can rot," one bellhop emphasized. "I'm not leavin' here till those spaced-out scar warriors blast off."

Irene Stitch laughed. "'Scar wars!' I love it! I feel like I been through Scar Wars. You ought to see where I got pinched.

"Hey! Can I, 'Reen?" a boy teased. "Be a good kid. Show us your pinch."

Irene ignored him, coyly, opening bags of potato chips and emptying them into a large bowl.

"Hotels suck!" another girl complained "Snow sucks! I should have went to live with my big sister in Alabama. I never knew a job was so bad."

"The-tips are good," Irene said, turning. "The money's good, if you can put up with the crap."

"Ya, if your waitressin'. Us guys don't get dink!"

"Don't get scar wars either," Irene giggled.

But cursing the people and the conditions had been a preoccupation of the past twenty-four hours. They now all agreed the problems in the hotel weren't theirs. Someone else could handle them. Given the opportunity, they would leave everything behind -- the hotel and their jobs -- immediately.

It was party time now. They each felt they deserved it. Eleven of them – six girls, five guys. The liquor bottles and mixers were lined up on the bureau top next to the peanuts, chips, cherries, olives and popcorn. There was no ice, but they had seen enough of ice and snow. They didn't need ice.

"Drink up. It's the only way to keep warm."

"I know another way," the bellhop said. The response to his comment was nervous giggle.

Although no one in the group had worked at the hotel more than six months, and one for as little as a week, they felt they knew each other well. Most had grown up in the surrounding towns and had met at school activities. Others had worked together for several weeks or more. And all felt a unique kinship brought on by the storm and their common hostility toward the conventioneers.

Each was lonely. Each was secretly afraid and missed home. None knew how to cope with events that shattered their previously carefree world. For most, this was the first time they had seen death, suffering, and general panic among a large group of adults. They quickly learned to fear these adults who were gripped by fright and foreboding themselves.

But there was one alternative to chaos. Since they had no experience in organizing adults, their only hope was to organize themselves, and a party was their most familiar form of organization. It gave them a comfortable sense of unity. It satisfied their instinct for friendship, peace, quiet and the familiar.

Now, sitting cross-legged in a circle on the carpeted floor with blankets over their shoulders, words at first were few. Reality was too close behind them for anything but light, crude humor. They told jokes, related the general horrors of everyday hotel work, and swallowed their first drinks rapidly.

As the warmth of the liquor spread through their bodies and into their nervous systems, they moved closer to each other and the cold reality of the day began to fade pleasantly into a fuzzy anticipation of evening.

*

The cruising speed of the snow cat soon diminished. Poor visibility and thousands of obstacles made the journey agonizingly slow.

"Nearly 2 p.m.. We've been at it for almost two hours and we're only about half way I'd guess."

Tragedy was everywhere along the highway. An occasional work team was seen on snowmobiles checking abandoned automobiles. Twice the glow of what appeared to be a distant fire could be detected through the swirling flakes. There was one temptation after another temptation to stop and help, but the reminder of equal troubles at home kept them going.

"I feel like a bastard," Maggie said, "but to stop means time away from home where we're needed. It scares me to death to imagine what we have to look forward to when we get back."

"Just what are your plans?" Ellen asked.

"I've been pondering that since we left. Frankly, they're pretty sketchy right now. First of all we're going to have brother Fitzy on our backs. He's going to want immediate transportation back to town."

"And I bet we'll be besieged by hundreds of people with just as many good reasons wanting a ride also. How're we going to handle it?'

Maggie shook her head. "No one gets a ride! We've got the sick and the wounded to care for first. And we have to get food and supplies from somewhere."

"I've been thinking about that," Ellen said. "What are the ethics of confiscating food and supplies from supermarkets and stores?"

Maggie thought for a moment. "That's a fabulous idea! Under these conditions I'd say we were perfectly justified. If we don't, hundreds of people will starve."

"I agree. And surely food and clothing will raise the morale of the people -- especially for those at the hotel who have nothing."

This was the nucleus of an overall plan for storm survival in Hollandson. During the next hour the women thrashed out a practical plan for organizing the town and helping ease the crisis.

"Without this machine, we have nothing," Maggie said. "Without transportation, people and supplies remain separated."

"We'd better insure it by carrying an armed guard," Ellen warned. "Survival is a strange phenomenon. The will to survive stops at nothing. Unfortunately, many people will see this machine as their only means of survival."

*

"We got a live one!" Sam Brownell shouted over to Phil. "She's here in bed and barely responding to me."

274

Both Brownell and Billings were knee-deep in snow, standing on the shed roof of the house. The first floor doors and windows were buried in drifts, so the pattern for the day had been to climb to the second floor and bang on the windows to attract attention of those who might be on the inside.

From the outside, this house looked deserted. There was no sign of shoveling, no sign of footsteps. There had been no obvious response to Brownell's window rapping. By chance, however, he had been able to see into the bedroom. It very definitely looked like an old woman, perhaps ill, lying in her bed. Her response to Brownell was the gentle movement of her arm.

"How're we gonna do this one? I hate to break the window. We'd never be able to get her out this way."

"Let's take a look at the porch door. That's partially protected," Phil suggested.

They leaped from the roof and waded around to the porch. The door was three-quarters covered with snow. Scooping with hands and arms, it was cleared in only a few minutes. Locked, they forced it, splintering the wood frame.

Through the dark, unfamiliar house they moved, as swiftly as they dared. Up the stairway they went where it was lighter because of the uncovered windows. She had a ghostly thin face, and her arms were nothing but wrinkled, skin-covered bones. It was evident she was suffering from malnutrition and exposure. She tried to smile at the men and then speak, but all that came out was a croak.

"Don't try to talk, ma'am," Phil said. "We're going to take you to a nice, warm place where you can have something good to eat." He had his fingers crossed. He hoped the neighbors would take her in for the time being.

In ten minutes the elderly lady was bundled in blankets and carried out to the snowmobile where she was lashed onto a toboggan. Slowly the machine towed its delicate cargo three doors down the road to where a young, childless couple had earlier in the day offered to take in anyone who needed help. Their home was warmed by a woodstove, and in minutes hot soup was brewing and the patient's eyes glowed with anticipation and gratitude.

"Merry Christmas," the men said to the family as they left. But as they said these familiar words, today they had taken on a greater depth. They suddenly realized that people they were meeting today really cared. A genuine Christmas spirit was developing, a spirit born out of one person helping another. There was every indication this would be a season of deprivation and suffering. But through it all an outpouring of human warmth was emerging.

"Merry Christmas," Phil repeated. It sounded very good, as if he had never spoken those words before.

Billings and Brownell were part of a team of eighteen volunteers, traveling in pairs, who were methodically visiting, house-by-house, the population of Hollandson. Their function was to raise the morale of those who felt alone and isolated by the storm yet who were capable of caring for themselves; and to rescue those who could not cope and deliver them to others who cared to share.

House after house was visited. The volunteers often had to force a cheerful, fun-filled spirit into their manner in the hope that others would pick it up. Thus far they had been successful, but the day was long and the work difficult.

For younger families, the disruption of everyday routine was less acute. They were urged to keep busy by giving every member of the family a project -- shoveling off roofs and porches, clearing doors and windows. Work generated heat. It also took the mind off broken and frozen water pipes, refrigerator-like house interiors, low food supplies, poor or nonexistent cook facilities, functionless toilets and boredom.

276

Rape.

The rumor spread through the hotel like a deadly gas, churning stomachs and quickening heartbeats. Fear, brought on by the unknown and inflamed by gossip, gripped the equanimity of the guests. Gone now was the carefree spirit and convention atmosphere.

The first indication came when a woman rushed up to an EMT in the lobby and spoke in an excited whisper. The EMT, with two others, walked hastily off with the woman, up the stairs and out of sight.

There had been two cases, in adjoining rooms. The victims had been unable to identify their assailants for they were stocking-masked. The girls were rooming singly. They had answered a knock on their doors, were grabbed by the throats, and a handkerchief shoved in their mouths. The rest was quick, violent and painful.

Attempts at organization of the hotel population during the day had failed. As the snow fell unrelentingly and weather reports continued their dismal predictions, the barometer of hope plunged into the range of despair. This morning's deaths set the tone for the day. Petty thefts, and now sexual violence, rocked the balance of human patience and understanding.

Concern for one's own individual safety threatened to dominate. Animalistic needs of food and warmth threatened to override Man's cultivated art of interdependence and concordance.

The fire in the lobby was comforting to those close enough to enjoy it. Those on the periphery were cold. As a result, other fires were built in less practical locations. The halls now became smoky. One fire, carelessly built on the carpeting, nearly spread out of control before it was extinguished by 100 pounding shoes.

Nerve ends were broken. People were overwhelmed by stress of the worst kind -- the inability to control one's own life.

The Governor was no help. He and his staff had locked themselves in their suite. Fitzwilliam would not mix with the "riff-raff." Since the cell phones went dead, consequently isolating him from the affairs of his office and the state, his temperament declined. His only hope, he continued to believe, was Maggie Billings. If and when she returned, he planned to commandeer transportation to Boston. He shivered at his fear of accompanying her this morning. That fear, he now felt, would have been far less sapping than the succeeding hours he had spent brooding in his room.

Nagging at him, eating at his thoughts, was the opportunity he was losing, had already lost, in directing state emergency plans in conjunction with The White House. The immensity of events unknown to him, carried out without him, was unbearable. He paced the floor, kicking at furniture, swearing at his incompetent aides.

The press had long since abandoned aggressive newsgathering. With communication cut off, they had now become part of the news themselves. It was an uncomfortable turnabout.

The Cloven Hoof Tavern was jammed with a spectrum of humanity. Drinks, on the house since the previous evening when the lights went off, had taken their toll. In the candlelight, many patrons had simply passed out from over indulgence. In order to make room for new patrons, it was popular entertainment to carry out those who had had their fill.

And there were occasional fights. Greedy individuals, harboring the desire to sequester a bottle for personal use, were intercepted and convinced that sharing the wealth was the proper conduct.

The hotel smelled foul. Fire, smoke, vomit, excrement and sweat filled the public rooms. With no running water, personal hygiene became difficult, often impossible.

For all practical purposes, the food supply was exhausted. With no deliveries since the storm began, with four times the anticipated hotel population, with thefts, and spoilage due to freezing and vandalism, little was left but powders, pastes and spices.

Dozens of people aimlessly wandered the halls, waiting, waiting for something to happen, something to bring order to their lives -- nervous, fearful, cautious of potential dangers yet to be released in the person across the room, down the hall, just around the corner.

*

Chandler Harrington was triumphant. He was relaxing in the Hilton, scotch and soda in hand, watching an old Perry Como Christmas Special. He cared nothing about the show. He had starred in his own production and was about to receive a multi-billion dollar reward for his efforts. He grinned to himself, over and over, reliving the week of high-level drama that had brought him this far.

The phone lines to New England were not functioning, the operator had told him. He was not able to get through to Randolph at Scan-Man. His grin faded as he thought about the New England snow conditions. He wondered if Randolph was really capable of handling the Scan-Man operation alone. Was he a star quarterback? Or was he simply a bright, temperamental yes-man?

He thought about the Bloodworth woman. She would remain on ice -- Harrington chuckled at his play on words. Everything could remain on ice for a few more days.

On the other hand he was eager to return to the office to pass along the good news to the directors. Oh well, he thought, he'd fly in after the weather cleared and give them a belated Christmas present. The infusion of money would make the stockholders exuberant. He could easily imagine tripling dividends. And then, of course, there would be the bonuses for the directors. Although he had actually sold the deal, it was their combined efforts that had paved the way.

Harrington's thoughts drifted back to the storm. His heavy, black brows dipped together toward his nose. How much longer could the storm last? He had expected it to be over by now. Certainly it couldn't continue, or could it? Recent reports said the depth was nearing six feet and mounting rapidly.

The phone rang, startling him out of his introspection.

"Chandler. John Ruben here. I'm afraid I have bad news for you." There was a pause and Harrington said nothing.

"I can't live with your secret. I simply called to warn you I have to go upstairs and let it all out."

Harrington sighed. It was always a pain having to deal with weaklings. "John. You're making a mistake. You're acting more like a soap actor than a Brigadier General. We're not conducting an evangelical retreat. We're talking about security of this country."

"You make it all sound so simple, Harrington."

"It is, if you let it be. Learn to relax, John. You'll live a hell of a lot longer."

"No. I've made up my mind."

"Look, John. Has the old Christmas spirit got you down? Don't forget this can mean a lot of cash. That cash can help ease the burden."

"You'll never understand, Harrington." Ruben sounded angry.

"Have you forgotten about the photos? It could ruin ... "

Harrington heard a click, followed by the dial tone. His jaw tightened. The veins on his neck stood out. He pulled an address book from his shirt pocket and punched a number.

"Glad you're there. This is Harrington."

"Yes boss."

"Now listen. Ruben's on his way to the Pentagon to empty his bladder. I want you to intercept him. I don't want to see him again."

"Gotcha."

"You know his habits. I think you can do it from a safe distance. But ... don't miss!"

"No problem, Mr. Harrington."

"Call me when you return." Harrington hung up, then went to the sideboard where he poured himself another scotch and added two ice cubes.

"You can't relax for a minute," he muttered to himself. "The bastards will turn on you every time."

*

Most of the McCullough's impromptu guests were showing signs of recovery. It had been a short walk -- perhaps only a quarter of a mile -- but it had been a violent one. The story Frank and Mabel heard horrified them. The fire. The freezing, exhausting struggle through the deep snow and drifts -- a monumental task, breaking through glass-sharp crust, the biting wind licking at their exposed flesh. Only through the necessity of their extreme movements to overcome the deep snow had that extra blood circulation been provided to keep away excessive frostbite.

"And I, like a damn fool, left my fur in the bedroom," Alice Stevenson complained. "That would have kept a couple

281

of us warm, but we probably would have wrecked it. Fortunately it's insured. And thank the Lord I wore my rings!"

Ralph Mitchell had not made it, however. He had a known heart condition. His only choices had been to remain near the burning house and eventually freeze to death, or to undertake the trek with the others.

The group trudged slowly at first so Mitchell would not unduly overwork himself. But slow walking meant a slow freeze for the others in their nakedness. They all speeded up, including Elaine, urging Mitchell to do the same. But he couldn't keep pace. He struggled for breath, unnoticed by the others in the high wind and blur of snow. He gasped, sucking in the below-freezing air. He fell forward several times, taking longer each time to get to his feet again. Gasping, sucking air deeply, he finally collapsed for the last time. Randolph and Stevenson hastily checked his pulse and said it was nonexistent.

Mitchell was a large, overweight man. There was no question he could not be carried, not even by Turk. His wife wanted to stay with the body but a hurried conversation and a gust of snow convinced her she would die with him if she remained. He would not have wanted that, they told her.

The death could not have made the ordeal more grim. After hauling the body to the side of the road, they all tried to move faster. It was then they heard McCullough's shouts.

Now, the heat of the house, combined with the hot soup and sandwich, had brought a welcome sleep.

It was 3 p.m.

Randolph awoke with a start. Dusk was beginning to hide the falling flakes. He shook Stevenson.

"Come on!" he whispered hoarsely. "We're going after Mitchell before it gets dark."

"Why? He's dead," Stevenson sleepily reasoned.

"Because we just can't leave him out there."

"I suppose we have to," Stevenson replied. "We can't leave the poor bugger out there all night. We'd never find him in the morning."

Randolph stood. He felt rotten. The exertion had scrambled his constitution, he thought. His mind was still in a muddle. He dreaded facing the snow again. He thought momentarily about Harrington and then blocked it out. He was glad now to have an excuse to forget about Scan-Man -- at least until Turk returned.

McCullough gave the pair his heaviest coats and wool trousers. The toboggan and rope were on the back porch, ready to go, until now used only to haul wood from the barn. He and Rolf watched from the porch as the two disappeared into the gray. He scratched his dog behind the ears and they both turned to go in.

Except for Robert and Francisco, who were playing Monopoly in the bedroom, the others were still asleep.

*

Stop number one for the snow cat was the police station. Chief Wilson was awed by the women's acquisition. "This is our savior," he shouted gleefully. "Where the hell did you steal it?"

"We'll save that story for later," Maggie said, controlling her own excitement. "Meanwhile, if you'd offer us a cup of coffee we'll tell you our plans."

"Thanks to the miracle of bottled gas and instant coffee, your request is granted." The chief's buoyancy was higher than Maggie had ever remembered.

For the next half hour the trio exchanged information and an overall plan making use of the cat was developed. The chief agreed to act as armed guard for the next few hours -- at least until the hotel delivery was completed.

283

"It might be rough," Wilson agreed. "I just hope force won't be necessary."

It was nearly dark when the snow cat arrived at the hotel. As they approached the entranceway, Maggie was puzzled by the strange, flickering light in the lobby. Was the hotel on fire? She asked herself in a moment of apprehension. They were flames without question, and they splashed crazy patterns on the snow in the cat's path. Yet she saw no excitement. Through the window the orange light reflected on motionless statues, not panicking human caricatures.

It was Ellen who interpreted the fire. "It looks like heat to me, Maggie. Civilization has now come full circle -- we've returned to the communal fire."

They pulled in under the shelter of the marquee. The insiders suddenly noticed the machine and crowded toward the electric doors that were now broken and sprung open. A heavy blanket covered a narrow passage. As the women turned to prepare to unload the supplies, Wilson let out a shout.

"What the devil?"

Fifteen or twenty people had left the hotel and were climbing onto the snow cat. Quickly Wilson unbuckled his revolver and pushed open the door of the cat.

"Everyone back inside!" he shouted. "Back into the hotel."

With the noise of the wind and that of the people themselves competing for attention to be heard, Wilson's voice was drowned. Now Maggie and Ellen had turned back and were frozen in place by the riotous scene.

"Damn it, Paul." Maggie said. "Fire a warning shot or something! These people are animals. They're going to tear this thing apart!"

Wilson hastily climbed out of the cab and, standing on the track, raised his arm and fired a shot into the air. The response was immediate. The crowd halted its assault and paused, waiting for something else to happen. Wilson provided it. He fired again.

"Please everyone," he said. "Everyone back into the hotel. We'll never organize anything if we don't get complete cooperation."

"Hey mister. All we want to do is help," one from the crowd shouted. They all chimed in. Could they carry anything?

"All we have is medical supplies here," Wilson said. "Go back inside. We'll explain everything in a few minutes."

During the next half hour the supplies were carried in and a central medical care station was set up. The medical technicians and whatever nurses and doctors were available were pleased to see the medicine, albeit hardly much more than rudimentary. Painkillers in the form of pills and Novocain were the most sought. Then came the demand for anti-infection vaccines, sterile dressings and bandages.

The chief remained with the snow cat, repeatedly rejecting innocent appearing requests to examine the machine. Just let one of these buggers in, he thought, and I'd have a wrestling match on my hands. The only interest they have is running off with it.

In the hotel, the approaches were more direct. Maggie and Ellen were plagued by dozens of people begging, crying, demanding and even threatening them in order to secure transportation. Their response was a universal no.

"No one is going anywhere yet!" Ellen spoke loudly. "You'll all have your chance." She knew, however, that it might be some days before that chance would come.

"But my six-year-old is at home alone ... " one woman wailed, tears streaking down her soiled face.

"There's not a soul here who does not have a crisis situation," Maggie said, relieving Ellen. "We have no choice

285

but to do the best we can with what we have. The most immediate need here is for organization. You can most effectively help yourselves by helping each other work toward the common good."

Maggie was surprised at her commanding voice. She was even more surprised at its results. Several people stepped forward, offering to help. She took them aside and explained the plan.

It was then that the governor and his retinue appeared. He walked up to Maggie with a broad grin and presented an affable back pat. "I'm ready when you are." he said. "Did you have any problems getting into town?"

Maggie looked at the governor and smiled. She felt a sudden need for sarcasm rising toward her tongue. She swallowed. "It was a very interesting trip, Fitzy. The jump out of the helicopter was, uh, memorable."

Fitzwilliam read Maggie's restraint. "Sorry, Maggie. I'm sure you did have problems. But I'm very pleased to see that you're back and were able to pick up the medicine."

"I have only you to thank. Really, Fitzy, the cat is going to be a boon to this town. I have a million uses planned for it."

The governor showed the slightest bit of discomfort and shuffled his feet. "When can we leave? My patience here is wearing very thin."

Maggie was tired. Her temper was bubbling just beneath the surface. She knew she now had to relinquish the snow cat for the few hours it would take to return his Excellency to Boston. She had delayed his departure long enough. If she irritated him, he might conceivably decide to confiscate the machine.

"Give me another hour. We must transport the worst of these victims to the hospital." She swept her arm in the direction of the stretchers "They have waited too long already. I understand several have died." `

"Of course," he said, amd swallowed hard. "We'll be ready in an hour." The governor turned and walked away, his aides, like ducklings, trailing behind.

The stretchers were readied for the first shuttle to the hospital. These were the most seriously wounded, those who had not already died from blood loss, shock or high fever due to infection.

*

Comradeship moved to arm-in-arm friendship. This melted into necking and petting and that degenerated into alcoholic intimacy. The warmth and apparent security of blankets, pillows and body-to-body contact permeated Room 413. Sexual intimacy came easy, for tomorrow was an uncertainty. Today, tonight, the moment, was all the eleven teenagers were certain of. Civilized inhibitions fell away as peer pressure took over.

The room was cold and damp. The liquor dulled the mind and body and heightened passions. They felt they had escaped to their own world, escaped from the watchful eyes of an adult chaos below.

*

Randolph and Stevenson located Mitchell's body without much difficulty. They followed the depression of their earlier tracks from McCullough's house along River Road. Despite six hours of snow cover, the body was in bold relief at the side of the road. They were surprised it was so close -- no more than 200 yards up the road. Mitchell had almost made it!

It was nearly dark as they brushed off the snow. They winced at the yawning, snow-filled mouth and the crystallized, staring eyes. The body was stiff, frozen in a crucifix where the arms had been extended when he was first

287

hastily pulled off the path. The arms now presented a problem. Mitchell was placed on the toboggan and tied in place, but there was no way the arms could be brought down to his sides. Pulling the sled through the soft snow, the arms acted like plows, making the pull next to impossible. The men paused for wind. "We'll never make it this way. We've gone only fifteen feet!"

They now tried determinedly to bend one of Mitchell's arms down to his side. It moved, slowly. Randolph maintained a steady pressure. Slowly it moved – nearly into place. Stevenson urged him on.

Then, with a snap that sounded like a dead limb broken from a water-soaked tree trunk, the frozen arm broke free in Randolph's hands. He fainted, and fell backwards in the snow. Stevenson gasped at the sight of the exposed raw flesh of the shoulder joint.

Stevenson walked around the toboggan to Randolph and slapped him gently on the face. Randolph sat up, looked at Mitchell again and puked between his knees.

Ignoring the second arm, they decided to pull the sled as best they could, having tucked the loose arm in Mitchell's pajama waistband.

It was a relief to see the glow of the kerosene lamp at the house. While Stevenson continued to pull the toboggan into the driveway and on toward the barn, Randolph ran ahead to get McCullough. He found him in the kitchen.

"Where do you want to put the body?" he whispered, breathing heavily.

Reluctantly McCullough followed, looking briefly at the body that was once again covered with a light blanket of snow. He looked away again and led the way to the barn, indicating a stall that was freshly covered with hay.

"We need a blanket to cover him. We can't leave him like this," Stevenson said. McCullough busied himself at the side of the barn. He pointed, without looking, to a heavy blanket over the stall divider. Mitchell and Stevenson rolled Mitchell in the blanket and secured either end like a giant sausage.

"He should be OK here as long as it stays below freezing. The trio returned to the house. Randolph looked very pale.

"I need a stiff drink," Randolph said. His mouth tasted sour.

"Sorry. We got no liquor. How about a coffee?" McCullough didn't look very well either. He still carried the distressed look he assumed when he first saw Mitchell's body.

*

Officer Commerwitz looked up in surprise from his novel as a giant of a man pushed through the police station door. His wool trousers were covered with tiny balls of snow and ice, as if he had walked a great distance.

"I need help." were his first words. "Lots of trouble."

"You and everybody else," Commerwitz said, dog-earing a page and dropping his feet from the desk.

Turk explained who he was and, rejecting an offer to sit, told about the Randolph family experiences during the day.

"You sure do need help, but there's nothin' I can do right now. Why don't you go over to the school? Get somethin' to eat and get some rest. We'll be makin' the rounds to the houses as soon as we can."

"I need help now!" Turk insisted, his face expressing the urgency Randolph had impressed on him. "The boss says he can't wait."

"Look, mister. Nobody likes to wait. I've been waitin' here all day. I don't like it. There's no choice. Your best bet is to go over to the school. You'll get help over there." Commerwitz was tired and irritable. The big man shuffled his feet, thinking of what he should do next. Commerwitz also wondered what the giant would do next. He fondled his revolver in anticipation of the worst. Then, the man turned and left, without a word.

Commerwitz shook his head in disbelief, settled back in his chair, feet back up on the desk, and returned to his book. He smiled. He was into the exciting part now.

*

The sun had just set, but the bright mercury vapor lamps in the north parking area took its place, radiating a dazzling, pink brilliance on the remnants of the snow that had fallen earlier in the week.

A red Toyota swung an arc through the nearly empty lot and pulled into slot 312, although there were three empty rows closer to the building. Headlights went out and a tall, uniformed figure stepped out, towering above the roof of the little vehicle. He had a blue braid over his right shoulder, a dozen ribbons on his breast pocket and two stars on each epaulet. A black, plastic nameplate read "Ruben" in white letters. He bent once more into the car to retrieve his brief case, straightened, slammed the door, and walked toward the building.

Behind him in the distance on a dark hillside, came a solitary flash of fire. The General fell to the pavement, in space number 212. As he fell, a sharp sound, similar to a backfire, or tire blowout, bounced across the lot. Silence followed.

His visored hat, decorated with "scrambled eggs," flipped off as his head hit the pavement, and rolled to one side. At the base of his skull was a small hole out of which a thick, red liquid oozed. He remained motionless. The liquid stopped flowing.

Harrington picked up the phone. "Yes?"

"Done," came the voice from the other end.

290

"It took long enough!"

"He musta thought about it for a while."

"Goodbye." Harrington smiled, feeling a sense of relief.

He picked up the television guide. Good, he thought, there were a lot of Christmas Specials tonight. He loved Christmas. It made him feel warm all over and even brought tears to his eyes.

He thought of his mother and father and how the three of them always spent Christmas Day together. Those memories went back fifty years. Year after year ---sitting in front of the Christmas tree -- how they loved to listen to their son talk of his accomplishments in the business world. They had lived just long enough to see him elected to chairman of the board -- how proud they were! And now, if they could only knew how he spoke before the President of the United States and how their son "Chandy" pulled off one of the world's biggest single financial coups. Mother and father would simply beam all over.

Christmas. It brought back warm memories.

*

It began softly -- a tiny, little-girl voice from a corner of the lobby. She was in her early teens a lovely Black girl whose ear was close to the portable radio she held at her shoulder. Her eyes were sad but her voice carried the joyousness of her mood. She was oblivious to her surroundings.

Silent night, holy night.

All is calm, all is bright.

Round ...

An elderly couple sitting next to the girl picked up on the carol. They were followed by others next to them. Soon nearly everyone in the lobby had joined in.

291

Almost instantly the mood in the room changed from that of self-pity and defeat to hope and a warmth for those around them. The reflection of light on the faces circling the fire gradually took on a look similar to that of the young girl's. Unwittingly, she had unleashed a cascade of Christmas carols. The lobby people swung easily from one to another to another.

The tension of the last few days was now relieved. The fuse was temporarily snuffed. Even those on stretchers waiting to be moved to the hospital seemed to rise above their pain and discomfort. Twisted smiles emerged through grimaces, and a determination was solidified that they were going to overcome any hardship that might beset them.

Even next door, 100 feet away in the tavern, the spirit was captured. A raucous "Jingle Bells," sung in full, off-key gusto, was a cheerful change from the beery atmosphere of minutes earlier. Some tavern patrons, for whatever reasons, left their bottles behind and joined the lobby people.

*

The storm had to be stopped. Had Randolph yet worked out the operation of the Searoc Beam? This thought was foremost in his mind.

Harrington's composure disintegrated in direct proportion to the length of time his call went unanswered. He could tell from the signal at the other end that he was connected. It was a standard communications line via satellite directly into Scan-Man headquarters. Whereas ground line calls were routed through the switchboard. There was always a team of technicians on duty. There was always someone to answer the call. This was the one room around which all Scan-Man activity circulated. Why was there no answer?

It was Christmas Eve. There was a blizzard raging. Headquarters was operating on internal power. These were no reasons for personnel to fail to fulfill their duties,
292

Harrington thought. All possible emergencies had been anticipated. The elaborate Scan-Man operations system was the result of the efforts of some of the greatest technical minds in the U.S. The system was designed to function independently of any outside influence -- and that included military conflict.

Teeth clenched, veins at his temples prominent and wriggling with muscle tension, Harrington disconnected his signal with an abrupt wave of his hand across the console. With fierce determination he launched a new call. The familiar buzz resumed. Seconds passed. No answer.

By God there had to be someone at Scan-Man! Where the hell was Randolph? Where were the other directors? Who was in charge? Who was running the show in his absence? During an emergency of any sort at least one director was required to remain at headquarters.

"Goddamn bunch of buffoons"

An answer.

"Who the hell is this!" Harrington barked.

Silence. "Hello? Hello!" he said, moderating his tone, trying to pull himself together, afraid that this person might hang up. This is Chandler Harrington calling from Washington. What's going on up there?"

"Oh. Mr. Harrington. This is Sam Polcari." Polcari was tired and irritable himself. His thoughts flashed back to the recent director's meeting at which he and his co-worker were, he felt, unjustifiably chastised. That meeting had eaten at him ever since. The succeeding days and nights of stress at Scan-Man had magnified his belief that his efforts were misplaced, unappreciated, unrewarded and unknown. Extreme conditions, coupled with his recent decision to look for employment elsewhere, released the hostility he had developed toward Scan-Man management.

"You probably don't remember my name, but my partner Jim and I met with you and the directors a couple days ago."

"Yes. Yes. I remember," Harrington said impatiently, sensing the hostility and wanting to avoid an argument. "Let me speak to your supervisor, Mr. Polcari."

"Jim and I took all that shit from your ill-mannered partner Randolph. If I ever ... "

This guy is insane, Harrington thought. How can I get rid of him and not lose the connection? "Is Mr. Randolph there?"

Polcari laughed. It was a shrill cackle. "No, Mr. Harrington. I have not seen any management around. There's just a couple dozen of us peons trying to hold things together. I don't know why we're here. Maybe we shouldn't be here. Do you want us here?"

Harrington was puzzled. Was this man sober? Was he drugged? Should he mollify him? "Polcari. Yes. You belong there. I'm depending on you like I never have before. I am personally grateful that you are carrying the ball the length of the field without the benefit of an offensive ... Is there someone else right there I can speak to?" Harrington recalled a similar telephone conversation in which he had called a neighbor. A very young child answered the phone and refused to relinquish it to anyone. "We're all very busy, Mr. Harrington."

Damn him! "Have you seen Margo Chin?"

There was a hesitation at the other end. Polcari's voice changed. "Margo is dead," he said.

Harrington was stunned. He wondered if this was part of the madman's joke. "What do you mean?"

"She's dead! We found her on the upper floors. We don't know what happened to her." Polcari paused. "Mr.

Harrington." His voice was excited. "It's been very spooky around here. I don't know how much longer we can take it."

"You don't know how she died?" The pitch of Harrington's voice was rising also.

"Jesus. Mr. Harrington. She was a mess. She had something stuck in her chest. There was blood all over the place. Oh, Christ, it was a terrible!"

"What else has been happening? What do you mean you can't take it any more? How about the snow? What's the XII report? Is the storm breaking up?" Harrington didn't know why he asked these questions. He knew most of the answers. There was no good news. Why was his intricate world falling apart? Where were his most trusted advisors? Margo Chin dead?

Polcari continued. "I don't know what they've been telling you down there, but I'll tell you things are a bitch up here. Nothing is moving. We are isolated. Those who aren't here won't be back because they have a good excuse. We wish we'd gone home. There'd be too much snow for us to come back here. There's over six feet of stuff out there and it's coming down like a bastard.

"The report from XII? The picture hasn't changed in days. The storm is stuck. Our weather people say as long as the storm is resting here, the Atlantic humidity will keep on pumping in. When the humidity hits the cold air you know what happens."

Harrington searched his mind for another name. It was the word "weather" that reminded him. "Is Ellen Bloodworth there?"

"Hey look, Mr. Harrington. Since you gave us hell, we haven't talked with her. And she was a nice girl too."

"'Is she there?' is what I asked."

"Damned if I know. I haven't seen her. Somebody said they thought they saw her last night. If she was here last night she must be here now, 'cause nobody's left. I mean we're all stuck here. Had to break into the vending machines for food. Got nothing else ... "

He wished he hadn't called. The pleasant Christmas Eve he was looking forward to was as deflated as a punctured football. All he had learned was that everything was out of control and no one was in charge. His hope of finding someone capable of operating Webster's Energizer, and therefore neutralizing the-storm, was rapidly fading.

"Mr. Polcari."

"Mr. Harrington," Polcari mimicked.

"You worked with Webster during the launch of XII, didn't you?"

"Sure."

"Didn't you assist in firing the Hole-in-the-Night?"

"Sure. You watched us, Mr. Harrington." "

"Can you operate the Searoc Beam?" Harrington felt uncomfortable mentioning these words to a stranger.

"I know a few things about it. You see, Mr. Webster, Jim and I worked as a team. Mr. Webster told us the countdown order of operations and we carried them out."

"I know that, Polcari. But can you and your partner operate the Beam without Webster?"

"No way." Polcari uttered his annoying high cackle again. "Mr. Webster had the operation memorized. He said it couldn't be programmed. Every activation is different, he said."

"That's too bad," Harrington sighed aloud.

"But we'll be glad to try, Mr. Harrington. Jim and I could work something out."

"Hold it! Hold it!" Harrington shouted. "Goddamn it! Don't you go near that goddamn Control Room!"

"But, if ... "

"Forget it, Polcari! Now you just go back to what you were doing." A shudder of fear ran through him. That was all he needed at this point, Harrington thought -- a madman at the controls. "Just forget I mentioned it."

Harrington sighed again. It seemed that his last hope was indeed shot. It all came back to Webster again. It looked like Webster had him cornered. For months the secrecy he insisted Webster maintain had been smugly satisfying to Harrington. That very secrecy had now backfired. The secret had been too well kept. It appeared that Webster alone had the knowledge of Searoc's operation. If anyone else was knowledgeable, Harrington didn't know how to identify him.

"Mr. Polcari. I want you to stay within earshot of this line. By the same token, if any dramatic changes take place up there, I want you to personally call me on the D-12 channel.

"I want you to keep me advised on all changes in personnel, weather, and internal systems. You're doing a great job, Polcari. You'll be rewarded."

Harrington wasn't such a bad guy, Polcari thought. It was good to hear a voice from the outside. Harrington was OK. It was Randolph he hated. "The only reward I want, Mr. Harrington, is a good night's sleep."

Harrington signed off. Questions, questions, questions. Where was Randolph? How could the crippling storm be halted? What had happened to Margo Chin? Could Scan-Man's system be held together by the crew alone, without management? Could Bloodworth still be used to manage the Energizer?

He felt an exhaustion crawl over him like a heavy blanket. He held the magnificence of a giant contract in one hand while in the other his hand his empire oozed like mud through his fingers.

*

Six hours of liberty had taken its toll. One girl rebelled. Her head throbbed. She was bleeding from the vagina. She was frightened. The reality of the bleeding, the nausea and complete separation from her parents, induced momentary hysterics.

The abrupt change from peace to vocalized fear tightened the stomach muscles of several youngsters. The complex mixture of indigestible foods and alcohol suddenly produced a rash of vomiting. Thrashing in the dimness of his flashlight, the bellboy heaved his juicy stomach contents across the length of three neighboring blankets. The girl wretching in the bathroom, and the sobbing of her bleeding friend, dramatically altered the atmosphere of their gathering.

The party was over.

One by one, two by two, they left Room 413. Some went to other rooms to sleep off their stupor, others returned to the adult world below where they might find help.

Irene Stitch was embarrassed. She should have known better. She was glad it was over.

*

It looked to Stevenson like Randolph had gone off the deep end. At first voicing his problems aloud, Randolph next gradually sank into a depression his friend could not help him overcome. Randolph was psychologically burdened by the crushing weight of frustrated responsibility. His world had gone sour. When he had begun to cry, Stevenson and McCullough helped him to a room on the second floor where they encouraged him to sleep. The only medication they were able to offer was a couple of aspirin. Stevenson remained by the bedside in a chair wrapped in a blanket The only heat the second floor received was what flowed up the stairs from the first floor.

Elaine Mitchell was in bed in another second floor room where Mabel had tried to make her comfortable. That

298

room was cold also, but a quilt, a heavy blanket and hot water bottle was more than adequate. She was grateful to Mabel and confided that she didn't think she would ever recover from the memory of the grisly way her twenty-five-year marriage had ended.

Marsha Randolph was still in pain on the living room couch, suffering from withdrawal symptoms from her heavy consumption of pills and alcohol the previous evening. Mabel, as time permitted, hovered over her as well. Administering favorite kitchen medicines that with some luck would cure a "swollen brain."

Alice Stevenson attempted to relieve Mabel in the kitchen by preparing dinner. But this kitchen was foreign to her. She was awed by Mabel's large, black stove and marveled at the even heat the wood fire produced. In addition, all of Mabel's cooking utensils were hand-operated.

"It's times like these they come in handy," Mabel explained. "Besides, those electric contraptions are always breaking down and they cost too blasted much. These jigamarandees never break. They're reliable. My mother gave me the lot, and that was fifty years ago!"

Robert and Francisco thoroughly enjoyed their evening. They followed McCullough around the barn as he conducted his evening chores. Robert proudly demonstrated his knowledge to the older Francisco who was having his first contact with farm animals. Retrieving eggs from under the hens was a thrill.

McCullough stood to one side and watched with satisfaction, if not a little anxiety, as the boys competed to see who could collect the most -- much like an Easter Egg hunt -- only these eggs were breakable, he reminded them.

Each of the boys had his turn at milking Henrietta. Three or four cats sat discretely by and McCullough showed how they'd open their mouths to catch a stream from the cow's teats. The skill, the boys learned, was more in the squirting than it was in the catching.

Returning to the house, the boys carried firewood through the fresh snow at the bottom of the snow trench, the sides of which were piled well over their heads. In the house McCullough helped them fill the kerosene lamps, wash the globes and trim the wicks. There was no end of chores on the McCullough farm. Everyone had the opportunity to keep busy.

*

"I'd like to say a prayer, if I may." There was a pause. "I'd like to say a prayer if you people will join me," the man repeated.

An individual, unknown to Puff had stepped in front of the fire in the hotel lobby. He was a handsome man, who stood with hands together holding a Bible, looking benignly at the group. The singing gradually dissipated until there was only the sound of the fire's crackle and distant voices in the tavern enjoying verse number fifty-seven of "Roll Me Over In The Clover."

Puff Chabus had returned to the lobby only minutes earlier after having suffered through her grief in her room. She now felt very much alone and in need of quiet companionship. The carol singing had attracted her and promised temporary satisfaction. She had long since pushed the conventioneers to the back of her mind. She didn't think she could face them now that Freddie had passed away. She turned her attention to this man with the remarkably commanding appearance.

The lobby people were silent, eyes also on the man "Oh, Lord, hear us tonight as we suffer through the disaster which has befallen us. Be with us and give us thy strength which we will need to endure the suffering that is yet to come."

300

Puff admired the control he had over the crowd and noted that nearly every head was bowed.

"We are sheep in Your pasture, a flock that does not understand what has happened. Give the sick among us the courage to bear the pain they carry. Give the healthy among us the patience and understanding to help our fellow human beings.

Oh, Lord ... "

The prayer completed, the carols resumed. Puff noted that the man sat alone, thumbing through his Bible. She crossed the room, introduced herself, and asked if she could join him. The smile across his rugged countenance welcomed her.

*

Maggie & Phil returned to their home on Great Road. The snowcat team had dropped them off on their way to Boston to fulfill the long-promised delivery of the governor to his office.

At Ellen's insistence, over Maggie's reluctance, the team had dropped Ellen off at Scan-Man headquarters. Ellen said she felt compelled to find answers to some of her most nagging questions. She said she might even spend the night at the office.

The snow had drifted against the rear storm door of the Billings household. It took several minutes to clear it away. The house was pleasantly warm and dry. Although the wood fires had died hours ago, the generator had kept the furnace running, maintaining the fifty-five degree setting.

Phil was exuberant over his survival arrangements. "I never thought we'd really need it, but it's certainly paid for itself already."

"I'm sorry I ever laughed when you installed that generator," Maggie said. "But don't you feel guilty?"

"How so?" Phil asked.

"We're so comfortable and everyone else is cold."

"Why should I feel guilty? We're simply being rewarded for our forward thinking -- our anticipation."

Maggie sighed. "I'm just thankful we're home and all in one piece." She laughed to herself. "It'll be a long while before I feel the urge to jump out of an airplane again."

"Especially if it's snowing," Phil added. "You continue to amaze me. I would never have guessed you two would do a stunt like that."

"I will insist that it was not a 'stunt.' It was a necessity that proved to be well worth it. I'm glad I didn't have time to think about it beforehand."

Phil and Maggie ascended the stairs, pulled extra blankets from the chest at the foot of the bed, and prepared for a normal night's sleep.

"Would you object if I join you tonight. . . Mrs. Billings?" Phil asked with the formal humor he used on occasion.

"You're not going to light the woodstoves?"

"The only fire I want to light is yours." He reached out and gently pulled Maggie down onto the big bed and nuzzled her neck and ear.

"You were magnificent today, Mr. Billings." she said, looking up at him. "I really am proud of you."

"You weren't so bad yourself, sweetheart," Phil responded. "If I had known you were performing sky acrobatics in a snowstorm ... You constantly amaze me."

Together they overcame their guilt and showered together under the spray of hot, steamy water. Drying rapidly, they then ran for the bed and crawled between the frigid sheets. Phil let out a holler. "Jesus! Your feet are cold!" Maggie snickered. "See if you can warm them up. In fact, I'm cold all over."

They pulled each other together tightly and enjoyed an intimacy each had long been without. They felt like newlyweds, but with the added satisfaction of having years of shared experiences. These experiences had their high points and low but they both knew the mean enjoyment level was pleasantly high.

"I didn't think you'd go through with it," Maggie said. "I never thought you could give up smoking."

"I guess I have. The only real difficult part was the first twenty-four hours. Since then I haven't thought about it"

And your body. It's so clean and smooth and smells so nice."

"You're full of compliments tonight. Thank you. I feel a hell of a lot better too. And if it means getting close to you like this more often, you can bet your left boob it will continue."

Maggie ran her hand along his stomach and chest. "My God. Even that pot of yours is disappearing. I can't get over the changes."

Phil tucked Maggie's feet between his legs then kissed her on the tip of the nose. Her feet were now warm.

Phil suddenly sat up. "Let there be light!" He turned on the bedside lamp.

"What are you doing?" Maggie asked, squinting in the brightness.

"Oh, nothing," he grinned. "Just gloating over the fact that we have electricity." He turned out the lamp.

"You're a nut, and I love it."

He snuggled under the covers and rested his head between her breasts. Maggie ran her fingers through his hair.

"I'm very happy," she said, "And tired."

*

It had been an exhausting day as well for the residents of the McCullough household. All of the guests had now retired after a light supper. The dishes washed, dried and put away, Frank and Mabel enjoyed the warmth and silence of their kitchen. Mabel peeled potatoes for tomorrow's salad and Frank carved another link in his wooden chain.

"What are you gonna do with that when you get it done?" Mabel asked, eyeing the long, delicately carved object.

"Give it away. I think Robert will like it. He's had his sights on it right along." Frank held one end out and over his head. "What do you guess -- four feet?"

He was relaxed. He leaned back in his chair thinking how grateful he was the snow had finally come. With a grin to himself, he thought it was quite certain his bulbs were now well protected. It was also a certainty that the ponds and reservoirs would be replenished this spring. The only reservations Frank had about the deep snow was the spring melt. He would pray that it would be a slow runoff. Otherwise flooding would counteract every benefit.

Mabel's thoughts dwelt on her Christmas Day surprise. She had checked on the cake today and it was holding up well. The frosting had not soaked in. Nine people. Well, at least they'd be able to put a dent in it.

Frank thought of the fun he'd had with the boys. They were good boys, interested in anything and everything. The problem was keeping them busy. He was thankful he'd found that pile of games. They would keep them occupied for days.

A frown overtook his smile suddenly as his thoughts turned to Mitchell's body in the barn. That poor man. It gave him a creepy feeling to know that he was in his barn, however, he was well hidden in the hay in an abandoned stall out of sight of the boys.

*

Christmas Eve. At midnight precisely, a light as bright as the sun broke through the heavy clouds over most of the New England region. It began as a narrow circle and rapidly expanded into an area that illuminated most of New England. It burned away, or pushed out to sea, all the cloud cover in exactly one hour. It then extinguished and the stars appeared. The North Star was brighter than usual.

Thousands of startled and terrified late-nighters witnessed this event. Many of them called it a Christmas miracle. The storm was over.

Some of those who saw the bright light at midnight recognized it from what they had read or heard about the first one that took place on December 19. Still, for all, it was frighteningly spooky and strange. And its source was still unknown. It was obviously a gift from Heaven following the snow from Hell.

TUESDAY, DECEMBER 25

As New Englanders awoke Christmas morning, they welcomed the sun for the first time in a week. With equal enthusiasm, they bid a cheerful farewell to the snowfall. The snow accumulation in many areas now totaled between four and eight feet, although rain and the effect of the snow's weight on itself had reduced this by a foot or two.

*

Maggie Billings woke, startled to see a bright morning. Icicles were dripping from the eaves. It appeared to be an Indian Summer. She couldn't believe it.

She shook Phil. "Hey! Wake up lazy and see the new world. The sun!"

Phil shook nighttime from his squinted eyes. "I can't believe it. That's the best Christmas present I ever had."

The snow cat team arrived at eight. Maggie was relieved to see them. She half feared her hard-earned prize, the giant snow cat, would be hijacked carting Governor Fitzwilliam back to Boston during the night.

Over coffee, the night driver told an incredible story.

"About midnight, just after dropping off the governor and his aides, a bright light broke through the clouds. It was blinding, just like the sun. It lit up the city like noontime. It was very frightening. We couldn't see the source of it like we can the sun. It was silent. It was warm. It was creepy. There was no explanation.

"There were a few people around and we all got together and puzzled over it. We didn't know what to do. And then it went out. Poof! And it was gone. After our eyes

306

adjusted to the dark again, we noticed the sky was clear and the stars were out. I'd guess it lasted for about an hour."

Maggie couldn't believe it. "You didn't stop at a watering hole while you were in town?"

"Aw, Maggie. Actually I don't blame you. It's the talk of the town. Everywhere we go people are us asking questions we can't answer."

*

It was almost noon -- dinnertime. Mabel was delighted to have the opportunity to prepare her biggest Christmas dinner in years. The table was set for nine and she had used her best silver and china.

"A funny thing happened last night," Frank McCullough said. "I got up in the middle of the night, as usual, and it was bright as day outside. And then it just went out like someone flicked a switch."

But not everyone was cheerful and excited this bright, sunny Christmas day. Ed Randolph was still in bed, given to frequent crying spells that totally disarmed those who knew him. Stevenson had given up his bedside vigil. He couldn't communicate with his Scan-Man partner.

The other guests had recovered reasonably well. Elaine Mitchell had rationalized that her husband, Ralph, was near the end anyway. They had many happy years of marriage. His frequent angina attacks were extremely painful and each had known it was only a matter of time. Her only regret was that it happened under these circumstances. On the bright side, however, she was destined to receive a large inheritance in cash and property. She figured she could survive very well on the interest alone. Things looked promising for Elaine.

Marsha Randolph, after twenty-four hours under Mabel's care, was fully mobile again. She remembered nothing of the house fire or the trek to the farm. Elaine and Alice had gently related to her all the grisly details of the day. She was thankful she couldn't remember the ordeal. It was the loss of the house and all her possessions that began to torment her.

Robert and Francisco were immune to everything. They had each other and were preoccupied with the large collection of boxed games McCullough had found in the attic. The boys had been banned from visiting the barn by themselves, but Frank had told them they could accompany him at chore time.

Randolph's condition had become the prime topic of conversation among the McCullough guests this morning. It was a mystery how this tough and abrasive leader of men had degenerated. His crying was infantile. Marsha, who was under psychiatric care herself, said she knew very well what the problem with her husband was. His crying was a reversion to childhood. She'd read a lot of books on the subject, she said. It appeared he had simply caved in under excessive pressures, real and imagined, pressures strong enough to overpower his mind that was not really as strong as his bold exterior indicated.

"Frankly," Marsha told the others, "I have little sympathy for him. For years I've tried to tell him to become human, but he'd never listen to me. He's tried to run his life and mine like one of his goddamned computers."

Peter Stevenson, on the other hand, thoroughly understood the pressures Randolph experienced in recent weeks. The two of them had discussed the problems at Scan-Man exhaustively. Stevenson, however, had been able to be more objective -- he was not President of the company; he was not the one Harrington was watching. These were not problems he cared to discuss with the three women.

Stevenson spoke with Marsha about the other pressures on her husband. He told her he did not think she was entirely reasonable in her callousness. He reminded her of Randolph's responsibility during the house fire. After all, he had rescued his wife at the possible loss of his son's life. He reminded her of Robert's story -- how Alberta had pulled Robert from his bed and had thrown him out the window. Robert said Alberta's clothing was on fire when she picked him up. It was surmised that she perished before she could jump. She saved Robert's life at the expense of her own. Now, Randolph had taken Alberta's horrid death personally.

Then there was the nightmare of his ordeal with Mitchell. The retrieval of that body would never be forgotten. The women had insisted Stevenson related all the details. Elaine accepted the death stoically and knew the ordeal was not yet over -- not until Mitchell was buried.

But most of all, Stevenson said, were the problems at the company -- complicated infinitely by the present storm. Although he said he could not go into detail, the lives of thousands and thousands of people rested on the outcome of this storm that now appeared to be over. Randolph's ability to continue managing events at Scan-Man was also in question.

Mabel and Frank found it difficult to mix informally with their guests. They were aware of some of the burdens each carried. They were also aware of the burdens that had now been brought into their home.

The McCulloughs welcomed their guests, faults and all. They were a strange bunch, they thought. While Stevenson and the three women talked earnestly in the parlor, Mabel and Frank talked just as earnestly in the kitchen. What would happen to the body in the barn? It certainly couldn't stay there. What was Mr. Randolph's problem? Was there a chance he might become violent? Was Marsha a druggy? What kind of drugs did she take? Why did she take them?

McCullough wondered if Turk had been able to walk all the way into town. It was doubtful. If not, what had happened to him? Mabel was saddened by Alberta's death -- all the more so because she had been heroic. She and Alberta food shopped together on several occasions. It was fascinating to see the huge quantities Alberta bought to satisfy the needs of the Randolph family.

In the end though, the McCulloughs shrugged their shoulders and accepted their guests at face value. They were newcomers to Hollandson. They had money, big houses and fancy cars, maids and chauffeurs. They led a life the McCulloughs found impossible to comprehend. Why weren't they happy with all their fancy things?

Mabel clanged the bottom of a large pan with her wooden spoon. "Dinner time! Come and get it!" She lighted the candles on either side of the holly centerpiece. The white linen tablecloth was spotless and the silver gleamed, thanks to the collective efforts of the boys and Frank.

As soon as everyone was seated, Randolph's empty chair was painfully evident. "I'll take him some goodies right after we finish," Mabel said.

McCullough broke that train of thought. "Let us join hands and pray." There was some hesitation and surprised exchanges in glances, but the others complied. Frank and Mabel already had their heads bowed.

"Lord, thank you most of all for the warm sun. Thanks also for this food and the companionship of our neighbors in the middle of this record-settin' blizzard. Help our friend Mr. Randolph get over his ills. And Lord, give everlastin' peace to Mr. Mitchell and Alberta. Keep a close eye on Turk and may he find a safe place to go. Thank you too, Lord, for makin' this house a safe place for anyone who looks for shelter. And we thank you for our health and happiness. Ah-men."

Mabel was given the usual compliments about the table and the completeness of the meal. She nodded graciously and said she was happy to have such a large group for Christmas. It had been a long time since her children had visited them. They were preoccupied with their own lives and

310

families, Mabel said. They told her they were happy and that was the main thing.

"Their lives are so much like yours," Mabel said. "So busy and complicated. I don't know how they do it."

Stevenson laughed. "It has become a busy and complicated world -- not altogether for the better, I must add."

"Depends what you're busy at," McCullough stated. "Mabel and me, we got simple needs. We fight off temptation." He dropped a piece of roast beef to Rolf. The dog caught it and moved another few inches closer to his master's chair. "I ain't no philosopher, but I learnt the difference between what I want and what I need. Too many people watch that TV too much. They end up wantin' everythin' they see on it."

Forks clinked against plates. Throats cleared. The pendulum clock in the background ticked away the seconds.

"Yep," McCullough said. "This is the biggest snow dump I ever seen. My ol' man told me about the winter of '88, but that don't stand up to this one." He threw Rolf another scrap. The dog inched closer and touched his nose to the table. McCullough thumped the table and the dog withdrew.

"I don't understand," McCullough said. "I don't understand why we got the dump we did. Ma Nature is pretty fickle, but the signs she gives are always right. The ones she gave me this week weren't for this big 'un."

"What signs were those?" Stevenson asked.

"I got me a weather vane. I got the clouds. An' I got a feelin' for dew in the air. These never let me down. And this week I got my usual signs, but they were wrong. It ain't never happened before.

"An' last night there was another sign I never saw before. It was about midnight and it was bright as day out. Then, like someone slammed the door, the light went out.

"An' this snowstorm. It too stopped like another door slammed. Nope. I just don't get it."

"There's a lot of things affecting the weather these days -- a lot of artificial things," Stevenson said, glad to be able to answer McCullough. "Take pollution, for instance. Some cities create their own weather -- rain, or even snowstorms – just by the pollution they create in the atmosphere with smoke and heat."

"I read somethin' like that in *Readers' Digest* a couple years ago. But this ain't no city. And New England's a mighty big place. I been thinkin' a lot about this. I wouldn't be surprised if the Russians got something to do with messin' up the weather."

Only Stevenson was intrigued by McCullough's comment.

"What makes you say that?"

"I don't know. The TV's had a lot of stuff on it about these space buggies. You got these, what do you call 'em, satellites up there, rockets and space men doin' all kinds of weird things. And then there's the cloud seedin' there're usin' in some states out west. It just makes you wonder."

Stevenson was taken aback by the old man's insight. He wondered how many other Americans might feel the same.

Mabel changed the subject as she cleared the table. "Now for a very special dessert we've been holdin' on to for a very special occasion. Come on Frank. I need help. You people just sit right where you are." Mabel giggled with delight at the thought of her surprise.

A few minutes later the guests heard the couple singing.

"Da da da-da, da da da-da." Through the door from the kitchen they came carrying a large, magnificently decorated wedding cake.

Mabel smirked as the guests helped them set it on the table. She then stepped to one side listening happily to the plaudits.

She placed her tiny arm around Frank's waist. "Frank and me made this with our own little hands. Frank carved the sugar bells all his self."

Robert and Francisco had been sitting quietly by themselves. Their eyes were popping at the sight of the decorations on the cake.

"OK, boys," Mabel said. "Come on up here. Let me give each of you one of these sugary hand-carved bells."

The boys approached the cake with huge grins. Mabel passed the bells to them and they returned to their chairs.

"Now, boys. Take a bite and tell us what it tastes like."

"Mmmm. Sugary lemon and lime. I like it," Robert purred. Francisco nodded and smiled.

McCullough spoke up. "And I have a present for the boys too." He held aloft two identical wooden chains that he had carved over the past year. "This was a six footer, but I wanted you both to have it so I broke it in half. Merry Christmas, boys."

The boys were overjoyed. For the last few days they had watched, admired and questioned the old man who worked so skillfully with his knife.

"Thank you Mr. & Mrs. McCullough," Robert said. Francisco nodded with a big smile.

*

A group was organized to help Jack Thompson operate the kitchen in the school building. Hot meals contributed to body warmth -- soups, frozen dinners, steaming vegetables, canned fruits and powdered milk. It was a Christmas Day feast of feasts.

Portable radios featured holiday music. The news broadcast was filled with the revelations of the "Great Light" last night. With the sun as the other great light, a spirit of thankfulness pervaded the room. Christmas meals had never seemed so much appreciated. Joyless depression now gave way to hope and optimism.

The roof shovelers returned to their task with renewed vigor.

*

"There's your transportation, fella," the school official told Turk, pointing to Maggie and Phil who had just unloaded a delivery. Turk spun around and walked determinedly to them.

"I need ride," he said, simply.

The pair looked up at him in surprise. There was something about him that was startling, maybe even threatening. This was one of perhaps hundreds of people who had expressed the same need, and the answer had always been no. But this one seemed different.

"Tell us about it," Phil said.

Turk's voice carried little animation. The chilling tale he related about the Randolph house fire and the man and woman who died carried no emotion.

"Did you say Randolph?" Maggie asked.

"Yes. Mr. Randolph needs a ride. He's in trouble. He needs help quick."

"Is that Mr. Ed Randolph, the one from Scan-Man?"

"Yes. Mr. Randolph needs help."

"OK, now. Look. You just wait here a minute. I want to talk with my husband."

Maggie and Phil stepped out of earshot. The big man's eyes remained on them.

"Randolph!" Maggie said in an excited whisper. "This may be our big chance to find out why he hasn't been at Scan-Man."

Phil was hesitant. Maggie was persistent.

"We've delivered the food," she said. "The next thing is house checking. Why not begin house checking on River Road?"

*

Peter Stevenson stood just inside the kitchen door. He was awed by the snow piled half way up the columns supporting the porch roof. He estimated the snow depth at eight or ten feet.

It frightened him to be imprisoned. The sun was encouraging but he was still stuck in this house with a finality that approached death. How long would it be, he thought, before this accumulation either melted or was removed so life outside could resume? He didn't want to imagine the realistic answer. If others were reaching out to save him, that would be one thing. But, when everyone was in the same predicament, that was something else. How much longer would McCullough's supplies last? They didn't seem to be worried.

He was hot. The kitchen was hot. What a paradox!

He had gone up to see Randolph after dinner. Marsha held Randolph's head while Stevenson was able to spoon in the soup. Marsha said she didn't have the patience to spoon feed her husband.

Randolph's eyes were blank. They were fixed and would not focus. He was pitiful. He needed medical care badly.

Stevenson's thoughts now turned to Scan-Man and what would happen if Randolph could not return to his responsibilities. Who would take over? Who was next in line for the presidency? Was he a candidate? He was the junior member on the board. He knew he was looked upon as one of the youngest and the brightest. Would he be taking Randolph's place?

If this was likely, Randolph's problems were now his. Did he want them? Would he accept the presidency if it was offered? Could he cope with Harrington's demands? Could he cope with the demands of such a fast-moving corporation? Did he agree with the decision of the directors in supporting Phase I/Phase II? Was it a conviction of his or did he simply vote along with the others?

The storm had given him plenty of time to think. There was, he thought, plenty of time.

*

Ellen slept late this morning. The walk home from Scan-Man had been tedious, but a lot of her questions had been answered. She had heard Maggie and Phil go out with the snowcat team, but she easily fell asleep again to happy dreams. She awoke at mid-morning with a big smile. The sun greeted her. She was very happy about everything. What a difference a day makes! She thought.

Merry Christmas to me. I so wish Nat was here.

Today, she resolved, was going to be her day of rest. She deserved it. The last few had certainly been exhausting.

*

Maggie was both ecstatic and apprehensive at the prospect of meeting Edward Randolph, the mysterious person, second in command of the Scan-Man organization. His report to the ASA at the hotel framed him as a tough-minded, hard-driving man. He intimidated her. Margo's apparent extreme loyalty to him, according to Ellen, was shocking. The technicians' whispered remarks about his temper were frightening. The intrigue enveloping Nat's project was awesome. This was the man whose desk Ellen raided. The power and influence Randolph wielded was beyond Maggie's comprehension. Could she face this giant among men?

Now, after arriving at the McCullough house, they found that Randolph was very ill, if not mentally barren. Maggie was tempted to laugh at the absurd contrast in the man from what she had imagined. Now she was ashamed of her levity in the midst of tragedy.

316

She turned to Stevenson who took her aside.

"He's apparently had some extreme form of mental breakdown, Stevenson said. "We should get him out of here and to some facility."

"There is no facility," Maggie said. "From what I can see you people have it made here. Not even the hospital can compete with this place."

Stevenson thought for a moment. "OK then. I'd like you to take me to Scan-Man to assume my responsibilities there."

Maggie saw her advantage. "You have your ride, but on one condition only." It was an impulsive statement. It was a statement uncharacteristic of her. She felt her heart speed up. She swallowed the bubble in her throat.

Stevenson hardened. "What the hell is this? Who the hell are you?"

Her pulse quickened still more. She refused to be intimidated. She had been through too much. "Where is Nat Webster?" she asked. Her voice was gentle and even. She looked Stevenson directly in the eye.

Stevenson was stunned. He sat. He looked away from Ellen. He gazed at the ghostly figure of Randolph.

Maggie felt something was working. She decided to take it another step. "We know what's going on with Scanner XII. There's no point in playing games with us."

Stevenson remained silent, flushed.

"Where is Nat Webster?" Maggie asked again, quietly.

Stevenson weakened. The isolation of the last few days had left him out of touch. The whole plan must have backfired. Harrington must have failed.

"You must know," he finally answered. "The poor bugger was incinerated in the car crash."

Maggie was stunned. "Then you really believe that?"

"What else is there to believe?"

Maggie was silent, thinking now of Ellen.

"I really liked the guy," Stevenson continued.

"So did his girlfriend."

"Where's Harrington?" Maggie asked.

Stevenson looked at Maggie curiously. "I thought you knew all about this."

Maggie hesitated, rapidly searched her thoughts. "I know enough to pin you on the wall for a while." She regained her composure when she saw Stevenson look away.

"Where's Harrington?"

"He's in Washington."

"How can I reach him?"

"I don't know. Look. I haven't been available for the last few days. I'm not in touch."

At that moment, Phil walked into the room. He looked at Randolph, then at Maggie and Stevenson. He sensed the tension in the air.

"What's happening?"

"He told me Harrington's in Washington. He doesn't know what's going on down there."

"Mr. Stevenson," Phil began. "We're very tired. This weather has not been very healthy for us. A lot of people are suffering out there. We know that Scan-Man is involved in weather modification. We are familiar with the Energizer and the use of the Searoc Beam."

Maggie joined in. "And my friend's life has been threatened twice at Scan-Man. We want to know what has been happening since Nat Webster died – uh, disappeared."

"I don't know anything. I've been stranded in this storm. Harrington only spoke with Ed, uh, Randolph. I wasn't in on it." Stevenson paused, shook his head and lowered it. In a soft voice he added. "I'm just sick of the whole thing."

Phil and Maggie looked at each other, raising their eyebrows.

318

"What do you mean you're sick of it?" Maggie asked.

"I guess I went along with this thing, but I assure you it was reluctantly. I guess I just followed the others."

"Who!"

"The directors. It was naked greed."

*

Stevenson changed his mind about returning to Sean-Man. He decided to remain at McCullough's with the others for the time being – at least until they were dug out.

EARLY JANUARY

"Here we are again, lady and gentlemen," the President began. "I trust you all have had a pleasant holiday. It certainly has been interesting.

"Over the past week or so I have studied Mr. Harrington's proposal for the counter measure to the 'Hole in the Night' with a great deal of interest. I have a couple of questions.

"On Christmas Eve, it appears New England experienced a 'Hole in the Night' similar to the one that took place over Greenland. Do you have an explanation for that, Mr. Harrington?"

"Of course," Harrington answered. "Its source has to be the same as the unknown source we have decided to meet head-to-head. The second attack reinforces the need for us to put every possible effort into speeding up our research before any further, more damaging attacks, take place. Time is short. The urgency could not be greater."

Senator Woark spoke up. "With this second mysterious event taking place, maybe now you will reconsider the possibility that the source could be that of an extra-terrestrial vehicle."

"Let me add here," the Honorable Lady Senator Robinson interjected, "that there have been two additional events since the first. One was the assassination of General Ruben right in our own back yard. This may also be related to these strange events. There may even be an enemy among us.

Pardon me. I mean generally speaking, not in our immediate midst."

"That is true," the President confirmed. "General Ruben was part of this secret committee. Who could have known?"

There was a long pause, as if in Memoriam.

Chandler Harrington spoke up. "I'd like to talk further about the financial need expressed in our last meeting. As I said last time, we at Scan-Man will be most happy to break the $41 billion into four payments as our research continues toward fulfillment a year from now. We would like to get the ball in the air ASAP."

"I'm sure you would, Mr. Harrington," the President said. "But before we go any further I want you all to hear what some other people have to say on the larger subject. The President gestured toward a side door.

"Let me present Mr. Nat Webster."

In walked Nat with two Secret Service men close behind.

Undoubtedly, the person most startled was Chandler Harrington. His face drained of all color.

Webster sat beside the President behind his desk. Two additional Secret Service men quietly entered from another door and stood at the rear of the room.

The President continued. "Mr. Webster has told me a different side of the story than you have Mr. Harrington. He tells me Scan-Man already possesses the Energizer and he has used the Searoc Beam to initiate the storm New England is experiencing. With the help of personnel at Scan-Man, Mr. Webster remotely initiated the Energizer and dispersed the New England storm on Christmas Eve.

"Do you have anything to say regarding this Mr. Harrington?"

Harrington didn't respond to the question.

"Mr. Webster has been acting under cover for several months. We have suspected that Scan-Man was acting in questionable ways."

Chandler Harrington had no words. He reached for his chest and fell out of his chair.

*

"Hi black an' white. Good to see you," Jack Thompson welcomed.

"I'm glad to see you're finally dug out and back in business," Maggie returned.

"I'm the lucky one, girls. Look at the mess up at the hotel. You think they'll ever rebuild?"

"Probably – if they have any insurance," Ellen added.

"Well, I wish them the best, whatever. The regular today?"

"Sounds good. It's been a few days," Maggie said.

Ellen and Maggie were quiet. They took inventory of the locals while waiting for Jack to deliver. The atmosphere was not much different from the last visit. It looked like things around Hollandson might even begin to get back to normal.

Ellen was the first to interrupt the silence. "I was so surprised and happy to get that call from Nat on Christmas Eve. Mr. Polcari, bless his devoted heart, took Nat's call and by chance I had gone in to work on Christmas Eve."

"You walked again!"

"I did. What else is a lonely single woman to do on Christmas Eve?

Maggie hung on Ellen's story.

"Nat spent the week in Washington, D.C. During that time he was able to hack into Scan-Man's system. When we got his call, Mr. Polcari and I worked at this end, and Nat at the Washington end. That's how we accomplished the Christmas Eve miracle."

"Well you can bet we are happy for you and him as well," Maggie said, "and greatly relieved after thinking he was dead. But who was it that died?"

"Nat's old VW was stolen that night. They were never able to identify the body, although they did save DNA samples, just in case. They found what was left of Nat's cell phone in the van. That's one reason he never called me. The other reason was the super secret mission he was on to trap Harrington."

"Secret mission?"

"I'll fill you in on the details later. What I can tell you now is Nat was involved in trapping Scan-Man in a plot to scam the government. That is why Nat has been so quiet for so long.

"On December 19, after verifying that the mission was going as he had planned, Nat flew to Washington. He contacted his friend Senator Conrad Cooper who was also in on the plan to trap Harrington. It took Cooper a few days to find a time that the President could meet with them. Holidays raise havoc with meetings. Nat and Senator Cooper met with the President soon after Harrington's initial meeting with the President.

"It all ended when Harrington saw Nat walk into that meeting."

"What happened to Harrington?"

"He had a minor heart attack. He recovered in the hospital. I believe he, and some of the Scan-Man directors are destined for a trial."

"What's going to happen at Scan-Man now?"

"Nat doesn't know. He is back at the office now trying to straighten things out and make sure all the employees are healthy. There are plenty of lesser projects to keep them all busy for the time being.

"We expect a new board will be elected and Nat may choose to become part of it. There are many unknowns about the long-range future of Scan-Man, not to mention the future of weather modification itself and the potentials of the Energizer."

"How are you and Nat doing – I mean as a couple?"

"Just great. He apologized for not contacting me, but with all the secrecy about this whole thing, he said his tongue had been tied. Nat knew it was especially tough for me, especially after he learned the guy who stole the VW might be misidentified as him.

"We're doing real well. There's a lot for us to talk over and get back to normal – whatever that is!"

"I have to ask," Maggie said. "What happened with Margo and you?"

"There was a preliminary investigation. Margo still had the screwdriver in her hand. Witnesses said the lightning bolt statue had always been on the window sill and it does appear she fell onto it when she attacked me. My fingerprints weren't on it.

"I also owned up to breaking into Randolph's desk," Ellen continued. "But since Randolph and others were suspect of greater things, I was not faulted for taking Nat's files."

"I hate to ask this question, really, but what happened to Mitchell's body?"

"I have no idea," Ellen said. "You'll have to ask Mrs. Mitchell about that."

Jack appeared again. "The black an' whites look very serious today. Everything OK?"

"They couldn't be better, Jack," Ellen said. "We'll see you tomorrow."

The women left, and were about to part when Ellen stopped them.

"I don't know why I hesitated to tell you, Maggie. You are, after all, my best friend."

The smile left Maggie's face. "What, Ellen?"

"Nat has received several death threats."

"What? Why?"

"He's been getting a lot of bad press about his involvement in creating this storm. Whoever wrote the threats doesn't like him or his technology."

"That's terrible. Has he gone to the police?"

"Yes. But Chief Wilson was undecided on how to handle it."

"Oh, my God. I feel so sorry for you and Nat. This is terrible."

"It is. Actually, I'm very frightened."

*

Maggie returned to her office, her head spinning with the latest revelation. Another weekly deadline was approaching for the *Bulletin*. Phil was busy closing out the newspaper's finances for the previous year.

Phil was in an upbeat mood. "Things look good financially for the *Bulletin*, Maggie. We might still be able to make a living at our labor of love."

"And I have good news too," Maggie said. "I wouldn't be surprised if our circulation increases. I have a lot of storm-related stories in mind that our readers might enjoy – or fret about -- particularly about Scan-Man. In the past week I feel I finally know something about Hollandson's largest employer – perhaps too much!"

"Do you think Scan-Man will pursue this weather modification stuff?" Phil pondered. "And how about its military ramifications? It blew me away when I heard that the – what do you call it – the Searoc Beam can melt an army tank!"

"I wonder if all that stuff falls into the category of local news that the *Bulletin* should carry." Maggie was thinking editorially.

END OF BOOK ONE

EPILOGUE

Planet Earth hangs in space as if from a giant mobile, constantly in motion with numberless other spheres. Earth, however, is unique because of its position on this mobile and the characteristics of the planet itself. It alone supports life. It alone is inhabited by a creature called Man.

Enveloping planet Earth is a six-mile thick mass of air called atmosphere that protects life on Earth from harmful space radiation and provides the planet with a variety of weather necessary for food growth.

The atmosphere itself is in perpetual motion, circulating and mixing as a result of the interchange of hot and cold air. This air moves in air streams from and to all parts of the planet. The meeting of two more air streams is what creates local weather.

The worldwide weather cycle is an extremely delicate and sensitive phenomenon, influenced by countless natural and unnatural forces. Man's survival on Earth is intimately dependent on the balance of extremes in climates. The environments at the North and South Poles are as unfit for human survival as the moon. The deserts of the world are similarly uninhabitable to the opposite extreme. Food crops cannot be cultivated at either. Man thrives best in temperate climates where moderation exists in all types of weather.

What happens when the weather patterns of the world are altered?

In the early nineteenth century the volcano Tambora, on the island of Sumbawa, Indonesia, erupted, spewing hundreds of millions of lightweight ash into the upper atmosphere. These billions of tiny particles had the effect of diluting the sun's rays, lowering the earth's general temperature as a result, adversely affecting the world climate for years.

Nuclear testing has been said to adversely affect world climate, not to mention the spreading of radiation around the planet.

Many of our large cities produce enough heat, through losses from streets and buildings, to produce their own mini climates. Hot air rising from a large metropolitan area meets a cold air stream passing overhead. The result is a very local rainstorm or some other form of precipitation.

The average temperature of Earth today is said to be 58 degrees. But at one time, through the last half billion years of Earth's history, the average temperature was as high as 72 degrees. Scientists tell us that on four known occasions the worldwide average temperature dropped to as low as 45 degrees.

Man and his food crops cannot withstand prolonged periods of high or low temperature extremes. Neither can he withstand too much rain, with resultant flooding, nor too little rain, resulting in drought.

*

Civilization has been, and continues to be, at the very mercy of weather. How incongruous it seems that technological Man, steeped in scientific knowledge, reinforced by computers, able to send manned spacecraft to the moon, successful in transplanting human hearts and other organs, has not yet learned to control the forces that so intimately affect his day-to-day life -- from the sudden summer rain squall, to the fall hurricane and tornado that obliterate the landscape and that in turn causes many deaths and much human suffering.

In truth, Man is afraid to attempt large-scale weather alternatives. Since weather is such an extremely complicated and unpredictable natural force, He does not know what the

328

consequences might be should a large-scale experiment fail. There is also a moral question here. Does one nation have the right to experiment with the weather that will eventually affect other parts of the world?

Weather in the northern hemisphere moves from west to east. It takes about two weeks for an air mass to circle the globe. Thus, an experiment of necessarily large proportions conducted in the U.S. could affect the rest of the northern hemisphere, in a chain reaction, within a period of only two weeks.

Although weather forecasting in recent years has greatly increased in sophistication, especially with the advent of weather satellites, Man has not yet learned enough to be precise in his predictions. If he is unable to predict what happens naturally, is it possible for him to attempt to control it artificially, and confidently predict the worldwide result?

ABOUT THE AUTHOR

Gerald Seaman lives in Massachusetts with his wife Carol. After a career in publishing at Little, Brown and Houghton Mifflin, he semi-retired to a small town and published a weekly newspaper. He then went on to found, with his stepson Tim Collins, "Popular Magazine Review" that later grew into EBSCO Publishing in Ipswich, Massachusetts.

Made in the USA
Charleston, SC
10 October 2012